Born in London, Alan Fenton was educated at Mercers' School in the City. Having won an open scholarship to Oxford he did two years National Service in the Royal Air Force, becoming a Pilot Officer, before going up to St Edmund Hall to read English Language and Literature.

On graduating, he worked as a trainee in business for a couple of years before writing a sketch for a children's television programme starring Ronnie Corbett. This led to a career writing comedy sketches and scripts for T.V. comedy series, Saturday Night Spectaculars and Sunday Nights at the London Palladium for most of the top comedians of the day, including Ronnie Corbett, Bruce Forsyth, Dickie Henderson, Roy Castle, Arthur Haines, Jack Douglas and Joe Baker, Dick Emery, Irene Handl, Des O'Connor and many others.

After several years of comedy scriptwriting, he drifted back into business. Working for a large American trading organisation he travelled the world, until he and a few friends set up their own company trading in metals and minerals, and ultimately in oil.

Leaving business a few years later, he wrote the *Shadow of the Titan*, his first novel, based loosely on his business experiences. Subsequently he wrote *The Call of Destiny*, the first book in the *Return of Arthur* cycle, and its sequel, *The Hour of Camelot*.

Alan Fenton lives in London with his wife and nine Pekinese dogs.

The CALL OF DESTINY

Alan Fenton

THE DOVECOTE PRESS

First published in 2006 by The Dovecote Press Ltd
Stanbridge, Wimborne Minster, Dorset BH21 4JD
First paperback edition 2010
ISBN 978-1-904-34978-5

Designed by The Dovecote Press
Printed in Spain by GraphysCem, Navarra

All papers used by The Dovecote Press are natural, recyclable products
made from wood grown in sustainable, well-managed forests

A CIP catalogue record for this book is available
from the British Library

1 3 5 7 9 8 6 4 2

THE WEAPON FORGED

*Yet some men say in many parts of England that
King Arthur is not dead . . . Men say that he shall come
again . . . I will not say that it shall be so, but rather
I will say, here in this world he changed his life.
But many men say that there is written upon his tomb
this verse: 'Hic Iacet Arthurus, Rex Quondam Rexque
Futurus.'*

SIR THOMAS MALLORY

Time Past, Time Future

ON THE SUMMIT of a hill in the county of Somerset stands a solitary church tower, bearing witness to the ferocity of nature and of man. It is all that survives of two churches that once stood here. The first was destroyed by an earthquake, the second by the command of Henry the Eighth. As sunset approaches, subtle details of stone and lichen, archway and niche, buttress and embrasure, are lost in the deepening shadows. Silhouetted against the evening sky the stark stone mass of the tower dominates the soft contours of the landscape, uniting earth and heaven.

A few yards from the base of the tower, on a mound that marks the crest of the Tor two motionless figures stand, one taller than the other. Seen from the valley below, their dark shapes loom, remote and mysterious. There is a haunting and powerful aura about them, as if they were not people but primeval monoliths or statues of pagan gods in an ancient burial ground. In some strange way they are beings apart, belonging not to the present time, but to time itself.

The hill is otherwise deserted, as are the woods at its foot and the countryside beyond. The red ball of the sun sinks below the horizon. The west wind that has gusted all day is suddenly stilled. Not a sound, not even a breath of air, disturbs the silence. Nothing stirs. In this hushed moment, the earth and all the planets that only an instant before wheeled round the sun, seem to hang motionless in space.

Slowly the taller figure raises his hand, as if to release the world from its spell, then touches the boy lightly on the shoulder. 'Shall we go? It's getting late.'

They begin the descent. 'Tell me more about him,' says the boy.

'He was a great leader,' his older companion responds. 'King of Britain, as they called it then. When he came to the throne the country was under constant attack by its enemies, both from outside and within.'

Down the steep track they jolt, each for a time absorbed in his own thoughts, the boy's head buzzing with questions. 'But what exactly did he do?'

'The world had gone mad. The king tried to bring it back to its senses, and restore meaning to people's lives. He wanted to give them courage and hope for the future. But to do that he first had to impose order on chaos.'

'How do you mean, impose?'

The man nods approvingly. 'You are right to question that word. He questioned it too. The thought of using force troubled him. But after much heart searching he decided that if mankind was to be saved, he had no other choice. He was given the power to do it, you see, power so formidable that many thought he had been sent to earth by God, or even that he himself was a divine being.'

'And was he?'

'No.'

'So he was just an ordinary man?'

A brief silence. 'He was a man, but no ordinary man. When he was young he found it hard to believe he had a special destiny. He wanted to lead a fun life and have a happy time, just as most people do. But as he grew older he came to understand that he was not the same as other men, and that the road he would have to take would be a different one.'

'Because of the power he had?'

'Yes. And because of the way he chose to use it.'

'How do you mean?'

'Other men would have used it for selfish ends, but not

8

him. He decided to fight the forces of darkness and chaos. He was a brave and cunning warrior; but he was also much more than that, a philosopher and a visionary, a wise and humane individual, gallant, just and honourable. Those who ruled by terror feared him. Those whom they terrorised, worshipped him. And in return he loved and honoured them, the ordinary men and women. He had a dream, a dream that one day the meek really would inherit the earth. But he knew they could only do it with his help.'

'Was there no one else they could turn to?'

'No one else whom good men and women would follow, no other leader who had the courage and strength of character to meet the challenge. Not that he was the only one who saw the world descending into chaos; there were leaders in other lands who feared for the future but were too weak, or too corrupt, or simply too afraid to act. As everything around them disintegrated, they stood by helplessly, resigned to self-destruction, accepting that mankind was doomed. They had abandoned all hope of changing anything; they no longer cared what happened. But he cared. He did everything in his power to create a new world for mankind, a world based on love and respect and justice.'

'And did he succeed?'

'For a while. Until things started to go wrong.'

The boy is impatient. 'But how? Why? I want to know everything.'

'It's a long story. Are you sure you want to hear it?' asks the man, teasing his young friend.

'You know I do!'

A loving hand rests lightly on the boy's head. 'Then you shall.'

A mole of thought furrows the boy's brow. 'Is it just a story? Or was there really such a person?'

'There was,' says the man, adding tantalisingly, 'and may be again.' The boy looks puzzled.

9

'There are those who say that if ever he is needed, he will come again.'

The boy's eyes shine. 'What will he do?'

In the twilight the first star shows itself. A pale sliver of moon floats above the horizon.

'Now there's a question,' the man says softly. 'What will he do . . . ? Well now, I imagine he will try to save mankind, just as he did all those centuries ago. Lord knows, we need saving.'

The boy nods in acknowledgement, though scarcely understanding.

'You never told me his name.'

'You know it already.'

'I do?'

'From the story books.'

The boy stands still and looks up at his beloved mentor, puzzled.

The man looks fondly down. 'You want a clue?'

'Yes.'

'You have the same name as that king.'

For a second or two the wide eyes dream, catching the starlight, then suddenly sparkle as he laughs with delight. 'Oh, that king!' On an impulse he cups his hands around his mouth and shatters the silence, crying out the name at the top of his voice. 'Arthur!'

The echoes wrap around him like a cloak in a swirl of wind . . . 'Arthur! . . . Arthur! . . . Arthur!', then tumble down the hill, fading as they fall, losing themselves in the twilight woods.

PART ONE

To Save the World

One

A TALL, GOOD-LOOKING MAN in his early thirties strode briskly along Pall Mall, headed up St. James's Street, pausing for a moment to peer through the window of his favourite cigar shop, and bounded up the steps of Grey's, the most prestigious of all London's private membership clubs. Pushing his way through the swing doors, he observed the tranquil scene inside with some amusement. Whatever upheavals and cataclysms had convulsed the world in the last three hundred years had left this hushed and elite interior undisturbed.

In the sitting area directly ahead, a few men lounged in button-back maroon leather armchairs, reading newspapers, chatting in subdued voices, or merely dozing. To the left, the famous bar (where it was said MI5 and MI6 once recruited spies) was almost empty. Not exactly what you would call a hive of activity, the young man thought. Most people would find the atmosphere stuffy and, in truth, so did he, but stuffy or not, Grey's was London's premier 'establishment' club, the one to which everyone who was anyone belonged. The question was, did he?

General Sir Roger Harding, KCVO, GBE, MC, DSO and bar, advanced towards him with outstretched hand. 'Congratulations, Pendragon! The committee has approved your application.'

Yes! Elation powered through Uther's body. With difficulty he restrained himself from punching the air triumphantly. Members of Greys did not punch air. 'Fantastic! Thank you, sir.'

'Don't thank me. Having the Marquess of Truro as your sponsor was the clincher.'

'If only he were still around to thank,' said Uther sadly. Lord Godfrey Whittaker had died of a gunshot wound to the head less than a month ago.

'Suicide, wasn't it?' enquired the general.

'Could have been an accident. Coroner delivered an open verdict. But you know . . . ' Uther lowered his voice discreetly, 'there were financial problems. I tried to help, but . . . ' – a shrug – 'Godfrey was a proud man.'

'How is his wife taking it?'

'Devastated, naturally.' Uther looked appropriately solemn. 'But Igraine's a strong lady. And of course she has the three girls.'

'Quite so.' A closer look at Uther. 'Ever been told you look like him?'

Uther nodded. 'Many times.'

'All very sad. Still, there we are. Life goes on. Like you to meet a couple of friends of mine.' The general gestured towards the bar.

'Delighted,' said Uther.

It was not yet noon, and there were only two other men in the bar. One was fiftyish, a wiry, compact man, with a neat moustache and close cropped hair – a civil servant he guessed, or a soldier in civvies? The other looked distinctly eccentric, not at all the sort you would expect to meet in Grey's. He was young, considerably younger than Uther – in his mid-twenties, perhaps – with blond, shoulder-length hair. He wore some kind of white smock, and over it one of those sloppy linen jackets with no shape and no collar. The jacket was too short, and the smock reached almost to his knees. Fish out of water. What was a weirdo like this doing here?

Drinks ordered, the general made the introductions. 'Colonel James Armstrong – Uther Pendragon.' Just as he thought. The man with the moustache was a soldier, his keen gaze and firm handshake expressing his forthright personality. 'James is Chief of the Joint Forces Weapons and Communications Research and Development Unit in Beaconsfield. Quite a mouthful, eh? Very hush-hush. A member of this club for how long, James?'

'Twenty years,' said the colonel, 'and every one of them a joy and a privilege.' He indicated the weirdo. 'My deputy, Merlin Thomas.' Expecting Thomas's handshake to be limp, Uther was surprised to find his hand held in a strong and controlling grip. For a moment he had the impression he was being detained and scrutinised. The eyes that studied him were green, luminous and hypnotic.

'We are trying to persuade Merlin to become a member of Grey's,' the general remarked. As he spoke, the weirdo blinked and released Uther's hand. Persuade! Who could possibly need persuading to become a member of Grey's? Uther was puzzled and irritated. Wasn't there a ten year waiting list for God's sake! In exceptional cases someone was able to jump the queue, as Uther had done. But what was so exceptional about Merlin Thomas? He looked as though he would be more at home in a field, with a crook in his hand and a flock of sheep at his heels, than here in the most distinguished club in London.

'Merlin was the outstanding Oxford man of his generation,' said Colonel Armstrong, as if answering the unspoken question. 'A true genius.'

'You exaggerate, James,' said Merlin Thomas, smiling.

'Does he?' said the general. 'Three double firsts before the age of twenty sounds like genius to me.'

'He is also the outstanding inventor of the age,' said the colonel. 'The country is indebted to him. We are very fortunate to have him at Beaconsfield.'

Uther was beginning to be irritated by the praise they were lavishing on the weirdo. Were they trying to put him in his place? Did they secretly resent the upstart South London boy invading these hallowed halls? Or were they simply envious of his wealth?

'Are you involved in the space race?' he asked, trying to make intelligent conversation, 'or are weapons your speciality?'

'Forgive me, but I'm not allowed to answer that,' said Merlin.

'Official Secrets' Act,' the colonel muttered.

After an awkward pause, the general abruptly changed the subject. 'Pendragon's a property developer.'

'What company is that?' asked the colonel.

'It's called Pendragon,' said Uther. 'My own outfit. You wouldn't have heard of it.'

Merlin intoned, as if reciting from an invisible text: 'Pendragon Property Development and Management. West End of London, 96-101, King George Street. Five floors. Private company registered in 1982 with an initial capital of two thousand pounds, now believed worth in the region of two hundred million. Major commercial developments in the City of London, the Docklands, Chelsea Harbour, Knightsbridge, Wimbledon, Manchester, Liverpool and Glasgow. Also fifteen apartment blocks.'

Uther laughed. 'Have you been swatting up on me?'

'Not really,' said Merlin. 'I expect I read about you somewhere or other. When I have nothing better to do, I soak up information on the Internet, or I memorise the Yellow Pages, trade gazettes, company reports, phone directories, that sort of thing.'

Uther wasn't sure if his leg was being pulled. 'You are not saying you memorise telephone directories, are you?'

'Used to, yes. To be honest I find them rather boring. I prefer Encyclopaedia.'

'Encyclopaedia,' repeated Uther dully.

'Yes.'

'May I ask how long it takes you to achieve this *extraordinary* feat of memory?' Uther's tone was now profoundly sceptical. 'A month? A year?'

'I should say – what? – a couple of hours?'

'Come now, Thomas,' said Uther with a smile, 'are you telling me you can commit an entire encyclopaedia to memory in two hours?'

'You misunderstood me.'

'Aha! Thought perhaps I had,' said Uther, winking broadly at the general.

'Not one encyclopaedia. A set of encyclopaedia.'

Uther's mouth gaped. Recovering his composure, he laughed scornfully. 'Who do you think you're kidding? Pull the other one, it's got bells on. Memorise a set of encyclopaedia in two hours! You expect me to believe that?'

He looked around for support but to his surprise no one was paying him the slightest attention. Why were they not backing him up when the man's claims were so patently absurd? He felt isolated and disoriented, being in a place he did not know, attempting to communicate with people he could not reach.

Suddenly he realised what was going on. It was all a joke, a pretty feeble joke it seemed to him, but a joke nonetheless. What a gullible fool he was. They had really got him going. But if it was a joke, why was no one smiling? The colonel was looking for an ashtray, the general was trying to attract the barman's attention. Both appeared to be seriously preoccupied. If not a practical joke, then, what could it be? Was it perhaps some sort of primitive initiation ritual that new members of the club were traditionally subjected to? Yes, that must be it. And the code of these grown-up schoolboys no doubt dictated that they act as if nothing odd were happening. Fine, anyone could play that game. No one was going to put one over on Uther Pendragon.

'Forgive me,' he said gravely, 'but now that I think about it, two hours does sound feasible – quite feasible. For a genius, that is.' That should fix them, he thought, with a complacent smile.

'I agree,' said the general. 'A couple of hours sounds reasonable enough to me. What's your view, colonel?'

'I would have thought two hours was very reasonable indeed,' said Colonel Armstrong, 'especially for a whole set. Frankly, I'd call it cheap. Was it on sale?'

'Actually, no,' said Merlin, 'I memorised it at full price.'

Uther's mouth gaped. None of this made any sense at all. Were they all stark staring bonkers? Or were they still sending him up?

'Even so, it's pretty incredible,' said the colonel. 'Didn't I say he was a genius?' he observed to no one in particular.

The back of Uther's throat was closing up. Were they all quite mad? He had never experienced a panic attack, but this must surely be what it felt like.

'I always say seeing is believing,' said the general.

'Damned right,' said the colonel, nodding vigorously.

'After you,' said the general.'

'No, after you, sir,' said the colonel politely.

Levitating about eighteen inches off the ground, and revolving slowly until his back was turned to them, the general floated out of the bar towards the members' sitting rooms, followed closely by the colonel.

Uther became aware that Merlin's huge green eyes were staring at him. For some reason he was finding it difficult to think rationally. 'What the hell's going on?' he demanded.

'Something wrong?' asked Merlin innocently.

The sweat bloomed on Uther's face. 'I seem to be hallucinating.'

'Quite possibly. I shouldn't let it worry you.'

'Did I just see what I thought I saw?'

Merlin hesitated. 'I can't be sure what you thought you saw. In any case, what you think you see is not always the same as what you see. And what you see is not always what is there.'

Uther put a hand to his head. 'Either I'm losing my mind, or you are some kind of illusionist. Are you?'

The brilliant eyes shone like two miniature moons. 'In a way.'

'Then,' said Uther, paying a rare compliment, 'you're the best I ever saw.'

Like an owl's, the eyelids dipped in acknowledgement.

Something strange was happening, something Uther did not understand. 'Who *are* you really?' he asked.

'I am Merlin.'

That he knew already. Was the weirdo being deliberately unhelpful? Uther frowned. 'What is it you want from me?'

'Your son,' said Merlin. He might have been asking Uther for a light.

'What on earth are you talking about?' asked Uther, mystified. 'I have no son.'

'Not yet.'

Those damned eyes were so big and bright, they seemed to possess him. 'Very well,' he said, humouring the man, 'let's assume that at some time in the future I have a son. Give me one good reason why I should give him to you.'

'To cheat fate perhaps.'

'There is no such thing as fate,' said Uther dismissively.

'It is written that he will overthrow you.'

That was too much for Uther's pride to take. 'Are you suggesting I should be afraid of my own son?'

'Is that so surprising? Many men are.'

'If ever I had a son, I would know how to control him.'

'Not this one you wouldn't.'

It was all rubbish, impossible to take seriously. There was no rhyme or reason to it. And yet . . . and yet, he sensed something about Merlin that defied reason, something spellbinding, buried deep in that entrancing voice, and in the depths of those hypnotic green orbs. He decided to put him to the test. 'I presume you are offering something in exchange?'

'You will become a member of Parliament.'

Uther shrugged. 'I hardly think I need your help to do that.'

'That will only be the start. You will be what you want to be.'

'And what is that?'

'Prime Minister.'

Dear God, how could he possibly know that? Uther's pulse raced. Excitement blazed in him like a flame, then quickly died. The man was a nutter. 'You can guarantee that, can you?' he asked, with heavy sarcasm.

'I can. If you promise to give me your son.'

'I told you,' said Uther irritably, 'I have no son. What's more, I have absolutely no intention of ever having one.'

'Then you have nothing to lose by promising to give him to me.'

There was, thought Uther, a certain crazy logic to that statement. 'What the hell,' he heard himself say, 'this hypothetical son of mine sounds like a troublemaker. Take him, then, since you seem to want him so much.'

Merlin inclined his head. 'Thank you.'

'You are welcome,' said Uther dryly. 'Mind you,' he added as an afterthought, 'nothing is set in cement.'

'May I ask what you mean by that?' There was a harder edge in Merlin's voice.

'I can always change my mind.'

Merlin shook his head. 'No, Uther. Once you give me your hand, you will never be able to break your word.'

'Who says?'

'Fate will not permit it.'

'Fate again,' said Uther disdainfully. 'You must be joking.'

Merlin extended his hand. 'Do we have a deal?'

'Why do you want him?'

'To save the world.'

Uther stared at Merlin. Was he serious? 'You expect me to believe that?'

Merlin repeated relentlessly. 'Do we have a deal?'

Uther raised his hand. Hesitated. Their fingers touched. They shook. The light in the green moons flared. Merlin sipped his beer. 'Four actually,' he said.

The general's eyebrows arched. 'Four what?'

'Double firsts,' said Merlin. 'Four, not three.'

'I do beg your pardon. Was it really?'

'Yes.'

'Even more remarkable. Apologies. I thought I read it somewhere. I must have been mistaken.'

'Not at all,' said Merlin politely. 'Believing is not always seeing.' He turned away to Uther and winked solemnly before turning back to the general.

Walking down the steps of Grey's out into the reassuringly familiar world, Uther Pendragon had the feeling that he had just returned from a long journey, though he was not at all sure where he had been. Once more the paving stones were solid under the soles of his shoes, the sunlight golden on the buildings. Then suddenly a cloud shut out the sun and a breeze blew down St. James's. The flag on the club veranda lifted and rolled. A muslin curtain flapped from an open first-floor window, and then hung limp. There was a crack of thunder. Umbrellas bloomed on the street and the first raindrops rapped the canvas awnings of the man's shop on the corner of Piccadilly. He hailed a black cab, pushing in front of a man who had hailed it before him, jumped in and watched in amusement as the red-faced loser thrust two fingers in the air. Ignorant yobbo. Life was good. Life was bloody good.

Sinking back he released a sigh of profound contentment. Stunning woman, Igraine. Now that Godfrey was out of the way, he would marry her – after a suitable interval, naturally. There might be gossip otherwise. Celebrity chat was what the mob lived on, wasn't it? Poor sods, what else did they have in their lives? Of course he loved her to bits, or he would never have done . . . what he had done to get her. The most beautiful woman in London, and a Dowager Marchioness into the bargain. Two presents in one gift-wrap. Walking her up the aisle would do him no harm, no harm at all.

Two

THAT EVENING, in exuberant good humour, Uther announced over a glass of champagne in the bar of his favourite dining club that he was now a member of Grey's. 'How about that? Not bad for a boy from the wrong side of the river.'

Igraine regarded him with fond indulgence. 'This is the nineties, darling. That sort of thing doesn't matter any more.'

'Easy for you to say, duchess.' Uther knew very well she was no such thing, duchess being his affectionate and slightly mocking soubriquet for Igraine. Nevertheless, the truth was that though he made fun of the aristocracy, titles impressed him. Igraine, Lady Truro; it had a certain ring to it; secretly he was hugely proud of escorting a Marchioness, even if, since the death of her husband, the Marquess, she was only a Dowager Marchioness. He was also proud of his own background, even prouder for having risen above it. Born in Peckham thirty-two years ago – father a railway worker, mother a cleaning lady – he had discarded the south London accent of his youth, together with outmoded working-class attitudes and socialist ideologies, much as a mountaineer, ascending from camp to camp, discards unnecessary baggage on the way to the top. A realist, he soon discovered that equipment and people indispensable at low altitudes became an intolerable burden in the rarefied atmosphere of the summit climb.

Achieving the status of the most successful property developer in London fulfilled an early ambition. But once he had made his pile, other considerations became pre-eminent. The daughter of a viscount and the widow of a marquess,

Igraine opened up for him an exciting new landscape of social acceptability and of power.

'They're lucky to get you,' she said, adding fondly, 'and so am I.'

They had met at a New Year's Eve party less than a year ago. Uther had a weakness for raven-haired beauties, especially when they were as luscious as Igraine; he had focused all his considerable charm on her. By the end of the evening she had fallen for him, and within a week they had begun an affair. She couldn't believe what she was doing; she kept reminding herself that she was married with three kids; women in her situation simply did not do that sort of thing. Yet however guilty she felt, her feelings were beyond her power to control. She was fond of Godfrey, but with Uther she was irrationally and ecstatically in love; nothing like this had ever happened to her before.

In character, Uther and Godfrey were as different as two men could possibly be. Godfrey was weak and indecisive, constantly in financial trouble, always cadging from his friends; Uther was strong, self-assured, successful, an independent spirit. Godfrey was the product of privilege, Uther the product of deprivation. In appearance, though, they were uncannily alike, the same height, the same heavy build, the same curly black hair, brown eyes and thick lashes. It was eerie and unsettling for her to be sitting opposite the living image of her dead husband. Godfrey was in his grave, yet here in the body of her lover he appeared again, a haunting reminder of the wrongs she had done him.

After dinner they sat in the bar. From time to time she gazed into Uther's eyes, or fondled his face, and once she undid a shirt button and slipped in her fingers to stroke and knead the warm flesh. Generally he discouraged such advances in public, concerned with what people might think. She, on the other hand, did not give a damn. Her love was tactile, passionate, spontaneous. Absurd, she thought, to be acting like some randy teenager; but absurd or not, she found it difficult to keep her hands off him.

There would never be a better time to tell him, she decided. It was July, and the baby was due in December. Surprisingly, he had not noticed anything. But then that was Uther, bless him. He would need careful handling. She began by referring to her symptoms, hoping he would swiftly diagnose her condition, but he was far too self-absorbed to respond to hints, unsubtle though they were. He had, moreover, drunk a great deal of champagne and claret; his brain was not functioning as well as it normally did. At the precise moment she dared to murmur the 'p' word, he had in his imagination planted his foot and a flag on the summit, and was presiding over a cabinet meeting in Number Ten. Receiving no reaction, she decided to postpone the revelation to another day.

Dozing on the way home in the taxi, he suddenly opened his eyes. 'Pregnant!'

'Yes,' she murmured.

'You!'

'Yes.' Her heart pounded in her chest.

'Dear God!' He closed his eyes again and didn't speak another word until they were back in her apartment. 'You do realise this is a total, unmitigated, bloody disaster, don't you?' he said, throwing himself into an armchair.

Igraine was stunned, unable to respond. How selfish could a man be? That the timing was inconvenient for both of them she was the first to admit. But an unmitigated disaster? 'We'll keep it quiet, darling, if that's what you want.' It was all she could think of to say.

'You said you were on the pill,' he observed petulantly.

So it was to be the blame game,' she thought. 'I was. I am.'

'Then how the hell . . . ?'

'I don't know.'

'You'll have to get rid of it,' he said abruptly.

Igraine felt sick; this was the man she loved more than life, the man for whom she had left her husband. The hurt and disappointment showed clearly on her face. She turned her back on him, partly to hide her feelings, partly because she could not bring herself to look at him.

'Darling,' said Uther, assuming a sudden disarming smile, 'I'm being a pig, aren't I? A selfish piggy-wiggy. I've been on my own far too long. Forgive me.' With that he took her in his arms and kissed her, and in an instant she was happy again.

Not a word more was said about the baby. Uther stayed over; something he rarely did, for fear some "sleazebag gutter press journalist" might be lying in wait for him when he left. Disappointingly for her, there was no love-making. As she put her arms round him he rolled away; seconds later he was snoring. His parting words the next morning – 'Whatever happens, we mustn't let it come between us' – echoed in her head all day. Come between us? That sounded ominously like a threat, a warning that this embryo developing inside her could destroy their relationship.

That evening Uther returned to Igraine's apartment later than usual, though much to her relief he was in a good mood. He had lunched with the chairman of the local Conservative Association who had promised that a suitable constituency would be found for him in time for the next General Election, sooner if possible. The weather was set fair, and the summit, albeit distant, in sight.

'I'm proud of you, darling,' she said, genuinely happy for him.

'He particularly emphasised my spotless reputation. The truth is, the party badly needs an injection of decency and integrity. We have been damaged by sleaze.'

'That's one thing they'll never have to worry about with you,' she said loyally.

Uther poured himself a scotch and sat on the sofa next to her, his arm draped across her shoulders. 'Well now, my dearest, that's rather what I wanted to talk about.'

Igraine tensed. She had always told herself that she would do anything for Uther, anything at all.

'This pregnancy – I know what it means to you,' he continued ominously, 'but the point is, if the press got wind of it, I'd be finished. *Kaput*. It wouldn't take them long to discover that you and Godfrey separated a year before he died. It would be pretty damned obvious who the father was. We would both be labelled adulterers.'

'If we tell the truth,' said Igraine, 'I'm sure they'll leave us alone.'

A sour smile. 'I fear you are being a touch naïve, duchess. The press doesn't give a damn about truth; what they care about is a good story, and if it involves adultery and sexual shenanigans, so much the better. That's what sells newspapers. They'll use smear and innuendo. They'll make Godfrey's death look as if . . . '

Uther's arm slipped from her shoulders as Igraine sat up. 'As if what?'

'As if it wasn't an accident,' – Uther avoided her eyes – 'or a suicide.'

Her eyes widened. 'What on earth do you mean?'

'Godfrey refused to give you a divorce,' said Uther, stressing every word.

'So?'

He was studying the carpet now. 'They'll say I had an excellent motive for . . . well, for getting rid of him.'

'But that's absurd!' Igraine protested. 'If they even hinted such a thing, we'd sue them.'

'A fat lot of good that would do. Mud sticks, Igraine. Think of the scandal. The story would run till the next millennium. You are happily married, you meet me, and five minutes later we have an affair and your husband leaves you and goes and lives in a crummy bedsit in Victoria. A year later he kills himself. Five months after his death, you have my baby. Fantastic! Guess who gets the sympathy vote, duchess. Not me, that's for sure. One way or another, they'd say I was responsible for Godfrey's death. They'd crucify me. You too probably,' added Uther for good measure.

'But it wasn't like that.'

'Nevertheless, it's what people will think,' he assured her.

'I don't care what people think,' said Igraine, sounding a great deal more confident than she felt.

'Lucky you, darling,' said Uther tartly. 'I have to care. A politician lives or dies by what people think.'

'Then why go into politics?'

'Because it's what I want.'

Her voice was low and intense. 'And *I* want my baby.'

'You can have as many babies as you like, Igraine, but not this one. Not if you love me.' And he stormed out, almost slamming the front door off its hinges.

Even in the depths of her misery, it occurred to Igraine that she could always start again. There had never been any problem finding men. The real problem was that she wasn't interested in other men; it was this one she wanted. Having just lost her husband, and with a young family to bring up – seven year old Elaine, five year old Margot, and "baby" Morgan, only three – she felt achingly vulnerable. Poor mites, there had already been the most appalling upheaval in their little lives. Now they were just getting used to Uther. No, she concluded, any other man would be unthinkable.

Uther bided his time, flattering himself that Igraine loved him too much to defy him. Yet several days passed and still he had no word from her. At last he was compelled to accept that somehow or other the problem would have to be resolved. Nothing was more important to him than his high political ambitions. He would never be Prime Minister if he were involved in a scandal. There was something else that had preyed on his mind ever since that strange and disturbing meeting with Merlin – those ominous words of his.

It is written that he will overthrow you.

Are you suggesting I should be afraid of my own son?

Is that so surprising? Many men are.

He phoned Igraine. 'We need to talk.' His voice softened. 'I miss you.'

'Me too,' she whispered.

For the rest of the day she waited for the doorbell to ring. Finally at ten o'clock Uther arrived, and as he entered the hall, came straight to the point. 'I was at fault, I confess it. *Mea culpa*. It would be wrong to . . . do what I suggested.' He took her hand. 'I love you, Igraine. I want to marry you. I couldn't bear to lose you.' Igraine's eyes filled with tears. Could he possibly need her as much as she needed him? 'I am going to suggest something, and I want you to consider it very carefully. Please don't answer me right away. Think about it first. Promise me?'

Igraine nodded dumbly.

'My proposal is this. You go down to the country as soon as possible. There's a place I know where you will be very comfortable. Everything will be handled with the utmost discretion. You will have the best care money can buy, and all in a superb setting – a beautiful house in lovely countryside in the heart of Somerset.'

Was he about to pronounce the death sentence on her unborn child? She could not look at him.

'A perfect place to have the baby.'

Her face lit up. Throwing her arms round his neck, she covered him with kisses. Gently he pulled away. 'Let me finish.' Her eyes searched his anxiously.

'You will have the baby, and then . . . ' – a moment of tense silence – 'I shall arrange to have it adopted. You needn't be involved. You may depend on me to find good and loving parents for the child.'

Igraine shrank from Uther, her body hunched, her fists held high, as if she were defending herself against a violent assault. 'Go to hell, you bastard!'

'I suggest we talk about this when you are calmer,' he said coldly. 'What I am proposing is a fair compromise. The child will have a good life, and you and I . . . we shall be happy again.'

Her voice grated in her throat. 'I won't let you take my son away from me.'

'Think about it, Igraine, that's all I ask.' Suddenly he realised what she had said. 'Your *son*? How do you know it's a son?'

'I had a scan. It's a boy,' she said, searching his face for the smallest hint of a change of heart.

'I don't want to hear any more,' he said, turning his back and walking away from her.

She followed, pleading, 'This is your son, your son and heir. Doesn't that mean anything to you?'

He looked at her with cold eyes. 'Think about what I said. I'll phone you in the morning.'

'Our own flesh and blood,' she said sadly. 'How can you ask me to give him away?'

'Believe me, it's for the best.'

She spat out the words. 'Best for your bloody career you mean.'

'Is it such a crime to want success?'

'No. But it's a crime to abandon your child.'

He shrugged. 'Happens every day, duchess. It's a funny old world. You're angry now, but you'll come round.'

How dare he patronise her? How dare he tell her how to think and feel? She was angry, angrier than she had ever been in her life, angry with him and angry with herself for being so mistaken in her judgement of him. She hated Uther for not being the man she had thought he was, and she hated him all the more because she knew he was going to get his way.

Three

January 1995

THE WAITING ROOM was sparsely furnished: two grey
polystyrene chairs, a white polystyrene table, its top
burned by cigarettes. On the table was a metal ashtray and a
copy of *Country Life* dated March 1992. The only decoration
on the grey-painted walls was a photograph of a young Queen
Elizabeth taken on the day of her coronation.

Uther lowered himself gingerly onto one of the chairs,
looked around the room and shuddered. Whilst he waited, his
thoughts drifted back a couple of weeks. To give Igraine moral
support he had driven down to Somerset and stayed at what
the Travel Agents had described as a Hostelry, whatever that
was; a synonym for a fleapit, presumably. On the afternoon of
the 22nd the clinic had phoned to say the brat was on its way.
Three days before Christmas – what a time to give birth. He
had hung around the fleapit a few hours; no sense in rushing to
the clinic, especially as he had not the slightest desire to watch
the 'proceedings'. Later, driving there, he had been caught in a
storm; first a wild wind, then distant thunder rolling closer and
closer, and then the storm itself breaking with such a banging
and clattering it might have signalled the birth of the world, or
the death. He had never known anything like it, the lightning
had lit up the streets as if it were day, and then the rain, like
a million tiny fists rapping on the car roof. The windscreen
wipers had packed up, and he had been stranded in the middle
of the village. Suddenly it was over – just before midnight –
and everything was eerily calm. Apparently that was when the
child was born.

Merlin entered briskly, shook hands with Uther, and sat at the table facing him. 'Offer you something? Tea? coffee?'

'No thanks.' Uther rested his hands on the table and examined his nails.

'Any problem finding the place?' asked Merlin politely.

Uther tried to concentrate his gaze on the Queen's portrait slightly to the left of Merlin's head. It was no good, the green orbs drew him back. 'Your directions were perfect.'

'Sorry about the red tape at the gate.'

'They certainly quizzed me. You chaps must be doing something pretty special here.'

Merlin turned his luminous eyes on Uther and made no comment.

'We met a few months ago,' said Uther. Being nervous was a new experience for him, and he didn't much care for it. 'I don't know if you remember me,' he added diffidently.

Merlin blinked. 'Indeed I do.'

'I expect it seems odd.'

Merlin directed a quick searching look at his visitor and waited for him to continue.

'My coming to see you, I mean.' Uther ruffled the pages of the tattered *Country Life*. 'You do understand this is all . . . highly confidential.'

Merlin inclined his head, waiting for Uther to come to the point.

Uther did not really know why he was here. Why here? Why Merlin? There was no rational explanation, except perhaps that there was no other place to go. 'This friend of mine I mentioned on the phone . . . ' Was it worth persisting with the charade? On balance he thought it might be, though Merlin was obviously no fool, and very likely guessed that the 'friend' was sitting opposite him. The pretence at least allowed him to address Merlin as an equal, rather than as a supplicant. 'I thought you might be able to help him. His wife wants to have the baby boy adopted, and he has agreed – reluctantly I may say.'

Merlin's eyelids drooped in the subtlest of acknowledgements.

'His main concern is to protect the lady's good name. He intends to marry her.' Uther shifted uncomfortably on the tiny chair. 'Naturally.'

Merlin's face remained impassive.

'The child was not – um – conceived in wedlock.' The archaic phrase somehow distanced Uther from the harsh realities of the situation, as indeed it was designed to. 'Normally this would present no problem, not in this day and age. In this case though, there are . . . complications.'

'What sort of complications?' The green eyes were focused unwaveringly on Uther.

'I prefer not to go into details, if you don't mind. Take it from me, there would be a scandal, a scandal that would destroy both their lives. Though as I say, my friend is less concerned with his own reputation than with that of his lady friend.'

No response. Uther found the absence of reaction irritating, showing a lack of respect, perhaps even a touch of scepticism. Again he asked himself whether he was doing the right thing in approaching this strange man. Why should he be able to help? Even if he could, would he keep his mouth shut? Panic stirred, his heart fluttered in his chest, and he was tempted to make some excuse and walk out. But that would be foolhardy, he had said too much to turn back now.

'Is this really your friend's child?' asked Merlin.

Uther was startled out of his reverie. 'Why do you ask?'

'Because if it is,' said Merlin, forcing the issue, 'then I fear there is nothing I can do.'

Uther was about to protest in the strongest terms, but Merlin's green orbs were turned on him, and in their blinding light, it seemed, nothing but the truth was possible. 'If you must know, the child is mine.'

Merlin nodded.

'I'm not sure, but I seem to remember you and I making some

kind of deal,' said Uther, who remembered it all too clearly, 'a deal I confess I never took seriously. And now here I am. A strange thing, life.'

'Isn't it.'

'Full of coincidences.' Uther was a proud man. It was humiliating to be sitting here, cap in hand – well, more like baby in hand. 'As it happens, I might be looking for a good home for my, um . . . '

'For your son.'

Uther was looking intently at the table now. 'Do you think you could . . . ?'

'When was he born?'

'The twenty-second of December, I think it was.'

'The winter solstice,' said Merlin.

'What does that have to do with anything?' Uther snapped irritably.

Merlin responded mildly. 'The winter solstice is about birth and rebirth.'

'Really?' said Uther indifferently.

'The sun is at its lowest point. The winter solstice is the longest, darkest night of the year. In the moment of greatest despair, a seed begins to sprout.'

Despair? Seed? What on earth was the man talking about?

'The storm had just died down?' enquired Merlin.

'There was a storm. Why all these questions?'

'I just wanted to be sure. So the boy is now two weeks old.'

'I suppose.'

'Wonderful.' Merlin beamed.

Uther saw nothing wonderful about it. Wonderful it would be if Merlin could spirit the brat away. Didn't he claim to be some kind of magician? That extraordinary business in the bar – it was all coming back to him now.

'Look here, can you help me or not?' asked Uther impatiently, making it clear by his expression and tone of voice that he found the whole business frustrating, not to say demeaning.

'There's a couple I know who would be happy to have the child,' said Merlin, unperturbed. 'They have a son about a year old, but the lady can't have any more children. They have been thinking of adopting for some time.'

'What kind of people are they?'

'She is a social worker. He is a schoolmaster.'

A social worker, a schoolmaster. My god, thought Uther, these are real people, a real man and a real woman with real jobs and a real son. And for all its strangeness, this was a real conversation he was having. Suddenly he understood the meaning of what he was doing; he was giving away his own son. Like the movement of some prehistoric creature in the depths of an uncharted lake, an unaccustomed and sombre emotion stirred the dark depths of his soul, and then was still. 'Is it a good home? I have to be sure. Good background and all that? Are they capable of . . . I mean, you're quite sure they'll look after him properly?'

'They are decent, unpretentious people,' said Merlin, 'moral, well educated and loving. Above all, loving.'

'Where do they live?'

A slight hesitation. 'In a small village in the Welsh countryside.'

Uther could scarcely conceal his distaste.

'In my opinion they would make ideal parents for your son.'

Feeling the need to regain the moral high ground he had so clearly lost, Uther shook his head in sham sorrow. 'Ideal? If only that were true. I fear the only ideal parents would be his own natural father and mother. You simply cannot imagine the pain this causes me. I wouldn't wish it on my worst enemy. But then life isn't fair, is it? Not on us, not on him. We are to be deprived of the joy of bringing up a son, and he, poor mite, will lose all those advantages I could have given him.' An anguished look was followed by another gloomy shake of the head. 'Ah well,' he continued with resignation, 'no sense in torturing oneself. The truth is, I'm too sensitive for my own good. It's a curse, you know, being tender-hearted. But then that's the way I am.'

Whatever he was thinking, Merlin's face revealed nothing. 'Do you want me to approach my friends?'

'By all means. Naturally I shall have to meet them to approve them – or not, as the case may be.'

'No.' The monosyllabic response was surprisingly firm.

'What do you mean, no?'

'Meeting them would not be a good idea.'

'My dear fellow,' said Uther imperiously, 'you surely don't expect me to hand over my son to complete strangers?'

'That is how it must be.'

Uther flushed with anger. Who the hell did this weirdo think he was, dictating terms to Uther Pendragon? He thumped the table with clenched fist. 'Not acceptable.'

'A normal condition of adoption,' said Merlin calmly, 'is that the adoptive parents and the birth parents do not meet.'

'This is hardly a normal adoption.'

'Would you like the other couple to know who you are?'

'None of their damn business.' Uther was affronted to observe the mini-disturbance at the corners of Merlin's mouth. This was no laughing matter. 'You are not suggesting there is any comparison between my rights and theirs?'

Silence.

To hell with it, thought Uther, that did it; he was going to walk out. He laid his hands on the table, pushed back his chair and prepared to leave. And if he left, what then? Where would he go? To an adoption agency? He would never be able to rely on their discretion. It would only be a matter of time before a greedy employee sold the story to the editor of some sleazy tabloid. To whom then? To a friend? An acquaintance? A colleague? Was there a person in the world he could trust apart from Merlin? No. Aggravating though it was he really had no choice. Best get it over with. That disturbing exchange at Grey's was in his head: *Why do you want him? To save the world*. Suddenly he had the odd feeling that the whole situation was out of his control, that it had all been decided a long time ago, long even before he met Merlin.

A few days later Uther drove to Merlin's cottage and handed over the tiny baby, carefully wrapped against the winter's cold. Uther glanced round Merlin's kitchen, with its simple pine furniture and stone floor. A fire burned in the grate. Uther shuddered to think in what squalor a teacher and a social worker lived in some drab village in the Welsh countryside. Was he condemning his own flesh and blood to a lifetime of poverty? Noticing a crib in the far corner of the room, his heart sank. Dear god, not even a nursery?

'Is there no room for the baby?' he enquired loftily.

Merlin spread his hands wide. 'All the room in the world.'

Uther sniffed. 'That is not what I mean.'

'I know what you mean.'

'What about money?'

'Money is not a problem,' said Merlin.

Uther waved a dismissive hand. 'I shall arrange something on a regular basis. A cheque or a bank transfer. No one need ever know where it comes from.'

'That won't be necessary.'

Uther seemed disappointed. 'Well,' he said, shifting his feet uncomfortably, 'then it's good-bye.'

Merlin nodded. 'Goodbye.'

After Uther had gone, Merlin warmed a bottle of milk and fed the tiny baby, cradling it in his arms. 'Welcome,' he whispered in its ear, 'welcome once again.' When the baby was asleep, he laid it in its crib.

It was bitterly cold, a crisp, bright January night. Merlin opened the back door and stood for a few minutes looking up at the sky alive with stars. Somewhere in the woods a barn owl hooted. Closing the door again, Merlin smiled. He knew that sound. The fire chattered in the grate. For a few moments he gazed into the flames, stirring the embers with a poker. Crossing the room, he stood by the crib, eyes closed, the palms of his hands pressed together as though in prayer.

The doorbell rang. Uther again. 'I almost forgot,' he said. 'His name is Arthur.'

'An excellent name,' said Merlin.

Four

To the west of Carmarthen, not far from Merlin's birthplace, and less than a dozen miles from the Bristol Channel, the tiny village of Ponterlally sits cosily in a fertile valley. At the east end of the valley, two flat-topped hills known locally as Adam and Eve overlook the forest called Eden. There, according to Ponterlally's official storyteller, golden-eyed lions hunt on moonless nights, and loose skinned elephants shuffle their ponderous dance at sunrise. Most villagers, however, see only hedgehogs, rabbits, squirrels, foxes, stoats, badgers and deer, and hear the raucous caw of crows at dusk and the hoot of owls in the snug hours of the night.

The village stream, called Lally, a distant relative several times removed from the river Severn, bustles through the valley, flowing down the shop side of the main street, under the stone bridge that tradition says was built by Julius Caesar, then south to join its tributary kinsfolk on the slow march to the sea.

In this valley of orchards, farms and fairy tales, lived the Hughes: young Hector and Elizabeth, man and wife, both born in the village, friends from childhood days. Elizabeth was a woman of strong character and emotions, and Hector a sensible fellow with a logical mind, both feet planted firm as oaks in the land of his birth.

At eighteen Hector went to the village school to teach, on the understanding that it was only a temporary commitment until he found his true vocation. Never a week went by that he did not ponder his future, until the day came, many long years later, when he was astonished to discover that what he had been doing all his life was what he had always wanted to do. Elizabeth, for her part, never had the smallest doubt that what she was doing was right for her. She was a part-time social worker, as well as being a wife to the man she had loved since she was twelve, and a mother to their only child, eleven months old Keir.

'The little darling,' she said, her pretty face glowing with happiness as she stroked the baby's tiny cheeks with the tips of her fingers.

'You know something? He looks like you,' she told Hector, who was about to point out the logical fallacy when he caught the look in Merlin's eye and thought better of it.

Merlin beckoned his friends to the kitchen table. Husband and wife sat opposite him, Hector with his arm round Elizabeth whilst she cradled baby Arthur. 'I want you both to promise me something. When Arthur is ready to hear it, you must tell him he is adopted.'

Hector liked to have the whys and wherefores of everything. 'How will we know when he's ready?'

'When the time comes, you will know. But whatever happens, you must tell him before his thirteenth birthday. Do I have your promise?' Merlin was looking at Elizabeth.

'I suppose so,' she said. 'Though why you men always want everything so cut and dried I shall never know.'

Merlin was content. 'You will make him a fine mother.'

'Will he want to know who . . . *they* are?' She could not bring herself to use the word "parents", for in her own mind Arthur was already her child, and she had no intention of sharing him with anyone.

'One day he will,' said Merlin.

'Who are they?' asked Hector.

Merlin smiled, knowing his friend as well as he did. 'I'm afraid I can't tell you that now.'

Hector sighed, frustrated. 'It's just that I like to have everything clear.'

'I know,' said Merlin. He reached across and patted Hector's shoulder affectionately. 'Patience, my friend. Everything will be clear in time.'

As Elizabeth rocked the sleeping child, her whole body was flooded by a wave of tenderness so powerful that she almost fainted. When her head cleared, she said, looking down at him, 'My son is special.'

'Yes,' said Merlin.

'Why us?' she asked.

'It is written,' said Merlin enigmatically.

For a full minute they did not speak. The bracket clock on the mantelpiece ticked self-importantly, the damp logs hissed and snapped in the flames. 'On the sixteenth of January,' said Merlin, breaking the silence, 'is the next full moon. I will tell you what you must do.'

When the night of the full moon came, the outside temperature was below zero. Hector stood at the kitchen door that led to the back garden. 'Be reasonable, Elizabeth, it's far too cold.'

She clasped the baby to her bosom. 'We gave Merlin our word.'

To Hector it simply did not make sense, and if a thing didn't make sense, you shouldn't do it. 'It's freezing out there. You want the boy to catch pneumonia?'

'We must do as Merlin told us. Don't ask me why. I just know it,' said Elizabeth, beginning to remove the baby's clothes.

'Are you out of your mind, girl? The poor mite will catch his death!'

'Stand aside, Hector.' She spoke quietly but with such authority that he moved away from the door, though still protesting.

'This is madness. I'll tell Merlin we did what he wanted us to do. He'll never know we didn't.'

'He'll know,' insisted Elizabeth.

Hector shook his head in bewilderment. 'It doesn't make

sense.'

'Some things don't.' With that she opened the door and went out to the garden followed by Hector, muttering angrily. The night sky was overcast, the moon and stars nowhere to be seen. Elizabeth held the naked baby high, and Hector, shrugging his shoulders in defeat, found himself speaking aloud the words that Merlin said would come to him.

'We offer you your son, Arthur, who has come again. We shall love him as our own; we shall prepare him as far as we are able. It is written that he will be wise and courageous and will perform great deeds. It is written that he will know much happiness, and much sadness too. It is also written that when his time comes he will be reunited with the Creator and with everything that lives and dies. We offer you your son, Arthur, who has come again.'

As Hector spoke, the clouds parted, and the full glory of the shimmering silver planet was unveiled in the eastern sky. 'We offer you your son, Arthur, who has come again. We shall teach him, as far as we are able, to know the planets and the stars and the galaxies, and all the heavenly bodies. We shall teach him, as far as we are able, to know himself, and to love his fellow men and all creatures. We shall teach him, as far as we are able, to fear nothing, neither life nor death. We offer you your son, Arthur, who has come again.'

Then the sky blazed with a light so dazzling that they were forced to turn away their faces. Gurgling with joy, the baby reached up his tiny arms as if to greet the heavens, kicking his legs and wriggling so hard that Elizabeth feared she might drop him.

Filled with wonder, they brought him back into the kitchen. Despite the biting cold outside, his little naked body was as warm as toast. Still Elizabeth was taking no chances; wrapping Arthur in a shawl, she sat in front of the fire and held him until he fell asleep. She was about to return him to his own crib, when on an impulse she laid him next to his adoptive brother.

Immediately, Keir began to cry.

Hector picked up Keir, put him across his shoulder and patted him gently on the back. When he stopped crying, he laid him next to Arthur again. For a few moments the two babies lay quietly side by side. But then, to Hector's surprise, Keir began to shriek louder than ever, fists clenched, face bright red, feet drumming the mattress. 'Poor baba's got wind,' said Hector soothingly.

Elizabeth shook her head. 'That's not wind,' she said, 'that's rage.' And the instant she put Arthur back in his own cot, Keir stopped crying.

Five

Having served ten years as Deputy Director of the Weapons and Communications Research and Development Unit, Merlin handed in his resignation. It was a disappointment, if not entirely a surprise to Colonel James Armstrong, Merlin's boss, and a major setback for the Ministry of Defence. Whilst Merlin was unknown to the general public, amongst researchers and scientists his name was magic. Britain now led the world in several important fields – robots, nano-technology, communications and weapons technology amongst others – and the explanation was simple: Merlin Thomas.

The Defence Minister was on the phone the next day. 'This is extremely bad news, James. The PM is seriously upset. It's no exaggeration to say that the United Kingdom owes its pre-eminent position in the world to Merlin, not to mention our economic prosperity. He has boosted our sales of weapons and technology several hundred percent. We simply cannot afford to lose him.'

No one knew that better than James Armstrong. 'I understand, sir, but I'm afraid he has made up his mind.'

'Then make him change it.'

'How?'

'Give him what he wants. Double his salary if necessary.'

James Armstrong sighed. In his experience politicians were invariably hardened cynics, judging others by their own dubious standards. 'It isn't a question of money.'

'Do I need to remind you that everyone has his price,' said the minister wearily. 'Discover what that is, and we have him,

James. It could be money, it could be a country house, it could be a generous *douceur*, it could be a title. For all we know he might settle for an Aston Martin. Whatever it takes. I mean what I say, James: whatever it takes. Am I making myself clear?'

He would have to be as big an idiot as the minister not to understand him. 'Yes, sir. Crystal clear.'

James Armstrong conveyed the minister's message as tactfully as possible, but as he expected, nothing could tempt Merlin.

'At least tell me why you're leaving. For my own satisfaction.'

'I have something more important to do,' said Merlin vaguely.

'What could be more important than serving your country?'

Merlin hesitated; there were things he could not discuss, even with James. 'Let's just say I have another master to serve.'

That was hard to credit. 'Does that mean you are going to work for the competition?'

Merlin smiled. 'In a way.'

'I must say you surprise me, Merlin. You are always saying the world is in grave danger, and here you are walking out on us. What has changed?'

It was a good question, and again, hard to answer truthfully. 'Nothing. The terrorists have the weapons and the technology to destroy us. Every year that passes brings mankind closer to annihilation.'

In spite of himself, James Armstrong shivered. 'Twilight of the gods? Ragnarok? *Götterdämmerung*?'

'Something like that.'

There were times when Merlin scared him, and this was one of them. 'My God, you sound like an Old Testament prophet.'

'I fear you don't take me seriously.'

'Indeed I do,' said James Armstrong earnestly. 'So does the PM.'

A sceptical smile. 'Only because I'm good for the country's arms trade. Believe me, James, there are greater priorities than exporting weapons. The time is fast approaching when we shall no longer have the capacity to take on the terrorists and the terror states. Our armed forces are weak and unprepared. The same is true of the rest of Europe, and even of the United States. Their soldiers don't want to fight, and as for their technology, it may be expensive, but it doesn't do the job.'

Merlin looked and sounded as sombre as Armstrong had ever known him. 'We need to strengthen our defences, no doubt about it,' he admitted.

'Being able to defend yourself is not enough,' said Merlin. 'If you wait for your enemies to strike, it is always too late. We have to hunt them down wherever they are – seek them out, and destroy them.'

If Merlin felt so strongly, then why in heaven's name was he resigning? 'This is no time to walk away, man. Stay and give us the means to destroy our enemies before they destroy us.'

'I can give you the means. What I can't give you is the will,' said Merlin sadly. 'We are in the hands of politicians who are not interested in the future of mankind. All they care about is getting elected, lining their pockets and promoting their image.'

So that was it. That was why he had resigned. Merlin had finally given up on the politicians. And who could blame him? James Armstrong tried one last desperate throw of the dice. 'I shall probably have to resign myself.'

'Why on earth would you do that?'

'The PM is furious with me. He thinks I'm responsible for your resignation.'

Merlin chuckled. 'You never were a very good liar, James.'

Armstrong raised his hands in surrender. 'Alright, I confess. It was a crude attempt at emotional blackmail. But do me one favour. The PM's PPS is desperate to see you. Go and talk to him. At least it would get them off my back. That much you owe me.'

Alec Pettifer, Parliamentary Private Secretary to the Prime Minister, crossed the room with a welcoming smile and an outstretched hand. 'A privilege to meet you, Mr Thomas. You have quite a reputation here. Do sit down.'

The two men faced each other across the PPS's imposing desk. The PPS prided himself on being a cool, twenty-first century man. He had seen most things, though never anything quite as bizarre as Merlin Thomas, quite the most oddly dressed individual ever to enter Number 10, even in these egalitarian days. What was he wearing? A knee-length sheet, and what looked like a hessian sack with pockets. As for that scraggy, shoulder-length blond hair . . . he looked more like a pop star than a major brain. Still, genius often came in strange packages. Twenty-five, and the greatest mind since Leonardo da Vinci, so it was said.

'I'll come straight to the point, Merlin. May I call you Merlin?'

He already had, hadn't he? 'Of course.'

'I am authorised by the Prime Minister to offer you a knighthood.'

'Why?'

Now the PPS had considerable experience in such matters. Offers of honours elicited varying responses; either fulsome gratitude, or incredulity, or some disingenuous expression of unworthiness was invariably involved. Never in his experience had anyone responded with a question quite so challenging, more than challenging – provoking. 'Are you asking me in what way you have earned a knighthood?'

'Not at all,' said Merlin, 'I have not the slightest doubt that I have earned it. I am questioning the Prime Minister's motives in offering it to me.'

Bloody impertinence. Who did this spook think he was? The PPS took a deep breath and resolved to remain calm. His speciality was handling awkward customers with skill and tact. 'The PM feels it is time to recognise your outstanding work in research. He believes, and I understand his view is shared by the President of the United States, that your contribution has been unique and invaluable in many fields, not least in the development of new weapons systems, satellite surveillance, communications, and micro-technology – to say nothing of your remarkable work with – um – robots.'

'What you say about my work is undoubtedly true,' said Merlin, who saw no point in false modesty. 'I was wondering whether the timing of the offer had any particular significance?'

'A simple case of achievement justly rewarded.'

'There are no conditions attached? Because if there are . . . '

'None whatsoever,' confirmed Pettifer.

Merlin considered. 'I am most grateful for the honour, then.'

'It is we who should be grateful. Your work at Weapons Research has been, and of course continues to be, of national importance.'

Merlin's eyes flashed. 'Continues to be? But I have handed in my resignation. Had you not heard?'

An unctuous beam. 'I believe there was some . . . chatter, though I never took it seriously. Anyway, I imagine that now . . . '

'Am I being asked to withdraw my resignation?'

Alec Pettifer shifted uneasily in his chair. He was not accustomed to being put in corners. A corner was not a convenient place from which to conduct good public relations. 'The PM expects nothing from his friends, nothing, that is, but loyalty. I'm not saying he would not be enormously . . . pleased, and . . . relieved, if you were to see fit to stay on another . . . what shall we say?' He was suddenly uncomfortably aware of the unsettling effect of Merlin's gaze. It was like being observed by two shining satellite dishes. ' . . . another year or two, perhaps? Entirely up to you, of course. Absolutely voluntary.' He bared his teeth, emphasising how voluntary it was. 'Shall we say . . . three or four years? So much work to be done. Your decision, naturally. The PM was adamant. No conditions, no deals. He has the very greatest respect for your integrity.'

'And my millennium proposals for research and development?'

'Are being studied.'

'What about my paper on the formation of a dedicated anti-terrorist task force?'

'That too is under consideration.'

'But not acted on.'

'Give it time, Merlin. The wheels of government . . . '

'How long?'

The PPS offered up the palms of his hands. 'We do what we can. The constraints of budgets, you know. People do so loathe paying taxes. Who can blame them?'

He was already congratulating himself on his people skills, and on a job well done. It could so easily have ended differently. Pushing back his chair, he clapped his hands on his knees and leaned forward, indicating that the meeting was over. 'Your name will be in the New Year's Honours' List. May I be the first to congratulate you.'

Merlin stood. 'Be sure to thank the Prime Minister. Tell him how much I appreciate his kind offer, which under the circumstances, and with regret, I cannot accept.'

In the act of rising, Alec Pettifer froze in a crouching position. 'You are turning down a knighthood?'

'I am.'

The PPS fell back in his chair. 'Isn't that somewhat arrogant of you?'

'I can see how it might look that way. I assure you, though, I don't feel arrogant. I feel only regret that my warnings are being ignored.'

At the door of his office, bridging the awkward moments of ushering out his distinguished visitor, the PPS remarked tartly, 'The Prime Minister will not be pleased. Is there anything you would like to say by way of explanation?'

Merlin considered the question. 'Tell the Prime Minister this: time is short. Every day that passes we lose ground to those who threaten the stability of the world. We must destroy them, or they will destroy us.'

'Are you not rather stepping out of your field, Mr. Thomas? These matters are, after all, best left to politicians.'

'Are they, Mr. Pettifer? What have politicians ever done to earn our trust? Tell me that. Can you think of one good reason why we should place in their hands the most precious thing we have – the future of mankind?'

'If I may say so, Thomas, you seem to take yourself a bit too seriously. But then you are young, very young. Politicians are not infallible, but they do have the experience, and on the whole they make good use of it. There have always been prophets of doom, and mankind has survived in spite of them. No doubt it will continue to survive.'

'That cannot be taken for granted.'

'You and Nostradamus, eh?'

Merlin shook his head. 'We are very different, he and I. Nostradamus was convinced that the end of the world was inevitable. I am convinced it is not.'

When Merlin had gone, the PPS breathed a sigh of frustration tinged with relief. The fellow obviously had a screw loose, several screws in fact. Didn't they say that genius was close to madness? Had he slipped over the edge? A knighthood? A straightjacket would be more appropriate.

When the news broke of Merlin's resignation from the Weapons and Research Unit, there were many in both the commercial and academic worlds eager to employ his services.

First, however, he had to be found, and that, for a time at least, proved impossible, for Merlin had disappeared. He seemed to have broken all contact with his friends and former colleagues, surfacing for brief periods in various parts of the world, never staying in the same place for long. No one knew what he was up to, though there were plenty of rumours: he was creating complex software programmes for the drug barons; he had become a master computer hacker; he was amassing a great fortune; he was on a remote desert island testing weapons of the future for the Chinese army. He was working for the Russians, he was working for the Americans, he was working for the Israelis, he was working for the Arabs. He was in South America, he was in Africa, he was in the Antarctic, he was on the sea bed, he was in space. When the unglamorous truth was revealed, it created both alarm and sheer disbelief; Merlin had become an assistant House Master at Glastonbury School in the county of Somerset.

That he had chosen an academic rather than a commercial career was not perhaps so surprising. What was more puzzling was that he had not offered himself to one of the United Kingdom's principal centres of learning and research. Had he done so, it was certain that every leading University in the land would have competed hotly for him. Quite apart from the inevitable academic glory, he would certainly have been showered with national honours and prestigious appointments; Chairman of this Royal Commission, President of that Council, and no doubt Tsar of whatever Committee or Association he cared to name. Yet for some inexplicable reason he had abandoned any notion he might once have had of making a name for himself, and in the process as good as labelled himself a failure. No one doubted that he would make an excellent schoolmaster, but oh what a waste of such extraordinary talents! It was a mystery to everyone who knew and admired him.

Six

O N A BLUSTERY DAY in late summer two boys were fishing near Ponterlally bridge. The eldest, a lad of eight, sat tense and straight-backed, his posture indicating deep concentration, left hand grasping the fishing rod, right hand firmly on the reel, never for a moment taking his eyes off the little red float riding the surface of the water, alert for the small dipping movement that would tell him a fish was nibbling at the bait. By his side, sprawled on his back, legs extended, ankles crossed, fishing rod balanced in the crook formed by his bare feet, lay his younger brother. His hair was white blond, his eyes a startlingly vivid blue, the colour of cornflowers, and they were looking not down at the river, but up at the sky. Keir found his brother's constant day-dreaming irritating. 'Where are you, for goodness' sake?' he asked, for the umpteenth time.

His younger brother did not answer. Where was he? How to explain that he was journeying to a place so far away that it was beyond the reach even of his restless imaginings? At this moment his mind was filled not with reels and floats and worms but with the vastness of the universe, where millions of solar systems and galaxies roamed, and black holes lay in wait to trap the unwary.

'Arthur!'

Some day, he dreamed, he too might be up there exploring those infinite tracts of space and time – times past and times future. It was possible, anything was possible if you believed, wasn't it? See there! And there again! Way, way up, in a sudden flare of time, he glimpsed his future in a flurry of white clouds as the wind whirled them across the sky.

'*Arthur*!' The name cracked like a whip in the morning air. Arthur's blue eyes widened as he sat up sharply.

'Where on earth are you?'

Arthur thought of trying to explain that he had not been on earth at all but decided not to; Keir would never understand. 'I was thinking.'

A scornful look darkened Keir's face. 'Thinking! Is that what you call it! You said you wanted to come fishing with me. Why aren't you fishing?'

'I am,' said Arthur. 'Sort of.'

'No, you're not. You're dreaming,' said Keir sternly. Although there was only a year between them, Keir was very much the elder brother. He took very seriously what he perceived to be his fraternal duty, a significant part of which was assaulting his younger brother either verbally or physically, or both. 'You want a fight?'

Arthur shook his head. He could never see the point of fighting. Besides, he always got the worst of it.

'You're a wimp, you know that?'

Arthur was silent.

'You watch out,' said Keir, 'or I'll thump you. You want me to thump you?'

'No.'

'Say you're sorry, then.'

'What for?'

Keir raised his fist threateningly.

'I'm sorry.'

Arthur pulled a handful of grass from the river bank. Throwing it into the water, he watched the green threads separate and drift downstream in the current. Watching him, the exasperated Keir wagged a stern finger. 'How many times do I have to tell you? Dreaming doesn't catch fish. There was one tugging on your line just now and you didn't even notice.'

'Was there?' Arthur lay back again, head resting on clasped

hands. He had noticed alright, and was secretly happy that the fish had got away.

Keir, who always worked diligently at everything, had no patience with his kid brother. There was something wrong with him, he never took anything seriously. If there was one thing Keir had learned from his father – if a thing was worth doing, it was worth doing well. Why was his brother so lazy? It was shameful. 'We've been here ages, and you haven't caught a single fish.'

Though Keir would never understand, Arthur was here to be with his brother, not to catch fish. 'Doesn't matter,' he ventured.

'Doesn't matter!' echoed Keir scornfully. 'If catching a fish doesn't matter, then what's the point of fishing?' Keir allowed himself a smile of quiet satisfaction; he was rather pleased with that remark, flattering himself that he had made an excellent point.

It seemed to Arthur that fish looked very happy in the river. So why not leave them there? That was his opinion, at least, but one he kept to himself when Keir was around. On the other hand, he was quite content to trot along with his older brother and be part of what he was doing. Despite everything, Arthur loved his brother, which was something else best kept to himself; Arthur had learned from experience that Keir was very touchy about anything to do with feelings. Once, when Arthur was much smaller, he had tried to kiss Keir on the cheek, and Keir had screwed up his face and jeered at him for being a sissy. Arthur had never forgotten that, but nevertheless nothing could alter the fact that for Arthur, Keir was the wisest, the most grown up, and altogether the best older brother any boy could have.

'Keir?' he whispered.

A sigh of exasperation. 'What!'

A nod up at the sky. 'Do you think *they* are watching us?'

Keir looked blank. 'Do I think who is watching us?'

'The aliens,' said Arthur.

Keir was thoroughly exasperated. His concentration had been disturbed yet again, and his brother was talking rubbish. 'How many times do I have to tell you? There's no such thing as aliens.'

'Are you sure?'

'Grow up.' Keir reeled in a fish. 'Even if there were any,' he added disdainfully, 'why would they waste time watching you?'

'I expect you're right,' said Arthur.

'Of course I'm right. They'd have better things to do.'

'Like what?'

Keir groaned with frustration. That was another irritating thing about Arthur, he was forever asking questions. Ending a conversation with him was like trying to wipe honey off your fingers. 'Like . . . well, you know . . . invading another planet or something.'

Arthur sat up sharply, eyes bright with excitement. 'You think they might invade earth?'

'Don't be bloody daft!'

'Why not?'

'Because . . . ' Keir floundered for the definitive response, the one that would wipe the sticky mess off his fingers for good. 'Because, stupid . . . because they are so many light years away from us that by the time they arrived, *we wouldn't be here any more.*'

Arthur lay back, closing one eye and then the other, observing his big toe move first to the left, then to the right. Why did it seem to move, when actually it hadn't moved at all? Or had it? How could you be sure? It was quite hard to be sure about anything. He was not even sure he understood what Keir meant, though it seemed like the wisest thing he had ever heard. He regarded his brother with a mixture of awe and astonishment. It was amazing; Keir was only eight years old, and already he knew everything.

'And don't ask any more silly questions,' said Keir, terminating the discussion. He tried hard to focus again on his rod and line but irritating thoughts crept in to his head disturbing his concentration. One of the most annoying things about Arthur was the way fish gathered by the river bank the moment he appeared. That never happened to Keir. There they were now, dozens of them, jostling and leaping a few inches from Arthur's bare feet. And what was he doing? Taking advantage of his good fortune? No. He could have bent down and scooped a handful into his basket. Instead, he was wriggling his toes, gazing at the sky and talking to himself. Once he even saw Arthur reach into the water, pick up a fish and stroke it. What's more, he spoke to it! He actually spoke to a fish as if it were a friend of his! The fish didn't even wriggle. He could easily have tossed it in the basket, but no, not Arthur. What did he do? He threw it back in the river again. What could you do with a ninny like that?

Keir lived to please his parents, Hector and Elizabeth. Getting things right was the best way he knew of earning their approval. Whenever he went fishing, he prided himself on catching at least five or six good-sized fish. Today, he had caught eight, a record. Unfortunately it was not in his nature to be satisfied for long. As he heaved the heavy basket onto his shoulder, he was whistling happily, but on the long trudge back, his spirits began to fail, and by the time the two boys got home, Keir was miserable. Why had he not caught more fish? he asked himself. He could have done, should have done. Glumly, he received his father's congratulations. 'Eight fish! And big ones too! Well done, Keir! Well done, indeed! Mum will be delighted. Run along to the kitchen and show her your catch.' Hector then made a big show of rummaging around in Arthur's basket, pretending to look surprised that it was empty. 'I expect they jumped back in the river, eh, Arthur?'

Arthur could come home with an empty fishing basket and still make his father happy. To Keir it made no sense. Dad was always going on about how everything had to be logical. How logical was it to be satisfied with failure? Was he not always telling his sons to use the gifts God gave them, and how they must do the very best they could? Yet here he was ruffling Arthur's hair as if he had done something to be proud of. At times like this, Keir hated his brother.

Fortunately, Arthur was not competitive, and excelled at nothing of any importance, though he did have a natural aptitude for ball games. At the local primary school he was opening bat for the first team, and much admired as a spin bowler; at soccer and tennis he also showed considerable promise. In general, though, there was nothing outstanding about him, except perhaps that he seemed to have a special relationship with animals; cats and dogs, like fish, followed him around; birds would fly down from trees and perch on his shoulder as he walked; on a horse, though he had never had a lesson, he was completely at ease. Some people said that horses spoke to him, though no one had actually heard them do it.

At school Arthur was well-liked, though no one took him seriously, least of all his teachers who had given him up as an academic prospect. Arthur found more to interest him in a shaft of sunlight than in boring lessons. What, for example, were those billions of specks of floating dust that appeared and disappeared as the sunlight came and went? To Arthur, it was obvious they were visitors from another solar system. Why else would they be beaming down through the classroom window? And what were they doing in a shaft of sunlight, scaled down to microscopic size? The only question was, were they friends or foes? It amazed him that the teachers ignored these sparkling motes floating in the air; or hadn't they noticed? He tried to warn his classmates, but knowing Arthur, they would smile and look away. They were too busy doing arithmetic and French and all that stuff. He couldn't help feeling they had all got it wrong, for what was more important; memorising the angles of an isosceles triangle, or making contact with a million extra-terrestrials?

Keir suffered no such distractions; he worked relentlessly, he paid attention, if he got it wrong, he did it again and again until he got it right. As a result he was invariably top of the class. No teacher ever said of him what they so monotonously said of Arthur – 'could do better'. Never once did Keir bring home a bad report, yet his demons were never far away; however glowing his parents' praise, it could never be enough, and however stern their criticism of Arthur, it could never be as harsh as he deserved. Had he been challenged, Keir would most vehemently have denied being jealous of Arthur. What reason could he possibly have to be jealous of him, when he was constantly proving himself to be better at everything he did?

The sad truth was, superior as Keir felt himself to be, that he was convinced his parents loved Arthur best, a fact which puzzled and infuriated him, especially as he had no idea what he could do to make them love him more than Arthur. For some reason he could not explain he had always looked on his younger brother as an intruder, sensing intuitively that he was born to be an only child, and had somehow been deprived of his rightful status.

Had Keir only known, his father was inordinately proud of him. 'Keir is the clever one,' Hector would say proudly. 'He's ambitious, and he's got guts. He'll be Prime Minister one day, you'll see. Arthur . . . ? He's a good lad. But he'll never amount to anything.'

Elizabeth would smile at her husband's predictions, and keep her opinions to herself.

Seven

FERDINAND TOZER, a wealthy industrialist and generous contributor to the Conservative Party, was waiting in the library to see Uther when a young girl walked in. It was Elaine, eldest of the Pendragon sisters. On her fifth birthday, Elaine had informed her parents that her chosen profession was the stage. That she was plain and a little pop-eyed did not bother her in the least. '*I shall be a great actress*,' she had announced. '*The queen will make me a dame, and I shall have masses of lovers.*'

She thrust out her hand. 'I'm Elaine,' adding helpfully, 'I'm fifteen.'

Tozer lifted his corpulent frame to an unsteady half-crouch, tweaked the proffered hand by the fingertips and fell back in his chair panting from the effort. 'Delighted to meet you, little madam.'

Elaine viewed the visitor coldly; if there was one thing she hated it was being patronised. She took a seat opposite Tozer, folding her hands demurely in her lap. 'My step-father phoned. I'm to entertain you.'

'Most kind.' Tozer sat nodding his head emphatically, emphasising how kind he thought it was.

Observing her visitor's uneasiness, Elaine presumed that he was probably here because he wanted something. Her step-father was an MP and had important friends, so people said. They also said he could do things for the right kind of people. 'Are you rich?' she enquired shrewdly.

Tozer's eyes widened. 'I suppose I am – rather,' he replied, pulling an apologetic face and wiggling his shoulders in embarrassment, as if to convey how deeply he regretted being rich.

That confirmed it, Elaine thought to herself. This man definitely wanted something from daddy – probably a knighthood or a lordship or something. She sized up her visitor, fixing him with an unwaveringly challenging stare.

Desperate to change the subject, Tozer observed soapily, 'You must be the eldest sister. Being so mature, I mean,' he added with a flattering smile.

'I'm fifteen. Margot's thirteen.' Knowing there were three sisters, Tozer was about to enquire about the youngest, when Elaine continued almost without a break. 'Would you like me to tell you a secret?'

'What kind of secret?'

'A secret about my step-father. A very important secret.'

Censure and curiosity battled in his head. Curiosity won. 'If you like.'

'You wouldn't use it against him, would you?'

Ferdinand Tozer's eyes narrowed. 'Certainly not.'

'She's a prisoner.'

Tozer leaned forward on his chair. 'Who is?'

'My sister. The youngest one. We've been told not to tell anyone if we don't want the same thing to happen to us.' Elaine looked down at her hands and sniffed.

Tozer looked unimpressed. 'Your father sent her to her room because she didn't do her homework. Right?' He cleared his throat importantly, ending on a high, challenging note.

'Wrong.'

'Then why is she a prisoner?'

'Daddy says she's mad,' said Elaine matter-of-factly.

This time Tozer could not restrain a chuckle that turned into a guffaw that brought on a prolonged fit of coughing. 'Come now,' he wheezed, red in the face, 'I wasn't born yesterday, my dear.'

Elaine stood up to go. 'I knew you wouldn't believe me. No one does.' She extended her hand with quiet dignity. 'Goodbye.'

Ferdinand Tozer prided himself on being a good judge of character. 'Sit down. Tell me more.'

Elaine did as she was told. 'Her name is Bertha Mason. Well, Bertha Mason Pendragon. She's the baby and dad picks on her. She howls and moans a lot, and she's a bit, well, simple. But she's quite harmless really.'

'How long has she been locked up?'

'Ever since she was a baby.'

'Where?'

'In the attic.'

'In the attic!' Ferdinand Tozer was shocked. 'That's outrageous! What does your mother say about all this?'

'She says this is the twenty-first century and people don't do things like that any more. Daddy wont listen. He says it would ruin his career if people knew he had a mad daughter.'

'But . . . but . . . ' Though Tozer was horrified, his brain was feverishly active, calculating how he could turn this extraordinary situation to his advantage. 'Why doesn't he put her in a home?'

Elaine's voice faltered. 'He's afraid someone might sell the story to the press.'

'Why are you telling me all this?' Tozer was suddenly suspicious again. 'Me, a complete stranger.'

'It's only a stranger I *can* tell. Father's friends won't listen to me.'

Tozer nodded. That certainly made sense, considering what he knew about Pendragon and his cronies. 'But what can I do?'

'You're rich, so I expect you're important. You can talk to father, make him set her free. She has a right to lead her own life and be happy.' Elaine gulped. 'Or as happy as she can be.'

'Of course she does.' This was dynamite. What would Uther

not give to keep his secret safe? 'Show me, my dear,' he said decisively. 'I want to see her.'

Elaine seemed a bit surprised. 'Now?'

'Now,' insisted Tozer, thrusting out his chest.

Elaine pondered a moment or two. 'I'll need a couple of minutes to make sure the coast is clear.'

It was considerably more than a couple of minutes before she returned, and as the seconds ticked by, the less believable her story seemed to Ferdinand Tozer.

Elaine was breathing heavily when she rushed in. 'Come quickly!' she hissed, grabbing his hand and pulling Tozer out into the hall and up three flights of stairs. It was the most exercise he had had in years. The top of a fourth flight of much narrower stairs was blocked by a low door. Elaine knocked a special knock. Rat – tat, tat, tat! Rat – tat, tat, tat! Ferdinand Tozer leaned against the wall wheezing and gasping for air. Elaine turned the handle and opened the door cautiously. 'Come!' she whispered, beckoning Tozer to follow her.

As his eyes adapted to the gloom he made out first a network of wooden beams supporting the roof and then a confusion of objects; a pile of suitcases, a few lamps and lampshades, a birdcage, a child's rocking horse, a baby's bath. The attic smelled musty. Ferdinand Tozer sneezed loudly, and as he did there came a low moan from the shadows somewhere to their right.

Finger to her lips Elaine whispered, 'She's very timid.' In a low voice she called, 'Bertha!' At first there was no response, and then came a faint scraping sound as of a chain being dragged across the floor. The sight that met Ferdinand Tozer's eyes was one he would never forget; a small figure crouched on the filthy attic floor, wrapped in a torn shawl, trembling arms outstretched, begging for who knew what? Food or drink, or simply love and understanding? The little mite's tired eyes were rimmed with what looked like blue and red welts; they were the frightened eyes of some tortured spirit that had never known peace of mind.

'Poor girl! Poor little girl!' Ferdinand Tozer's eyes moistened. It was a long time since he had been moved to tears. He held out his hand but the pathetic creature shrank back into a dark corner, eyes full of terror, fingers scrabbling at her mouth. It was then he saw the padlock on her tiny ankle and the chain that shackled her to one of the rafters.

'Good God in heaven! This is inhuman! This is . . . ' Words failed him.

'She tried to set the attic on fire,' explained Elaine. 'It was just to attract someone's attention, but father said she was a danger to herself and everyone else and chained her up.'

'Monster! Cruel Monster!' said Tozer in a hoarse whisper.

As they descended the attic steps Ferdinand Tozer heard a sound that made the hairs rise on the back of his neck and all the way down his spine – peal after peal of demoniacal laughter that must surely have come not from a little child but from a tormented soul in hell. He had intended to threaten Uther Pendragon with exposure and offer to keep silent in exchange for whatever promise of honours he could extract from him. His conscience now demanded that he abandon that cynical scheme, and do everything in his power to ensure that Pendragon – brutal, degenerate beast – was punished for his crime. Life imprisonment would surely not be too much for him. Never had Ferdinand Tozer felt so good about himself, so righteous was his indignation, so just his cause.

When finally he confronted the wicked perpetrator of the sickening crime, the amusement with which Uther greeted Tozer's angry denounciation was as unexpected as it was shocking. Convinced that this monster was the son of Satan, Tozer responded with bitter insults and solemn threats. Yet in the middle of his righteous tirade, Uther abruptly left the library and reappeared holding Morgan, his youngest daughter, by the ear. The sight of Morgan clutching a filthy old shawl, the telltale smudged red and blue cosmetic circles round her eyes, and several of her front teeth blacked out, was one that branded itself like a hot iron on Ferdinand Tozer's memory.

He was not the first to be taken in by Elaine, though that was no consolation to him at all. Having gulped down the best part of a bottle of Uther's finest twenty year old Malt Whisky, Tozer's driver helped him, still shaking his head in bemusement, into his Bentley.

Uther's embarrassment was tinged with secret amusement, for whilst he had little time for his step-daughters, whom he considered spoilt, wilful and absurdly privileged, they were at least entertaining. 'Naughty but funny, eh, duchess?'

Igraine was not so sure. 'Why Bertha Mason?' she asked her husband.

Uther found that an odd comment coming from Igraine, an intelligent and well-read lady. 'Quite appropriate, I thought. A demented female imprisoned in the attic and all that.' He grinned. 'Serve Tozer right. If he had read *Jane Eyre*, he would have known it was a practical joke.'

'It wasn't Elaine's idea, you know. It was Margot's.'

Uther handed his wife a gin and tonic. 'How do you know?'

'She told me. Seemed rather proud of it.'

Uther opened a can of tomato juice. 'So?'

'You don't find that strange?'

'Should I?'

'Elaine is the passionate one. She's the one who adores wildly romantic novels, not Margot.'

Uther spiced his Bloody Mary with a few drops of Tabasco. 'I'm not with you, duchess.'

'Think about it. Margot is the most calculating of the three girls. She never acts on impulse, and she never does anything without a reason.'

Uther sipped his drink thoughtfully. 'You think she's telling us something?'

'A guilty secret. An abandoned child. Parents afraid the

63

world might discover the truth. Isn't it all a little too close too home?'

A sharp pain stabbed Uther's chest. Just for a moment he felt breathless, and then the feeling passed. 'You're not suggesting she knows anything?'

'Bit too much of a coincidence, isn't it?'

'But how could she?'

Igraine shrugged. 'She might have overheard us talking. Margot's smart. She's quite capable of putting two and two together.'

'Should I talk to her?'

Igraine shook her head. 'Absolutely not. It wouldn't achieve anything, and it might make matters a lot worse.'

'That girl is going to give us trouble,' said Uther, not for the first time.

Not only was Margot smart, she was also the most beautiful of the three sisters. With her black hair, big brown eyes and creamy complexion she seemed as pure and innocent as a Madonna. The reality, as Uther knew, was very different. Margot combined innocence with sensuality in a way that many visitors to Brackett Hall found remarkable, not to say disturbing. When she was around, wives and girl-friends watched their partners closely. Perched on a man's lap, she would entertain him with childish chatter, tossing her hair from time to time so that its soft waves brushed his face. Giggling girlishly, she would bury her head coyly in his neck and whisper secrets in his ear. She would hold his hand, (she was obsessed with hands), caressing it affectionately, or touch his cheeks with pouting lips, all the time confronting the other guests with her eyes as if to say, 'What's wrong? Nothing. Nothing but your nasty mind.'

When Martin, the head gardener, died, his successor was Tom Beddows, a young man in his early twenties, good-looking, cheerful and uncomplicated. Margot took a fancy to him and would trail him round the gardens, chattering incessantly, leaving him now and then to chase a squirrel or turn a cartwheel on the lawn. At first Tom found Margot's constant attentions a distraction, yet to his surprise he missed his young friend when she went away to boarding school. Distraction or not, he had grown accustomed to having her around.

With the holidays Margot returned, as if no time had passed at all. In those few short months, though, Tom noticed the change in her. Whereas she used to skip behind him turning cartwheels, now she walked demurely by his side, tossing her black hair, slipping him an occasional sidelong glance. Before, she had shown artlessly, as a child does, that she liked him; now he could no longer read what was in her mind.

The day before her school summer term began, Tom was eating his lunch on the Victorian ironwork bench by the big lawn, and she was sitting next to him. He liked that; it was the first time she had shown her friendship for him in such a companionable way. For a while she watched him eating, and for some reason this made him nervous. Pushing aside his last sandwich only half eaten, he wolfed an apple in four bites, slopped a mug of tea from his thermos flask and gulped it down.

'I'm going back to school tomorrow. Will you miss me?' she asked.

Had he answered immediately, he would have said yes, and that would have been the end of it; but uncertain how to respond, he hesitated. Avoiding her eyes he busied himself clearing up the debris of his lunch. By chance, it seemed, their hands touched. The unexpected physical contact made him recoil so violently that flask and mug, apple core and remains of sandwich were tossed on the grass. Confused, all he could do was sit there looking at the mess. Seeing how agitated he was, Margot burst out laughing. Tom was hurt. 'I'm sorry,' she said contritely, 'I didn't mean to laugh. But you look so miserable.'

For a few moments they sat staring at the lawn, Tom sullen, Margot wondering how she had offended him. 'Are you angry?'

'Why should I be?' he muttered.

'Why won't you talk to me then?' She turned to face him, her eyes willing him to speak.

For a few moments he was silent. Then he looked away, mumbling ungraciously, 'I've no time to sit around talking to children.'

'I'm fifteen,' she said indignantly. Most days she practised telling lies in front of the mirror in her bedroom.

He picked up the mug and the thermos flask.

'Do you think I'm pretty?' she asked him softly.

Pretending not to hear, he scooped up the scraps of bread and the apple core and stuffed them in his plastic lunch box.

'Do you, Tom?'

He clicked the lid shut. 'I wish you wouldn't talk like that, miss.'

'Why not? It's a simple question.' She put her head on one side and eyed him seductively. 'Do you?'

He said something under his breath.

'I didn't hear you.'

'I said yes, didn't I?'

For a while they sat without speaking, then, without warning, she took his hand in hers; when he tried to draw it away, she tightened her grip. For a young girl she was surprisingly strong. 'How big your hand is,' she murmured, caressing it gently. 'I love big hands.' Neither the smile nor the coquettish look that accompanied the words were hard to read. Flushing bright red, Tom snatched his hand away.

In an instant her mood had changed. She jumped up, graceful as a ballet dancer, and spun round and round on the tips of her toes. Tiring of that, she turned two perfectly controlled cartwheels, revealing in the process slim legs and a pair of white knickers. Tom looked guiltily away. Such thoughts; what was the matter with him? Look at her, skipping round the lawn, a carefree, innocent child.

'Good-day, miss,' he said gruffly, and rushed off in the direction of the lake.

'Good-bye, Tom!' she cried after him, watching him disappear from view. Lifting her skirts, she whirled round and round until she was so dizzy that the lawn reared up and tumbled her. For a while she lay on her back, eyes closed, waiting for the earth to stop moving. When finally it came to rest, she sat up and giggled. 'Dear Tom,' she murmured wistfully.

As the days passed, Tom convinced himself that he had been imagining things. What had seemed at times deliberately seductive behaviour was nothing more than the natural way of a girl at the confusing age of puberty. All the same, he wished she hadn't taken his hand in hers. The thought of physical contact between them disturbed him. Perhaps he was being foolish, but for him the touch of her hand had tainted something wonderful between them, something precious and innocent. For some reason he felt ashamed, as though he had committed a sin. It was not as if he had done anything to feel guilty about, but it was enough that he felt guilty. That night he went home and proposed to his steady girl friend. A few weeks later they were married.

It was the following year before he saw Margot again, and he was startled by the change in her. She was no longer a child, she was taller, her slim hips swayed as she walked, her long dark hair fell loosely about her shoulders. With her head carried high, she moved with a natural, unselfconscious grace and an indefinable air that told the world, "I am beautiful, and I know it." His heart beating fast, he went to greet her, wiping earth from his hands and bobbing his head deferentially.

She held out her hand. 'Hello, Tom.'

'You don't want to shake my dirty hand,' he said churlishly.

As if she hadn't heard him, she took his hand in both of hers and held it for a long moment. Gently, he eased it away. 'I'm off to get some more bulbs.'

'I'll come with you.' Quickly she fell in step beside him. For a few moments they walked together without speaking a word.

'I got married,' he blurted out.

'I know.' She pouted. 'Beast!'

'Known her a long time.' Why, he was thinking, did it sound like an apology?

'Oh, Tom,' she cried happily, dismissing all talk of so mundane a subject, 'it's brilliant seeing you again! It's been so long! I'm sixteen already. Think of it. Sixteen!' Catching the meaningful sidelong glance, his face burned bright red.

'Sit down and talk to me.' She pulled him to her on the lawn.

'I don't have time to talk, miss,' he protested.

'Oh you!' she scoffed. Her eyes softened and before he could stop her, her arms were round his neck and her mouth close to his. He knew his only hope was to push her away but his body refused. Once, twice, three times, she touched his lips with hers, tantalising him, her brown eyes smiling a mocking smile. 'Kiss me, Tom,' she whispered. 'You know you want to.'

The blood surged in his veins, his head swam, and he almost fainted. Grabbing hold of her, he kissed her roughly, pulling her harder and harder to him, limbs shaking uncontrollably in a frenzy of torment and desire. As his whole body stiffened, he threw back his head with a cry, not of joy, but of despair and pain, like a wounded animal. When he looked at her again, she was studying him with serious eyes. 'It's no use pretending anymore. Is it, Tom?'

And that was just exactly it. He thought of handing in his notice but he had a wife to support and a child on the way. He knew what he ought to do – turn round and leave this place for ever. But he could not; the truth was, he yearned for Margot, every nerve and sinew in his body crying out its need.

All the time she watched him with those big brown eyes, and then, as if she knew what he was thinking, she nodded. Without a word, she walked towards the big potting shed behind the greenhouses; as in a spell, he followed her. Inside,

68

she stood facing him, boldly meeting his gaze.

'For God's sake, Margot, this is wrong,' he pleaded.

'Dear Tom,' she said, holding up her arms to be undressed, the way a child does.

Gently he removed her clothes. When she was naked, he knelt at her feet. 'If you're not the most beautiful thing I ever did see.' He ran his hands over her small, hard breasts, her swelling stomach, her thighs. Kneeling there, he was torn between desire and shame, desperate to make love to her and praying for a miracle to save him from this mortal sin. Margot looked down at him and raised an eyebrow. 'Have you brought me here to worship me, Tom?' she asked mockingly. Kneeling beside him, she began to undo his trousers.

He was lost; demented with desire, he thrust her down and took her savagely. It was more like an act of revenge than of love. As he drove into her, he cursed and swore, loathing himself and her, while Margot lay serenely on her back, eyes closed, lips parted, with a half smile on her angelic face. When it was over, he saw to his horror that her thighs were covered in blood. She had not uttered a sound, much less cried out. Overwhelmed with remorse and guilt he asked himself again and again – what had he done? What had he done?

During the tortured weeks that followed he tried everything he could to stay away from her, but there were few places to hide on the estate, and she always succeeded in tracking him down. Although she made it more than obvious what she wanted, he refused to go with her again.

'Don't you love me anymore?'

He told her he could never touch her again, and that he was bitterly ashamed of himself. It was a clumsy and insensitive rebuff, and he knew it. At that moment she became like a child again. 'Must I be ashamed too?' That only made him feel worse, for it was not her who should feel ashamed. His lust had perverted a near child's romantic dream of love. He reported sick, then after a few days, returned to the gardens to look for her.

69

She was waiting for him on "their" bench. Determined to say what had to be said, he sat beside her, but before he could utter a word she was kissing him passionately, her fingers thrusting between his legs. Scarcely knowing what he was doing, he grabbed her and threw her from him savagely. She fell back, hit her head on the lawn and lay there, not moving, eyes closed. For one terrible moment he thought he had killed her. The panic rose in his throat, choking him, his mouth gaped as he gasped for air like a drowning man. A sharp pain gouged his head and he cried out in agony. Margot opened one eye, then the other. Slyly she grinned at him. He stared down at her as though he were seeing her for the first time. 'I keep thinking you're an innocent child. But you're not, are you?'

'Am I not, Tom? What am I then?'

For a second his face was distorted by hatred and contempt. 'You're a monster!'

Margot sat up, her face expressionless. Smoothing down her dress, she nodded her head several times in a knowing way, as if nothing in the world could ever surprise her. She stood and looked at him as she had never looked at him before, her scrutiny thoughtful and frightening in its detachment. This was not his Margot, this girl who walked away and never once looked back.

Never would Igraine forget the sight of Margot, dishevelled, dress torn, face scratched, moaning pitifully and tearing at her hair as though demented. That such a thing could happen to her angelic daughter was beyond her comprehension. Uther fired Tom on the spot. That, he made clear to Igraine, was the end of the incident as far as he was concerned.

'Incident! It was rape! We must call the police. The man's a pervert, a paedophile. If he's not punished, he'll do it to someone else's child.'

Uther shook his head. 'Drop it, Igraine. Do you really want your child to go through the trauma of cross-examination by the police, and then court proceedings with all that sick publicity? Our first duty is to protect Margot.'

Igraine knew Uther was right, though for all the wrong reasons. "Your child", he had called her, not "our child". Nothing could be clearer. He didn't see it as his problem. And yet it was hardly surprising, for this was the man who could sacrifice his own son on the altar of his ambition. Why should he hesitate to do the same thing to his step-daughter? Protect Margot, indeed! She knew exactly who Uther was protecting. 'It's your bloody career you're thinking about.'

'What if I am? I'm trying to claw my way up from the back benches. The last thing I need is a scandal.'

'Margot has done nothing wrong. She is the victim. So are we. How could anyone make a scandal out of that?'

'Easily. Imagine the sanctimonious claptrap, the media's moral censure – the parents who allowed their beautiful young daughter to spend her days with a hot-blooded gardener! They'd say we were either indifferent to Margot's wellbeing or unbelievably naïve. Either way they'd condemn us.'

'If we don't call in the police, Margot will think we don't believe her story. It's important she knows where we stand.'

Uther nodded. He knew what he had to do. 'You are right, duchess,' he said, 'absolutely right. I'll have a chat with her.'

Uther stood by the library window with his back to Margot. 'Good gardeners are hard to find,' he said, directing his words at the ornamental gardens.

'You don't give a shit what he did to me, do you?' She spat the words at him.

'Tom wouldn't hurt a flower, let alone a young girl.'

'He raped me!' she screamed.

Uther turned to face her. 'Did he, Margot? Or was it you who raped him?'

She burst into tears. 'I hate you! I hate you! You don't know me at all!'

'Oh but I do, darling,' he said calmly. 'Don't forget, I've seen

71

you in action. I know what you can do to men.'

She started to protest but he waved her quiet. 'I warn you, Margot. This game you play with men, it's a dangerous one. One day you'll pay for it. You never know what a man will do when he loses control. This time it only cost you your virginity. Next time, you might not be so fortunate.'

'I don't know what you're talking about.'

'Don't you? Let me explain then. I had my suspicions, of course, so I went looking for evidence. I found it in a drawer in your bedroom. By the way, a small tip for the future. Under your knickers is not a very intelligent place to conceal your diary. Appropriate perhaps, intelligent no.'

Margot's eyes flickered.

Uther waved a red book at her. 'Recognise it?'

'Give it me! It's mine!' She made a grab for it but he held it out of reach.

'A mistake to record everything in your diary. It makes it crystal clear you planned Tom's seduction from beginning to end. I must say I found it fascinating, if a little over-written in the pornographic passages. I imagine your mother would find it shocking.'

Margot clenched her fists and stamped her foot in frustration. 'Give it back!'

'I prefer to keep it – as insurance, you understand.'

'I know plenty about you and your lady friends.'

'Well, well, we are grown-up, aren't we? Do I take it you are threatening to blackmail me?'

Margot maintained a resentful silence.

Uther regarded his step-daughter coolly. 'Nice try, darling but you haven't a hope in hell. Your mother knows all about me and my extra-mural activities. She may not admit it but she knows. On the other hand she knows absolutely nothing about you. Think how fascinated she would be to discover who you really are.'

Margot sidled up to him. 'Don't be cruel,' she murmured,

'Uther, darling.'

He felt himself being drawn into those darkly beautiful eyes. 'My God, Margot, you really are bewitching.' He shook his head ruefully. 'And when it comes to a pretty face, like most men I'm a fool.'

Margot hooked her fingers inside the waistband of his trousers and pulled him close. Standing on tiptoe, she closed her eyes and put her mouth up to be kissed. For a moment Uther saw nothing but rosebud lips. He bent down. But then, an instant before their lips met, he shook himself, and the spell was broken.

'But not that big a fool,' he muttered.

Eight

2003

At the start of the Easter holidays the Hughes family drove to the Devon coast for a long weekend. Hector woke early, opening the door of their caravan onto a perfect spring day, the blue sky unblemished by a single cloud, the air fresh with the smell of the ocean. Elizabeth was still asleep. Not wanting to disturb her, Hector woke the two boys quietly, and took them for a walk, leaving a note for Elizabeth to say they would be back in an hour or two. As they followed the narrow track that ran the length of the cliffs, Hector stopped, squinted his eyes and pointed.

'Way up there. That tiny speck. See it?'

'What is it, dad?' asked Keir.

'It's a golden eagle.'

Arthur was impressed. 'Wow! Can it see us?'

Hector nodded. 'It can see a mouse in the long grass.'

Above them a skylark warbled its timorous song.

'It's following us,' said Arthur.

Indeed it seemed to be, for as they walked the bird kept pace with them, its tiny wings fluttering in a frenzied blur, hovering and darting by turns, trilling nervously, almost as if it were warning them. Hector shielded his eyes from the sun as he searched the sky. The eagle had disappeared. A breeze ruffled a patch of ocean and then died, leaving it smooth again. A mile or two out, a cargo ship moved slowly past, heading out into the Atlantic. For a few moments they watched it from the cliff edge. Far below, the beach curved in a long crescent between two promontories. For most of its length it was deep in shadow, but at the north-western tip the sand glistened like gold in the morning sunlight.

There was not a sound to be heard, nothing stirred, not a mouse, not a blade of grass. The silence was eerie. Hector felt a sudden sharp stab of fear in his stomach. In that instant the light of the sun was blocked out as the eagle stooped in an almost vertical dive, its curved beak and deadly talons reaching down towards Hector's face. Convinced he was about to be torn to pieces, he tried to run, tripped and fell heavily. Fearful that his sons might also be attacked by the wild bird, he shouted to them to take cover. But there was no cover, only fields of long grass stretching in either direction as far as the eye could see. In shock, scarcely knowing what he was doing, Hector staggered to his feet. Sky, cliffs and fields spun round him, his knees folded, his head fell back and he collapsed, dazed and bewildered.

Keir ran to his father. 'Dad, are you alright?'

Hector shook his head to clear it. 'Fine, fine. Help me up, Keir. Let's get the hell out of here before someone gets hurt.' But then, looking up, there was the eagle circling a few hundred feet up. 'Stand still,' he told Keir. Somewhere he had heard that an eagle only attacks a moving prey.

Arthur was walking slowly along the track some way behind them, shielding his eyes from the sun. He too was watching the great bird circling lower and lower. Keir ducked down, making little moaning noises, trembling with fear. Hector crouched by him. 'Don't move, son, whatever you do.' He called out to Arthur. 'Art! Stay where you are!'

The eagle hovered directly overhead, so close that Hector could see its fierce yellow eyes gleaming in the sunlight. Clasping Keir protectively, he shielded the frightened boy's head with his hands, certain the bird was about to attack again. Suddenly Arthur was running inland through the long grass, shouting at the top of his voice. For God's sake, what was he doing!

Hector watched helplessly as the eagle banked and dropped

like a stone on Arthur who froze, not moving a muscle. The murderous talons were inches from his face, but at the last second the great bird braked effortlessly, its tail feathers brushing Arthur's head, then sped away inches from the ground, wings shadowing the long grass. Over the sea it lifted and soared into the blue sky until once more it was a tiny speck high above them.

Again a menacing silence. Never in his whole life had Hector been so afraid. Where was the eagle now? Had it given up and flown away? He peered at the sky, but the sun was in his eyes and he could see nothing. And then, dear God, there it was, circling lazily overhead, round and round and round, as though it were taunting them. He shouted across to Arthur, 'Lie down, Art! Cover your head!' But the warning came too late, for like a thunderbolt the eagle dropped again on Arthur, and this time it seemed nothing could save him. A split-second before the steely talons struck, Arthur flinched. A razor-sharp claw slashed his face.

Hector cowered, expecting to see his son torn to pieces. But to his amazement, instead of administering the *coup de grace*, the eagle hovered directly over Arthur's head, stroking the air serenely with its massive wings before folding them and landing on his shoulder. There it stood, shifting its weight from one foot to the other, head turning from side to side, yellow eyes peering angrily about. And Arthur, showing not a trace of fear, stroked the eagle's breast feathers. The eagle opened its wings and spread them over Arthur. Moments later it lifted itself a few feet in the air, circled him three times, uttering a sonorous cry, *Kluee! Kluee! Kluee!*, banked left, then right, climbed steeply into the sun and disappeared from view.

Hector ran to Arthur and anxiously examined his face. The left cheek was bleeding but miraculously the eagle's talons seemed only to have inflicted a superficial wound.

'We must get that seen to right away.'

'What's all the fuss about?' said Keir. 'It's only a scratch.'

Hector frowned. 'Let's go, boys. That face needs dressing, Arthur.'

Keir shoved Arthur in the chest. 'Serves you right for being such a sissy.'

'I'm not a sissy.'

'You are. Coward!'

Tears of anger stung Arthur's eyes. 'I'm not a coward, I'm not.'

'Yes you are. You ran away.'

'That's enough, Keir,' said Hector sternly.

Although Keir did have a point. Arthur's taking off like that had certainly provoked the eagle to attack him. The boy had panicked but who could blame him? He was only nine years old.

'You nearly had us killed.'

'Leave him alone, Keir,' said Hector sternly.

Keir fumed and muttered all the way back. Arthur, never unhappy for long, threw stones and chased butterflies. Walking quickly to the caravan, Hector silently thanked God, though he was far from being a religious man. More than once he laid his arms on his sons' shoulders and told them how much he loved them. Arthur was obviously too young to understand what terrible danger he had been in. Even so, it was astonishing how relaxed he was.

Her usual unruffled and efficient self, Elizabeth rushed Arthur to the local hospital where his cheek was dressed and he was given an anti-tetanus shot. The doctor warned him he would have a small scar on his left cheek that most probably would never completely disappear. Keir sulked, disgusted at the attention being paid to his younger brother. Arthur remained quietly unconcerned about the whole business.

The more Hector thought about what had happened, the more puzzled he was. There were questions in his mind, questions he had no answer to. How to explain the eagle's behaviour? Why had this wild creature attacked them in the first place? And why had it perched on Arthur's shoulder like some domestic pet? Elizabeth needed no explanations, and would not hear a word against Arthur. 'Arthur is special,' she said, as she often did. 'It could all have turned out very differently. All I care about is that you and the boys are safe. That's quite enough for me.'

But it was not enough for Hector; for him everything had to make sense. He had always been an earthbound man, a man who believed only in what he could see and touch. Sometimes he allowed himself to believe in abstract concepts, but these were chiefly related to scientific theories which, in his considered opinion, had been irrefutably proven. Having nagged for days at the problem, he finally came up with a theory that provided the only rational explanation of the events of that extraordinary morning. Waiting till the boys were back at school, he went to see Merlin at his cottage. It was always worth hearing what Merlin had to say on any subject – not that he would be able to find any flaw in Hector's reasoning. All the time he was recounting the story of the eagle, he had the strangest feeling that Merlin already knew it. But if he did, he said nothing, listening carefully to every word.

'An amazing experience,' said Merlin when Hector had finished. 'I imagine you have a logical explanation?'

Hector preened. 'As a matter of fact, I do.'

'And that is?'

'Sex.'

'You don't say,' said Merlin dryly.

'Remember, it is spring. Making the assumption that the eagle was female, I would say that from a few thousand feet up she got confused, and mistook Arthur for a potential mate. I know it may sound far-fetched but I have heard of such things. On taking a closer look, she discovered her mistake and flew off. That's all there was to it.'

Merlin's expression was inscrutable.

'You agree?' asked Hector.

'I am not an expert on the mating habits of eagles,' said Merlin, 'but your theory sounds logical enough.'

Hector was clearly delighted to receive what sounded like the great man's imprimatur.

'There is only one problem,' said Merlin.

'What's that?'

'If you are right, then the normal neutral relationship between man and raptor was distorted by a random eruption of hormones. That would mean that everything that happened was due to chance.'

'I'm sure it was,' said Hector, for that is what he wanted to believe.

'It might well have been,' said Merlin, 'had the eagle swooped only once and then flown away. But it did not. It attacked three times. One mistake – possible. Two – highly unlikely. Three – inconceivable.'

Hector looked crestfallen.

'Also, each time the eagle stooped, it did something different. The first time, it attacked you. That could have been sheer chance, I grant you. But the second time, it attacked Arthur. And the third time again.' Those penetrating eyes focused on Hector. 'Why was that, do you think?'

'That's easy. Because Arthur took fright and ran. He became a moving target. He provoked the eagle.'

Merlin nodded. 'Very plausible.'

Hector beamed. Merlin was beginning to come round to his point of view.

'Another question,' said Merlin thoughtfully. 'Why did the eagle scratch Arthur's face the second time? Why not the first time?'

'Maybe it tried to and missed.'

'An eagle does not miss.'

'This one did.'

'Very well, let's suppose I am wrong. Let's say it did miss the first time. What about the second time? Why did it only scratch

Arthur's face when it could easily have inflicted much greater injury, or perhaps even killed him had it wanted to? Was that chance too?'

Hector shook his head in bewilderment; instead of taking his hand and guiding him to *terra firma*, Merlin was leading him into a quagmire. He was beginning to wish he had never come. 'If the whole thing wasn't chance, what else could it have been?'

'A test, perhaps?' suggested Merlin.

A puzzled frown. 'What kind of test?'

'A test of Arthur's courage and resourcefulness.'

What was Merlin getting at? 'I don't follow you,' said Hector irritably. 'Whose test? And what for?'

The two men faced each other across the table in Merlin's kitchen. Hector's mug of tea was warm in his hands, the table solid under his elbows, the floor stone, the furniture pine, and everything around him as commonplace as could be. He had come here for an explanation as ordinary and accessible as Merlin's kitchen. What he was getting was anything but.

It was as if Merlin had read his thoughts. 'What is it you want from me?' he asked.

Hector sipped his tea. His own theory was weak, far-fetched, one he would like to believe in but couldn't. What he needed from Merlin was a rational explanation of that extraordinary and disturbing encounter with the eagle.

'Reassurance.'

Merlin smiled. 'I'll do my best.' He moved over to the hob, returned with the pot and refilled their mugs.

'The first time the eagle attacked you, what happened?'

Hector closed his eyes, reliving the scene; and so terrifying was it that even here and now in Merlin's kitchen it was all he could do not to shield his face from the predator's murderous talons. 'I stumbled and fell. I nearly passed out. Keir ran over to see if I was alright.'

'And Arthur?'

'Art was behind us on the track, looking up at the sky.'

'What happened next?'

Why all the questions? 'Where is all this leading?'

'Bear with me, Hector,' said Merlin gently.

'The eagle appeared again and started to circle. I was sure it was going to attack me.'

Merlin leaned forward, eyes bright, every muscle in his body tense. 'You were sure it was going to attack you. Not Arthur.'

'No. It had attacked me once, and it was directly over me again.'

A satisfied nod. 'What did you do?'

Hector clasped his hands together to stop them shaking. 'I told the boys not to move. Then I saw Arthur running in the long grass and shouting like a maniac.'

Merlin bounced with excitement. Hector had never seen him so animated. 'He left the track and ran into the field?'

'Yes.'

Merlin leaned back in his chair and sighed a contented sigh. 'And when the eagle attacked him, what did he do?'

'One moment he was running away in blind panic, the next he was turned to stone. I suppose he was paralysed with fear.'

'You think so?' Merlin's eyebrows arched. 'What happened then?'

'The eagle was circling directly overhead. I shouted a warning to Arthur.'

'And then?'

'The eagle attacked him again, and this time it scratched his face. I thought it was going to kill him.'

'What did Arthur do?'

Merlin's relentless questioning compelled Hector to relive traumatic events. He was close to tears. 'I can't remember.'

'You can't remember anything at all?'

'No! . . . yes! . . . he . . . he flinched,' Hector stammered.

'Why? Why did he flinch?'

Absurd question. 'Because the eagle scratched his face.'

'No.'

'What do you mean, no?,' said Hector indignantly. 'I saw it with my own eyes.'

Merlin soothed the air with his hands, calming Hector. 'You saw Arthur flinch. But he didn't flinch because the eagle scratched his face. *The eagle scratched his face because Arthur flinched.*'

A long silence. 'I have not the remotest idea what you are talking about,' said Hector wearily.

Merlin leaped up and paced the kitchen excitedly, back and forth. 'Listen to me, Hector. When Arthur saw that the eagle was about to attack you, he shouted and ran. That was not panic, he did it deliberately to distract its attention. And that is exactly what happened. The eagle attacked him and not you. So you see, Hector, far from panicking, your son risked his life for you. When the eagle attacked him a second time, he was certainly scared but he didn't run, did he? He didn't even try to shield his face; all he did was flinch. For that momentary weakness he paid a token price. He will bear the mark of the eagle's talon for the rest of his life, not as a badge of shame, but as a sign that he is human.'

Hector was deeply confused. This was not what he had come to hear; it was far from being reassuring. How could a nine year old boy show such courage, such amazing presence of mind? Every logical cell in his brain, every reasonable fibre of every nerve and muscle in his body cried out that Merlin must surely be mistaken. And yet . . . and yet . . . whatever the dictates of reason, intuition was sending him a different message, Elizabeth's words were in his head: *Arthur is special.*

Merlin slumped on his chair again. Observing the turmoil in Hector's head, he was deeply sorry to have been responsible for it. His friend had come to be comforted, and he had given him cause for unease. 'Consider what happened after the third attack,' he said softly. 'Was that not even more astonishing than anything that preceded it? The most dangerous predator in the skies stands peacefully on a small boy's shoulder. Why, Hector? Why did it hover over him? Why did it circle him?'

Hector didn't know and he didn't want to know. He should have stayed at home and tried to make do with his own poor theory. There would have been doubts but he could still have slept at night. Nervously his hands folded and unfolded on the table. He had gone too far to stop now. 'You tell me why,' he said fearfully.

'The eagle perched on Arthur's shoulder as a sign that he has been chosen. When the eagle spread its wings over him it was telling Arthur that he will always be protected. And when it circled Arthur, the king of the skies was paying homage to a defenceless young boy on behalf of all creation.'

Chosen? Protected? Homage? Arthur was his son, a normal child, nothing more. Hector crossed the room and looked down at the empty crib that still stood in the corner.

Merlin stood beside him, his hand on Hector's shoulder. 'Do you remember when you and Elizabeth carried a tiny naked baby into the garden on that freezing winter's night?'

'Shall I ever forget it?'

'Elizabeth held him up to the heavens, and you said what you had to say. Do you remember what happened then?'

'The clouds parted,' murmured Hector.

Merlin dipped his head in acknowledgment. 'The clouds will always part for Arthur.'

'There's no rhyme or reason to it,' Hector complained. 'It doesn't make sense.'

Merlin smiled. 'Must everything make sense? You want to analyse and define, you want to draw the length and breadth and height, you want to pluck out the heart of the mystery. But you can't, Hector, no one can. Arthur is of the earth, as all men are, but he is not earthbound. His relationship with God's creation is metaphysical, a thing of infinite beauty and mystery.'

Tears glistened in Hector's eyes. 'He's just a boy, Merlin, just a boy. He's my son. I can't think of him in any other way.'

'It's a simple matter of faith,' said Merlin.

'Not so simple.'

Merlin smiled the kindest and gentlest of smiles. 'It is if you believe.'

Hector rubbed his eyes with the back of his hand. 'I don't,' he said stubbornly.

It was as if Merlin had not heard him. 'In a few years' time, when Arthur is fifteen, there will be a second sign.'

'What kind of sign,' asked Hector suspiciously.

'You will recognise it when you see it,' said Merlin, 'and when you do, you will be convinced that Arthur has been chosen.'

'For what, Merlin? Chosen for what?'

'Why,' said Merlin, as if it were the most obvious thing imaginable, 'to save the world, of course.'

Nine

2004

KEIR AND ARTHUR were growing up fast and soon they would be leaving Ponterlally Primary School. They were both enrolled for Glastonbury, a fine school with an excellent reputation, and besides, Merlin was keen for them to go there. The only problem was the entrance exam. Keir would certainly pass it. But Arthur? Hector worried about his younger son. Arthur was a dreamer who did not take to schoolwork at all, and was regularly near the bottom of his class. In many ways, Hector would rather Arthur went to the local state school where there was no entrance exam and the academic pressure not so great.

It was early days, of course, but when Hector thought about Arthur's future, his head began to spin. What would he do with his life? How would he earn a living? What career was open to a lad with the attention span of a dragonfly, whose only interests were sport and animals? 'Tell me, Arthur,' he would ask him, 'what do you want to do when you grow up?'

'Don't know,' the boy would respond.

Why didn't that surprise Hector? 'There must be something.'

Arthur would pull a rueful face more eloquent than words. 'What could I do? I'm not much good at anything, really.'

'You can do whatever you want to, if you work at it,' said Hector, always ready to shore up Arthur's confidence.

Arthur's blue eyes clouded over. 'Do you really think so?'

'I do.'

Arthur thought hard. 'I'd quite like to be a vet.'

'Good idea.'

Thank God, Arthur had both feet planted firmly on the ground. He was not all that bright but at least he was sensible. It might be better if he did not go to Glastonbury, as a boy could get some very strange notions listening to Merlin.

'You don't believe all that stuff about Arthur being chosen to save the world, do you?' Hector asked Elizabeth.

'Yes, I do,' she said.

In Hector's view Merlin's influence on Elizabeth was far too strong. He was the one putting fancy ideas into her head about Arthur. 'Just because Merlin says so?'

Hector ought to have known by now that Elizabeth had a mind of her own. No one was going to tell her what to think or what to do. 'You should know better than that,' she said huffily.

He was puzzled. Did Elizabeth know something about Arthur that he didn't? 'Why do you believe it?'

'Because I believe it, that's why.'

Surely there had to be a reason for believing, some logic, some rationale? 'What evidence do you have?'

'You and your evidence,' scoffed Elizabeth. 'I know Arthur. That's quite enough for me.'

Frustrated, Hector resorted to sarcasm. 'It's not what I'd call a career,' he said, 'saving the world. Not exactly a recognised profession, is it? Even if it were, there wouldn't be any money in it.'

'You can scoff as much as you like,' said Elizabeth. 'It wont change what I think.'

'I'm sorry, darling.' Hector put his arms around Elizabeth. 'It's just that I worry about the boy. What's he going to do with his life? He's talking about being a vet now. That's all very well, but vets have to take exams just like doctors. If only he weren't such a hopeless student.'

Elizabeth kissed her husband firmly on the mouth, wiped off the lipstick and patted his face. 'You're a good man. Now stop worrying. And don't you go bothering Arthur about his future. He's only ten, after all. When the time comes, he'll do what he has to do.'

'How do you know that?'

She wanted to explain but she could not. How to explain instincts and feelings? 'I just know. Some things can't be explained.' Whatever the truth about Arthur, Elizabeth was sure of one thing; he had been given to them for a reason. Whatever it was that made Arthur special had something to do with that cold winter's night when the clouds parted for him. For her that would always be a treasured memory, one to be locked away in her heart, too precious and too fragile to be shared with anyone but Hector.

In the autumn of 2004, at the age of eleven, Keir went to Glastonbury school, having sailed through the entrance exam. Arthur would have to wait another year.

Keir came home for the Christmas vacation very much the superior elder brother. He and Arthur went fishing at the usual spot near the stone bridge across the Lally. Elbows on knees, chin on hands, Arthur stared at the float, his thoughts wandering downstream with the current. This lazy little tributary at his feet joined another and another, until a dozen or more tributaries merged into a great river. Crammed with boats, white sails swollen in the breeze, the river flowed faster and faster, until finally it surged into the Bristol Channel and the sea. The sea! What would he not give to be out there on the Atlantic swell. Or in space. Or in the foothills of the Himalayas. Or anywhere in the universe, anywhere but school.

'What will you do when you grow up, Keir?'

'Haven't decided yet, have I? I expect I'll have my own company – something on the Internet, probably. I'm going to be a billionaire,' Keir boasted, 'that's for sure.'

Arthur was impressed, and rather overawed by his brother. After a time he plucked up the courage to ask, 'Would you like to know what I'm going to be?'

'Not really. I expect you'll tell me, though.'

'I'm going to be a vet.'

'You'll never pass the exams,' said Keir cruelly.

'Do vets take exams?'

Keir raised his eyes to heaven. 'Do fish swim?'

Arthur stared hard at the sky. The clouds were wet and blurry.

For a while Keir concentrated on his fishing, and Arthur on his dreaming. 'What's Glastonbury like?' he asked finally, more to please Keir than because he really wanted to know.

'Brilliant.'

'Lots of sport and things?'

'Look here, Arthur,' said Keir, 'it's no use thinking they're going to let you in just because you're good at sport. Glastonbury is for chaps with brains.'

Arthur did not like the sound of that at all. 'Do you think I'll pass the entrance exam?'

'Not a hope.'

Arthur stiffened his jaw to stop his lower lip trembling. 'Why not?'

Keir was pitiless. 'Because you don't know anything, that's why.'

Arthur thought that was a bit unfair. 'I may not know much about history and Latin and stuff, but I know a bit about animals, and quite a lot about birds.'

'Terrific,' said Keir, with heavy sarcasm. 'When they ask you about Archimedes Principle you can do your bird imitations.'

'Is the work very hard?'

'Hard?' A scathing look. 'Hard!' Another withering look to ensure he had Arthur's complete attention. 'You could not even begin to imagine in your wildest dreams how hard it is.'

Arthur looked glum. His float dipped once, and then again. Easing it gently away from the fish, he reeled in his line and cast it far upstream. This outrageous transgression of the fishing code did not pass unnoticed. 'Don't you want to catch a fish?'

'I'm waiting for a big one,' said Arthur, grinning nervously.

'Is that so?' Keir reeled in another fish. 'Not only is the work ex-*cep*tionally hard,' he continued, with savage emphasis, 'but there's a *huge* amount of it. When I say huge, I mean huge as in *colossal*. Most boys can't keep up. And I'm talking about the clever ones. I don't want to discourage you but I really don't see how you could possibly cope. You'd be miserable at Glastonbury. Take my advice and go to some other school where the academic standards are not so high.'

Arthur looked at his brother enviously. 'I wish I was clever like you.'

'Well, you're not,' said Keir. 'But that's life. Men are not born equal. We can't all be clever.'

That little mole of thought burrowed around the top of Arthur's nose. 'If I was to start doing my homework . . . '

'If I *were* to start doing my homework.' Keir wagged a reproachful forefinger at Arthur. 'There, you see. How can you expect to get on in life if you don't know your grammar?'

'What did I say wrong?'

'You should have used the subjunctive.'

'Is the subjunctive important, then?'

Keir's lip curled. 'Of course it is, ignoramus. What kind of question is that?'

'If I *were* to do my homework,' said Arthur carefully, 'do you think I could get into Glastonbury?' Like a hungry dog, his eyes feasted on Keir's face, pleading for a titbit.

Keir kept his kid brother waiting. Opportunities like this were not to be squandered. 'I tell you what,' he said.

'Yes?' said Arthur eagerly.

'If you *were* to study really hard.'

'Yes?'

'If you *were* to do your homework every day.'

'Yes?'

'If you *were* to stop dreaming.'

'Yes?'

'And if you *were* to start concentrating.'

'Yes?' Arthur's mouth gaped with anticipation.

'You still wouldn't have a cat's chance in hell of passing the entrance exam.' Keir writhed on his back, shrieking with mocking laughter, bicycling his legs ecstatically in the air. Overwhelmed by a profound sense of inadequacy, Arthur threw chunks of grass in the water and watched them drift downstream with his hopes.

But Keir was wrong; Arthur passed the Glastonbury entrance exam; what's more, he passed it easily. Hector was astonished, Elizabeth not at all. Arthur was happy about it, though perhaps less surprised than might have been expected. When Keir came home for the Easter vacation, he took his revenge on Arthur by being even more superior and patronising than ever. No amount of tender loving care from his parents could reconcile him to the fact that Arthur would be joining him at Glastonbury. Would he never be free of the little wretch? Elizabeth did her best to reassure him. 'It will be alright. You'll always be in a higher form than Arthur. You're a year older than he is, and that's one thing that will never change.' True enough, but small consolation for Keir.

It was not long before he picked a fight with Arthur and gave him a black eye. When Hector asked him how he got it Arthur said he had walked into a door. Hector knew differently and wanted to confront Keir, but Elizabeth persuaded him not to interfere. 'It will only make things worse.'

'Then how do we stop him bullying Arthur?' he asked, and was surprised at his wife's respons e.

'It's not up to us. It's up to Arthur to stop him.'

Hector looked doubtful. 'He'll never do that.'

'When he's ready he will.'

Secretly Elizabeth doubted the wisdom of sending both boys to the same school. As a mother, she understood Keir's chronic jealousy of his younger brother, and it troubled her to see his pain. It troubled her conscience too, for if Keir was the child of her womb, Arthur was the child of her heart.

Ten

THE COTTAGE was half a mile from the shore. The only other indication that there was, or ever had been, human life on this barren island, were two ramshackle barns open to the sky, the ruins of an ancient castle, and an abandoned lighthouse at the end of a rocky promontory reaching out into the sea. Ravaged by wind and ocean, the island was flat and featureless, with here and there – the only touch of colour – a ragged clump of purple heather. Tall wild grass grew everywhere, cowering from the westerly gales that blew the year round. The sandy beaches, ribbed by wind and tide, were stalked by long-legged birds in search of food. As Merlin tramped across the fields, seagulls floated above him, greeting him with doleful cries. It was a desolate place this, he thought, but with its own sombre beauty.

The old man showed no surprise when Merlin entered, greeting him courteously.

'I am glad to see you,' said Merlin.

On either side of the open fire were the only seats in the room, two Windsor chairs, one empty, the other occupied by the old man. At his feet a black Labrador slumbered. Merlin sat in the vacant chair. 'I imagine you have few visitors,' he said, to get the conversation going.

'None. None but you.'

The Labrador uttered something between a sigh and a groan. Without moving his head, he opened his eyes and contemplated Merlin, then, apparently satisfied with what he saw, closed them again.

Merlin tried once more. 'This island. Is it marked on the maps?'

'It is on some,' replied the old man laconically.

'It's not easy to find.'

A shrug. 'Who would want to?'

Merlin gave a little smile. 'Who indeed?' He was certain the old man knew why he was here.

'You live alone?'

'There are no other people here, if that's what you mean. But I am not alone. I have Robbie.' He indicated the Labrador.

'Are you never lonely?'

'Loneliness is a state of mind.'

'Even so, isn't it strange never to hear the voice of another human being? It's so quiet here.'

The old man smiled. 'You wouldn't say that if you were here in an autumn gale, or in the winter, when the rollers crash at the foot of the cliffs. As for voices, there are many on the island – the wind, the sea, the birds and animals, and of course Robbie here. And then there are other voices . . . ' The old man drifted away on the tide of his memories.

'Other voices?' repeated Merlin curiously.

'Voices from the past. But I don't deny it, there are times when I long to hear a human voice – once or twice a year, perhaps – and then I'm off to the mainland.'

'This is your island?'

'It has been in my family for centuries. Once it was the subject of much gossip and speculation but that was long ago. Now no one remembers us; they have forgotten we exist. No one tells the old stories any more.'

'What kind of stories?'

The old man lifted the kettle from the hob and poured Merlin a mug of a dark coloured brew that might have been tea, though by its smell it was clearly something else. He sipped it cautiously. It tasted of the sea.

'A thousand years ago, or so they say, this island was ruled by a great king, the greatest that ever lived. Here he built a castle surrounded by a wide moat, with walls a hundred feet high and fifty feet thick, and turrets and towers so tall that their tops touched the clouds. At full moon the king can still be seen riding a white horse at the head of his knights – a hundred and fifty of them. The noise of their hooves on the drawbridge is like thunder, and the sound of their voices unearthly, like spirits from another world.'

Merlin leaned forward, intrigued. 'Have you ever seen them?'

'I have seen the shadow of the cliffs on the water at full moon, and the white foam horses galloping across the ocean. On stormy days I have seen the waves reach up their turrets to the sky. On calm days, when the sea gulls float and dive, I have listened to them talking of other places and other times. "I could tell a tale!" they cry. "Such a tale! Such a tale!"' The old man chuckled. 'Have I seen the spirits? Indeed I have.'

Merlin was confused. 'Yet you seem to be saying that all these stories have a perfectly rational explanation.'

For a long time the old man did not reply. 'Perhaps,' was all he offered to disturb the silence.

Merlin persisted. 'This king you spoke of . . . did you ever see him?'

Another lengthy silence. When he broke it, the old man did not answer directly. 'You saw the castle?'

Merlin warmed his hands on his mug of tea, or whatever liquid it was. Watched closely by the old man he took another tentative sip and tried hard to look as though he were enjoying it. 'I passed some ruins on the way. From what I saw of the one tower that still stands, and the remains of the walls, it was certainly a big one.'

The old man bent to the Labrador, his face softening as he stroked it. 'There was a castle here once, of that there is no doubt, some say as long ago as the sixth century. There was a great king here too.'

Merlin tensed. 'How do you know?'

The old man hesitated, as if he were debating with himself. 'I have seen a knight walking the ramparts at full moon. Let me be clear: I did not imagine it, I have seen him, not once but many times. It is obvious he is someone of importance, for he is clad in golden armour, and everyone about him treats him with great deference. Sometimes he walks alone, sometimes with two or three of his knights. I have also seen him with a lady, and from time to time, in the company of a man with long hair and a flowing white robe.' A sly look in Merlin's direction. 'Much like you.'

'The knight in golden armour.' The green orbs shone brightly. 'Was it the king?'

A long silence. And then: 'It was the king.'

'How can you be sure?'

Again his host seemed reluctant to respond. 'Once, when the north wind blew, I thought I heard the lady address him by name. Who knows? It could have been an owl hooting.'

'What name?' asked Merlin.

'Or a seal barking on the rocks.'

'What name?' asked Merlin again, barely concealing his impatience.

The old man was silent for long moments. 'She called him Arthur,' he said at last.

Merlin let out a sigh. 'So it was him. I knew it.'

'And you are Merlin?'

A slight bow of the head in acknowledgment. 'I am.'

'What is it you want of me?'

Merlin lifted his hands. 'I think you know.'

The old man fondled the Labrador's ears. 'Men say he will come again.'

'So I have heard.'

'They say that if he does, this island will be his kingdom, as it was in ancient times.'

Merlin said nothing.

'You are not here for the sea air, I imagine.'

'I am not,' Merlin acknowledged with a smile.

'So what will you give me for this desolate isle?'

Merlin spread his arms wide. 'The world.'

'If I wanted the world, I would not be here.'

'I will pay any price you ask.'

'You are speaking of money?'

'If that is what you want.'

'What would I do with it? I have an appointment with death, one I have no option but to keep.'

'Life, then?'

The old man's eyes sparkled. 'You could do that, magus?'

A nod. 'For a time. Quite a long time, perhaps.'

'That is certainly tempting . . . very tempting. Life is beautiful, and so very short.' The old man pondered some more, leaning back in his chair, closing his eyes.

The fire crackled and flared as it ate into the driftwood. A wonderful thing is a fire, thought Merlin. In their caves his ancestors had sat round just such a fire, warming their bodies, and no doubt dreaming, as he was dreaming now. For a time he was with them, watching the play of flame and shadow on their strong, enduring faces.

The old man stirred. 'No, I think not. I have almost lived the years allotted to me. Soon I have a journey to make, and God willing I shall hear the gulls' tale. I am ready, or as ready as ever I shall be. And whether the end comes today or tomorrow, what difference will it make when it comes?'

The Labrador groaned and laid his head on his master's feet.

'Then tell me your price?'

'Why concern yourself? Wait until I die. It will not be long, I promise you, and then you can have my island for nothing.'

Merlin shook his head. 'Honour demands that I pay the price.'

The old man nodded approvingly. 'Then,' he said, 'know

that my kingdom will not be sold for any wordly thing.'

It was as Merlin expected. 'For what, then? What will you sell it for?'

'For love.'

Even the magus was puzzled. 'What riddle is this?'

'You are good at riddles. Solve it.'

Merlin eyes clouded as he withdrew into his head. For love? Whose love? And for whom? What could it mean? Last of his line, the old man had no kin, nor any friends, it seemed, so it was not their love he was talking about. Puzzled, Merlin watched him stoop again to fondle his beloved dog. Of course! What a fool he was! The answer to the riddle lay at the old man's feet.

'When you cross over to the next world,' said Merlin, 'Robbie shall be my companion, and I shall love him till the day he dies.'

The old man smiled. 'Merlin the wise,' he murmured. For a few moments he said nothing, though Merlin could see there was something on his mind. 'You must come quickly when I summon you.'

'You have my word,' said Merlin.

And with that the old man seemed content.

Eleven

MORGAN WAS only seven when she first claimed to be able to fly. Locking her bedroom door, she climbed out of the third floor window and stood on the narrow parapet waving her arms as if they were wings, and shouting, 'I can fly! I can fly!'

Since Uther was at the office and Igraine shopping in the village, it was left to Elaine and Margot, William the butler, the cook, and a few panic-stricken housemaids, to handle the crisis. Standing on the lawn, they pleaded with Morgan not to jump but she ignored them all. Eventually it was cook who managed to coax her back into her room with a promise of sticky toffee pudding and vanilla ice cream. When Uther came home and heard what had happened, he stopped Morgan's pocket money for six months and after that there was no more climbing out of windows. Morgan, however, was stubborn, and never ceased to believe she had special powers.

'I can do anything I want,' she told Margot defiantly.

'You couldn't make a man fall in love with you,' said Margot.

'If I wanted to I could.'

'No, you couldn't,' said Elaine. 'Your bum's too big, and you've got a moustache.'

This mockery only made Morgan more determined to demonstrate her supernatural powers. In the middle of the night she would creep into their bedrooms and leave a variety of animals on her sisters' pillows, together with a brief explanatory note. A snake, perhaps: snakebite for the gift of tongues. Or a tortoise: a tortoise kiss to make you immortal. Or a snail: a snail's slimy caress to make you as beautiful as Helen of Troy. What more could they want? And why were her sisters so horribly ungrateful when all she was doing was trying to help? Didn't they want to live for ever? Didn't Margie want to speak Greek and Latin, French and German, Russian and Chinese? Didn't Elaine want her face to launch a thousand ships? Didn't they want to fly?

As the years passed, Elaine and Margot became increasingly wary of their younger sister, even though they both knew she would never dream of lifting a finger against them. Although the youngest, she was by far the tallest and strongest of the three, with broad shoulders, a gruff voice and a square jaw. In manner and appearance she was in fact less like a girl than a boy, and a pretty tough one at that. Normally placid, she had a violent temper when crossed, and her tantrums were alarming; she would scream in a harsh, tormented fashion, her eyes wild and unfocused, as though she were possessed. She was only two when the family doctor murmured something about fits, though all the usual tests were negative.

Then there were her pets. From a very early age, Morgan gathered about her an odd collection of guinea pigs, hamsters, snakes, several species of poisonous spiders and insects, a tortoise, white mice, a talking mynah bird and a number of gerbils. If owning such creatures was not in itself all that unusual, her relationship with them most definitely was; her pets were her 'familiars', her assistants in secret rituals performed in her bedroom in the dead of night: black masses, incantations, conjuring the dead, casting of spells and various unspecified altar ceremonies. No one, not even her sisters, was allowed to witness them. Nevertheless, in such an unusual household no one found her particular form of eccentricity especially disturbing – or not until the affair of the gerbils.

It happened when she was thirteen years old. In the early hours of a grey January morning Morgan marched into Elaine's bedroom and deposited a gerbil on her pillow. 'Mary's dead,' she announced.

Still half asleep, Elaine shrank from the corpse. 'Go away! And take that disgusting thing with you.'

Morgan's lips trembled. 'I loved her.' Picking up the corpse, she kissed it tenderly, two large tears rolling down her face. 'She was such a darling gerbil.'

Elaine was unsympathetic 'Get out!'

As Morgan was about to close the door behind her, she hissed over her shoulder, 'It was murder.'

In the darkness, Elaine stiffened. 'Murder?'

'Tom did it.'

Elaine switched on the bedside lamp and sat up. 'What are you talking about, Moggy? Who is Tom?'

Morgan shut the door, stomped back into the room and sat on the bed. She looked as though her whole world had come to an end and Elaine did not have the heart to turn her away. The corpse was produced from a dressing gown pocket and lovingly stroked. 'Tom is Mary's husband. This is Mary. *Was* Mary.' Morgan began to sob.

'Gerbils have friends, Moggy. Lots of friends. They don't get married.'

'Tom and Mary did. At the high altar in my bedroom. I married them myself. It was a lovely service. "Do you take this gerbil . . . till death us do part . . . " All that stuff. Afterwards they had a reception and speeches and a cake and everything . . . and then they had three beautiful babies. Now he's gone and murdered her.' She held the little lifeless creature in her lap, stroking it and sniffing loudly.

Elaine considered the departed with distaste. 'How did it happen?'

Morgan blew a trumpet blast on her nose. 'He broke her neck.'

'Moggy, you are silly! How could a gerbil do that?'

'You don't know Tom. He's very strong, and he's got a

99

wicked temper.'

'It might have been an accident,' suggested Elaine. 'I suppose animals have accidents, like human beings do.'

'It was no accident. He murdered her,' said Morgan emphatically.

'Moggy darling,' Elaine assured her, 'animals don't murder each other.'

'Tom did. He has a lover, that's why he did it. Her name is Delilah. She's a real bitch. She's been after him for ages, always shoving her bum in his face. He fell madly in love with her. She's why he killed Mary.'

Elaine was not sure where all this was leading. 'Supposing he did murder his wife,' she said, humouring her young sister. 'What's to be done about it?'

'He has to be punished.'

Morgan insisted Tom must pay the penalty. The affair promised to be mildly entertaining, having all the essential elements of drama and romance that appealed to Elaine, and to a lesser extent to Margot. Investigations were completed, charges laid, legal representatives appointed and a trial date set. It was held at midnight in Morgan's bedroom. Elaine, counsel for the defence, and Margot, counsel for the prosecution, appeared in Chanel jackets borrowed from Igraine's dressing room, their lips black, their eyelids purple. Morgan, the judge, was wrapped in a red table-cloth, with a roll of cotton wool at her neck and a Restoration wig her step-father wore at fancy-dress parties. Beside her on the table lay the black bowler hat Uther had sported to cut a dash in the city when he was a young man. On the accused's chair in a small cage was Tom, the gerbil, scratching nervously, responding to some primeval instinct warning him that he was in trouble.

It was swiftly established by Margot that Tom had a wandering eye and had taken that tart, Delilah, as his mistress. Potentially the most damning piece of evidence was a taped message from Mary, the murdered wife, allegedly recorded just before she died. She confirmed that on several occasions she had refused her husband's request for a divorce and that each time he had beaten her up, until finally, in a fit of rage, he had broken her neck.

Elaine, the defending counsel, lodged an objection to the tape on several grounds. Firstly, that gerbils could not speak English; secondly, that Mary could not have known her husband had broken her neck because she would have been dead at the time, and thirdly, and most potently, that the taped voice sounded suspiciously like the judge's. Her objection being summarily over-ruled by the judge, the outcome of the case was no longer in serious doubt.

In vain the defending counsel strove to establish that one gerbil was incapable of breaking another gerbil's neck. She was told by the judge that she knew nothing about gerbils and was talking complete nonsense. This line of reasoning being discredited, counsel fell back on her last line of defence: this was not murder, she argued, but a crime of passion, and should therefore be regarded as manslaughter.

The judge summed up, following which the jury, consisting of three baby gerbils, a rat, two white mice, a hamster, a guinea pig, a grass snake, a tortoise, a bird-eating spider and a talking mynah bird, was asked to consider its verdict. Not surprisingly there was no response from their cages for a long time.

'This is silly,' said Elaine. 'We'll never get a verdict out of this lot.'

'Silence!' said Morgan. Once more she addressed the foreman of the jury, the talking mynah bird: 'I ask you again. What is your verdict?' After another lengthy delay, the mynah bird squawked something unintelligible.

Turning to the accused, the judge enquired, 'Have you anything to say before sentence is pronounced?'

'I object!' said Elaine.

'On what grounds?' asked the judge.

'The verdict was unclear. In fact I thought he said not

guilty.'

'That's impossible,' said the judge.

'Why is it impossible?'

'Because I only taught him to say guilty. So there!' The judge then stuck out her tongue at counsel for the defence.

'This trial is a farce,' said Elaine in disgust. 'I'm going to bed.'

'No one is allowed to go to bed before I pass sentence.'

'Then get on with it,' said Margot. 'It's one o'clock and I'm tired.'

Morgan put on Uther's bowler hat. 'Tom Gerbil, I sentence you to death.' As an afterthought, she added, 'By hanging . . . and it has to be by the neck.'

'I object!' said Elaine.

'On what grounds?'

'The death sentence was abolished years ago.'

'Yes,' said the judge, 'but not for gerbils.'

The judge then invited both counsels to witness the execution. They were to assemble before dawn the following morning.

'You must be joking,' said Margot. 'No one's getting me up at that hour.'

'Me neither,' said Elaine.

The play was over and the curtain had fallen. The masquerade had been enormous fun but now they would have to find something else to entertain them. No one would be getting up early, of course. The whole thing would be forgotten in the morning. But it wasn't. Morgan's powers of persuasion were formidable, and Elaine's and Margot's curiosity got the better of them. In the dark depressing hour before dawn they found themselves by the old apple tree, all three sisters shivering in their flimsy dressing-gowns. The sky was overcast, the air damp and bitingly cold.

Morgan took a pair of leather gloves from a Sainsbury shopping bag, pulled them on, and removed Tom from his cage. The poor little gerbil was shivering too, though whether from fright or from cold it was impossible to tell. 'He's quite happy really,' said Morgan cheerfully. 'He ate a hearty breakfast, just like condemned prisoners are supposed to. And he had an extra helping of gerbil food. Didn't you, Tom?' she said, chucking him under the chin. 'And a whopping piece of apple. Yes, you did, you naughty boy.' Whereupon she turned her back on them.

Eyes shining, shuddering and giggling by turns, Elaine and Margot had forgotten the cold. Morgan turned round again and showed them Tom. His tiny feet were tied together with string and he was jerking his head and wriggling his body in a vain effort to be free. 'There, there, Tom,' said Morgan, putting him back in his cage, 'no need to be upset.'

For a moment Elaine and Margot were disappointed, thinking this must be the end of the drama. But there was more to come. They watched fascinated as their baby sister plunged her hand into the plastic bag and produced a length of rope with a slip noose already tied at one end. The noose she flung over a branch so that it dangled about three feet from the ground. The other end of the rope she wound round the trunk of the apple tree and knotted it.

There was a hint of alarm in Margot's eyes. 'What is she doing?'

'It's all make-believe,' said Elaine, reassuring her sister.

Morgan opened Tom's cage and took him out again, clasping his body firmly in the leather gloves so that only his tiny head was visible. Twisting this way and that, the gerbil tried to bite her fingers but his teeth could not penetrate the gloves.

Elaine yawned. 'Let's go to bed now, Moggy.' The gerbil's eyes bulged with terror. He had stopped struggling and was uttering high-pitched squeaks, as if he were pleading for his life. 'Moggy?' No response. Elaine's voice sharpened. 'Moggy! I know this is make-believe, but that's enough now. Put Tom back in his cage.' Morgan did not seem to hear. Slowly, and with great care, she removed her right hand from the gerbil, and with a quick movement flipped the noose over his head. 'No!' said Margot, suddenly fearful. 'You're hurting him.'

The creature gave a plaintive shriek that changed to a gurgle as Morgan pulled the noose tight. 'Take it off, Moggy. Take the rope off.' Elaine's voice was oddly calm and reasonable, as though she were trying to pacify a madwoman.

Morgan looked up and nodded. At last, they thought, they had got through to her. She was about to put an end to the macabre charade. But Morgan had nodded for another reason. In the dark sky the first pale gleam of light had appeared. 'It's dawn,' she said, and let go the gerbil. For a few moments it dangled by the neck at the end of the rope, struggling, at first frantically, then feebly.

Elaine made a grab for the gerbil but Morgan was too quick for her. Seizing the little creature's body with both hands, she pulled down sharply. They heard the crack as its neck snapped.

Suddenly Margot understood. 'My God!' she whispered, 'that's what she did to Mary!' Elaine and Margot huddled together and watched, horrified and fascinated, as the limp corpse of the gerbil slowly revolved at the end of the rope, first one way, then the other, until finally it was still. They turned and ran back to the house, arms around each other, shivering from cold and shock.

When her sisters had disappeared in the gloom, Morgan cut down the dead gerbil. 'There, Tom,' she said, kissing the tiny broken body and pressing it to her cheek, 'it's all over now. I had to punish you, didn't I? I did it for Margie. You shouldn't have put your thing in her, Tom. You really shouldn't have.' Laying the corpse carefully on the compost heap, she followed her sisters back to the house.

Twelve

MERLIN HAD been hired to teach mathematics and science at Glastonbury School. In practice, though, he taught every subject under the sun, including some that were not on the curriculum of any school in the land. As he had promised Hector and Elizabeth, he kept an eye on Keir and Arthur, and in particular, for his own reasons, on Arthur.

Keir hated sport but was a solid, if uninspired, student. Arthur was an excellent all-round cricketer, a fine scrum-half and a promising tennis player. Academically he held his own, although his heart wasn't in it. The classroom was no more congenial to him than a cage to a wild animal, and he spent most of the time peering out of the window wishing he were anywhere but where he was.

When first he came to Glastonbury Arthur was invited to tea by his housemaster, as were all new boys. Merlin was pouring tea when there was a whir of wings, and an owl perched on his wrist. 'Ah.' Merlin laid down the pot and stroked Virgil's chest feathers. 'This is Virgil.'

Arthur's eyes were big. 'He's a barn owl, isn't he?'

'That's right.'

'He's beautiful.'

Virgil puffed up his feathers proudly until he was twice his normal size. When Arthur held out his hand Virgil took two fingers in his beak and nibbled them gently. Then he jumped onto Arthur's shoulder and began to inspect his hair. Merlin beamed. 'He does that to me. He's never done it to anyone else.'

How different the two brothers were, Merlin was thinking as he watched the owl and the young boy. A year ago he had introduced Keir to Virgil, and Keir had made what he obviously thought were owl sounds. Instead of responding, Virgil had turned his back on him. Not wanting Keir to feel rejected, Merlin had tried to explain that birds and animals needed to be treated as individuals, just as human beings did. But Keir was not interested. What was the point of an owl or a blackbird? What use was a fox or a mouse or a weasel? Now fish were something else. Fish you could catch and put in a basket and take home and eat.

As Arthur settled into his first term Merlin left his academic studies in the hands of other teachers, believing there were more important things for him to learn than anything to be found in books. If Arthur wanted fun, then that was what Merlin would provide, and so he concentrated on making learning fun, and Arthur learned without knowing he was learning.

With the magus there were no formal lessons. Merlin might, if he felt like it, mumble 'Astronomy' or 'Geography' or 'History' or 'Zoology' to give Arthur some idea what it was he was about to experience, for that is what all Merlin's lessons were; there were no lectures and no exams, only experiences. Master and pupil would go for long excursions in the country at weekends and talk about anything and everything, though never about schoolwork. Most of the time Merlin was the best company in the world, cheerful and ebullient. Occasionally, for no apparent reason, a black mood descended on him and the magus would withdraw into himself like a tree in winter. Arthur would be concerned and finger the small scar on his left cheek as he sometimes did when he was troubled, wondering where his friend and teacher had gone; but then suddenly the dark cloud would lift and Merlin was alive again, sprouting words and gestures like spring leaves.

From time to time he would show Arthur one of his conjuring tricks, or so he called them. But where in this world or any other was there a conjurer like Merlin? 'Astronomy' he would say, slip his hand into his pocket and pull out first a miniature Sun, and then in quick succession, Mercury and Venus, Earth and Mars, Jupiter, Saturn and Uranus, Neptune and Pluto. A wave of the hand, and there wheeling overhead, was the solar system. Soon Arthur knew the night sky like the back of his hand – the Great Bear and Orion's Belt, Taurus the bull, Aries the ram, Cancer the Crab and the scales of Libra. He would lie awake on a starlit night and dream himself into space, and into time past and future, until his spirit left his body and floated among the stars.

A mumbled 'Geography', a nod of the head, and there were the Victoria Falls, or the Pyramids, or Venice, or St. Petersburg, or the polar icecap. Studying an atlas was fine but having the world come to you was surely better. History? The wink of an eye, and there was Nelson or Socrates, Julius Caesar or George Washington. For other boys history was dead and gone; for Arthur it was alive and here and now.

Botany and Zoology? Merlin taught the lad all there was to know about the natural world and by the time he was thirteen Arthur knew the name of every flower and shrub, every bush and tree, every insect and butterfly, every bird and animal. In the dust Merlin would draw the outline of wild geese and goshawks, robins, blackbirds and nightingales. A flick of the fingers, and he would send them flying. In no time at all Arthur knew the birds of the air better than he knew the palm of his own hand, every detail of every feather, every speckle of every egg, every note of every warble.

Animals came next. Merlin would raise his hand and conjure up a lion or an impala, a tiger or a bear, a wolf or a reindeer. Fortunately none of them showed the smallest inclination to eat Arthur, for the power of the Magus confined them to their world.

Then followed the patterns and functions of plants and trees, stones and rocks and clouds, streams and oceans, black holes and galaxies, so that soon Arthur was as familiar with the boundless universe as he was with his own small room.

When Arthur had learned enough to know that he would never know enough, Merlin decided it was time to give his young protégé some practical experience. 'Do you know what it's like to be a dog?'

Arthur laughed and shook his head, and the next thing he knew, Merlin was stooping to pat him, asking, 'Who are you?'

'I am a dog,' growled Arthur, wandering, nose to the ground, to smell out any rabbits in the neighbourhood. Never had he imagined that life could be so interesting. What smells! He could smell the whole delicious, odorous world! What was more, every smell signified something tremendously important. And what sounds! Such wondrous sounds! He could hear every note that every bird sang, every step that every creature took, every breath of wind, every creak of every branch, every rustle of every leaf. He could even hear Merlin breathing.

'Yes, I know what it's like to be a dog.'

'How do you know?'

'Wasn't I a dog once? Or did I imagine it?'

Merlin chuckled. 'You imagined so hard, you imagined yourself out of your head. That's the first lesson, Arthur. Most people are trapped inside their heads, all they care about is themselves, all they know is themselves. You have learned how to escape from your head.'

After a time Arthur could imagine almost anything – what it was like to be an owl like Virgil, or a blackbird, or a thrush, or a plant or a tree, or a fish (he was very thoughtful after that experience), or a field mouse, or a mole, a hedgehog or a squirrel, an otter or a badger, a bee or a snail – what it was like to be almost anything, in fact, anything that lived in the whole wide, vibrant, excellent world.

One day, Merlin said, 'Imagine being a lion.'

That was a real challenge, for apart from Merlin's conjurings, he had only seen pictures of lions. But to his own surprise, he heard himself roaring, 'I am a lion.'

'Or a warthog?'

'I am a warthog,' he grunted.

'Imagine what it is like to be a lion killing a warthog.'

Arthur's expression was fierce and cruel.

'Or a warthog torn to pieces by a lion?'

The young lad's eyes were clouded and full of pain.

'I'm scared, Merlin,' he confided, on the way back to school.

'Excellent!' said Merlin cheerfully. 'That shows how well you are doing. It can be a frightening business living in someone else's head. It doesn't matter whose head it is, head of predator or prey, beggar or king, young or old, good, bad or indifferent, black or white. But believe me, Arthur, it's the only way forward, a man can run to the end of the world and back again, he can explore the outer limits of the universe, but he will never escape from his own head. Unless . . . '

'Unless?'

'Unless he can imagine a way out of it, just as you are learning to do. Remember, Arthur, a man can know everything, and understand nothing. When you understand that, you might learn to understand other people.' He laid his hand affectionately on Arthur's shoulder. 'Who knows? You might even learn to understand yourself.'

'Do you believe in God, Merlin?'

'I believe in creation.'

'Who created us?'

'I don't know. I don't have to know. I only know we were created.'

'Why do we die?'

'Because we have to change.'

'How do we do that?'

'When our time comes, we return to earth. There, with the rocks and the stones, we learn patience and the mystery of eternal life.'

'You believe in eternal life, then?'

Merlin gave the question some thought. 'I believe that the life force is eternal. But everything has a beginning and an end – sun, moon, stars, galaxies, black holes, comets, the planet earth which we inhabit, the universe itself. That is the great paradox, Arthur. Nothing survives that does not change.'

'Does God change?'

'I don't know,' said Merlin, laughing. 'It's one of your better questions though.'

'It was you who taught me to ask them.'

'Don't ever stop,' said Merlin.

Thirteen

A WEEK BEFORE Arthur's thirteenth birthday, Hector reminded Elizabeth of the promise they made Merlin all those years ago. She stopped knitting. 'What promise was that?'

'We agreed to tell Arthur he's adopted. We said we'd do it before he was thirteen.'

'Oh, that!' Elizabeth resumed her knitting, clacking the needles noisily.

Hector would not be put off. 'We gave our word.'

Another burst of agitated clacking.

'It's time he knew, Liz.'

Elizabeth laid down her knitting. 'He's our son,' she insisted obstinately, 'and that's all he needs to know.'

'Of course he's our son. But we adopted him and there's no use pretending we didn't. Even if we hadn't given Merlin our word, it would be wrong not to tell him.'

Suddenly Keir was in the room. 'Tell him what?'

Hector jumped. 'How many times have I told you not to listen at doors?'

'What is it you have to tell Arthur?' insisted Keir stubbornly.

Hector hated to lie but how could he tell him the truth? 'It's a private matter – nothing that need concern you. Alright?'

'Fine.' But Keir was not convinced. Something was going on and he was determined to find out what.

For the next few hours Elizabeth debated fiercely with her conscience, dropping a few stitches and more than a few tears.

That afternoon she beckoned Arthur into the kitchen and shut the door.

'There's something I have to tell you,' she said, bustling about making tea. 'It's private.'

The longer Arthur waited, the more puzzled he became. What was so private that she couldn't say it in front of dad? Or in front of Keir, for that matter? And why was his mother, normally so efficient, creating such a drama over a simple cup of tea? First she forgot to put the tea bag in the cup, then she knocked over the milk jug. He watched with some anxiety as she stooped to wipe up the milk. Was there something wrong with her? He felt cold and afraid. Whatever it was she had to tell him, he did not want to hear it.

The words that finally crept out so hesitantly were not the ones she had rehearsed. 'I just wanted to tell you . . . to tell you . . . that . . . you are my very own son, and I love you very much.'

It was not clear to Arthur why that would make his mother cry, but being a feeling person, he understood that for some reason she needed love and comforting. 'I love you too, mum,' he said, hugging her.

Elizabeth was a little ashamed of herself. She could scarcely look Hector in the face. 'I tried to tell him. I just couldn't.'

'Then I shall have to.'

She knelt at his feet and laid her head on his knees. 'I'll do it.'

'Promise?'

'I promise.'

He had his doubts about that promise, but he hated to refuse her anything.

The days passed, and Elizabeth could not bring herself to do. it. Hector was worried. He did his best to persuade her how much better it would be if Arthur learned the truth from them rather than from someone else. She seemed to agree, and she renewed her promise to tell Arthur but so passionately did she want Arthur to be her own flesh and blood that she had almost convinced herself he was.

By the time the two brothers next went fishing, Keir's persistent eavesdropping had been rewarded; he had discovered his parents' secret. Moreover, he knew they had not shared it with Arthur. Lying on his back, hands clasped behind his head, Arthur watched his beloved clouds race the wind across the sky. There was a time, not so long ago, when he would have seen more than clouds in those white scraps of cirrus. When he was seven years old, what else would they have been but ships from outer space? Now that he was thirteen and a man – or so Merlin said – he had to admit they were nothing more than clouds. He was not at all sure that he liked growing up.

Keir cast his line. 'I always knew it.'

So heavy was the burden of silence that in the end Arthur felt obliged to respond. 'Knew what?'

'That you were not my brother.'

Arthur sat up, his attention fully engaged. 'What did you say?' he asked, not sure he had heard right.

'I said you are not my brother. And mum and dad are not your parents. They adopted you. You are no relation to any of us. None at all.' Keir's voice rose triumphantly. 'I knew you weren't one of us. I always said you were different.'

For a few seconds Arthur stared at his elder brother in disbelief, then his face folded in grief and pain, and tears sprang from his eyes.

'Cry baby! Cry baby!' chanted Keir. This was positively the best moment of his life. Nothing, absolutely nothing, would ever give him greater satisfaction.

'I don't believe you,' said Arthur. But he did not know what to believe. For days he was in torment. Was Keir lying? His first thought was to ask his parents, though Keir had warned him not to say anything to them – 'My parents,' he called them, rubbing salt in the wound – or they would throw Arthur out of the house and he would have no home at all. Arthur knew that could not be true. Elizabeth and Hector loved him. It was not what they might do that troubled him, it was what they might say. What if they said it was true? What if he really was adopted? In a way he preferred living in uncertainty. He did not want to know. But in the end the strain of not knowing became too great and at breakfast a few days later he blurted out, 'Keir says I'm not your real son.'

Elizabeth and Hector looked at each other in shock. Hector put down his cup. 'Your mother and I need to talk to Arthur alone,' he told Keir. But as Keir got up to leave the kitchen, Elizabeth shook her head. 'No,' she said, 'let him stay. This involves all of us.'

Arthur had his answer. There was nothing more to be said. 'So it's true.'

Feeling his pain, Elizabeth suffered with Arthur. If only she had listened to Hector. 'Yes,' she said, 'it's true.'

'Why didn't you tell me?' asked Arthur wretchedly.

'Dad wanted me to. I'm so sorry. I was afraid.' She opened her arms.

'Afraid of what?'

Her voice was low. 'Of losing your love.'

Arthur went to her and hugged her. 'You could never do that, mum. Don't you know that?'

Elizabeth burst into tears. 'I was scared of hurting you – the way Keir has done.'

Keir sat with head bowed, raging. Wait till he got the little shit alone!

'You see, Arthur,' said Elizabeth, clasping her younger son tightly, 'we adopted you when you were a tiny baby. You were only ten days old. We have never thought of you as anything but our own flesh and blood. The law says you are our adopted son but we don't. We never have, do you see? You are our son, just like Keir. As far as we are concerned, there is no difference.'

Keir was close to tears. 'He's not your son! He's not my brother!'

'He is, and he always will be,' said Elizabeth firmly.

'That's because you love him more than me.'

'That isn't true,' said Hector. 'We love both of you the same.'

After a long silence, Elizabeth said, 'I was wrong, Arthur. I should have listened to your father. I'm really sorry you had to learn the truth this way. But I'm glad you found out, even if you didn't hear it from me. I never carried you in my womb but from the first moment I laid eyes on you, you have been a part of me, part of my flesh, part of my bones, part of my heart. You are my son, my very own son. No mother ever loved a child more than I love you.'

'I am your father, Arthur,' said Hector. 'I love you with all my heart and soul.'

Then Elizabeth and Hector took both their children in their arms and hugged them. Arthur hugged them back, but Keir held himself stiffly, his head filled with bitter thoughts.

Hector said hesitantly, 'I'm afraid we don't know who your – your birth parents are. We can find out, if you want us to.'

Arthur shook his head. 'No.' He was not ready to accept that he had any other parents.

Neither Hector nor Elizabeth rebuked Keir for the wrong he had done his brother. Keir suffered torments, not because his conscience troubled him but because Arthur bore him no grudge. Indeed he went out of his way to show his older brother the affection he still felt for him. Keir accepted it as his due, and gave nothing in return. Perhaps Arthur tried too hard, or Keir too little, but whatever the reason, Keir was more jealous of his brother than ever.

There was, however, one significant change in their relationship. Never again did Keir try to bully Arthur. Nothing was said, there was no confrontation, no threats or counter threats, it was simply that he noticed something different about his younger brother, something indefinable, revealing itself in small ways – a look in the eye, perhaps, or a touch more confidence in the way he carried himself – insignificant enough, but a clear warning, none-the-less, that Arthur was not a child and would no longer tolerate being treated like one.

Fourteen

2008

ON MOST WEEKENDS Merlin took Arthur on long rambling walks in the country. Sometimes they discussed where they would go, sometimes Merlin had no destination in mind. It might then have been fortuitous that they found themselves at the foot of Glastonbury Tor late one Saturday evening, although, as Arthur well knew, Merlin rarely left anything to chance.

As they reached the top of the Tor the red ball of the sun slipped below the horizon and the western sky glowed red. As the shadows deepened on the ruined church that crowned the summit, the dark mass of its tower dominated the landscape, uniting earth and sky. The west wind that had gusted all day was suddenly stilled. Not a sound, not even a breath of air, disturbed the silence. In this hushed moment the earth and all the planets that only an instant before wheeled round the sun seemed to hang motionless in space.

'Shall we go?' suggested Merlin, 'it's getting late.'

As they made their way down Merlin began to speak of a great king who ruled Britain many centuries ago.

'What king was that?' asked Arthur.

'You want a clue?' Merlin loved riddles.

Arthur grinned. 'Definitely.'

'His name . . . ' – a teasing pause – 'was the same as yours.'

'Oh, King Arthur! The Knights of the Round Table and all that old stuff,' said Arthur scornfully. 'They rode round knocking each other off horses and rescuing damsels in distress.'

Merlin smiled. 'True, but there was more to it than that. This country was besieged by its enemies, brutal and merciless men who pillaged and murdered and terrorised anyone who stood in their way. And the troubles were not just here; the whole world was sliding into chaos, the tribes that ruled Europe were disintegrating, society was fragmenting, families were breaking up, and few people believed in God or morality any more. The real power was passing into the hands of the wicked, and there was no one courageous enough to stand up to them – no one, that is, but King Arthur.'

'I wonder what he was really like,' mused Arthur, his eyes dreaming.

Merlin slid a mischievous glance at his protégé. 'You can imagine what it's like to be a dog or a lion or a snail. Why not try to imagine what it was like to be King Arthur?'

Arthur sped down the hill, hopping from one foot to the other, leaping rocks and grassy mounds, nimble as a mountain goat. 'Did he really try to save the world?'

Merlin was having difficulty keeping up. 'It's a – foof! – a long story. And you know something? Foof! We haven't seen the end of it.'

Arthur stopped, waiting for his mentor to catch up with him. 'How do you mean?'

A grateful hand rested on the boy's shoulder. 'There are those who say he will return.'

Arthur was off down the hill again. 'But it's just a story, isn't it?' he sang out.

'Who knows?' said Merlin mysteriously.

Arthur jumped, caught his foot on a rock, tripped, fell, rolled and was up again in an instant. 'You think there really was such a man?'

'Yes, I do.' Merlin was planting his feet with caution now. It was getting dark. The stars were beginning to reveal themselves. 'What exactly he did, and precisely who he was, no one knows for sure. But yes, I believe there was such a man.'

As they moved on down towards the foot of the Tor, Arthur said wistfully, 'it might be fun to save the world.'

'You have the right name for it. Why not have a go?' Merlin could not make out the expression on Arthur's face, but he sensed that the young boy had not dismissed the challenge. Arthur's eyes shone, catching the starlight. Cupping his hands to his mouth, he shouted at the top of his voice: 'Arthur! Arthur! Arthur!' The echoes swirled around him, rolled down the hillside and faded away in the dark woods below.

The next day they explored the ruins of Glastonbury Abbey, where, it is said, in 1191, the bones of King Arthur and Queen Guinevere, were found. 'The Tor was once a hill on an island,' explained Merlin. 'According to legend, the island was called Avalon. It was the place where the mortally wounded King Arthur was taken to be healed of his wounds. These ruins are on the site of an even older church, built, they say, by early disciples of Jesus. They even say Joseph of Arimathea came to Britain some thirty years after the crucifixion, and that here, at the foot of Glastonbury Tor, he threw his staff on the ground. It took root and budded, and that was the birth of the famous Glastonbury Thorn that flowers every year at Christmas. Here they built the old church, and here Joseph buried the Holy Grail.'

Man and boy rested on a log, and for a few moments wandered with their thoughts.

'Merlin?'

'Hum?'

'The Holy Grail. No one ever found it, did they?'

Merlin shook his head. 'No. Some say Galahad deserted Arthur to look for it, some believe Lancelot himself made the pilgrimage and saw the Holy Grail. But just as Moses was not allowed to enter the promised land, so Lancelot was not permitted to enter the room where the grail stood.'

'Why not?'

A slight hesitation. 'Because he had committed the sin of

adultery. He had slept with Guinevere.'

'Don't say that, Merlin,' said Arthur, suddenly angry. 'Lancelot would never betray his king.'

Merlin looked at Arthur in astonishment. In the rebuke there was such authority, that it was hard to believe it came from a thirteen year old boy.

'In any case,' continued Merlin, 'King Arthur thought the search for the Holy Grail was a waste of time.'

Arthur hugged his knees. 'And was it?'

Merlin peered far into the distance, beyond the cornfield and the hedges bordering it, beyond the distant woods, beyond the horizon, beyond anything on earth that Arthur could see. 'The search for the Holy Grail is the search for perfection. Man may never find it, but he will never stop looking for it.'

'Who was the better man – Galahad or Arthur?' asked Arthur suddenly.

'Depends what you mean by better,' said Merlin. 'They were very different. Galahad never stopped believing in man's essential goodness. Arthur, on the other hand, was convinced that man was part good, part evil, and that the way to save the world was not to look for the Holy Grail but to destroy the wicked. He had the will, and he was given the means to do it.'

'Excalibur?'

Merlin nodded. 'The ultimate weapon. Only Arthur possessed it. Only he could use it.'

'Why was that?'

'He did what no one else was able to do. He drew the Sword from the Stone. That meant only he was physically and spiritually strong enough to wield Excalibur.'

That little mole of thought burrowed in Arthur's brows. 'But Camelot was defeated in the end.'

'Yes.'

The blue eyes were troubled. 'So King Arthur failed.'

'Did he? Who can say?' said Merlin, standing and stretching, signalling it was time to move on. 'Maybe the struggle is more important than the outcome.'

That did not satisfy Arthur. 'But did King Arthur really change anything?'

Merlin held out his hand and pulled Arthur up. 'Can man change his own nature? King Arthur was a man, and like all men imperfect.'

'Even you, Merlin?'

'Even me.'

A quizzical look. 'What about me?'

Gently Merlin reached out and touched the scar on Arthur's left cheek. 'Even you,' he smiled.

Skirting the cornfield they made for the woods and back to school, Merlin's white robes trailing behind him in the breeze. 'King Arthur carried in himself the seed of his own destruction. That seed was his son, Mordred. But just as Arthur was not wholly good, so Mordred was not wholly evil. In a way the conflict between them symbolises the endless struggle in man's soul between good and evil.'

Suddenly Arthur felt weary, as if he were carrying the burden of the world on his young shoulders. 'So much to learn.'

'All you really need to know is that everything has a purpose, and every man a destiny.'

'Including me?'

'Especially you,' said Merlin.

Arthur was far away now, his eyes wistful, as if his thoughts were concentrated on some future sadness. Merlin had never seen that look before and it troubled him, for he cared deeply about his young friend. For a moment he found himself wishing that Arthur's destiny had been different, and that he could have been like other boys. But then Arthur was back from wherever it was he had been, and once again he was smiling, those magical blue eyes of his sparkling like a mountain stream in sunlight.

Fifteen

As THE YEARS PASSED, Uther had grown more and more frustrated with his step-daughters. They were all problematic, although of the three, Margot was his most immediate problem. Once the seductive nymphet, now a mature and lusciously beautiful young woman of nineteen, she was feared and resented by virtually every woman she met, often with good reason. Most of Uther's male friends, both married and unmarried, lusted after her, a good many having, he strongly suspected, found their way into her knickers. The thought was deeply disturbing to him, not because he gave a damn about morality in general, or Margot's well-being in particular, but for fear he might be accused of being a bad father.

A man for whom an immaculate public image was crucial could not tolerate such a potentially explosive state of affairs, that much was clear; what was less clear was what he could do about it. He and Igraine had never seen eye to eye on the subject of the girls. She was convinced all her daughters were perfect, especially Margot; was it her fault men tried to take advantage of her innocence?

Margot is as innocent as Lady Macbeth,' said Uther caustically.

Igraine was outraged. 'How can you say such a wicked thing? She's just a baby.'

'Margot was never a baby. She was born a hundred years old.'

'Don't be absurd.'

Uther frequently asked himself whether he would have

married Igraine if he had understood exactly what baggage she was bringing with her. Well, it was too late now. 'I warn you, duchess, if we don't do something soon, she'll end up in deep trouble. And so shall we. That girl's power over men is frightening.'

'Why is it,' asked Igraine indignantly, 'that women are always cast as sirens, and men as helpless victims? Margot can't help being beautiful, anymore than men can help being chronically unfaithful.'

Uther winced. 'Is that by any chance a hint?'

Hands on hips Igraine demanded, 'Who is May Middleton?'

'Why do you ask?'

'Who is she?' Igraine insisted.

A bland stare. 'My personal assistant.'

'How personal?'

'For god's sake, Igraine,' said Uther, assuming the reproachful expression of the maligned, 'May helps me in the office.'

'I hear she helps you outside the office as well.'

'That's a dirty lie!' It was astonishing to him that Igraine had even heard of May, let alone suspected anything. He would have to be more careful in future. 'My God, what people will do to discredit a successful man.' He took her in his arms. 'You do know you can trust me, don't you, duchess?'

'Of course,' she said, backing off, preferring to avoid a confrontation that would be humiliating for both of them.

'It's high time Margot got married,' he went on, as if nothing had happened. 'It would be the best thing for her, and a great relief for everyone else.'

'People don't arrange their daughters' marriages anymore. This is the twenty-first century.'

'So they tell me,' he said dryly. 'I'm simply suggesting we introduce her to a decent man before she finds herself an illiterate yobbo soccer player, or a drug-crazed pop star, or some filthy fortune-hunting jet-setting creep.'

She had to admit he had a point; she could not keep her beloved girls at home much longer, though she could not imagine what life at Brackett Hall would be like without them. For all Igraine's feminist convictions, it was still, she had to admit, a man's world. Uther had his career but what did she have? Not even a lover, though she had often thought of taking one. It was not the sex, and certainly not the shabby intrigue that attracted her; it was simply that she needed to feel someone really cared for her. Far from helping, being surrounded by friends and admirers only heightened her acute sense of loneliness. There was no one she felt able to confide in, being far too proud to admit to her friends that she knew about Uther's "indiscretions".

Uther considered his wife. His duchess was a remarkable lady, and still, at forty-three, a dish. There were lines around her eyes and mouth, of course, though somehow those tiny flaws added to her appeal. Her eyes still glowed as they did when she was young, except that now they had that resigned, slightly melancholy look he had noticed in other women of her age. Was it because she knew she was past her best? Or did it have something to do with her naughty husband? The last thing he wanted was to hurt her, but life was to be lived, and you only had one shot at it. Maybe he wasn't quite the man he used to be either, but if you had May Middleton you didn't need viagra.

'I hate to say it, duchess, but Margot is becoming notorious. The gossip columnists love her, the paparazzi won't leave her alone. It's only a matter of time before some scandal or other breaks.'

Igraine sighed. 'If only she would find a good man, someone to love, someone who would love her and take care of her.'

She had given Uther an idea. 'Leave it to me,' he said, 'I know just the man.'

Lennox Lotte had succeeded his late father as chairman of one of London's most successful trading and investment houses: presentable, well educated and with excellent social connections, he was nevertheless timid and rather inexperienced where women were concerned, or so Uther had heard. Probably just as well, he reflected. Ideal, in fact. An experienced man might think twice before marrying Margot. Arranging to meet Lennox at a friend's dinner party, Uther and Igraine were impressed. The question was, would Margot be? And even if she were, would she not simply eat Lennox up and spit out the pieces, as she invariably did with men? What would certainly have astonished her parents had they known, was that Margot had decided, young though she was, that it was time to settle down. What advantages were there, she asked herself, in being single, that a married woman could not equally enjoy? None. What sacrifices would she be making in exchange for lifelong independence and security? None. None that she could think of, and anyway here at home she was suffocating. Mumsy was a darling, though much too possessive; Father was a pain. It was time to fly the nest. There were only three conditions: to qualify as her husband a man would have to be rich, good-looking and a competent lover.

In this receptive frame of mind then, she found herself at the Pendragons' next dinner party sitting next to a highly eligible young man. Since her parents had never once mentioned him, she immediately concluded that he had been put there for a good reason.

'M-my name is L-Lennox L-Lotte.'

He was certainly good-looking. The stammer was . . . well, different . . . rather endearing, actually. One down. Two to go.

'And what do you do?'

'I am chairman of a p-private t-trading and inv-vestment c-company.'

'How interesting. Private, you said?' She toyed with her seabass. 'Does that mean you own it?'

'It d-does.'

G-good looking and l-l-lots of l-l-lovely l-l-lolly. Two down. One to go.

Lennox Lotte had heard somewhere that the Pendragon

girls had a reputation for being "unusual", but nothing in his sheltered upbringing could possibly have prepared him for Margot. Lavishing on him all her charm, she ensnared him with her feminine wiles. He was first intrigued, then enraptured, and finally enslaved. From the top of the table, Uther discreetly kept watch, astonished and impressed, not for the first time, by Margot's power over men; he almost pitied the poor fellow. Lotte was totally intoxicated, though he had scarcely touched a drop of alcohol.

As coffee was served, Lennox found himself being whisked off by Margot. As the two young people left the room, Uther drew on his cigar with quiet satisfaction, and directed a solemn wink at Igraine.

'What do you think?'

'I thought you said he was shy.'

Uther grinned. 'He is.'

A tour of the great house ended in the grand Hall of the Zodiac. Together they walked down the long white marble floor, the echoes of their footsteps rebounding from the mirrored walls and vaulted ceilings. In the centre of the hall Margot stopped and looked down. His gaze followed hers. There in a circle, exquisitely inlaid in rose pink marble, were the twelve signs of the Zodiac.

'Do you know your sun sign?'

'I'm a Virgo.'

'Of course you are. Stand there, then. On your sign.'

He stood, a little apprehensively, in the segment containing the zodiac sign of Virgo. Margot stood two segments away from him in the sign of Scorpio.

'Scorpio.' She smiled a smile of such demure and innocent charm that Lennox's heart seemed to somersault in his breast. 'Some say it's a dangerous sign, not to be trusted.'

'I w-would t-trust you with my l-life,' he stuttered.

She extended her arm. Reaching out and taking her hand

he held it in both of his as carefully and tenderly as if it were a damaged bird.

'I have n-never m-met anyone l-like you,' Lennox Lotte confessed.

Her eyes widened. 'Am I so terrible, then?'

'You are l-laughing at m-me.'

Holding hands, and with Libra between them, they were still a couple of feet apart.

'Libra is the sign of lovers.' Her demurely lowered lashes veiled her eyes. 'We are separated by love, you and I.'

Lennox took a step forward, and pulled her gently towards him. Now they were both standing in the Libra segment. 'N-not any m-more,' he said, and boldly kissed her.

As he opened his eyes again, he could not help noticing that their embrace was reflected in a dozen mirrors lining the great hall. A dozen times it brought home to him the enormity of what he was doing – taking advantage of a young and innocent girl. He experienced a pang of shame.

Her eyes gleamed coquettishly up at him. 'Lennox?'

'Yes?'

'Would you like to have sex with me?'

Shocked as much by the crudeness as by the unexpectedness of the invitation, he was quite unable to respond.

'We shall do it here in Libra,' she said, nodding her head like a battery-operated doll. 'What could be more appropriate?'

He stood looking at her, senses roused. Scarcely taking her eyes off his, she unzipped his trousers and helped him remove them. Hoisting up her skirt, she tore off her knickers and pulled him down on top of her. The coupling was brisk and on Margot's part noisy, her amplified cries of pleasure resounding round the marble hall.

'I'm s-so t-terribly s-sorry,' he said, when it was over. 'I should n-never have . . . what m-must you think of m-me?'

'Actually, I think you're rather good.' Three down, Margot was thinking. None to go. 'We had better go back or they'll be wondering what we are up to.'

As she clicked down the hall nodding away to herself, she asked him, casually, 'Are you going to propose now?'

'Pr-propose?'

'You see, I never gave myself to anyone before. Of course, if you don't love me . . . ' She thrust out her lips in a pout.

'Why yes,' he said hastily, 'of c-course I d-do. I think you're w-wonderful.'

'Then hadn't you better pop the question?'

It took a few moments for Lennox to get his tongue round the words. 'W-will you m-m-marry me?' he stammered.

'Yes,' she said promptly.

Looking her intended up and down, she noticed that in his confusion he had left his flies gaping. Kissing him, she zipped him up. The gesture had about it a brusque, almost brutal finality. Leading him briskly into the drawing room, she made the announcement without preamble. 'Lennox and I are engaged.'

Conversation ended abruptly. The room was silent. 'I am going to be Mrs. Lotte,' she added, in case there was any doubt about the matter. Taking hold of his arm, she led her intended to her astonished parents, her smile clearly saying, "There, aren't you pleased with me? Have I not given you exactly what you wanted?"

Uther was astounded but cautiously pleased. Cautiously, because the self-satisfied smile on Margot's face seemed to suggest that she knew something he did not.

'Poor Lennox,' he said to Igraine, a week before the wedding. 'He looks shell-shocked.'

His wife thought that was unfair. 'He looks like a man in love to me.'

'No doubt. Still, one can't help feeling sorry for him. Wait till he finds out what she's really like.'

Igraine's chin lifted defiantly. 'I don't know what you mean, he's lucky to get her. She's beautiful and talented, and she'll make a wonderful wife and mother.'

'Beautiful, yes. Talented, undoubtedly. A mother? Never. Margot is far too selfish for that.' But Uther was mistaken. A few months after the marriage, Margot fell pregnant. Inevitably though, she blamed Lennox. 'How could you do this to me?' she wailed.

Lennox was distraught. 'B-but I thought we w-wanted a b-baby?'

'We!' shrieked Margot. 'You mean *you* wanted one!'

'You know I only w-want w-what you w-want,' he said, and meant it; but it was no use. Margot sobbed and sulked and was inconsolable. Motherhood was the last thing she wanted. She was terrified, her life was over, she was condemned to be a milking cow. Poor Lennox suffered her sulks and tantrums for days that dragged on into weeks, and was at last desperate enough to ask his father-in-law's advice.

Uther smiled his world-weary smile. 'Try jewellery.'

'Margot isn't the s-sort of w-woman you can b-bribe with b-baubles,' protested Lennox.

'She most certainly is not,' agreed Uther. 'Baubles would be a grave error. We are talking serious jewellery here.'

Lennox went out in his lunch hour and bought a Van Cleef and Arpels emerald necklace with matching bracelet that cost a small fortune. To his relief, Uther had given him sound advice. As the tips of Margot's fingers caressed the jewels, she was miraculously transformed. Sulks? What sulks? Tantrums? Where were these tantrums? 'Van Cleef and Arpels! You shouldn't have, darling.' Clawing his shirt and trousers, she purred with feline contentment. It was a mutually satisfactory solution to what had threatened to become a major problem. Lennox was happy, and Margot had established an important precedent.

The baby was a boy. They called him Gawain. He had white lashes and a fuzz of red hair. Margot was at first dismayed, then found it rather chic. None of her friends had redheads, and she adored being different. Lennox was delighted and proud to be a father. Margot made it clear she would not change the baby's nappies; that was what nannies were for; nor would she breast feed it. The very idea was repellent. And one child, by the way, was quite enough.

Sitting on Margot's bed in the clinic, Lennox was ecstatic. 'I l-love you, M-Margot,' he crooned.

She patted his hand. 'I know.'

'And you l-love m-me, don't you?'

She said nothing.

'You d-do, d-don't you, d-darling?'

She played with his fingers. 'I'm mad about your hands. You have such long fingers. You know what they say about men with long fingers.'

Lennox persisted. 'Do you l-love m-me, M-Margot?'

Margot thrust his hand aside. 'No, Lennox,' she said, 'I do not. I thought I made that clear before we walked up the aisle.'

Taking her hand, as he had done when they first met, he clasped it with great care, as if it were a wounded bird, when in fact it was he who was wounded. 'I expect I d-didn't b-believe you,' he muttered.

'You should have,' said Margot coolly.

'You will l-love me, M-Margot. One d-day.'

She was merciless. 'No, I will not. I'm fond of you, but I shall never love you. It's not about you, Lennox, it's about me. I don't do love, I'm not capable of loving anyone. I don't have those sort of feelings. I don't even know what you mean by love.'

'Then,' said Lennox, 'I shall j-just have to l-love you enough for b-both of us.'

To everyone's amazement Margot doted on her baby, just as her husband doted on her, and Lennox consoled himself with the thought that despite her protestations, Margot was learning to love.

Sixteen

2008

MERLIN WAS taking an evening walk in the woods that lay to the west of Glastonbury. It was that magical hour when the world is hushed, poised between day and night. A black Labrador slipped from the shadows and stood facing him. Merlin stopped. The dog lifted its head and barked twice, and as Merlin walked towards it, trotted along the path ahead, always maintaining the same distance between them. When Merlin stopped again, the dog stopped, turning its head to look at him. 'Robbie,' whispered Merlin, knowing he was being summoned.

Two days later he landed on the island and made straight for the old man's cottage. The old man sat by the fire with Robbie at his feet. 'You have come to claim Camelot,' said the old man. It was a statement, not a question.

'Yes,' said Merlin.

'Will it be as you promised?'

'It will be as I promised.' Merlin stooped to pat the Labrador. 'Robbie shall be my friend and companion, I shall love him and care for him until the day he dies.'

The old man nodded his approval. 'And when he dies?'

'His ashes will be buried here on Camelot as a sign and a symbol of its ideals.'

'And they shall be?' The old man intoned the question as if it were part of a litany.

Merlin repeated solemnly, 'Truth. Justice. Love.'

'Do you swear it?'

The magus raised his right hand. 'I swear it on Arthur's

life.'

The old man smiled contentedly and lay back in his chair. 'Then Camelot is yours.' Merlin held the old man's hand until, barely an hour later, he heaved a sigh and died.

Throughout the day, Merlin gathered moss, clumps of peat and driftwood. Where the long grass met the beach he built a great mound measuring ten feet square and two feet high, and when the sun set and the sky was streaked with red, he laid the old man on the funeral pyre. As the flames embraced the corpse, Merlin knelt in prayer. By his side Robbie, the black Labrador, kept vigil, never once stirring, brown eyes staring sadly into the flames. The fire burned that night and most of the following day. At first, the flames leapt high, then gradually fell back. As the sun went down the following evening, a wind gusted from the west, inspiring a last flurry of life in the dying embers, whirling the sparks upwards to the first stars.

By the next morning it was all over. When the heart of the fire was cold, Merlin collected the old man's ashes. As the magus walked away, Robbie stood and stretched, then a little unsteadily, for his limbs were stiff and he was weak from fasting, followed at the heels of his new master.

Before he left the island Merlin visited the cottage and took one last look round. The old man had accumulated scarcely any possessions in his long life, and nothing of monetary value – a few sticks of furniture, a kettle, some pots and pans, two large wooden spoons, a knife and fork, herbs grown at the back of the cottage, a few well-thumbed books, the pages yellowing with age and foxed with damp. Merlin sat by the empty grate and let his mind drift back to the past and forward to the future. He had both the means and the skill to do what had to be done, though he would need help. First, however, there was a firework display to organise, the greatest the world had ever seen – a very special illusion that would fool everyone, he flattered himself.

A few weeks later a number of military and civil stations

around the world picked up faint signals, indicating seismic activity in the Atlantic Ocean. By no means an infrequent occurrence, it was immediately established beyond doubt that the disturbance was a natural one and that no country had broken the global ban on the testing of nuclear weapons.

Several commercial aircraft crossing the Atlantic, and also a container vessel and an oil tanker, reported seeing a big explosion about a hundred and fifty miles west of Land's End. This was followed by a series of lesser explosions accompanied by dazzling, multi-coloured lights, rising several hundred feet into the air, the phenomenon resembling a giant pyrotechnic display. The obvious conclusion was that there had been a significant shift in the underwater terrain created by, or resulting in, a volcanic eruption. Confirmation of this came when streams of volcanic ash and traces of plant life were observed floating on the surface of the sea in the vicinity of the reported disturbance.

Scientists did not know precisely what had happened, but one thing was clear; the explosion or eruption had been sufficiently powerful to cause the total disintegration of a small island. Such natural phenomena were by no means unheard of. More than one small island in the Indian Ocean had suffered a similar fate. The original location of the island was of course known, yet a search by satellites, ships and aircraft, revealed nothing. It had disappeared without trace.

Seventeen

Following his triumphant, and somewhat unexpected, success with Margot, Uther turned his attention to his eldest daughter. He had no illusions, Elaine would be a hard nut to crack. She had personality in abundance but was certainly no beauty. He had heard that such attachments as she formed were passionate but brief, usually with actors or stage hands with highly developed pectorals. As to her views on marriage, she had made them crystal clear: who needed to settle down with some mindless moron whose aspirations were money in the bank, a fat bonus at the end of the year, a trophy wife with big tits, liposuctioned thighs, collagen-enhanced lips, two kids, a house in town, a Range Rover and holidays in the boring Caribbean or the even more boring French Riviera? Who needed to settle down at all?

Uther disapproved of actors; as far as he was concerned they were all faggots and layabouts with dubious values and worse morals. Acting was not an appropriate profession for any decent girl, most certainly not for a Pendragon. Margot had married well, and Elaine would damn well do the same, or he would know the reason why.

Elaine rarely spent the night at home in Brackett Hall. On one of the rare occasions that she did, Uther waylaid her at breakfast.

'And where were you last night?'

'I'm really not sure, dad,' said Elaine, who adored baiting her step-father. 'But wherever it was, I had an ecstatic time.' She slurped her coffee. 'You know what I mean,' she added with a huge wink, just in case Uther had missed something.

Uther sniffed disapprovingly. 'Time you stopped messing around and found yourself a suitable husband.'

'What exactly do you mean by *suitable*, father?' Elaine enquired.

'Anyone but an actor,' said her father pointedly.

'I see,' said Elaine. 'A murderer, a rapist or a child abuser perhaps, but not an actor.'

Uther sighed wearily. 'Very comical, Elaine. As you well know, I mean someone with a good background and a steady job, a man who will support you and be a decent father to your children.'

Elaine wrinkled her nose. 'I'm sorry, I don't have time for all that bourgeois crap. Besides, I don't believe in steady relationships. I prefer to play the field.'

Uther's patience, never his strong point, was soon exhausted, and he hinted that if she did not find (or allow her parents to find) a suitable man to marry, he would cut off her allowance. She had six months, he said.

Elaine called his bluff. Within a week she had moved out of Brackett Hall and into a short-term bedsit in Camden Town. Igraine was wretched. To lose one daughter was bad enough, to lose two, and in so short a time, was nothing short of catastrophic. She berated her husband. 'You drove her out of the house – you and your obsession with marrying off the girls.'

Uther would not accept any blame. 'Nonsense, duchess. It was her decision entirely. The birds are flying the nest, that's all, one of those things that happen in families.'

The truth was that he was quite pleased to see the back of Elaine, married or not; now he only had Morgan to worry about. He had a soft spot for his youngest step-daughter, she had guts, she was refreshingly different. She was also vulnerable and needed looking after; just as long as he wasn't the one who had to do it. From time to time Uther would look at Morgan dispassionately, prepared to be generous, hoping to discover some physical attribute that might appeal to a potential suitor, but he never did, there was just too much of her. Everything about her was big – her shoulders, her hips, her legs, her tummy. Then, of course, there was her face. What could you say about her face? Downright ugly? Unkind. Charmingly ugly, then? Intriguingly ugly? Engagingly ugly? Her eyes bulged, her mouth was enormous, her upper lip bristled. The village kids, cruel as only kids can be, would follow her along the street chanting, 'Mog, Mog, face like a frog!' And Morgan would threaten good-naturedly to turn them into toads and rats, melt their eyeballs and rip out their tongues, threats, needless to say, immediately reported back to their parents who, like their children, were convinced that Morgan was a witch.

Uther knew what it meant to struggle against the odds. No doubt poor Morgan would have to do the same. He would dearly have liked to find her a good man but was almost resigned to the fact that she would never leave home. So that when long-stemmed red roses began to arrive at the house addressed to Miss Morgan Pendragon, it was, to say the least, a shock.

'What's this all about, duchess?' he asked his wife, waving at her the latest offering of roses.

'I have no idea.'

The roses, Uther discovered, came from Arran Gore. The family was well known in Yorkshire; not too much money but gentry and very respectable. Wasn't he a solicitor or an accountant or some such? Where had he met this young man? The Conservative Dinner? The Red Cross Ball? One of those do's. Nice enough chap as he recalled; why would he be interested in Morgan?

Which was exactly what Morgan was asking herself. Gloomily she consulted a mirror, and found nothing to reassure her. It was, she concluded cynically, probably a hoax. As it turned out, it was not. Arran Gore phoned Morgan to ask her out to dinner and Morgan decided to play along, if only to see when and where the humiliating game would end. From that moment Brackett Hall was in turmoil, and as the day approached, the atmosphere in the house grew more and more strained. The only one who seemed entirely relaxed was Morgan herself.

On the appointed evening, Arran Gore duly presented himself at the front door of Brackett Hall and was shown into the sitting room. He was a shortish man, thirty-five or so, well-spoken, pleasant, quite good-looking and altogether very presentable. Igraine thought him rather too conventional for Morgan, though behind his quiet manner she sensed the inner strength of a man who knew what he wanted; Uther thought there might be too big an age difference, Morgan, after all, being only nineteen. There again, an older man might be just what Morgan needed. What young man could handle her? Chatting to his hosts whilst waiting for Morgan to come down, he made it clear that he thought her the most stunning and original lady he had ever seen. At first Uther thought he must be joking but then, seeing how serious Gore was, he wondered if the man might not be deranged. There were crazies everywhere you looked these days, and who knew what hole this one had crept out of? A crazy might well find Morgan attractive; she was more than a little crazy herself.

Igraine had no such misgivings, Arran Gore would do just fine. For days now she had fussed around her truculent and uncooperative youngest child, offering advice on make-up, perfumes and hair-do's. That morning she had finally found her the right dress, an elegant, well cut little black number that flattered Morgan's large frame and bosom. A discreet application of make-up disguised the prominent eyes, the froggy mouth and the shadow on her upper lip. With her long black hair coaxed to frame her face, reducing it to more normal proportions, Morgan was a work of art. With the light behind her, she looked almost attractive. Igraine complimented herself on a job well done.

But alas when Morgan joined them in the sitting room, she was wearing not the neat little dress that Igraine had so carefully chosen for her, but what appeared to be a witch's costume. It was long, black and shapeless, frayed at the hem, and tied savagely at the waist with a length of rope, emphasising her wide hips. On her head was jammed a conical witch's hat, her cheeks were white as a clown's, her eyes rimmed with black, and the hair her mother had so carefully blow-dried and shaped, now hung in greasy clumps about her neck. Uther turned away in embarrassment whilst Igraine advanced on Morgan, intending to smack her face; but Morgan swept past her, greeting her date with an incongruously gracious smile. In stunned disbelief, Uther and Igraine watched the surreal mini-drama unfold. Arran Gore bowed, and with a courtly gesture kissed Morgan's hand. Not by so much as a twitch or quiver of his face did he indicate that he found her appearance in any way unusual. 'You look wonderful,' he said.

For a moment Uther and Igraine were struck dumb by this spectacular lie. Uther opened his mouth to speak, but before he could say anything, Morgan had grabbed Arran Gore's hand and dragged him out of the house.

To everyone's amazement, the man came back for more. He escorted (his word) Morgan to the theatre, to concerts and to restaurants, and when it became obvious that he was not to be put off, Morgan gave up trying to traumatise him. Within a few weeks she had adopted a more reasonable style of dressing, and was even beginning to take some care with her hair and make-up. He was, after all, the only man who had ever paid any attention to her, and for that she was ready to reward him. Nevertheless, she remained deeply sceptical, finding it hard to understand what any man could possibly see in her. In vain she reminded herself of the advice she had always given her sisters: "If you believe in yourself, you can do anything." Even if, by some miracle, he truly loved her, she was determined not to love him in return, for fear she would be heartbroken when he tired of her; for tire of her he most assuredly would.

But he did not. On the contrary, Arran Gore remained a constant and most persistent suitor. His attentions made her happy, but they also troubled her, as Morgan was convinced that no one, not even her parents and her sisters, had ever or could ever, love her. She was so undemanding that she was quite content to love them and expect nothing in return. What did love mean anyway? It was just a word. People always said they loved each other, didn't they? But did they really mean it?

Over dinner one evening Arran proposed. How many times had she fantasised about that moment? How many times had she pictured herself gazing at him adoringly, taking in his every word? But when, miracle of miracles, it actually happened, she could not even look him in the eye. Instead she looked down at the table and played with a bread roll.

'You know how I feel about you, Morgan. From the first moment I saw you flash past on your motorbike, I couldn't stop thinking about you. Then, when I came to pick you up on our first date, I was certain you were the one. Guts and humour and a proud spirit, that's what you have. I never met a girl like you. You might think I'm a bit old for you, and I may not have set the world on fire but, well, I'm not such a bad fellow when you get to know me. I'll make you a good husband, I promise you that.'

How could she help but be touched? Could it really be that for the first time in her life someone truly loved her? If so, she was the most fortunate woman in the world. Margot and Elaine were beautiful and gifted but what did she have? Nothing compared to them, neither looks nor talent; and yet she was more than fortunate, for here she was being offered marriage by a truly nice man – not perhaps the most exciting man in the world, a touch old fashioned, a bit short, a little too old, but what did all that matter? He wanted her, and for that she was grateful. Taking a deep breath, she looked him in the

eye and heard herself say. 'I'm sorry, Arran. I can't marry you.'
She was shaking. Her heart pounded remorselessly against her
ribcage, as if punishing her for her stupidity. Never had she felt
so wretched and confused.

'Can you tell me why?'

She shook her head in bewilderment. 'I don't know. I just
can't.'

'I shan't take "no" for an answer,' said Arran. And he
didn't.

'Why does he keep asking me?' Morgan lamented to her
mother.

'He's in love with you.'

'He can't be. I'm ugly. And now all this worry is making me
fat.' She looked at herself head on, then sideways, in one of the
sitting room mirrors. 'God, look at my tits. I really must go on
a diet. Maybe I could have them shrunk. I was reading about
a new laser flesh-liquidiser the other day. I could have my hips
and bum done at the same time.'

'Arran likes you the way you are, darling,' Igraine insisted.
'Besides, looks aren't everything, as I keep telling you. Arran
loves you because you are different.'

Morgan knew exactly what that meant. Different meant
protruding teeth; different meant a big bum and facial hair.
'Anyway, I shall never get married. All that . . . business.'
Morgan pulled a face. 'The whole idea scares me. Women
should not have to submit to things like that. If that's love, you
can keep it. I shall never do it, not with anyone.'

Igraine smiled. 'My dear, there's a great deal more to
marriage than sex.'

'Such as?'

'Practical things. Having a roof over your head for one.'

Morgan scratched her upper lip noisily. 'I already have.
Father has seen to that.'

'There's companionship,' suggested Igraine.

'I've got you and dad. I've got Elaine and Margot.'

This was not going to be easy. 'There's children.'

Morgan mimed vomiting. 'I prefer dogs.'

Every week, sometimes twice a week, Arran would pick Morgan up and take her to a restaurant or to his club. Every week, over coffee, he proposed. And every week she would turn him down, chiding him affectionately. 'This is getting to be a habit, Bore. How many times is that?' With great good humour, he had accepted the nickname. As long as she married him, Morgan could call him anything she liked.

'I've lost count,' he admitted.

'Isn't it time to give up?'

'I'm a stubborn sort of chap,' said he quietly. He was also an endearing sort of chap, though she would rather die than tell him so. A bit stiff, a little over formal perhaps, but then, as he had often explained, his forebears had been army people. A Gore had fought with Wellington at Waterloo, he once told her proudly. No doubt he too had been a stubborn sort of chap.

The more she thought about him, the more she admired him and the less she understood why he wanted to marry her. 'What's your game, Bore?'

A puzzled frown. 'Game?'

'You should marry the girl next door.'

'You *are* the girl next door,' he said. He tried to take her hand but she pulled it away.

'Oh pooh,' said Morgan.

Perversely she had reverted to her former maverick style of dressing. Tonight, for example, her large hips and backside had somehow squeezed their bulk into a narrow strip of black leather two sizes too small for them, and had spent the evening struggling to escape. Every time she moved or spoke or took a mouthful of food, her black leather suit protested, its creaks and groans warning of intolerable stress. Her spiked hair was pink, her face a white mask, her lips purple, and her eyes, like those of some nocturnal creature caught in a spotlight, peered anxiously at the world through dark circles of black mascara.

The girl next door? Perhaps not. Arran had to admit she had a point.

'You just want me because you can't have me.'

'I shall go on wanting you until I can. Then I shall want you even more.'

Clearly she ought to do the decent thing and send him packing, but somehow she could not bring herself to do anything quite so extreme. Dear old Bore would be most horribly upset. Might he not do something dreadful if he thought he had lost her forever? And though of course she couldn't possibly marry him, she did rather enjoy his company in an odd sort of way.

One evening over dinner, Arran was talking about some legal case or other he was working on, and she was looking at him, not hearing a word he said, almost as if she were watching a silent movie. Observing him as he spoke, she noticed for the first time how the corners of his mouth moved when he smiled, and that funny habit he had of putting his head on one side when he was thinking. This is a good man, she thought, a kind man, kind and gentle and sincere, the sort of man you can trust; and he wanted her. She felt faint. An unaccustomed distillation of tenderness blurred her vision, disturbing her equilibrium.

'Yes,' she said.

'I beg your pardon?'

'Yes, I will marry you.'

And that was that. No one could possibly have been more surprised than Arran, unless of course it was Morgan. As Elaine put it after the wedding, Morgan had finally demonstrated that she really could fly. Or if she had not exactly taken flight, she had done something just as amazing; she had taken a walk up the aisle.

Eighteen

2009

MERLIN LOVED the wild and sea-tossed coast of northern Cornwall. Recently he had talked about it so enthusiastically that Hector suggested the family spend a couple of days there during the school holidays. 'There's the old castle at Tintagel, and lots of walks and incredible views and marvellous beaches. We'll take the car and leave the caravan behind – do it in style. Merlin recommended a bed and breakfast place. Full English breakfast and comfortable beds.'

'I don't remember him mentioning Cornwall before,' said Elizabeth curiously, knowing from experience that Merlin never said anything without a reason. Why was he so keen for them to visit Cornwall?

'You know how he is,' said Hector, who for once needed no explanation, 'he gets these passions. Tintagel is his latest passion, that's all. How about it?'

'Fine with me. Let's try it.'

The following week, Elizabeth, Hector and the two boys set off early in the morning. By nine a.m. they were turning into the driveway of an old Cornish house, its stone façade flaking and mellowed with age. Breakfast was everything Merlin had promised it would be. 'Exercise is what we need now.' Hector drained the last drop of coffee, stretched and yawned. 'How about a walk to the castle and back?'

The wooden stairway that linked the mainland with the causeway was not for the faint-hearted. It descended so steeply that looking down from the top it seemed like a step-ladder. Although it was July and the sun was warm, the fitful Atlantic breezes gusted sharply first from one direction then another. The two boys were unconcerned but Elizabeth and Hector clutched the guide ropes as they made their way cautiously down. At the bottom of the stairs, a narrow causeway led to the promontory on which the castle stood. Another set of steep and narrow steps as fearsome a challenge as the first, climbed to the sky, curving first right, then left towards the entrance of the ruined castle.

Crossing the drawbridge, Hector, Elizabeth and the two boys passed through a gateway once guarded by a massive iron portcullis. To their right, and far below, was a shingle beach overhung by precipitous cliffs on three sides. The two boys and their father stood looking down the cliffs to the beach where the sea had carved out huge caves. Elizabeth could hardly bear to look. 'Do be careful,' she said nervously.

Hector pointed. 'You see the biggest cave. There, on the left, where those boulders are.'

'I see it,' said Keir.

'That's Merlin's cave.'

Arthur grinned. 'Quite a coincidence.'

'Ever ask your housemaster where he got his name from?'

'I did once,' said Arthur. 'He said he got it from the same place Merlin did.'

Hector smiled. 'That's my Merlin.'

'Was this King Arthur's castle?' asked Keir.

'I'm afraid not. These ruins only date back to Norman times. If Arthur lived at all, it was in the sixth century, several hundred years earlier.'

'What do you mean *if* he lived?' Arthur seemed surprised. 'Is there any doubt about it?'

'No one seems quite sure. Some scholars think he was a historical figure, some don't.'

'All the same, wherever you look, there's something that links this place to Arthurian legend,' said Elizabeth. 'I believe he was here. I feel it.'

'Anything is possible,' said Hector, 'but I can't help thinking a lot of these stories were invented for the tourists. The lady at reception assured me that King Arthur's round table is buried in Bossiney Mound at Bossiney Castle. What's more, she claims she has actually seen it rising from the mound at full moon! It makes you wonder what else folk round here see at full moon, especially with a few pints inside them.'

'Merlin says King Arthur was a real person,' said Arthur.

'Maybe he was, maybe he wasn't. One thing for sure, though, a lot of people want to believe he was.'

'That sculpture, or whatever it is – up there, on the highest point,' said Keir, 'is that very old?'

Hector chuckled. 'The Sword in the Stone? It's not even as old as you are. I'm told the local Council commissioned it for the millennium, and apparently there was a lot of opposition. After all, there isn't the slightest evidence connecting this site with Arthur. Still, there it is, large as life. Who wants to take a look?'

Elizabeth shook her head. 'I think I'll walk down to the beach and explore Merlin's cave.'

'The path looks pretty steep. I'll come with you,' said Hector.

'I want to see the Sword in the Stone,' said Keir.

Arthur said nothing but he followed Keir. The higher the brothers climbed, the further they could see: to the south-east, Tintagel, and beyond to the bleak hills of Bodmin Moor; to the north-west, the great expanse of the Atlantic ocean; to the north, the steep descent to the beach and Merlin's cave. Up here the capricious breezes now joined forces, and the wind was so strong that Keir and Arthur were almost tumbled over several times. Progress was slow but at last they reached the flat peak of the headland. The stone on the summit was about six feet square, and on it was set an anvil. Projecting from the anvil was the hilt and a few inches of sword. Three or four kids were playing round the sculpture, climbing onto it and trying to pull out the sword. As one by one they failed the others laughed and jeered. Tiring of their game, they moved off in the direction of the path that led down to the beach, leaving the brothers alone.

'It's bigger than it looked from down there,' said Keir. 'Quite impressive.'

'It is,' agreed Arthur.

Keir rapped the sculpture. 'Made of bronze.' He read the inscription aloud. WHOSO PULLETH OUT THIS SWORD OF THIS STONE AND ANVIL, IS RIGHTWISE KING BORN OF ALL ENGLAND. Climbing onto the stone, he grasped the hilt of the Sword and gave it a token tug.

'Forget it,' he said scornfully. 'Nothing could shift that.' But for some reason, even though he knew it was impossible, he could not resist trying again. This time he grasped the sword with both hands and heaved with all his strength, arching his body so that the back of his head almost touched the stone. Moments later he collapsed, groaning. 'That hurt!' he muttered, nursing the red weals on the palms of his hands. 'Stupid. Don't know what made me do it.'

Arthur turned away towards the path. Keir slid off the stone. 'Your turn. Don't you want to be King of England?'

Arthur smiled and shook his head. Keir could not resist adding spitefully, 'Now's your chance to prove you're so damned special, like Mum is always saying you are.'

'I don't have to prove anything,' said Arthur. Keir had long since lost the power to torment him.

'What are you afraid of?' said Keir, determined to provoke some reaction.

Arthur found a direct challenge like that hard to resist. Jumping onto the stone, he laid his right hand on the sword's hilt. After a moment or two he turned to his brother, as if appealing to him.

'Get on with it, man,' said Keir waving his arms, urging his brother on.

From the sea the west wind rose suddenly and raged round the headland. Head flung back, his long blond hair streaming in the wind, Arthur held onto the hilt of the sword with both hands to stop himself being blown off the stone.

As suddenly as it rose, the wind dropped. Tensing the muscles of his right arm, Arthur drew the sword from the anvil. In one swift movement he raised it high above his head, lowered it to kiss the hilt, and slid it back in place. As he did so, a group of tourists appeared over the brow of the hill, a man and woman and three teenage children. They were looking at him oddly. Had they seen anything? Without a backward glance at Keir, Arthur hurried down the path in the direction of the beach.

For a few moments Keir was so stunned he could barely move. His face deathly pale, his expression half incredulous, half fearful, he followed Arthur like a dog following its master, every few moments erupting in irritable bursts of words, all the time breathing heavily, as much from the shock of what he had just witnessed, as from the jarring pace that Arthur set.

'How did you do it? How did you do it,' he babbled. 'Tell me how you did it! It was loose, it must have been, it was loose wasn't it? It was me that did it. All that pulling loosened it . . . Arthur! Answer me! Wait! What happened? You think you can fool me? Well you can't. I know your tricks. You can't bear to be ordinary, can you? You want everyone to think you're something special . . . You're going to tell Mum and Dad a pack of lies! Well don't think they'll believe a word of it, because they won't . . . Arthur! Listen to me, you little shit! Stop! Stop! . . . They won't believe you, I tell you. I won't let them. I'll say you're a liar . . . *I'll tell them I did it!*'

At a bend in the path below, Arthur stopped and looked up at his adoptive brother. 'Tell them what you like.'

Down on the beach, Keir rushed frantically here and there, searching for his parents, determined to get to them first. Arthur wandered about, kicking pebbles disconsolately. At last, Keir caught sight of Hector and Elizabeth in the half light of Merlin's cave. Long before he reached them, the words were tumbling from his mouth. Hector shook his head in bewilderment. 'Calm down, son, calm down. Let me get this straight. Who pulled the sword from the stone?'

'I did.' Keir's eyes challenged his father.

A giant wave crashed on the shore, its roar echoing menacingly in the cave. High up in the vaulted roof the wind wailed like a soul trapped in hell.

'You did?'

'Yes.'

'You pulled the sword from the stone?'

'Yes.'

'How did you do that?'

'How should I know,' said Keir sullenly. 'Thousands of tourists must have tried the same thing. I expect they loosened it.'

'I see.'

Elizabeth said nothing. When they were out of the cave, and Arthur had joined them, she asked Keir, 'Do you want to do it for me and dad?'

Keir blinked. 'No point in climbing all the way up again.'

'We have to climb up anyway. It's not much of a detour.'

'Fine,' he muttered.

It was lunchtime and the headland was deserted. The fickle weather had changed and a massive storm was moving in from the Atlantic to the shore, the advancing clouds drawing a black pall over the sunlit ocean. In their shadow the sea was restless now and flecked with white. By the Sword in the Stone they stood facing the wind, hands deep in the pockets of their windcheaters, hair flying.

'Show us how you did it, Keir,' said Hector.

'This is silly.'

'Show us.'

With Hector and Elizabeth watching intently, and Arthur's attention apparently concentrated on the ground, Keir rolled his large frame onto the Stone, grasped the handles of the sword with both hands and pulled so hard that even in the wind that howled round him, the sweat ran down his face. After a few seconds he gave up and looked out to sea with blank eyes. Seizing the hilt of the sword once more, he heaved, this time with the full weight of his body behind his arms, lying back almost parallel with the stone. A third time he pulled, so fiercely that the veins on his neck stood out, and it seemed as if his arms must surely be torn out of their sockets. But for all his efforts, the sword held firm in the anvil, moving not even the tiniest fraction of an inch. Finally his strength deserted him, his arms went limp, and releasing the sword with a groan, he folded to his knees. He was so exhausted that for a full minute he remained there crouched by the anvil, his damp forehead resting on the cold stone. Wincing with pain, he eased open his hands. The palms were flecked with blood. 'It was a freak, that's all,' he muttered. 'One of those things.' His eyes shifted nervously from one to the other. 'It won't move now. But it did.' Elizabeth turned away, Hector looked uncomfortable. 'It moved, I tell you,' protested Keir, 'it came right out.'

Seeing they did not believe him, he appealed to his brother. 'Tell them, Arthur.'

Arthur was silent.

Elizabeth dug her hands deeper into the pockets of her windcheater and shivered. 'It's cold, and it's going to pour with rain.' She walked quickly away. A few seconds later Keir followed her. Hector did not move. Nor did Arthur.

'Well, Arthur?'

No reply.

'Tell me what really happened,' said Hector.

Arthur touched the scar on his cheek. 'Let's go, Dad.'

Hector had no intention of going anywhere – not until he had learned the truth. 'Did someone pull the Sword out?'

Arthur shifted uneasily. 'Please, Dad, let's go.'

'I'd like to see you try it first.' Hector pointed at the Sword.

'I'm waiting.'

For a long moment father and son looked at each other.

'Coming then?' said Arthur brightly.

Hector shook his head. 'I'm not moving from this spot.'

'You'll catch your death of cold.'

'What if I do?' said Hector, folding his arms.

It was a battle of wills, each knowing how stubborn the other could be. In the end it was Arthur who gave in. Jumping onto the stone, he set his hand on the Sword. Grunting and puffing, he made a show of straining to pull it out. 'There,' he said. 'It won't budge.'

'Are you sure?'

'You saw me trying to pull it out.'

'I saw you trying not to,' said his father.

Arthur said innocently, 'I don't know what you mean.'

'You never lied to me before.'

The sea was calm now, the wind had dropped. Storm clouds hung low over the ocean, their long fingers reaching down to the water. Soon the rain would come. Arthur laid his right hand on the hilt of the sword and gently drew it out. For a moment he held it high above his head, and then, as if embarrassed by what he had done, quickly replaced it. Turning, he found himself alone, Hector was nowhere to be seen. A myriad stars and galaxies glowed in the arched canopy of the night sky, but as he looked down, there far below him, it was day. The Atlantic waves rolled green and grey in the rapidly shifting light, as the rays of the afternoon sun, filtering through the clouds, swept the surface of the ocean. Everything about him was quiet and still. He was afraid. He wanted to call out in the hope someone might respond but he did not, knowing there was no one there. Standing in the dark night on the summit of this bleak outcrop of land, he felt uncannily alone, as if he were the only one left alive on the planet. Never before had he felt such dread, nor so profound a sense of isolation.

But then, on the mainland side of the promontory the light

of a candle gleamed, and then another and another, until soon
a seemingly endless procession of candles wound its way down
the precipitous wooden stairway and across the causeway. As
the column of lights approached, it disappeared now and then
behind dark masses of cliff face. Slowly, unhurriedly, it wound
its way on and up towards the headland where Arthur stood by
the Sword in the Stone.

His mouth dry, a pulse hammered the back of his throat
as the ghostly procession of candles approached. As the first
candle passed through the castle gateway, he caught the glint
of armour and heard the tramp of marching men. These were
no ordinary footsteps, for the harsh and fearsome sound that
echoed louder and louder in the courtyard of the ancient castle
was the clash of metal-clad feet on flagstones.

As the first knight came into view, Arthur saw that he
was covered from head to foot in glistening armour, his face
concealed by a lowered visor. Ignoring Arthur, he went straight
to the stone, poured a drop of hot wax, and stood his lighted
candle on it. Laying both his mail-clad hands on the sword's
hilt, he pulled with all his strength. The sword did not move.
Turning to Arthur, he raised his mailed fist in salute, then
taking up his candle, walked on, making way for the next
knight, who did exactly the same as the first. One by one,
the knights tried to pull the Sword from the anvil, and one by
one they failed. As each knight saluted Arthur, picked up his
candle and left the headland, another took his place. A moving
necklace of lights encircled the cliff tops beginning at the top
of the stairway on the land side of the promontory, down the
stairs to the causeway, up the cliff face, through the gateway
of the castle to the Sword in the Stone, descending by the path
to the beach, where finally, in Merlin's cave, the last candle
disappeared from view.

'Arthur! Where are you? Wait for me!' But Arthur was
nowhere to be seen, and Hector was standing alone by the
sculpture. Had Arthur really drawn the sword from the anvil?

If he had, there must surely be some rational explanation for it. Hector was a powerful man, broadly built and muscular, fit and strong for his age. He climbed onto the stone. Laying his hands on the sword's hilt, he tensed every muscle in his body, from the tips of his fingers, through his hands and arms and shoulders, down into his chest and stomach and thighs to the soles of his feet. Concentrating all his strength and all his will, he leaned back and pulled, his face contorting with the strain. The sword would not budge.

For a few moments he relaxed, breathing deeply, feeling the power flow back into his muscles. Setting his knees against the anvil, he pulled a second time. Again he pulled, and again, and yet again, until the veins jutted from his neck like cables. The muscles in his arms and legs and back ached. His hands burned like fire. The sword remained firm and immovable, nothing could shift it.

Looking about him, Hector saw that the sky was clear again. The storm clouds had vanished, and yet there was no wind to blow them away. He heard Merlin's voice, heard it as clearly as if he were standing next to him. 'The clouds will always part for Arthur.' Suddenly he understood that this was the second sign prophesied by Merlin. Thoughtfully he set off after his adopted son.

Near the bottom of the second flight of steps, a man in an official looking cap and uniform stopped the Hughes family, first Elizabeth and Keir, then Arthur, then Hector. He was polite but insistent; they were to follow him to the office to talk to his boss, it would not take long but there was a matter that had to be cleared up. In the cramped room, the two boys and Hector stood in line with the man in uniform, Elizabeth sitting on one of the only two chairs. Behind a grey vinyl-topped desk covered with cigarette burns sat the man introduced as the boss.

'What's up, Bill?'

Bill intoned without emotion. 'These people interfered with

the sculpture – The Sword in the Stone.'

'Evidence?' the boss demanded.

'They was reported,' said Bill.

'Who reported them?'

'A family. They 'ad to go, but I got their name and address.' Bill laid a scrap of paper in front of his boss. 'That's it there. Three kids and two adults. Quite disgusted the parents was. Yobbo behaviour they called it. Said it was one of these two youngsters did it.' He nodded in the direction of Keir and Arthur. 'One of 'em pulled the Sword right out of the anvil and waved it in the air. Must 'ave damaged the sculpture. Act of vandalism.'

The boss leaned back in his chair and pressed the palms of his hands together. 'Pulled the sword out and waved it in the air?'

Bill nodded. 'That's right.'

Without even glancing at it, the boss screwed up the scrap of paper on his desk. 'Checked the sculpture have you?' he enquired.

''Ad to stop this lot, didn't I? 'Aven't 'ad time to check it, 'ave I? But I will. I'll check it now, if you like.'

'Don't bother.'

'Why not?' said Bill.

'Because,' said the boss, emphasising his words, 'those people did not see what they thought they saw.'

Bill scratched his head. 'They was categoric.' He jerked his thumb at Arthur and Keir. 'One of them lads pulled the sword out.'

The boss shook his head. 'There's not a man alive could do that.'

'Why do you say that?'

'Because there's no sword to pull out,' said his boss triumphantly. 'You can't pull out what isn't there, now can you?' His steep brows challenged anyone to contradict him.

'But I've seen the sword a thousand times,' protested Bill.

'No you haven't, Bill. What you see – what everyone sees – is a hilt and a few inches of sword sticking out of an anvil. So naturally you think there's a sword inside the anvil. It may look as though there is, but there isn't. The whole sculpture is one solid piece of bronze. I thought everyone knew that; the sword is an illusion. Just like the story of King Arthur, if you ask me.' Standing up politely he leaned over his desk and extended his hand in turn to Elizabeth, Hector, Keir and Arthur. 'Sorry you've been troubled, madam, sir, young lads. Bill here was only doing his duty. I hope there's no hard feelings.'

Hector stirred himself out of his trance. 'None at all.'

'Amazing how gullible people are,' said the boss, shaking his head incredulously, 'even in this day and age. You wouldn't think we were living in the twenty-first century, would you? There's still a lot convinced King Arthur really lived. Not that I'm complaining. Where would the tourist industry be without him?'

No one in the Hughes family ever mentioned the disturbing events of that day again, as if not acknowledging them would mean they never happened. Hector was the sole exception. He gave a full account to Merlin, who showed no surprise at all. 'Tell me, Hector,' he said, with a mischievous gleam in his eye, 'do you have a logical explanation this time?'

Hector shook his head ruefully. 'I wish I had, but I haven't. I should have believed you five years ago when Arthur saved my life. I should have known when the clouds parted for that tiny baby. I've been a fool.'

'Indeed you have not. It isn't easy for any of us to accept the things we do not understand.'

'What does it all mean?'

'It means,' said Merlin happily, 'that the prophecy is fulfilled.'

Hector never doubted Merlin again. He was immensely proud and a little in awe of Arthur, but from that day on he had lost his peace of mind, fearing what the future might have in store for his beloved adopted son.

Nineteen

Summer was surrendering to autumn, and already the air was heavy with the smell of fallen leaves and damp grass. Back at Glastonbury after the summer vacation, Arthur was spending the weekend with Merlin at his cottage. Arthur had never spoken of that day at Tintagel Castle and the extraordinary affair of the Sword in the Stone, and Merlin had carefully avoided the subject. What Arthur needed, he believed, was love and nurturing, not challenging. The boy already had more than enough to cope with.

Supper was cleared away. A fire burned in the grate, the logs cracking from time to time, throwing up showers of sparks. Arthur and Merlin played Scrabble. From time to time the magus muttered fiercely to himself and scribbled formulae on scraps of paper, returning to the game as if nothing had happened. Virgil perched on Merlin's shoulder, eyes shuttered, hoo-hoo'ing softly whenever his master fondled him. Seeing that Merlin's attention was distracted from the game, Arthur lay on the floor and gazed into the fire. For some reason he sensed sadness in the air. He scratched Robbie's tummy, stroking the dog's ears and kissing him on the nose, and Robbie made grateful noises in the back of his throat. Encircling his muzzle was a ring of white. When had he grown old? Arthur wondered. The brown eyes were shadowed with blue cataracts, the lithe body padded with plumpness, the glossy coat dry and patchy. When had all this happened? Why hadn't he noticed it before? How old would Robbie be? Ten? Twelve? More? He wasn't sure and had never thought to ask. What did age matter anyway? All he remembered was that Merlin had said something about taking Robbie over from a friend who died.

'We humans are never ready,' said Merlin, without looking up, 'but animals are. They seem to know when the end is near. What's more they know there is nothing they can do about it, so they just accept it. Very sensible of them.'

'Robbie is fine,' insisted Arthur vehemently. 'He'll live another ten years, won't you, Robbie?' The black Labrador had become an inseparable part of his life. He went to bed feeling wretched and lay awake for a long time. Dreams disturbed his sleep. He could not remember what dreams exactly except that Robbie was in all of them. Opening his eyes the next morning, he was delighted and a little relieved to see the old dog standing by his bed looking up at him, his tail wagging so furiously that it wagged his stout body with it. If anything he seemed younger and more active than he had the night before. What was wrong with Merlin? All that talk of death. Was the magus feeling the passing years?

While Arthur washed and pulled on his clothes, Robbie grabbed his shoes and disappeared under the bed with them. Briefly he reappeared to help himself to a sock, and made off with that too, all the time growling ferociously. Arthur grinned happily, and when finally he recovered his shoes and socks, made his way downstairs, Robbie trotting behind him, nudging the back of his ankles with his nose as if to hurry him up.

Once outside the cottage the Labrador ran off. Merlin was nowhere to be seen. He was an early riser, and often took a walk before breakfast, so Arthur put on a windcheater and went to look for him. He strode across the fields, the wind behind him, nudging him playfully in the back. Occasionally he looked round, disturbed by the uneasy feeling that he was being followed. In the distance, carried on the wind, Arthur could hear Robbie barking. He turned. There was nothing to be seen but the corn swaying, and in the lower meadow a drift of smoke. He walked towards it, slowly at first, then faster and faster. Fear gripped his stomach as he caught the scent of burning wood.

With his long white robes and shoulder-length hair, Merlin might have been an Old Testament prophet, or a philosopher in ancient Greece. On his shoulder was Virgil, unperturbed by the flames. Arthur gazed into the fire as he had the night before in the kitchen, except that these flames were Robbie's funeral pyre.

'When?'

Merlin put his arm round Arthur. 'Last night. About an hour after you went to bed.'

'But that's impossible! I saw him this morning. I couldn't have imagined it, he was playing with me. He ran off with my shoes and socks like he always does when I stay with you. You remember that, Merlin, don't you?'

'I remember,' said Merlin, squeezing Arthur's shoulder.

Arthur looked down at his shoes. No tooth marks. He pulled up his trouser leg, left and right. No holes in his socks, no marks of any kind.

'He was there,' he repeated stubbornly, 'I know he was.'

'He died around midnight.'

'But I saw him, Merlin.'

'I'm sure you did. Robbie loved you. He wanted you to remember the many happy hours you spent together, not just the last few sad ones. That was his gift to you. That was his way of saying good-bye.'

The grief welled up inside Arthur and sprang from his eyes. 'But I don't want him to be dead, Merlin. Please don't let Robbie be dead. You can bring him back, I know you can.'

Merlin bowed his head and Arthur turned away to hide his tears.

'There is nothing wrong in showing your grief,' said Merlin gently. 'Quite the contrary, in fact.'

Arthur's body heaved with sobs as Merlin held him. After a while Arthur was calm. 'Are you sure?' He nodded at the flames. 'Are you sure that's Robbie in there?'

'Only flesh and blood and bone.'

'What else is there?' said Arthur bitterly. 'I'll never see him again.'

'The fire will burn all day,' said Merlin. 'What the wind doesn't take we shall keep. One day you will return Robbie's ashes to his master.'

Arthur was tempted to ask who, if not Merlin, was Robbie's master but the moment passed, the question was not asked, and Merlin offered no explanation.

It was Arthur's first experience of death. It made him think about things he had never wanted to think about before. He thought about Hector and Elizabeth, and how important they were in his life. The day would come when he would lose them too; flesh and blood and bone.

Then he had another thought, every bit as disturbing. The parents he had never met . . . what if they were to die without his even knowing them?

'My parents . . . ' he began hesitantly.

'You mean Hector and Elizabeth?' said Merlin.

Arthur shook his head. 'The others.' He did not know quite what to call them, nor even how to think of them. His real parents? No, real was not the right word. How could they be real when they had played no part in his life? His natural parents? No, not natural either. What was natural about parents who abandoned you?

'Why did they give me away for adoption?'

'That is a question you must put to them. I can tell you how to contact them but you must decide if that is what you want to do.'

It was a question Arthur had asked himself a hundred times. During the weeks that followed not a day passed when he did not think about the parents he had never met. Did he want to meet them? Yes. Was he afraid to meet them? Yes. Would it change his life? Probably. How would they react to him? How would he react to them? Did it matter? Did any of it matter? Yes, of course it did. Whatever the consequences, he had to meet them, if only to know why they had given him away. Even if it meant hurting the two people he loved most in the world? Yes. Enough. He was thinking too much, doing too little. He reached a decision. He would ask Merlin for their phone number. He would call.

Igraine was sipping coffee and wondering what to do with her afternoon; Margot and Morgan were married, Elaine had left home, Uther was storming around being a politician. She had lots of friends, though none very close, for she was not the sort of woman who cared to share her secrets. Being on her own was what she had become accustomed to; it was a condition she neither liked nor disliked. As with most things in her life she had learned to accept it. When the phone rang she happened to be sitting next to it. 'Hello?'

There was no response. Someone was there though, she could hear him breathing. A man. Her first thought was that it must be one of *those* phone calls, a stalker perhaps or a sexual pervert. Her voice a little unsteady, she asked timidly, 'Who is it?' Still there was no reply. 'If you don't answer, I'll put the phone down.' Again that unnerving silence.

Suddenly she was not afraid any more. She knew. How she knew she could not tell. She just knew. Her heart pounded against her ribs, her hands trembled, the handset slipped from her grasp. For a few dazed moments she stared blankly out at the gardens. Something white, a newspaper or a plastic bag, rose on a gust of wind and drifted by the window like a spirit from the past.

Dropping on hands and knees she searched frantically for the phone. 'Oh God, let him still be there!' Retrieving the phone from under her chair, she whispered into the mouthpiece. 'Is it you?' There was a click. The hum of the dialling tone filled her ear.

'Arthur,' she murmured. Laying the handset back in its cradle, she clasped it to her bosom, swaying from side to side, as if she were rocking a baby to sleep.

Twenty

2013

THE COMMEMORATION BALL, known to Oxford undergraduates as the Commem, is held every May, towards
the end of the academic year. By tradition it commemorates
the University's many founders and benefactors, though it is
fair to say that at this point in their lives the thoughts of most
undergraduates are focused not on their elders and betters
but on their end of year exam results, their degrees and job
prospects. For one brief night, though, the Commem offers
them the chance to forget such weighty matters and relax.

Arthur was eighteen, and this was his first year at college.
Being a handsome and charismatic young man, he was popular
with the opposite sex, his mop of blond hair and cornflower blue
eyes causing many a heart to skip a beat. Until now, however,
there had been no special girl in his life; passing fancies, yes,
but not true love; that was a state he had never experienced.
Not that he had consciously shunned it, it was simply that he
was more inclined to fun than to serious entanglements. And
so, like many of his friends, when the evening of the Commem.
Ball arrived, he was footloose and fancy free.

The gardens and quadrangles of the college were crowded
with undergraduates, staff and guests, men in dinner jackets,
ladies in evening dresses. As the sun sank below the spires and
towers of Oxford the shadows lengthened on the lawns, and
the evening air was heavy with the sweet scents of spring. A
more romantic setting could hardly be imagined. Lennox Lotte
could not recall when he was last at a dance of any sort. Being
clumsy on his feet, he had never much cared for dancing. It

never occurred to him to ask why Margot wanted to come to the Commem. Ball. She did, and that was good enough for him. She was a gorgeous girl, a marvellous wife, and an excellent mother to Gawain, Agravaine and Gaheris, their three sons. He would do anything for her, anything at all. As luck would have it, the master of the college had been a close friend of his late father, so it had been easy enough to arrange an invitation.

Whatever happened he was determined to enjoy himself, as much for Margot's sake as for his own. However, shortly after walking though the college gates and meeting the master, he and Margot were separated. There was some jostling, nothing serious, just some high-spirits in the quad, and the next moment she was gone. Lennox was nervous, Margot would certainly feel out of place amongst all these youngsters. Who did she know? Not a soul. He located the master again. 'Where c-could she have g-got to?' he enquired anxiously. 'Not to worry, Lennox,' said the master reassuringly, 'she's bound to turn up soon. Such crowds, you know. Try the gardens,' he suggested helpfully.

There were several hundred people in the gardens, none of them Margot. He looked around the college but could not find her. She was not in the library nor in the Junior Common Room nor in the dining hall where the dancing would begin at eight o'clock, and he could only hope that sooner or later she would come looking for him there. If there was one thing she loved, it was dancing. That thought lifted his spirits. She would be in the hall, of course she would, ready to dance her heart out when the Ball began. Helping himself to another glass of champagne, he wandered disconsolately about the college gardens, killing time till the dance started.

At ten minutes to eight he hurried across the lower quadrangle to the dining hall. Outside the heavy oak doors a crowd of people had formed a queue, waiting to get in. Looking around, Margot was nowhere to be seen. When the doors opened, he rushed in and positioned himself close to the entrance, so that he would not miss her when she arrived. But to his growing consternation, she did not.

The Master and the President of the Junior Common Room briefly welcomed the guests, the band struck up and the dance was under way. Outside Lennox roamed the quadrangle with a heavy heart. Still no Margot. What a bore. Where could she be? He would give her a piece of his mind when she turned up. What did she think she was doing walking out on him like this? It was inconsiderate – no, more than that, it was irresponsible. He did not know a single, solitary soul. Not that he wanted to, surrounded as he was by kids. Surely undergraduates had never looked as young as this before, most certainly not in his day. The whole thing was a dreadful mistake. Why on earth had she been so keen to come? It was beyond him.

The pushing and shoving that followed the arrival of Lennox and Margot had not been accidental. The instant she walked through the porter's lodge into the upper quadrangle, Margot had attracted attention. It was not surprising, as she had taken particular care with her make-up and choice of dress and had never looked more alluring. All about her, voices were hushed and heads turned in her direction. Surrounded by several undergraduates, she and Lennox, by a deft and entirely deliberate manoeuvre, were separated.

The next moment Margot was in the centre of a group of young men, one of whom, with his dark hair, flashing eyes and roguish grin, was particularly good-looking. He bowed theatrically. 'May I be of assistance?'

'I'm looking for my husband.'

'I'm sure he won't mind if I borrow you for a while,' said the handsome young man, demonstrating his bravado for the amusement of his cronies. 'Allow me to show you round the college.' With exaggerated courtesy he offered her his arm.

'No really, I ought to find him. He was here a moment ago. Have you seen him?'

'Over there!' responded the young men in unison, each pointing in a different direction, and amusing themselves enormously in the process.

Despite her obvious reluctance, the handsome student, who now held her firmly by the arm, began to propel Margot in the direction of the college gardens. His persistence was beginning to scare her, and it showed on her face.

As he was leaving the quadrangle with a reluctant Margot in tow, a young man blocked their path. 'Where are you off to, Edward?' he asked.

A fanciful wave of the hand. 'I'm taking this lovely lady to wonderland.'

'And where might that be?'

A sly grin. 'I'll let you know when we've found it.'

Though the young man spoke quietly, there was a hint of warning in his voice. 'I don't think she wants to go there.'

Edward stood his ground defiantly. 'Who are you to say what she wants?'

'Why don't you ask her?'

'Why don't you get lost?' For a moment it looked as though he was going to start a fight.

'Let her go,' said Arthur quietly.

'Why should I?'

'Because she's our guest, and you're a gentleman.'

For a moment longer Edward stood his ground, then nodded and released Margot's arm. 'See you around, Arthur,' he said, and moved back to his friends.

So swiftly had Arthur reacted to Margot's predicament that he had not really looked at her. The instant he did he was smitten. Black hair framed the oval face, delicate features and glowing skin of a Pre-Raphaelite beauty; never had he seen anyone so lovely. A little smile of gratitude lifted the corners of her mouth, and in her luminous brown eyes was an expression so tender that the blood sang in his veins. 'That was very gallant of you. Thank you.'

'Nothing to thank me for,' said Arthur. 'He meant no harm. High spirits, that's all.'

'Thanks all the same. It's good to know the age of chivalry is still alive and kicking.' She stood on tiptoe, slipped her hand behind his neck, gently pulled his head down, and kissed him on the cheek.

He blushed. 'I expect your husband's waiting for you.'

A slight pause. 'What makes you so sure I'm married?'

'I thought I heard you say . . . '

'An excuse to escape from that young man.'

His spirits rose and instantly sank. 'But of course you must have . . . '

'What must I have?'

'A date. I'm sure you have a date.'

Margot lowered her eyes demurely. 'I did come with someone.' Observing Arthur's dejection, she quickly added, 'A relative. A close relative. Not really what you'd call a date. Anyway, he has disappeared.'

'In that case,' said Arthur, hopeful again, 'I might just be the luckiest man in the world. May I – um . . . ?'

'Yes?' she said encouragingly.

'May I be your escort tonight?'

It was such a deliciously old-fashioned way of putting it. And he was cute, quite irresistibly cute. For one thing, such an exceptionally handsome young man would normally be a touch conceited, arrogant even; not this one. There was no hint of posturing, no effort to impress or beguile. On the contrary, he appeared to be not only entirely unaffected but also completely at ease with himself and the world. Moreover despite his unassuming manner, he stood out from the crowd, and not just because he looked like a Greek god. She had noticed how the other students treated him with respect; he had spoken quietly but they had listened.

'I'd be delighted,' she said gravely. 'Margot Lotte.' She held out her hand.

He clasped it as gently as if it were a new-born puppy. 'Arthur Hughes,' he said.

164

She nodded. For a moment Arthur was puzzled by that nod. It occurred to him to ask if she had heard his name before, but then the thought was gone. For the next hour he hardly stopped talking. Never had he felt so relaxed in a girl's company. He told her about his childhood and about life in Ponterlally, he talked a great deal about Merlin, again a name that seemed to mean something to Margot, though when he asked her if she knew him, she shook her head. To his own surprise, he spoke of being adopted, something none of his friends knew.

Most of the students and their guests had drifted towards the lower quadrangle by now, and the gardens were almost deserted. They strolled around aimlessly, not knowing or caring where they were going, so involved were they with each other. After a time their fingers touched, and soon they were walking hand in hand. Every now and then Arthur would look down at the lovely woman at his side and marvel. How could his life have changed so dramatically in so short a time? His heart surged with happiness.

They sat on a bench under a May tree, its white blossoms so densely packed, so fat and flawless, that they were surely at the very peak of perfection. What could be more beautiful, thought Arthur. If only those blossoms would stay just as they were now. 'I shall never forget this moment,' said Margot quietly. 'I shall put it in a cupboard and lock it up. And when I'm old and grey, I'll take it out and look at it, and everyone will know poor gran is dreaming her favourite dream again.'

She had read his mind and he was happy, but also a little afraid. Did love come so quickly, and if it did, would it last? As if to confirm the ephemeral nature of things, the sky darkened and there was a crack of thunder. Without warning the rain came, a heavy spring shower, warm and dense. For a time they were protected by the overhanging blossoms, but soon they were beaten from the tree and the petals scattered on the grass. There was nothing now to protect them from the rain, and if they stayed where they were they would be soaked to the skin.

'Let's make a run for it,' said Arthur. He looked at his watch. It was after nine o'clock. The ball had started over an hour ago. 'Time to dance.'

For a second she leaned against him, then quickly moved away, as if embarrassed by her own daring. 'Would you mind very much if we didn't. Not just yet, I mean. Later.'

'Whatever you say. What would you like to do?'

'I'd love to find somewhere to dry off and freshen up. After that we can dance as much as you like.'

He thrust the intruding thought from his mind; he had a room in college. Any suggestion in that direction, though made in all innocence, might well be misinterpreted. He was wondering what to propose when suddenly she jumped up and ran into the full force of the driving rain. To his amazement she began to turn the most perfect cartwheels on the lawn, exposing white pants and shapely legs.

'Come on, let's see you do it!'

'No chance!'

'Spoilsport! Try!'

He attempted a cartwheel, and fell on his back roaring with laughter. Margot stood over him, hands on hips, legs wide apart. 'What fun!' she cried. Holding out her hand, she pulled him to his feet, and then suddenly to her. Caressing the back of his neck, straining her body to his, she kissed him passionately. Abruptly she pulled away from him, and throwing her arms wide, declaimed at the top of her voice:

'"There was a roaring in the wind all night;
The rain came heavily and fell in floods;
But now the sun is rising calm and bright."'

'Arthur,' she said, 'do you love me just a little?' Eyes shut, she lifted her face to the heavens and let the rain stream down from her forehead to her chin. He tried to tell her how his heart was bursting, and that no one in the history of the world had ever loved as much as he did, but the words would not come, and he stood there, spellbound, gazing at this entrancing girl, with her wet hair embracing her cheeks, her rain-soaked ball-gown clinging to her slim body, and her beautiful face shining in the last rays of the setting sun.

For as if in miraculous response to the poem's message, the clouds parted and the rain stopped. He reached out to her but she was off again, whirling about the lawn, prancing and leaping like some woodland nymph. Whoever this girl was, she was not of this world. Suddenly she stumbled and fell awkwardly, lying with eyes closed and bosom heaving. He knelt beside her, fearing for a moment that something terrible had happened. Gently he touched her face, and as he did so she growled and sharp white teeth closed firmly on his fingers. From beneath long lashes her brown eyes regarded him with the most mischievously seductive expression. 'Well, do you? Because if you say you don't, I shall eat you up and spit you out.'

'You know I do.'

'Then say so.'

'I love you,' he said earnestly, bending his head to hers. When he opened his eyes again, she was looking up at him and smiling. Had she been watching him while he kissed her?

Pushing him away, she sat up. 'I'm absolutely drenched.'

Once more the forbidden thought nudged his brain.

'Do you live in college?'

'Yes, I do.'

'Then why don't you take me back to your room so I can dry off and do my hair and make-up and stuff, and then we can go and dance.'

He was enormously relieved that it was she who had suggested it. Having met this lovely girl only a couple of hours before, and being a chivalrous young man with rather old-fashioned views about such matters, he could not help but feel responsible for protecting her reputation. Taking her arm he somehow managed to wind a circuitous route back to his staircase without being spotted. His satisfaction at the success of his tactics was somewhat diminished by the fact that Margot seemed entirely unconcerned whether she was seen or not.

His digs were on the first floor, overlooking a small quadrangle at the front and an ancient cemetery at the rear of the college. It consisted of a small bedsit with an adjoining bathroom. The largest piece of furniture in the room was a bed, a fact that clearly embarrassed him. Margot peered through the leaded glass windows at the cemetery. Arthur stood behind her. 'Does it worry you?'

'Not really. Death only happens to other people, doesn't it?' Despite her brave words, she shivered.

'You're cold. What am I thinking of?'

Shepherding her to the bathroom with a bundle of towels, he shut the door behind her. Whilst she was presumably drying off her dress on the towel rail, and repairing the rain damage to her hair and make-up, he stripped down to his underpants, put on a dressing gown and lit the gas fire. He calculated that Margot would be at least five, probably ten or fifteen minutes. He would give his clothes a few minutes to dry, then put them on again.

Sitting in an armchair he looked at his watch. It was unusual for him to be so precise but there was too much at stake to take any risks. Whether his clothes were dry or not, he would be dressed when Margot opened that door. Forty seconds, fifty, a minute. And ten, twenty, forty, and fifty. Two minutes. And ten, twenty . . . A combination of the heat of the gas fire, the excitement of the evening, and the regular counting of seconds, made him drowsy. His head began to nod.

When he woke he was in bed with Margot.

'I swear I never meant this to happen,' he said, biting his lip at the banality of the words.

'Didn't you, darling?' Once, twice, three times she kissed him on the mouth, long, thoughtful kisses. 'I did.'

Arthur flushed, feeling stupid.

She traced the outline of his face with her finger. 'How old are you?'

'Nineteen,' he admitted self-consciously. He was almost too shy to ask her the same question. 'And you?' he asked after a while.

She shuddered. 'Twenty-five. An old lady.'

'Grandma.' He kissed her.

Her tongue savoured his chest with long, lingering licks.

He glanced at his watch. 'Oh no,' he groaned, 'it's three o'clock. You've missed the dance.'

'I haven't missed a thing,' said Margot.

In the morning he found himself on the floor. Margot was asleep in the bed. Her beauty pummelled his heart. He dressed, made some coffee, and gently woke her. But it was not coffee she wanted. An hour later she took her first sip.

'It must be stone cold. I'll make some more.'

'It's fine.' She was looking at him in an oddly searching way, as if she were seeing him for the first time.

'I never saw such deep blue eyes. They are quite wonderful.'

He was embarrassed.

'You really are a very handsome young man, Arthur,' she said admiringly. 'You obviously have excellent genes.'

'I never knew my real parents.'

'I know.'

Once again her reaction puzzled him. 'How do you know?'

'I – I suppose because you said you were adopted. I just assumed you hadn't met your real parents.'

He drove her to the train station in good time for the ten o'clock to London. 'Let's sit in the coffee bar,' he suggested. He had so much to say to her, so little time to say it.

'If you want.' She gave a half smile as he led her to the farthest, darkest, corner table.

'We can talk here,' he said, looking round to be sure no one was listening. 'It's more private.'

'Why does it have to be private?'

He found it an odd question. 'Oh, you know.'

She shrugged. 'As you wish.'

It was the first time he had ever been in love. Everything had happened so quickly, it was hard to take in. And now she was leaving him. 'When can I see you again?'

She held his hands in hers and stroked them. 'What beautiful hands. So strong, so fine.'

'When, Margot?' he persisted.

It was as if she had not heard the question. 'I shall never forget you.'

'I won't give you the chance to.'

She eased her hands away from his. 'You mustn't say that.'

He was hurt and confused. 'Why not?'

'Please don't make it difficult for me, Arthur.'

'I don't understand,' he stammered.

'I can't see you again,' she said, avoiding his eyes. 'Not ever. Not in that way.'

'But we're in love, aren't we?' He took her hand and pressed it passionately to his lips. 'I couldn't – not see you again. I never want to be with anyone else. I thought you felt the same way. Last night . . . you told me . . . you said you loved me.'

'Did I?' She said it as though she had forgotten. 'I'm sorry, but I really can't see you again.'

He was desperate. 'That's not true. It can't be.'

She started to get up. 'I shall miss my train.'

'Don't go.' He reached out to her. 'Stay with me.'

Her eyes were suddenly cold. 'You are being tiresome, Arthur,' she said disdainfully. 'I thought you had more sense. You'll be telling me next that I'm treating you like a one night stand.'

'Don't mock me,' he said in a low voice, 'I'm serious.'

She pulled a face. 'Are you, darling? How boring.'

He shook his head ruefully. 'I apologise. I'm making a fool of myself.'

Her expression softened. 'You could never do that.'

'At least tell me why.'

She thought for a moment. 'You'll be shocked.'

'Try me.'

She grasped the back of her chair and stood looking down at him for a long time. 'I'm married,' she said finally.

The blood drained from Arthur's face, the scar on his cheek burned. 'It isn't true.'

'I'm afraid it is.' Poor boy, how she had hurt him, her Greek god, her handsome prince. She went to him, took his face in both her hands and gazed into his eyes so intently that she might have been looking into his soul. 'Don't you understand?' she said fiercely, 'it wasn't my fault, or yours either. Life makes us do bad things and then it makes us suffer for them. It was fate. There was nothing we could do about it. It was meant to happen.'

From somewhere he heard himself asking, 'Do I know you?'

'Who knows anyone?' She bent and kissed him softly on the lips. 'Good-bye.'

He looked up at her hanging over him in her ball dress like a beautiful white canopy. 'I'll see you off,' he said, trying to delay the dreadful moment.

'No.'

His heart was breaking. 'Must you go?'

'Dear Arthur,' she murmured, and walked quickly away.

Lennox was standing at the barrier looking worried and exhausted. When he saw Margot his eyes lit up. With relief came anger, and he began to shout at her.

'What d-do you th-think you are p-playing at, woman, d-disappearing all night! Where the hell have you b-been? I've b-been out of m-my m-mind with worry.'

'And who can blame you, my poor darling?' said Margot, soothingly, as if she were indulging a wayward child. 'You must be starving. I know I am. We're going to spoil ourselves and have a lovely breakfast on the train, a huge English breakfast with all the trimmings.'

Taking his arm, she skipped along beside him up the platform. 'Now you must tell me everything, I insist you do. Were you really out of your mind with worry, my sweetheart? Are you very angry with me? Is my great big strong husband going to spank his naughty Margot? Has she been wicked, then? Of course she has! But when you've heard all my trials and tribulations, you'll forgive me, I just know you will, my sweety lamb. Poor darling Lennox,' she cooed, 'I'll tell you all about it on the train. Now you're never going to believe what happened to me . . .

Twenty One

SHE WAS WITH HIM every hour of every day. During the last two weeks of term he sat every morning under the May tree, bare of blossoms now, and heard her voice calling him across the college lawns. At night he felt her soft flesh against his, and lay shivering in ecstasy as she caressed him with her predatory little tongue, whispering the same lies she had whispered that night in the darkness of his room: 'I love you, Arthur. I'll never leave you.'

Now, with hindsight, he realised that he had all too willingly deceived himself. How naïve he had been to think a woman as sophisticated and experienced as Margot could ever have fallen for a callow undergraduate. Yet if he had been foolish and presumptuous, he had been harshly punished for it. He told himself that he was not the first man to suffer such humiliating rejection, and no doubt would not be the last. That however was small consolation. It hurt. It hurt all the more because he had fallen in love, and because the *coup de grace* had been administered with such callous, and, he suspected, practised efficiency.

There was something else . . . a question that nibbled away at his subconscious mind, finally to rise to the surface. Was their meeting pure chance? Or was there something more to it? Her words kept coming back to him. *There was nothing we could do about it. It was meant to happen.* What could Margot have intended by them?

For all his pain, he dreamed of her, and contrary to all logic and common sense, still yearned for her. He understood only too well that he was indulging in a kind of romantic self-deception, and that it hardly mattered that the woman he had gone to bed with was not the real Margot. For the real Margot was not the woman he loved; he was in love with the woman she pretended to be. But whoever Margot was, he never expected to see or hear from her again. In the summer vacation, however, to his surprise, he received a letter forwarded to him by his college. Before he opened it, and although he had never seen her handwriting, he knew it was from her. How his heart raced! How his hands trembled as he tore open the envelope!

Dearest Arthur,
I bet you didn't expect to hear from me again! I've been thinking lots about you, wondering how you are and whether you have forgiven me. I do hope so.
I have something important to tell you. Can you meet me at the Café Royal in Regent Street next Thursday at four o'clock?
Margot.

He was half an hour early, and as the minutes passed grew more and more nervous. What was the important thing she had to tell him? That she loved him after all? Could that be it? Had she left her husband? His heart thumped in his throat. Suddenly there she was, walking across the room towards him, smiling. How beautiful she was! He jumped up, feeling the old passion stirring in his blood. If she felt any embarrassment at seeing him again, she certainly did not show it. Instead she threw her arms round him and gave him a big hug, stepped back and studied him. 'As handsome as I remembered. And oh, those beautiful blue eyes! They give me goose-pimples! How wonderful to see you, darling.'

No sooner had they ordered tea than she dragged him onto the dance floor. They danced cheek to cheek, and as they danced she pressed her thighs against his and caressed the hair at the nape of his neck until he almost fainted with longing for her. 'I'm so glad you're still a teensy bit fond of me,' she said, evidently happy to have lost none of her power over him.

'How is your husband?' he asked defensively.

She gave him a reproachful look. 'Don't be cruel.'

'Aren't you afraid he might see us together?'

'What here!' She giggled. 'Lennox wouldn't be seen dead at the Café Royal – much too kitsch for him. Besides, we're not doing anything really wicked, are we?' She looked up at him. How well he remembered that provocative look. Before he could stop her, she was kissing him. 'At least, not yet,' she murmured mischievously, her lipstick smudged, her dark eyes blurred and sensuous.

Abruptly she stopped dancing. 'Our tea will be getting cold.'

He guided her back to the table. As she sat down, she asked, 'Would you like to fuck me?' as if she had been offering him a biscuit.

Arthur swallowed hard. 'You said you had something important to tell me.'

Swallowing a last morsel of chocolate éclair, she licked the cream off her fingers with long, lingering licks. 'I'm pregnant.'

'That's wonderful,' he said, concealing his jealousy at the thought of another man making love to her.

She beamed. 'Dear Arthur, only you could be so naïve.'

His face showed first incomprehension, and then, as the truth dawned, shock.

'That's it, darling, you got it in one.' Strangely, she seemed quite unconcerned, as if it were someone else's baby she was talking about. 'I know it's yours, you see, because Lennox was rather difficult after Oxford. He wouldn't have sex with me for ages, poor lamb. Then he was away in the States on business.' A quick shrug. 'So there it is.'

'I'm so sorry. It's entirely my fault.' He squared his shoulders. 'You can count on me.'

'Can I darling?' Was she mocking him?

'To do the right thing I mean.'

She clapped her hand to her mouth. He could scarcely believe it. There she was erupting into giggles, as if she hadn't a care in the world. 'Oh dear,' she said, when she had recovered her composure, 'I *am* sorry, Arthur, I didn't mean to laugh at you, really I didn't. But, well – the right thing! How sweet. How gallant. How chivalrous. And what might the right thing be? An offer of marriage?'

He responded huffily. 'If that's what you want.'

'There is the slight problem that I'm already married,' she said, still teasing him. 'But then, that was not what you had in mind, was it?'

'Actually, I . . . what I meant was, if you should decide to . . . you know . . . then I would naturally . . . pay whatever . . . '

'Poor lamb. It hasn't turned out well, has it? Not what you expected at all. I'm not the girl you thought I was. I would like to be,' she said, wistfully. 'I really would. You were so in love with her.'

'I still am – in love with you, I mean.'

'No, you're not. How could you be? You have no idea who I am, no idea at all.'

She was right of course. Maybe it was love he had fallen in love with, though it wouldn't hurt any the less if that were true.

'Arthur Hughes,' she said thoughtfully, adding for no apparent reason, 'I wonder what your real name is.' She took his hand, holding it tenderly in what he took to be a condescending gesture, more about pity than about love. He was overcome, first with embarrassment, then with remorse for being embarrassed. Abruptly he pulled his hand away.

It was clear the rejection offended her. 'So you want to get rid of it, do you?'

'I don't know what I want, Margot. To be honest, I haven't taken it in yet. I need time to get used to the idea of being a father.'

'What would you say . . . ' – over her teacup her dark eyes taunted him – 'if I had the baby?'

Arthur was uncomfortable and hated himself for it. 'How would you explain it to your husband?'

'Lennox?' An airy wave of the hand. 'I could always tell him the truth.' Relishing Arthur's uneasiness, she said, with mock horror, 'Surely you wouldn't expect me to lie to him?'

'I'm not suggesting that. All the same, I . . . '

'You are dithering, Arthur.'

It was true. He was not making sense. 'Give me a few days to think about it.'

'What is there to think about?' She sat back in her chair, her eyes challenging him.

What he really wanted was for the baby to go away. He knew that was wrong but he was nineteen years old and a student. What were the options? He could leave Oxford and take a job. Margot could get a divorce, they could get married and she could have the baby. But it was obvious she didn't want that, that she didn't love him. What future would there be for them?

'You don't think,' he said hesitantly, 'you don't think it might be better if . . . '

She cut in brutally. 'You want the baby killed?'

He looked shocked.

'I'm sorry if my choice of words offended you. I should have been more elegant. Let me see, now. You want me to have an abortion. Does that sound better?'

Arthur shook his head despairingly. She seemed to take pleasure in tormenting him.

'No? Well then, how else can I put it? Should I see someone about it? Is that better, my darling? Should I see someone about it?'

'I know I'm making a mess of it,' he said quietly, 'but nothing in my life has prepared me for anything like this.'

'I see. Let's all be sorry for Arthur, shall we? Poor lad, he's just an innocent teenager and Margot's a twenty-five year old slag. So naturally it's her decision and her responsibility.'

'That's not the way I feel at all,' he said indignantly.

'In heaven's name, how *do* you feel?' As heads turned in their direction, Margot lowered her voice to an intense whisper. 'You certainly don't want to face facts, do you, lover boy? I'm pregnant. There's this living thing inside me. If I decide to get rid of it, some sleazy abortionist is going to stick a metal claw up my vagina and crush his, or her, head.'

'You must have the baby,' he said decisively.

'Sure?'

'Quite sure.'

'I am a tease, darling, aren't I?' she said contritely. 'I don't know how you put up with me. Another éclair?'

He shook his head, confused. How calmly she was taking it, as if none of it were real.

She helped herself. 'I shall have an abortion,' she said, sucking her fingers. 'Alright with you?'

'Yes,' he said, but so quietly that she had to strain to catch the word.

Around them the waiters bustled, clattering away the debris of afternoon tea, already laying out the tables for dinner. Arthur paid the bill and they hurried out of the restaurant into Regent Street. He said awkwardly. 'Please let me help.'

'Money is not a problem.' She stood on tiptoe and kissed him lightly on the lips. 'Just remember, darling, it's what you wanted.' Before he could reply, she was walking briskly away from him. Without warning he was wracked with pain, as if some wild beast were tearing out his stomach; in all his life he had never felt so wretched and ashamed. He had a sudden urge to run after her and tell her he had changed his mind; but it was too late. She had disappeared in the crowd.

About to leave for the office one morning, Lennox a tidy

man, forever cleaning up after his wife, picked up a letter from the sitting room carpet. It was from the gynaecologist's receptionist confirming an appointment for Mrs M. Lotte that very afternoon.

'N-Nothing wrong, is there?' He looked so concerned that even Margot felt a stab of conscience. How to respond? Should she say she was having a check-up, hinting darkly of a dread disease? And when the abortion deed was done, she would say it had been a false alarm, only some minor infection needing antibiotics. Brilliant! His relief should be worth at least a diamond bracelet.

'I'm pregnant,' was what she actually said. It was as much of a surprise to her as it was to Lennox.

'That's w-wonderful, d-darling.'

'I wasn't going to say anything. To tell you the truth, I was thinking of having it – seen to.'

Lennox was appalled. 'An abortion!'

'I thought you wouldn't want another baby. Besides, I didn't want to bore you with woman's stuff.'

'W-woman's stuff!' The protruding vein at the side of his forehead was throbbing. 'What a-b-bout m-man's stuff! I d-did p-play a m-modest role in its conception, d-didn't I?'

It was obviously intended more as a statement than a question. Still, there would never be a better opportunity to tell him the truth. It was tempting. Should she? Should she not? She wavered, savouring the moment. But then she thought, poor darling, he was so innocent, so vulnerable, so bloody naïve, she couldn't do it to him. 'Of course you did, darling, and I enjoyed it enormously. It was unforgivable of me not to consult you. I'll cancel the gyno.'

Hugging her affectionately, he asked, 'When is it d-due?'

Margot hesitated. Lennox had blundered into dangerous territory. The baby was due in February the following year. 'I never was any good at maths. Let me see,' she said vaguely, 'March or April, I think.'

It was absurd to have a baby so soon after giving birth to Gaheris, and yet, the more she thought about it, the more the whole thing appealed to her perverse nature. It amused her to reflect that the child in her belly was not her husband's, and it aroused her to think that it was Arthur's. If Lennox wanted to believe the child was his, let him; who was she to disillusion him? Why sink a man with the truth when he was content to swim with the lie?

It was a boy, and the name they gave him was Mordred. Lennox had been hoping for a girl, but Margot had always known she was destined only to have sons. Morgan had told her, and Morgan knew about such things. The infant supposedly due in April surprised everyone but Margot and her gynaecologist by arriving in February, and was, naturally enough, remarkably well developed for a seven month baby. Margot assumed Lennox was too happy to notice; but she was wrong. He had noticed, and the doubts gnawed at his mind. After several false starts, he finally expressed them. 'M-Mordred was b-born s-several weeks   p-prematurely, was he not?' he observed without warning one evening, when he had been drinking more than usual.

'Was he, dear?' The response was soft as a cat's purr. 'Since when were you an expert?'

'I'm not. The d-doctor said M-Mordred was a p-perfectly normal b-baby. D-definitely not p-premature.'

Margot considered her husband for some moments, and there was menace in her gaze. 'Well now, you've discovered my shameful secret,' she said at last.

'Secret?' Lennox flushed all the way down to his collar.

'All these years I've been having a passionate affair.'

His face was ashen. 'Am I n-not the f-father, then?'

'That would be telling, wouldn't it?'

'For God's sake, Margot,' he pleaded, 'stop torturing me. Who is Mordred's father?'

She eyed her husband scornfully. 'The plumber, of course!

Who else would it be? You know how I adore plumbers. All those huge muscles and spanners and things.'

'What k-kind of n-nonsense is this?'

'The same kind of nonsense as yours, my darling. Smoke without fire.'

'I never said M-Mordred was n-not m-my son.'

'Didn't you? I thought you did.' In a flash she had abandoned her derisive manner and had assumed her baby girl pout. 'How could you be so cruel? Don't you know I would never betray you?'

'Of c-course I d-do.'

She clawed at his chest, murmuring, 'Why would I need a lover when I have the best stud in London?'

'Oh God, M-Margot, I'm so crazy a-b-bout you. P-please forgive me. I'm such a f-fool.'

When he thought about it later, Lennox felt vaguely uneasy, for the fact was he had not been satisfactorily answered. His wife had made certain he would never raise the subject again, yet she had not given him peace of mind. Smoke without fire, she had said. What had she meant by that? Everyone knew there was no such thing. The inconsistency reflected the confusion in his mind. There was no fire, or so she expected him to believe, yet the smoke was there for everyone to see.

Twenty Two

IN HIS FINAL TERM at Oxford, when he ought to have been feeling confident and positive about the future, Arthur was apprehensive and disillusioned. Never had he felt so isolated. His birth parents had abandoned him, Margot had betrayed him, and Merlin, once his god, now had feet of clay. Though still teaching, Merlin spent more and more of his time in those mysterious facilities of his at Glastonbury. When Arthur asked questions, Merlin was evasive, hinting at "preparations", promising vaguely that one day all would be explained. Arthur did not appreciate being treated like a child, nor did he like being taken for granted, for whatever Merlin was planning, he appeared to assume that Arthur would one day be involved in it. That Arthur found disturbing and demeaning. He was his own man, and no one, not even Merlin, had the right to tell him what to do with his life.

An unexpected visit from Keir did nothing to improve Arthur's state of mind. Over a glass of wine in his rooms it was soon obvious that his older brother was there for one reason only – to put him down. 'Let's face it, Arthur, all this . . . ' – a disparaging wave of the hand at the ancient domes and spires of Oxford – 'all this is pure theatre, fantasy. There's nothing tangible here, no future, no career. Look at me. I shall be a director of IPC very soon – biggest Internet Service Provider in the world. Now that's real. This is all wind and fart. Never understood why you were so keen to come here. I never wanted to, as you know.'

A blatant lie, though Arthur decided not to challenge it. The fact was that hard-working, plodding Keir had not fulfilled his early promise, failing to win a place at Oxford, or indeed at any other university.

'One of us has to live in the real world. I can see I shall just have to make pots of money, not for myself, you understand, but for those two wonderful people in Ponterlally who sacrificed so much for me. And of course for you too, Arthur . . . excellent wine this.' A sly look in Arthur's direction. 'But I don't need to remind you, do I? You have even more reason to be grateful to them than I do.'

To Arthur it had very much the sound of a prepared speech. The jibes were barbed and well-aimed. 'After all, they took you into their home out of the goodness of their hearts. Did they ever make you feel unwanted? Of course not. Quite the contrary, in fact. They went out of their way to treat you like one of the family.' Keir shook his head sadly. 'When I think how hard they worked. And what have they got to show for it in the twilight of their lives? Precious little . . . what a splendid Burgundy this is, wish I could afford wines like this . . . No, they don't have two beans to rub together. Everything they had they gave us. To you and me, Arthur.'

Arthur had taken enough. 'You are my brother, Keir, and I love you,' he said, 'but that doesn't give you the right to lecture me on my responsibilities.'

Keir sat back in his chair, gaping open-mouthed in mock outrage. 'I am mortified, Arthur. Truly mortified. Lecture you! Nothing could be further from my mind. We have taken different roads, you and I, that's all I'm saying. You have chosen the high road to glamour. And I, the low road to hard graft.'

Out of family loyalty, Arthur somehow contrived to tolerate his brother, but his student friends who found him insufferable, felt no such obligation. Like many people insensitive to the feelings of others, Keir was himself highly sensitive and found it hard to endure the disdain of these young men. Even harder to take was the respect they so obviously had for Arthur. They were his friends, yet somehow more than friends, for Keir saw not just affection in their eyes when they looked at Arthur, but something close to hero-worship. Without seeming to exercise authority, he was clearly their leader, and they followed him as if it were the most natural thing in the world.

Edward Campbell, the student who had unwittingly brought Margot into Arthur's life, had become one of his closest friends. It was he who inadvertently mentioned the Steeplejacks.

Keir was intrigued. 'Who are they?'

'Just a club,' said Campbell carefully.

'You can trust Keir,' said Arthur.

Campbell grinned a little sheepishly. 'Some undergraduates play rugby, some row, some booze, some even work. We climb buildings.'

'They climb towers,' explained Arthur, 'church spires, sheer walls, whatever. And they name all of them after famous mountain peaks – K2, Everest, Makalu, Mont Blanc, the Matterhorn, the Eiger, and so on.'

Keir was looking at Arthur disapprovingly. 'You do this?'

'No, I'm not a member. I couldn't do what they do.'

'Glad to hear it.' Keir was baffled. 'What's the point of it all?'

Edward Campbell chuckled. 'It's like Mallory said about Everest; we climb them because they're there.'

'Surely there has to be a better reason than that,' said Keir incredulously.

Edward shrugged. 'I expect you're right. It's about recognition as much as anything. Everyone wants to be a hero, don't they?'

Keir was puzzled. What was heroic about climbing a wall? It was trivial, childish. He scorned Campbell, he scorned all of them, yet oddly enough he found himself envying them. Their lifestyle may have been superficial, but it was certainly adventurous. For the first time he was overcome by a depressing sense of the dullness of his own existence. There had to be something more to life than the Internet. If only someone cared enough to notice him, it would have made a difference, but no one did. The truth was, he had as much chance of becoming a director of IPC as he had of – well, of climbing Everest.

The old envy flared up inside Keir like a flame, consuming him with rage and bitterness. Who admired him, as those bright-eyed students admired Arthur? Who hung on his every word? Who looked at him the way they looked at Arthur? For heaven's sake, they treated him as if he were a king! It was too much to bear. Was he destined to live in Arthur's shadow forever? That evening Keir was preoccupied. The merrier Arthur and his friends became, the more morose he was. Once or twice Arthur asked if anything was bothering him but Keir rejected him in his usual surly fashion. Dinner at The Trout was followed by a tour of Oxford's pubs. By eleven o'clock the party was breaking up, and one by one the friends made their way back to their colleges.

Back in his rooms Arthur collapsed on his bed. No sooner had he fallen asleep, it seemed, than his mobile was ringing. It was Edward Campbell. 'Better come quickly.'

Arthur glanced at his watch. It was two-thirty in the morning. 'What's up?'

'He's only half way up the library, that's all.'

'Who is?'

'Your brother.'

The sky was partially clouded, lit intermittently by a three-quarter moon. In the deep shadow of the courtyard Arthur and his friends watched, hardly daring to breathe, as a man inched his way up the lower part of the dome that crowned the great rotunda of the library. From time to time the moon appeared, lighting up the circular building. There was no doubt about it – it was Keir.

'He seems to know what he's doing,' said Edward. 'He's already made it a hundred feet up the North Face, and that's got to be one of the hairiest climbs in Oxford.'

'I can't believe this is happening. What about the dome? How difficult is it?'

'Steep and slippery. It's covered in copper sheets.'

Arthur muttered anxiously under his breath.

'How much experience does he have?' Edward wanted to know.

Arthur had never seen Keir climb as much as a tree. 'Not a lot.'

A keen look. 'Worried about him?'

'He'll be okay,' said Arthur, trying to sound a great deal more confident than he felt.

'Is he sober?'

Arthur hesitated. 'More or less.' At eleven o'clock, when Arthur had left him at his bedroom door, Keir's speech was slurred.

A burly, compact figure, followed by a second and a third, appeared out of the darkness. The Proctor's Bulldogs were famous for aggression, fleetness of foot and tenacity. Once they caught you, they did not let go. 'Friend of yours, Mr. Hughes?' The Bulldog nodded towards the dome.

'No,' responded Arthur, accurately, if misleadingly.

'Ah, Mr. Campbell! What a pleasure seeing you here! Steeplejack, is he?'

'Nothing to do with us. He's not even a member of this place.'

The Bulldog looked disappointed.

For some time Keir had not moved.

'You sure he's alright?' whispered Edward Campbell, but when he looked round Arthur was gone.

The door at the back of the building was unlocked. Arthur rushed into the library and up the stairs two at a time. Reaching the circular gallery, he ran round it to a window on the south side of the building just below where he calculated Keir would be. It was open. He called up. 'Keir? You OK?' There was no reply.

Half in, half out of the window, he peered into the night, and there was Keir, spread-eagled on the dome. Arthur spoke quietly in order not to startle his brother. 'It's me, Keir. Arthur. You okay?'

Once again, no response.

'Come on down,' said Arthur calmly.

'No.' Only one word, but enough to know that Keir was very tense. Arthur wiped sweat from his face. If his brother slipped now, he would hurtle off the dome, and there was nothing to stop him until he hit the paving stones below. No one could survive such a fall. He tried again. 'Move down a little. I'll grab you and pull you in.'

'No.'

'Take your time,' said Arthur reassuringly. 'You'll be fine.'

'Can't . . . can't move.'

In a sudden flare of moonlight he caught a glimpse of Keir's face. To his horror, Arthur saw that he was terrified. 'Hang on, Keir, you'll be fine.' He kept his voice calm and confident.

'I'm going to fall!'

'No you're not. Don't move.' If he couldn't talk his brother down, there was nothing for it, he would have to help him down. 'I'm coming up to get you.' Facing into the building, he eased himself through the window and grasped the lintel at the top. He was standing on the sill now, knees braced against the window frame. Reaching up, he began to explore the smooth surface of the dome. High above his head his fingers located a ridge no more than half an inch wide where two sheets of copper were lapped and joined. His fingers and hands would have to bear the weight of his body. Keir must have done it, but his upper body was stronger than Arthur's. Closing his eyes, Arthur concentrated, preparing his mind for the trial to come. Hooking the tips of his fingers over the tiny ridge he breathed in, tensed his muscles, and lifted his body up and out. For a few seconds he held on, and then could hold no longer. But even as his fingers lost their grip, his toes touched the ledge at the top of the window. He was standing on the lintel.

Slowly he inched his head to one side, at the same time flattening his body against the dome. To reach Keir he would have to pull himself several feet higher. But how? What if Keir had a panic attack and lost his hold? Best not think about it. If he looked up he could just see Keir's feet at the extreme limit of his vision. But he dared not move his head again for fear that even the tiniest backward movement would unbalance him and send him crashing to his death. From here the dome looked even steeper than it did from the ground. Despite the cold, sweat dripped from Arthur's forehead, stinging his eyes. He began to tremble. He was no climber, that was for sure, he didn't belong here. In a moment the dome would throw him off, and the paving stones would rise up and slam into his body, and he would be dead. In the silence he called out, 'Merlin!' There was no reply, no arms to hold him, no voice to comfort him. He was on his own, his own man. He closed his eyes until his head cleared and his limbs stopped shaking.

Calm, he must be calm. Focus, he must focus his mind as never before. Think only of the next few inches of copper sheet, nothing else mattered. Hands and arms taking the strain, he grasped the ridge and pulled himself up and off the lintel. Scarcely any foothold now. Nothing to stop him falling but the pressure of his toes against the dome and that tiny ridge of overlapping metal above his head that his aching fingers clung to. Directly above, his frightened brother moaned quietly.

Using his toes and the inside of his knees and thighs as leverage, Arthur pulled himself up inch by inch, the tips of his fingers still locked on the tiny ridge of metal sheet . . . up and up, now his hips were resting on the ridge. He could pull no more. If he tried to push himself up on it, he would thrust his body away from the dome. His only hope was to find the next ridge, yet it took all his nerve to release his hold on the first one. With infinite care he slid first one hand then the other up the surface of the dome. With his arms fully extended, his fingers scrabbled frantically as high as he could reach. There was no ridge. Fear exploded in his chest. His left leg cramped, twisting under him as the muscle spasms wracked his calf. He was going to fall! 'Merlin!'

A familiar voice spoke softly in his ear. 'I am here.'

'Is this the end?'

'The power is yours, Arthur.'

Somehow he found the will to do what only moments before had seemed impossible. Reaching up his right hand another agonising millimetre his scrabbling fingers touched a ridge of metal sheet and hooked over it. The fingers of his left hand found the same ridge, his hips slid fractionally down and away from the first ridge, and the full weight of his body hung by his fingertips. In seconds he would have to let go. He tried to think of anything but the agonising pain in his fingers and the cramp tearing at his leg.

The cramp eased, both his legs were functioning again. Bracing his knees, he jammed his toes against the dome for leverage and support, easing the strain on his fingers. One last cautious pull, and the top of his head was no more than a few hands' breadths from Keir's feet. Panting, face and neck streaming sweat, he rested his cheek against the cold metal. 'Listen to me, Keir. I'm just below you . . . directly below. Here's what you do. You are going to ease down to me very, very slowly, until your feet are resting on my shoulders. I have a good, safe perch here. You'll be fine. When you've done that, I'll tell you what to do next.'

'Can't . . . ' Keir whimpered. 'Can't move.'

'Yes you can. You made it up here. You can make it down. When I give you the word, relax your body and let yourself go. Use the toes of your sneakers and the palms of your hands to control your descent. Nice and gently, mind. I'll tell you when I'm ready. Wait for the word.'

Keir was in too much of a panic to take in what his brother was saying. Before Arthur had a chance to brace himself, Keir's feet thumped down on his shoulders, and with them the full weight of his two hundred pound frame. For a second Arthur held on, but then his fingers lost their hold on the second ridge and they were sliding to their death.

Out in the night he heard someone call, 'Elbows!' He dug his elbows into the dome slowing his slide the tiniest fraction. But it was enough, for in that moment his hands located the first ridge, the same ridge he had used to pull himself up from the window. The combined weight of the two men now hung from his fingertips. He would have to let go. Now! Now! Was he directly above the window? If he was they had an outside chance. No time to look down, no time for thought. If he had strayed to one side or misjudged the distance nothing could save them.

He let go and his toes thumped the lintel above the window frame. It was a reprieve. For how long? The tips of his fingers were bleeding. Agonising pains stabbed his neck and shoulders. He stood on his precarious perch, cheek pressed against the dome, chest heaving, trying to work out his next move. Somehow he would have to find the courage to abandon his toehold on the lintel. But how to get back through the window? Above him he heard a sob of fear.

Relinquishing his hold on the ridge, he anchored his hands round Keir's ankles. They were linked now. If he lived, Keir lived; if he died, Keir died. The instant he eased his toes off the lintel he would descend in a free fall. With the dead weight of Keir's two hundred pounds on his shoulders, he would have to jack-knife his legs inwards at precisely the right instant. If his timing was perfect the momentum would propel him through the open window, and Keir with him. If he made the tiniest miscalculation, they would plunge past the window to the courtyard below.

Closing his eyes, he prayed, the prayer lasting no more than a few moments in which he hung poised like a trapeze artist midway between life and death. He prayed to the God he imagined, and to the stars and planets and galaxies wheeling in the orderly disorder of the universe, he prayed to all those he loved, to Hector and Elizabeth, to Merlin, Virgil and Robbie, he prayed to the friends he had known, and to the parents he had not. And as if in answer to his prayer, there surged through his body a feeling of such confidence that he knew with complete certainty that Merlin was right – the power was truly his.

Opening his eyes, he took a deep breath, slipped his toes off the lintel and jack-knifed down. With stunning force he landed on his back, and in that instant of agony his spirit left his body. Standing over him was a black-clad figure and a man in a long white robe. As Merlin shook his head, Death turned away.

The weight on his chest was suffocating. When he opened his eyes, he was lying on the stone floor of the gallery with the unconscious Keir on top of him. So great was the pain that he must surely have broken every bone in his body. Everything hurt, his back, his neck, his legs, his hands, his fingers, his head, even his eyeballs. But what did it matter? He was alive! Gloriously and miraculously alive! He was not a shattered corpse on the paving stones. Dear God, he was alive! Keir stirred. Carefully, painfully, Arthur eased his brother off his chest. The physical relief was enormous; he could breathe freely again. Rolling forward to a kneeling position, he moved first his shoulders, then his back, then his legs, arms and hands; nothing seemed to be broken. It was incredible; he was unhurt, bruised and aching but unhurt. A hand touched his shoulder.

'You saved my life.'

'You nearly had us both killed,' said Arthur wearily. 'What were you doing up there?'

'I must have been drunk. I would never have tried it if I'd been sober. I'm not that stupid.'

In the shadow of the library, Arthur greeted Edward Campbell with a bear hug.

'Thanks for that shout of "elbows". It was you, wasn't it?'

'You'd have got down without it.'

Arthur grinned. 'A lot faster, though.'

'You're a bloody hero.'

'Nonsense.'

Edward offered Keir his hand. 'That was quite a climb.'

'I didn't make it.'

'You didn't do the dome but you made it up the façade, and the North Face of the Eiger is one of the toughest climbs in Oxford.' One by one they shook his hand, looking at him, he could have sworn, in that special way they looked at Arthur.

Saying goodbye to Arthur the next morning, Keir was ill at ease, fearing his brother might have something to say about the previous night. But in the end, it was not Arthur who said it, it was Keir. 'You know, don't you?'

Arthur nodded. 'The door at the back of the library was forced, and the window underneath the dome was open. It didn't take a genius to work it out. You broke into the library and used the stairs . . . then out of the window and onto the dome. You never climbed the North Face.'

'I could have done if I'd been sober.'

'That's not what you said last night.'

'You're not going to give me away, are you?'

'No.'

Keir smiled sardonically. 'No, of course not. It would never do to tell the world your brother is a cheat, now would it? It might stain your spotless image.'

'I risked my life for you,' said Arthur quietly.

'I never asked you to.'

The enormity of the rejection silenced Arthur. Turning his back on Keir he walked quickly away. Despite everything Arthur still loved his brother and could not help wondering when and where he would see him again. He sensed that Keir was neither as happy nor as successful as he pretended, and he knew that sometime in the future destiny would bring them together again.

The next morning Arthur was passing Blackwells on his way to a tutorial, when he was momentarily blinded by a flash of sunlight. For some reason he turned back, and there in the bookshop window was a hologram of Merlin's head.

'Could you please appear?'

'I have appeared,' said Merlin.

'All of you, I mean.'

'No time. Besides, I'm in the Atlantic at the moment.'

'What do you want?'

'To congratulate you.'

'For what?' said Arthur.

'Come now, you know very well,' said Merlin's talking head. 'What is braver than overcoming your fears? What is nobler than risking your life for your fellow man?'

'You too, Merlin? You make me sound like some kind of hero. And I'm not. I'm quite ordinary.'

'Is that so? Well let me tell you, young Arthur, you can't escape your destiny by denying it. You can modify it, you can tweak it a little bit here and there, but you can't change it. In the end you'll just have to accept it. When you know who you are, that is.'

'I know exactly who I am,' protested Arthur.

'Do you? Do I have to remind you of the story of Oedipus? He also thought he knew exactly who he was. It was prophesied that he would kill his father and marry his mother. So what did he do? He escaped to Thebes thinking he could change his destiny by running away from it. And what happened? He ran right into it. He killed his father, Laius, king of Thebes, and he married his mother, Jocasta.'

'I can't believe I'm standing in the street listening to a hologram lecture me on Oedipus. You're too much, Merlin.'

'Do you acknowledge your destiny?'

Arthur's jaw set pugnaciously.

'Do you, Arthur? Or are you as stubborn and pig-headed as ever?' The green eyes glowed.

'Well . . . up there on the dome . . . when I was praying . . . '

'Yes?'

'Something happened . . . I never felt stronger or more confident.'

'Never?'

Arthur hesitated. 'Once, perhaps.'

Merlin's hologram head beamed happily through the window at his beloved protégé. 'And when was that?'

'I'd rather not say.'

The orbs flashed. 'When was that?'

'When I . . . when I drew the Sword from the Stone.'

'Ah, so that was you, was it?'

A slight hesitation. 'You know it was.'

The clouds obscured the sun, and in that moment of transformation Merlin was gone, and Arthur was alone again.

Twenty Three

2015

WITH HIS STUDENT days behind him the time had come for Arthur to make a decision about his future. What was he to do with his life? Business did not appeal to him, nor did any traditional profession he could think of. Somehow he did not see himself earning a living as an accountant, a lawyer or a doctor. An idealist, the sort of young man who wants to help his fellow men, he toyed with the idea of joining the Red Cross or some organisation that helped the poor and underprivileged in Africa or South America. However that would still leave him somewhat financially dependent on Hector and Elizabeth and he had lived off his parents long enough. It was time to start earning his keep, time to enter that real world Keir was always talking about. Until he finally settled on a career he took a number of short-term jobs – sales assistant in a clothing store, relief postman, hospital porter, waiter in a restaurant. His earnings supported a modest lifestyle, including the rent of a bedsit in South London.

More than once he had been on the point of contacting his birth parents. Almost five years had passed since he put the phone down on his mother – or at least he presumed it was her; that was still on his conscience. Somehow he had not been able to summon up the courage to speak to her, but the time was fast approaching when he would have to do the inevitable.

Meanwhile, he did everything he could to reassure the Hughes. 'You are my parents, the two people I love most in the world, and always will.' Despite his assurances, Elizabeth could not endure the thought that her beloved son might soon be embracing his natural mother. He could tell her ten times a day that no one would ever take her place but she would never believe him. Before Arthur could take the fateful step, however, there were questions to be asked, questions only Merlin could answer.

'Why did their marriage break up?'

'There were financial problems, I believe,' Merlin responded cautiously. And then, seeing that Arthur was not satisfied . . . 'There may have been other reasons too.'

'Such as?'

'I can only tell you that Godfrey Whittaker moved out of the house and was living in a small hotel in Victoria. It seems he was chronically depressed.'

'My poor father.'

Merlin made no comment. It was his duty, as he saw it, to answer Arthur's questions, not to give answers to questions he never asked. If Arthur wanted to know who his biological father was, he would certainly tell him. Much better, though, if he heard it from his father.

'When did my mother remarry?' asked Arthur.

It was the first time he had asked that question. Who could say what resentments Arthur had stored up against his mother and step-father? 'About twelve months after Godfrey died,' said Merlin.

'So soon.' The implied censure was clear enough but Merlin did not react. Abruptly Arthur changed the subject. 'And my adoption? How did that come about?'

Merlin sent his mind searching back nineteen years to the events of those momentous days. 'You were two weeks old. Uther asked me to find a good home for a baby boy.'

'You didn't try to change his mind?'

'No, Arthur. It was something that had to be done. A week later he brought you to my house and I handed you over to Hector and Elizabeth who were very happy to adopt you. From the moment they saw you they loved you. The rest you know.

Those are the facts.'

Sparse facts. There was more, much more that he needed to know. Arthur took time off from work and drove down to Ponterlally to be with his parents . . . if only they really had been his parents, if only everything were as simple as that. In every important way they *were* his parents, though he could no longer think of them in quite the same way. He was so confused, so uncertain where he belonged, that he could scarcely look them in the eye. It was unreasonable and unfair, and he hated himself for it but the fact was that he was angry with Hector and Elizabeth, as if somehow it was *their* fault they were not his real parents, as if indeed *they* were the ones who had abandoned him. He could feel his whole world changing, and that made him desperately sad.

Every morning he would wander along the banks of the Lally to the spot near the stone bridge where he and Keir had passed so many happy hours, Keir fishing, Arthur lying on his back, dreaming. The moment he sat down, shoals of fish thronged the water's edge, reaching up their heads, mouths gaping expectantly. Scattering fish food on the water, he stroked their snouts gently with the tips of his fingers. Thinking he knew them, he greeted them by name, until he remembered with a pang that they could not possibly be the same fish he had known all those years ago. Lying on his back, legs outstretched, ankles crossed, head resting on clasped hands, he watched white wisps of cloud drift across the sky, and dreamed the dreams he had dreamed when he was a boy.

After a few days at Ponterlally he decided not to contact his birth parents after all. The next day he changed his mind again, and again the next, until he no longer knew what he wanted to do. He was curious to meet them, if only to learn why they had abandoned him, yet he was afraid to meet them too, in case they told him things he had no wish to hear.

What sort of parents, he kept asking himself, gave away their own child? Merlin had offered no reason, no chronic sickness, no lack of material resources, no sudden catastrophe to explain such a callous act. Why then had they rejected him? That was the question he needed to ask them. Did he really want to hear the answer? Was there some sinister explanation? Some genetic or inherent flaw in his own character or body? Could it be that in some way he *deserved* to be rejected?

Most days he would wander over to the primary school and stand leaning on the gate imagining he was a child again. Nothing had changed, Arthur told himself, everything was the same; the same battered old school building, with its red brick walls, its grey slate roof, its smoke-blacked chimney stack, the same playground with the same swings, the same climbing frame, the same rocking horse and elephant and fire-engine he used to sit on, the same slide he used to slide down. Those children he now saw dimly through the classroom window – were they not his old friends? Was Keir not there too, eyes forever glued to the blackboard? And was there not in that same classroom a small boy who saw nothing of his teachers and heard nothing of his lessons, dreaming away the hours tracking aliens from outer space, ready at a moment's notice to challenge a billion invaders in a shaft of sunlight?

If only he could stop time, or even turn it back. If only he could stay in Ponterlally and be a child again, be as carefree as he was then, for a year, a month, a week, even for one single, precious day. Life was so much happier then, so much less complicated, so much less cruel. Poignant memories flooded in on him, moving him to tears. He longed to embrace his youth once more, but everything has an end. Time present and time future had to be faced. He was a man now.

Suddenly all his doubts left him and his mind was made up. One morning he came back from the river, hugged Hector and kissed Elizabeth so fondly that she cried, partly from happiness, partly because she too knew that the old life was over, and that nothing would ever be the same again.

Twenty Four

2015

THIS TIME, when Igraine answered the phone there was a voice at the other end, and a name attached to it. She begged Arthur to come and see her that very day.

There was an uncomfortable silence in the sitting room as mother and son stood looking at each other. 'You cannot imagine how many times I have dreamed of this moment.'

'Me too,' confessed Arthur.

She lifted her shoulders awkwardly. 'Shall we . . . ?' She sat in the corner of the sofa, Arthur opposite her in an armchair.

'Let me look at you.' She studied the son she was seeing for the first time. 'You won't be angry with me if I say something personal?'

He smiled. 'I'll try not to be.'

'You are quite the handsomest young man I ever saw.'

'You don't think you might be just a little prejudiced?'

'Not in the least.' Igraine searched for the right words. 'I wish I could express to you how happy I am. I had given up hope of ever seeing you.'

'Well, here I am,' he said flatly.

'Yes, here you are,' she said. She wanted to take him in her arms, yet looking at her son across the coffee table, the distance between them seemed as unbridgeable as the gulf of years.

'Why did you have me adopted?'

She had expected the question, but not so directly and not so soon. 'You don't believe in wasting time.'

'We could talk about the weather if you prefer.'

'So angry?'

'Angry is not the right word. Puzzled, certainly. Hurt, perhaps.'

'No. You are angry. How could you be anything else?' She stood at the bay window looking out at the lush lawns, the well-tended flower beds, the rose garden, the gazebo, the ornamental lake and the woods and fields beyond; everything perfectly laid out, everything in its proper place. Unlike her life. Hers had been a privileged existence, she had everything a woman could reasonably ask of life, everything but peace of mind. Since she gave her son away, hardly a single day had passed without her conscience troubling her. She hoped he might forgive her, even perhaps in time learn to love her. More than anything, she wanted an end to lies.

'When I look at you now, Arthur,' she said, 'I don't know how to answer your question, I don't know how I could ever have given you away. All I can say is that you were a baby then. I didn't know you, I hadn't learned to love you. It was wrong of me, I should never have done what I did. But do please try to understand. I know you must feel desperately hurt and rejected, but you see it wasn't you I gave away. It was someone else, someone I didn't know.'

'It was your son,' he said bitterly.

Igraine bowed her head. What could she say? 'When Godfrey died, I was lonely, Arthur, so very lonely. He deserted me when I needed him most. Oh yes, you can look shocked, but that is exactly what he did. He left me to face the world alone, with three young children and another one on the way.'

'Why do you think he . . . ?'

'Who knows,' she said wretchedly, 'who knows why anyone takes their own life? He was faced with financial ruin.'

'Was that the only reason?'

'I knew he had problems, but he would never discuss them. He was brought up in an old-fashioned school, you see. His father died leaving a lot of debts, and after that it was all downhill. Godfrey became introverted and morose, not at all the sociable, charming man I married. We had no fun, no social life, nothing. I didn't mind so much for myself, but there were the girls to consider. We hardly had the money to pay the school fees. Things were difficult, very difficult.' She paused, observing her son's sombre expression, wondering what he was thinking.

'Go on,' he said.

'We gave this New Year's Eve party,' she continued. 'It was Godfrey's idea, though how he was going to pay for it I never understood. I should have talked him out of it, but . . . ' She shrugged. 'I thought it might cheer everybody up. I even persuaded myself he must be doing better. Perhaps he thought of it as his final fling. Who knows? Anyway, he chose that very night to tell me he was bankrupt. It was a nasty shock, I can tell you. He had given me no real warning. I knew things were bad, but not that bad. If only he had taken me into his confidence before, I might have been able to help him. We had a row. I – well, I threatened to leave him.'

'Did you?'

She shook her head. 'I couldn't. He told me something else that night. He said he had stolen money from his club – he was the treasurer of Greys, you know – well, borrowed it was what he said, but I knew what he meant. I never discovered exactly how much, but apparently it was a great deal.'

'What did you do?'

'What could I do? I wanted to help him but I didn't know how to. Anyway, Godfrey didn't want to be helped – not by me, at any rate. It was New Year's Eve, and my world had collapsed. It was the worst night of my life.'

'Was that when he left home?'

She shook her head. 'That was much later. No, New Year's Eve was the night I met a man who looked like Godfrey's twin.' On a tripod table by the armchair stood two silver-framed photographs, one of Godfrey, one of Uther. 'See for yourself.'

Arthur studied them. 'Incredible. Which is which?'

She pointed at one. 'This is Uther.'

'How could you tell them apart?'

Her face flushed scarlet. 'It was fate, Uther turning up out of the blue like that. If it hadn't been for him, I don't know what we would have done. He was simply wonderful, kind and thoughtful and generous. He adored Godfrey, of course, everyone did, and he respected him enormously, thought him such a gentleman. It was Uther who settled the business of the missing money – how exactly, I don't know. I only know he saved Godfrey from disgrace, and then he helped him out financially. Not just once, either. Finally, when he realised Godfrey was never going to make it on his own, he gave him a job in his property company. For a time our lives were transformed.'

'For a time?'

'Godfrey was a proud man. I don't think he was ever comfortable working for a friend. It wasn't long before things started to go wrong.'

'In what way?'

She hesitated, as if she had said more than she intended to. 'There was Uther . . . successful, confident, rich. Poor Godfrey. I think he felt inadequate.' Arthur's face showed his discomfort. It hurt to hear her talking about his father in that disparaging way.

'You make him sound such a failure.'

'I'm afraid he was, at least financially. Though if money had been the only problem, we would have managed, somehow or other.'

'What other problems were there?'

Igraine shifted uncomfortably on the sofa. She had said too much, and now was being pushed where she did not want to go. 'He – imagined things.'

'What sort of things?'

Lord, why these questions? Why, after all these years, did he have to know everything, and so quickly? Arthur was young. How could he possibly understand what she had endured? 'It doesn't matter. It's not important.'

It was her evasiveness that gave him the clue. He saw it in her eyes. 'He was jealous of you and Uther. That's what you mean, isn't it?'

'Dear me, what a suggestion.' She tried to laugh it off but the laughter sounded forced. 'Mind you, men do get jealous sometimes. Yes, I suppose he might have been jealous of us.' She looked away, avoiding her son's keen look.

'Might have been?'

'Supposing he was, what then?' There was an edge of impatience and irritation in her voice.

He studied the photographs again. The two men were so alike that at first sight they might well have been twins, and yet, on closer examination, they were really very different. There is a glint in this one's eye, and a toughness about the mouth and jawline that clearly says, this is a confident man, a man who knows what he wants and means to get it. This other one is a gentle man, lacking the inner strength to endure the worst the world flings at him. The eyes of the first challenge you, the eyes of the second stir compassion. He picked up the photograph of Godfrey Whittaker, Marquess of Truro. Thinking of all the misfortunes he had suffered, he pitied him with all his heart. How he wished he had known him.

He glanced at his mother, unaware that in his eyes there was a look of reproach, gone in an instant, but not before her watchful eye had caught it. She burst into tears, but they were more tears of temper than of sorrow. 'How can you be so distant?' she complained. 'You haven't kissed me. You haven't even called me mother. I am your mother, after all, whatever happened in the past. You have no right to cross-examine me, no right at all.'

'I believe I have. And you have the right to answer, or not to answer, as you choose.' It was a cold reaction to her heated outburst.

'Whatever you may think, I never gave Godfrey any cause to

be jealous of me,' she said, lifting her head defiantly. 'He may have imagined the worst. But what was I supposed to do?'

'Is that why he shot himself?'

Igraine jumped up and paced the room, wringing her hands. 'How can you say such a wicked thing! It's cruel! Cruel!'

'Sit down, mother.' The words rang out like a command. It may have been the tone of authority in his voice, or because he had called her mother for the first time, but she obeyed instantly. 'Forgive all these questions,' he went on gently, 'but I want to try and understand my father's state of mind, and why he committed suicide.'

His father? For a moment Igraine was confused. Of course! Arthur assumed that Godfrey was his father! In all the trauma of the meeting, she had overlooked that crucial fact.

'From what you tell me,' he went on, 'his financial problems were solved. So he had only one reason to be depressed that I can think of; he thought he had lost his wife to another man. What other explanation could there be?'

She slumped back on the sofa. So he did blame her. Suddenly she was weeping, this time not tears of anger but tears of remorse. When she spoke again, Arthur had to lean forward to catch the words. 'Godfrey and I were devoted, but we were never . . . oh, he loved me in his way but he was not a passionate man. And then suddenly, there was Uther. I never meant it to happen, it just did. Those two men . . . you can't believe how much alike they looked. Even more alike than the photographs.

'In a way it was like falling in love with Godfrey all over again, except that . . . how can I put it? Uther pulsated with life and energy. He *needed* me to love him, he needed me so much to love him; and so I did, you see. What else could I do? It was as though I had been waiting for him all my life. I never believed in fate before, but oh, I am certain it was fate. How could it have been anything else? I couldn't help myself. I *did* love him. I loved him passionately.'

For a while the great drawing room was so quiet that through the open windows they could hear the breeze sifting through the avenue of beech trees. Arthur broke the silence. 'So my father must have known, or at least he must have guessed that you and Uther – that you were lovers.' The word burned like acid in his mouth.

Igraine hesitated. For a moment she was on the point of telling him the truth. But then her courage failed her. 'Not while Godfrey was alive,' she muttered. 'I was never unfaithful to him.' Pray God she would be forgiven for the lie, pray God Arthur would believe it.

'I am not here to judge you, mother.'

She reached out her hand and touched his cheek. 'Oh Arthur, I am sorry. So sorry. If only I had the time all over again. It was a terrible thing we did to you, a terrible thing we did to ourselves. I would give anything to be able to make it up to you. But I can never do that, can I?'

'What's done is done. We all have to live with it. At least explain to me why you had me adopted.' She tried to take his hand in hers but he eased it away. 'Why, mother?'

She shook her head helplessly. 'Not just like that, not after all these years. It didn't make sense then, and when you ask me to make sense of it now, I can't. There are no easy explanations and too many questions to answer. I need time, time to think, time to remember, time to get used to having my son back.'

'I only want to know why you had me adopted. Surely that can't be so difficult to explain? Everything else can wait.'

A long silence. Then Igraine said in a low voice, 'It was not my doing.'

He was standing over her. 'Whose then?'

Her mouth opened and closed but the words would not come. 'It was Uther,' she said finally, her voice trembling. 'He made me do it.'

'Made you? How could he do that? You could have said no, couldn't you? Why didn't you? All those months you carried me. Didn't you feel anything for the child growing inside you?

Didn't you feel anything when I was born?' Arthur's voice broke, the tears leaped from his eyes as they used to when he was a boy. 'Tell me, mother, what *did* you feel? Did you feel anything at all for me?'

'How can you ask? Of course I did.'

'Then how could he *make* you give me away? Why didn't you insist on keeping me? Why couldn't you just love me?'

'Stop! Stop! You're breaking my heart!' Covering her face with her hands, Igraine began to sob.

'You didn't love me, did you, mother? That's the truth of it.'

She took a few moments to regain control of herself. Hands twisting in her lap, she pleaded with her son. 'Don't say that, Arthur. Please don't say that. Say I was weak, I admit I was weak. Say I was afraid of losing the man I loved. I was. But don't say I didn't love you. I agreed to have you adopted, and yes, it was a wicked thing to do. But I've suffered for it, Arthur. I've paid a dreadful price for it every moment of every day of my life.'

She had offered excuses, but no satisfactory explanation. 'Why did you give me away, mother?' he asked her yet again.

Igraine knew by the determined look in her son's eye that he would not leave her in peace until she had given him his answer. 'Uther made me do a deal,' she whispered.

'What sort of deal?'

Igraine looked down at her hands. 'He made me agree to have you adopted. I was desperate, you see. I couldn't live without him. At least that's what I told myself. What can I say? I was young and foolish.'

'So my adoption was the price you paid to keep your marriage intact.'

Her hands were clenched so tightly that the knuckles were white. 'It was the price I paid for your life.'

A long silence. Mother and son looked at each other as if for the first time. 'Try not to judge me,' she pleaded.

He paced the room, turning everything over in his mind. After a time he sat beside her and took her hand.

'Shall I see you again?' she asked.

'Yes, of course. But I need time to take all this in.'

'Will you see Uther?' She squeezed his hand, willing him to say yes.

'What's the point?'

'You two ought to meet, for your sake, as well as his. He needs forgiveness just as much as I do, don't forget that. And you, Arthur, you need to forgive.'

She was right, of course. But was she being altogether honest? He left with the feeling that something was being concealed from him. Until he discovered what it was, his mind would never be at rest.

When Uther came home that evening he wanted a full report on Arthur's visit.

'He thinks Godfrey is his father.' It was the first thing she thought of.

Uther frowned. 'Why didn't you tell him the truth?'

'I couldn't.'

He was genuinely puzzled. 'Why not?'

Even after all these years it was still hard to say. 'If I had told Arthur you were his father, he would have worked out that I must have been sleeping with you while Godfrey was alive. As it is, he thinks we only became lovers later.'

'Really, Igraine,' said Uther disdainfully, 'there are times when I despair of you. You have what you dreamed of these many years – you have your son back. You also have the chance to wipe the slate clean and start again. And what do you do? You lie to him!'

Igraine was close to tears. 'If I hadn't, he would think I was responsible for Godfrey's death. I couldn't bear that.'

Uther's lip curled. 'How like you not to see the wood for the trees.'

'What do you mean by that?'

'What does it matter if he knows we committed adultery? What does any of it matter? What matters is that we tell him the truth.'

Igraine flushed with anger. 'That's rich coming from you! You were the one who wanted to see your son dead rather than tell the world the truth. Or had you forgotten?'

No, he had not forgotten, but that was then and this was now. 'It's wrong to lie to him, Igraine.'

It was the last straw. 'How dare you lecture me, you sanctimonious bastard! I suppose you never lie?'

'Not if I can help it.'

'You can't help lying to me, is that it?'

'Meaning?'

'Our marriage is one big lie.'

'I really have no idea what you are getting so excited about,' said Uther coldly. 'Our marriage is no more of a lie than anyone else's. You have everything you want.'

'Except a faithful husband.'

'I am an excellent husband. I look after you, I am generous, not to say indulgent. I think I do my duty.'

'Oh really? Was it your duty you were doing when Arthur came to see us this morning?'

'I wanted to be here, but unfortunately I was detained at the House.'

'Whose house? One of your many girlfriends? May Middleton's perhaps?'

It was clear to Uther that he was getting the worst of this exchange, a change of tack was needed. He had been shrewdly cautious in promoting his political career, advancing with care up the treacherously icy slopes that led to the highest office in the land. All around were precipitous drops and deep crevasses, one false step could mean the end of everything, and he was well aware that in politics there were no second chances. Igraine was crucial to his advancement, her beauty and her social connections conferred on him a certain celebrity status in the House of Commons. No one ever refused an invitation to Brackett Hall. Pendragon was known to have an excellent chef and the best wine cellar in England. 'Duchess,' he cooed, 'you know that isn't true.' He shook his head despairingly. 'Why, oh why, must we always fight? It's so terribly depressing, and so unnecessary. If this argument was my fault I am truly sorry. If I have done anything to hurt you, please forgive me.' He struck his breast. '*Mea culpa*. I am such a clumsy oaf. Let's face it, that's all we men are, clumsy oafs.'

'Don't try that unctuous shit with me, you hypocrite! You devious, lying shit!' When she had screamed and ranted and sobbed the bitterness out of her system, she pleaded with him. He was Arthur's father. He must be the one to tell him. 'We shall have a son again,' she said, wiping away her tears. 'He'll come and live with us, and you will give him a job. Oh, it will all be so wonderful. Please, darling, tell him you're his father. Do this one thing for me.'

Uther shrugged. Who said women were the stronger sex? 'If that's what you want, duchess.'

Twenty Five

SHOOTING HIS CUFFS self-importantly, Uther surveyed the dining room of Greys. All around were the distinctive sights and sounds of an exclusive London club: walls hung with portraits of distinguished past members, tables gleaming with crystal and silver flatware, the room humming with discreetly controlled conversation punctuated by the occasional explosive burst of laughter.

'I don't mind telling you, Arthur, there are some per-itty important people in this room. I doubt there's anyone here who isn't in *Who's Who*.' He sipped his glass of claret. 'Except for the waiters. Mind you,' he added roguishly, 'I shouldn't be surprised if some of them weren't in it too.' Uther bounced in his chair, enjoying his little joke.

It was the first time they had met, or at least the first time for twenty years. Uther considered Arthur – excellent bone structure, athletic build, a fine looking young man. Walking into the dining room with him he had felt a rush of pride. At every table heads turned and everyone looked at Arthur. That shock of blond hair and those startlingly blue eyes attracted attention. But there was more to it than that, the youngster carried himself well, almost, you might say, regally. There was about him a calm composure that conveyed a sense of inner strength; a rare quality, that. This was no gauche youth, this was a young man at ease with himself, taking in his stride what was certainly an unfamiliar experience and could easily have been an intimidating one. Uther had to admit, he was impressed

After ordering he came straight to the point. 'I owe you an

apology, Arthur. *Peccavi*, I have sinned. I am deeply ashamed of being a party to your adoption.' The apology was handsome enough, but it was not apologies Arthur wanted, it was explanations. 'Can you ever forgive me?'

Instead of answering the question directly, Arthur countered it with one of his own, the same he had asked his mother several times. 'Why *did* you have me adopted?'

Uther looked surprised. 'Did your mother not explain?'

'She said you made her do it.'

'Did she now?' Uther set down his wine glass. 'Well if that is what she said, far be it from me to contradict her.'

Arthur was left to work that one out. The response was shrewd, falling short of a challenge but leaving Igraine's claim open to doubt. 'I can only say I believed that what we did was for the best.'

Arthur swallowed a few more mouthfuls of whatever it was he was eating and laid down his knife and fork. He had no stomach for food today.

Uther watched in silence. 'I hear you got a first.'

'Yes.'

An approving nod. 'Well done.'

'Thank you, sir.'

Later, when coffee was poured, Uther lit the largest cigar Arthur had ever seen, waved the match in the air long after the flame was out, directed a long, indulgent stream of smoke at the cherubs on the ceiling and leaned back in his chair with the look of a man about to deliver himself of something portentous. 'Tell me now, my boy, what do you intend doing with your life?'

'Somehow or other I shall have to earn a living,' said Arthur.

'One of those tiresome imperatives,' agreed Uther dryly. The edge of sarcasm was not lost on Arthur. At least, he thought, Uther had not mentioned the real world.

'You will find the real world rather different from Oxford.'

Arthur bit his lip. 'So I've been told.'

'Anything in mind?'

'Not as yet.' What was all this about, he wondered, and anyway what right did his step-father have to discuss his future with him?

'What about politics?'

'I'm afraid I know nothing about politics.'

'Splendid. There is no better qualification for politics,' said Uther grandly, 'than knowing nothing about it. There are far too many politicians who think they know it all. Look at me, I never knew anything, and I still don't. And I am Secretary of State for Trade and Industry, with some hope of becoming Foreign Secretary in the near future.'

Arthur grinned. Against his natural instincts he was beginning to warm to the man. 'Somehow I don't think politics is for me,'

'I dare say you are right,' said Uther. 'It's a precarious game.' On reflection, the last thing he wanted was having his son compete with him in his own back-yard. With a swift change of direction he enquired, 'Keeping the wolf from the door are we?'

'Just about,' said Arthur.

'How, if I may ask?'

This was beginning to feel like an interrogation. 'I'm temping here and there.'

'Temping!' Uther made the word sound like a virulent disease. 'And what does that involve?'

'At the moment I'm working as a hospital porter. It doesn't pay much but it's interesting.'

Uther's lip curled distastefully. 'My dear boy, you can't wheel dead bodies around for the rest of your life, there's no future in it. I suggest you find something that makes better use of your talents. Have you ever considered going into business?'

'No.'

'Hmm. Well, as it happens, I might be able to offer you something rather good.' The tip of Uther's cigar glowed red, and yet another stream of smoke was directed at the winged cherubs. 'You may know I own a property company.'

'Yes, I do.'

'I made a bundle of money in the early days, I don't mind telling you, but in recent years things haven't gone so well. Frankly, since I went to Trade and Industry I haven't had much time to devote to business. If they make me Foreign Secretary I shan't have any time at all. I'm looking for someone to run things. Interested?'

'I know nothing about property either,' replied Arthur regretfully.

'No problem. I can teach you. You're a bright young chap. If you do well, I'll give you half the company. It's a one in a million opportunity to make yourself a fortune. What do you say?' Uther leaned back, puffing away at his cigar, and contemplating Arthur through narrowed eyes. He was congratulating himself. An inspiration, a stroke of genius. If it worked out, both of them would make money; if it didn't, he had lost nothing. Either way he would have his son where he could keep an eye on him.

Arthur delayed his response, not because he was seriously considering Uther's proposition but because he did not want to offend him. 'Please don't think me ungrateful,' he said finally, 'I just don't think business is for me.'

'I see.' Uther did his best to hide his disappointment. 'What did you have in mind, then?'

'I would like to see the world – have some adventures.'

'Indeed? And how do you intend financing this global adventure tour of yours?' enquired Uther sardonically.

'I was thinking of joining the army.'

Uther stubbed viciously at his cigar. 'Dear God. Is this by any chance Merlin's idea?'

'I discussed it with him, yes,' admitted Arthur.

'Now there's an example of a wasted life,' said Uther, wagging his finger at Arthur as if he held him personally responsible. 'What would he know about careers? Why a brilliant man like that threw his talent away on schoolmastering, I shall never know.'

Arthur was silent, refusing to be drawn, which irritated Uther even more. The stupidity of it, turning down the offer of a lifetime for a career in the army! But then, come to think of it, was it really so stupid? For Arthur, yes. But for Uther? On second thoughts, perhaps it was not such a bad idea. It had at least one attraction – it would keep his son out of his hair. Not that he had ever for a single moment taken Merlin's so-called prophecy seriously. Still . . . 'I suppose if that's what you really want,' said Uther doubtfully.

'So you approve?' No sooner had he asked the question than Arthur regretted it. Who was this man to approve or disapprove of his plans?

'Can't say I'm thrilled. Not much future, I would have thought. Why do we need an army anyway? No one left to fight bar a few crazies. This is the twenty-first century.'

'Merlin thinks the world is a more dangerous place than it was in the twentieth century.'

'No doubt Merlin knows better than I do,' said Uther, with heavy sarcasm. 'He's a schoolmaster and I'm merely a humble politician.'

'I did think of joining "Aid without Frontiers",' said Arthur. 'They're international and non-political as you know, and they do a lot of good work.'

Please God, thought Uther, not good work, anything but that. He flashed a dazzling beam at Arthur. 'What a splendid idea! I respect a man with a social conscience. I can see you're an idealist, as I was at your age. You want to put the world to rights, feed the hungry, clothe the naked, succour the sick, that sort of thing. Shows your heart's in the right place. Take my advice, though, stick with the army. If you do well, and I'm sure you will, you'll have something on your CV that means something.'

'Thanks for the tip.' He was thinking he may have been overhasty in judging his step-father. From now on he would try to keep an open mind.

Until today, Uther's conscience had never troubled him; now, however, with the benefit of hindsight, his reasons for having his son adopted seemed less than compelling, almost trivial. He was beginning to think it would have been nice to have a son, to watch him grow and see him develop into this engaging young man. He could have influenced him, guided him, given him the benefit of his advice and experience. Well, it was all done and dusted now. Too late for regrets.

'More coffee?'

'I'm fine, thanks.'

'Glass of port?'

'No thanks.'

No, of course not, this young man was far too controlled to be drinking at lunchtime. Uther considered lighting up another cigar but decided against it. Idly he brushed a few bread crumbs off the tablecloth. It was time.

'Your mother was very insistent we meet.'

'Yes.'

'To be honest, I was rather hesitant about the idea . . . in all the circumstances. I only wish they had been different. Still, I imagine there's a time in most men's lives when their past comes back to haunt them.' Uther glanced nervously out of the window at Green Park, as if the ghosts of his own past were lying in wait out there, ready to pounce on him the moment he stepped out on the street.

Arthur made no comment, sensing his step-father had something important to tell him. Uther leaned forward and placed his hands flat on the table in a decisive gesture.

'Do you know why she was so keen on our meeting?'

'I imagine she wanted me to get to know my step-father.'

'Not quite.'

'You mean that wasn't the reason?'

'I mean I'm not your step-father.'

A puzzled frown. 'Who are you, then?'

Uther looked Arthur directly in the eye. 'I am your father.'

Arthur stared back at Uther blankly, unable to take in what he had said.

'I am your father, Arthur,' repeated Uther.

The conversation in the dining room was hushed; at a nearby table someone delivered the punch line of a joke, and there was a sudden burst of raucous laughter.

'That's not possible.'

'I realise this may come as a surprise to you, but the fact is you are my son.'

'Surprise?' Arthur snatched at the word, as though it were a lifebelt in a stormy sea. For a few moments he sat in a daze. 'My father is dead,' he said at last.

'Who told you that?'

'Merlin. At least I think he did. But anyway, my mother – your wife – she confirmed it.'

A quizzical look. 'Did she? Perhaps you only heard what she wanted you to hear.'

'I assumed – that is,' stammered Arthur, 'I always thought . . . '

A brisk nod. 'That Godfrey, Marquess of Truro, was your father.'

'I was born six months after he died.' Arthur was trying to remember his mother's precise words. 'Didn't Mother tell me that you and she . . . that you . . . ?' He broke off, too embarrassed to continue.

'That we only became lovers after Godfrey's death?'

'That's what she said.'

A rueful grimace. 'I'm afraid she lied.'

'But why?'

'Scared you might think badly of her, I imagine. Don't be too hard on her, Arthur. None of us is perfect. We all tell porky pies from time to time. Meeting you after all these years was a trauma for her. She intended to tell you the truth, she wanted to tell you the truth. When it came to it, she funked it, that's all.'

Arthur looked intently at the tablecloth, not trusting himself to look at Uther who continued. 'We were young and in love, if that's any excuse.' Arthur's thoughts whirred uselessly in his head like the broken mechanism of a clockwork doll. 'Suddenly she was pregnant. My fault, of course,' admitted Uther magnanimously, 'I should have taken precautions.' Arthur flinched and Uther knew instantly he had said the wrong thing. 'Not quite the point, eh? I should never have touched her in the first place. That's what you're thinking, isn't it? You are right, of course.' Uther smote his breast dramatically. '*Peccavi*. I have sinned. I have committed fornication. Beat me. Knock me down. Stamp on me.'

Arthur looked up, his eyes full of resentment. 'You make it sound like a joke.'

'Do I? Well, perhaps that is my way. I do assure you, though, it wasn't the least bit funny when your mother told me she was pregnant.'

'It's all clear to me now,' said Arthur. 'Godfrey found out about you and mother. That's why he killed himself.'

'There is not one shred of evidence to support that theory,' said Uther icily. 'Let's face it, Godfrey was a weak man. He couldn't cope.'

Arthur said nothing, Uther sensing his disapproval. 'Why are you so concerned about Godfrey anyway? He wasn't your father. I am. I do hate clichés, Arthur, but let's face it, blood is thicker than water.'

'You didn't let that worry you when you had me adopted.'

'I have already apologised for that.'

'That wipes the slate clean, does it?'

'Judge me if you must,' said Uther. 'But like it or not, these things happen even in the best regulated families. They are beyond our control, or they seem so at the time. Was it so terrible what we did? Or was it the most natural thing in the world?'

'The most natural thing in the world?' echoed Arthur

scathingly. 'I was your son. Yet your first thought was to get rid of me. I couldn't understand why you and mother gave me away, but I do now. I was an embarrassment to you, wasn't I? The timing of my birth was inconvenient. Your adultery would be in all the papers and it would be the end of your political career. You were determined to avoid a scandal, even if it meant killing your own son. And when your wife wouldn't agree to do that, you gave me up for adoption. Was that the most natural thing in the world? Or the most unnatural?'

Uther looked sheepish. 'Can't say I blame you for feeling aggrieved.' Aggrieved. A bland word to describe the way he felt, thought Arthur. 'Let me be candid with you, Arthur,' said Uther, lying smoothly, 'I did think about my career, I won't deny it. But that was secondary. It was your mother I was most concerned about. The press would have blamed her for Godfrey's death and destroyed her reputation. Socially she would have been finished. Can you understand that?'

'Yes.'

'But you can't forgive.'

Arthur tried to answer honestly. 'The man I am now has to forgive. But that child you rejected – I'm not sure he can.'

'Let me tell you something about that child,' said Uther. 'I know who he is now, but I didn't then. I never thought of you as a child, much less my son. You had no form, no shape, no name. You were a foetus, that's all, nothing I could relate to. What can I say? I was wrong. It seemed like the right decision at the time.' Uther paused, scrolling back the years in his head. 'Ten days after you were born, you were wrapped in a blanket and shawl and handed to me. I never looked at you. Not once. If I had . . . who knows, I might have weakened. Seeing you now . . . ' It was as close to a plea for forgiveness as Uther would ever get, and Arthur knew it. 'Will you take my hand?'

'Of course.'

Father and son shook hands awkwardly.

'Would you care to reconsider my business proposal?' enquired

Uther, seizing what he perceived to be his best and probably last opportunity. 'Half my property business in exchange for your commitment to the Company?'

'It's a most generous offer,' said Arthur, hesitating, 'but as I say I'm not sure I'm ready to . . . '

'Accept favours from your father? Is that what you are thinking?' Uther could tell from Arthur's expression that it was. 'Well you've got it wrong, my boy. This is not some kind of handout, I assure you. I should expect a hundred percent commitment and performance from you.'

'As I said, I know nothing about business.'

'So what!' said Uther dismissively. 'I shall teach you everything you need to know – and a hell of a lot more,' he added with a sly wink. 'After all,' he said, his voice softening, 'we are father and son. That changes everything, does it not?'

It did, but it was clear to Arthur that his father was laying a trap for him, a honeyed trap but a trap nonetheless. If ever he was to find his true destiny, he would have to preserve his independence. Nothing was more important than that. 'Give me some time to think about it,' he said.

Which meant, Uther knew, that his son was determined to do his own thing, whatever that might be. 'Take all the time you want,' he said grandly. 'Meanwhile you shall come and live with us.'

'I have a bedsit across the river.'

'Give it up. You can have your own apartment in Brackett Hall. Come and go as you please. You shall have a mother and father again. Igraine will have her baby back and I shall have a son and heir. Think, Arthur, think of the doors I can open for you – business, politics, law, whatever damned profession you choose. Hell, go ahead and join the army, if that's what you want. I'll support you whatever you do.'

Arthur shook his head. 'Thank you, sir, for being so understanding. But I really would prefer to stand on my own feet.'

'At least come and see us – stay the weekend. Your step-sisters are dying to meet you.'

'I look forward to meeting them too.'

'Come any time. Come as often as you like. Feel free to treat Brackett Hall as if it were your own home. Damn it, man, it is your own home!' Uther was elated. Life had given him a second chance, it had brought back the son he once so casually rejected, and, what was more, without any embarrassing repercussions. It was all very satisfactory, and more, far more, than he deserved.

But then a dark thought shadowed his joyful mood; Arthur was back in the fold, so what if he decided to take the name Pendragon? If he did, the media would be onto it in a flash and with their usual frenzied efficiency the tabloid press would sift through the dirt. Searching questions would be asked about his affair with Igraine and his reasons for giving his son away for adoption, not to mention the whole sordid business of Godfrey's death. Godfrey would be seen as the victim, and Uther as the man responsible for his death. He would be made to look a complete shit. He could imagine the headlines. "Minister re-united with son he rejected twenty years ago . . . Uther Pendragon confronted with his past . . . Wife's adultery drove husband to suicide . . . Tory Grandee puts politics before parenting . . . "

Signing the bill, he said casually, 'I imagine you'll be keeping your present surname.'

Arthur was taken aback. 'I only just discovered I'm a Pendragon. I shall need time to think about it. Does it matter?'

'Changing your name would inevitably invite speculation by the yobbo press. This is our business, not theirs,' said Uther. 'No one need know I'm your father.'

Arthur's jaw jutted, his eyes flashed angrily. Uther could have kicked himself. He had blundered.

'Are you ashamed of me?'

'My dear boy, how can you ask me such a question? Ashamed

of you? What nonsense! I couldn't be more proud of you.'

'Then show it.'

'Listen to me, Arthur . . . '

'No, father,' said Arthur, 'you listen to me. I never knew who my real father was, now suddenly I do. It's like coming out of a dark tunnel into the light. You are my father and that makes me a Pendragon.'

'Of course it does,' said Uther uneasily. 'All I'm saying is let's keep it in the family.'

'No, let's not do that. You are my father and you are going to tell the world that I'm your son. You rejected me once. I won't let you do it a second time.'

Uther could not remember the last time anyone had told him what to do, let alone so emphatically. He had made the mistake of underestimating his son. In future he would have to be more careful. This was a young man to be reckoned with. He would make a staunch friend; and a formidable enemy.

'I am justly rebuked,' he said humbly.

'That was not my intention,' Arthur assured his father.

'Nevertheless you are absolutely right.' He would just have to make the best of a bad job. Rather than let the press uncover the story, he decided to give the story to the press.

"Believing as I do that politicians have an obligation to uphold the very highest standards of honesty and integrity, I would like to share with my constituents, and with the public at large, my joy at being re-united with my long lost son, Arthur Pendragon. To my shame he was given up by me for adoption when he was a baby. The circumstances were the following.

When I was a young man I fell deeply in love with my beloved wife, Igraine. At the time, she was unhappily married to Lord Truro. Though she and he had long been estranged, and were husband and wife in name only, he refused to give her a divorce. We began an affair and she became pregnant. Her husband was experiencing financial problems, and was also suffering from the chronic depression that ultimately led to his suicide. She felt it her duty to stand by him, refusing to desert him in his time of trouble. I freely admit that she was also concerned not to expose me to the condemnation of the public and of my peers. I, for my part, was equally anxious to protect the reputation of the woman I loved.

I therefore persuaded her, much against her will, to keep the baby's birth secret, and to have it adopted by a caring and loving couple. It was the most painful decision we have ever had to make – one, I may say, neither of us has ever ceased to regret. Having our son back in the family after so many years has been some consolation to us, and has made us the happiest and proudest couple in the world.

Times have changed. The world we live in is far more aware and far less judgmental than it was when I was a young man. Not for one single moment would I consider doing now what I felt obliged to do then. That is not an excuse, merely a simple statement of fact. I take full responsibility for my actions, submitting myself to the judgment of the electorate. If it is their decision, or the decision of my Party, that I should resign as a Member of Parliament, then I shall not hesitate to do my duty."

Neither the public nor the Party decided anything of the kind, nor did the Press. Their guns had been well and truly spiked; every newspaper in the land was behind Uther, their stories focusing rather on his courage in revealing the truth than on the facts of the revelation. His assessment of the mood of the times had been flawless. Columnists praised him for having learned the lesson most politicians never learn; he had come clean. What's more, he had done it without waiting for the truth to be dragged out of him. Not that it was the real truth, it was Uther's truth, a counterfeit so good it was almost indistinguishable from the real thing.

Twenty Six

SHORTLY AFTER meeting his father, Arthur joined the army. His short leaves he spent in Ponterlally with Elizabeth and Hector, both of whom, to his delight, were as warm and loving towards him as they ever had been. His change of surname at first troubled Elizabeth but she soon got used to it. 'You are still my Arthur,' she said, hugging him until he was red in the face, 'and you always will be.' Hector, being a realist, saw it as the most natural thing in the world that Arthur should become a Pendragon; it signified that his and Elizabeth's task was done, and well done too, for it was largely thanks to them that Arthur had regained the inheritance to which he was entitled.

Having a weekend pass, Arthur accepted Igraine's invitation to stay at Brackett Hall. It was a visit he anticipated with mixed feelings; with Hector and Elizabeth he was at ease, with Uther and Igraine he was not, for there were too many unresolved issues. Nevertheless he looked forward to seeing his birth parents again, and of course to meeting his three step-sisters for the first time.

Arthur kissed his mother affectionately. Igraine was overjoyed. 'I can't believe I shall have you to myself for two whole days.'

'And how is Elizabeth?' Igraine had asked to meet Elizabeth but her approaches had been politely rejected. She had not pressed the point.

'She's fine.' He would have preferred to pass on Elizabeth's love or best wishes or even regards but she had not sent them, and what was the point of lying?

'I should like to have met her.' Igraine smiled, a forlorn smile it seemed to him. Why was she sad? Was it only because of him? He knew so little about her. He tried to look at her objectively, to see her not as his mother but as a woman. She was beautiful; she must have been over fifty, though she certainly did not look it, her face still the face of a young woman, her hair – even if with some artificial aid – still glossy and raven black, her body slim and shapely. In those dark eyes there was that same touch of melancholy he had noticed in her smile, a wry acceptance of the passing years, a hint of secret yearnings and of dreams unfulfilled. As if to give the lie to his sombre reflections, she suddenly came to vibrant life, crying out happily, 'And what a splendid uniform! How smart you look!' Hands clasped she gazed at him adoringly. 'How the girls must chase you. You really are the handsomest young man I ever saw.'

Arthur grinned. 'You exaggerate.'

'Not a jot,' she insisted.

'You, on the other hand, without any exaggeration, are certainly the most beautiful woman in the country.'

'What nonsense,' cried Igraine blushing.

The "monsters", as Igraine affectionately dubbed her grandchildren, were duly assembled to meet their long lost uncle. Gawain, the eldest, was much the liveliest and most endearing, a stocky, freckled-faced lad, with flaming red hair, and a challenging gaze. Agravaine, the second born, was pale, plump and wining, clinging to his grandmother's skirts. Gaheris, the third brother, was a big, swaggering fellow with a loud voice. Mordred, the youngest, retreated under a table, from where he observed Arthur with darkly suspicious eyes.

And the girls? Where are they?'

'Dying to meet you.' At that very moment Elaine appeared, struck a theatrical pose with arms spread as if to say, "Da-dum! Here I am and here you are!", and gave Arthur a hug.

'You must have been listening at the door,' said Igraine, smiling affectionately at her eldest.

'An actress,' said Elaine, 'always makes her entrance on cue.' She stood back, took a long look at Arthur and cooed admiringly, 'My but you really are a dish!'

Arthur did not know what to say. Murmuring something that he hoped sounded like appreciation, he considered how best to return the compliment. If nature had not blessed Elaine with beauty, it had lavished on her both vivacity and charm. 'I know very little about the theatre, Elaine,' he admitted, 'but enough to know that you have star quality.'

Elaine melted. Arthur could not have said anything to please her more. 'Friends for life, darling,' she gushed.

Morgan's entrance was more subdued but equally impressive in its way. She strode in and gave Arthur a bear hug that made him wince and left red marks on his face. When she released him, he studied her with interest. His heart went out to her; Morgan was the most engagingly ugly woman he had ever seen. Her eyes bulged, her mouth was huge, and was that a hint of a moustache on her upper lip? Studying her outfit, he now understood why her embrace had been so painful. Her large frame was encased in a skin-tight black leather suit hung with several pounds of steel – buttons, badges, brooches, tassels, studs and chains. Her hands writhed with steel serpents, from her ears steel witches dangled, and both her nose and lips were pierced with steel rings.

Morgan stared right back at Arthur, her steel-encrusted lips parting in a gleaming smile. 'I'll bet you never saw anything like me before.

Arthur laughed. You are definitely an original.'

'Take care, Arthur,' said Elaine. 'Morgan's a witch.'

Igraine hated it when anyone made fun of Morgan. 'Nonsense dear.'

'Oh but I am, mother,' said Morgan. 'I can give you the power of tongues,' she informed Arthur. 'Or I can teach you to fly if you like. I'm teaching Elaine to fly,' she said proudly, 'aren't I, darling?'

'I'm playing Peter Pan in Exmouth next month,' explained Elaine.

'The stupid producer wants her to wear a harness,' said Morgan. 'He makes us so angry, doesn't he darling?'

'Of course he does, precious,' said Elaine, humouring her sister.

Morgan took Arthur's hand in hers. 'I see an island,' she said after a moment or two, 'a white island in a grey sea.' Though Arthur had no idea what she meant, the hairs rose on the back of his neck. Her words both excited and disturbed him.

'Your wife will be beautiful, and young, very young,' continued Morgan.

'Do stop, dear,' said Igraine uneasily, 'I'm sure you must be boring Arthur.'

'Not at all,' said Arthur. Far from being bored he was anxious to hear more.

'She will make you very happy and very sad,' said Morgan.

Igraine had lost patience with her youngest. 'Arthur doesn't want to hear any more.'

Morgan bowed her head, stuck out her tongue and dug the toes of her shoes into the carpet like a child who has been rebuked. Elaine came to the rescue and took her younger sister for a walk in the gardens. Igraine slipped her hand through Arthur's arm and drew him to the door. 'There's a beautiful young lady waiting for you in the library.'

'Fantastic. Let's go and see her.' Arthur was wondering if the third sister was as eccentric as the other two.

'She said you were to come alone, made quite a point of it, wants you all to herself. She was quite tearful at the thought of meeting her brother for the first time. Such a sensitive child.'

He knocked on the library door and went in. The afternoon sun shone obliquely into the room. At the big bay window a young woman stood looking out at the gardens. Turning, she walked over to Arthur and looked up at him with a half smile on her lovely face. 'I shall put this moment in a cupboard and lock it up,' she murmured. 'And when I'm old and grey, I shall take it out and look at it.'

'You! What are you doing here?'

Margot's eyes mocked him. 'Is it so surprising? This is my home, after all. Or it was before Lennox carried me off.'

'Your home?' He stared blankly at her, not yet understanding, or perhaps not wanting to. Slowly the look of incomprehension turned to shock as the blood drained from his face. 'You!'

Margot waved her hand dismissively. 'Don't be silly, Arthur, who else could it be?'

'*You* – Margot! *That* Margot!'

'In the flesh, darling.'

'Dear God!'

'Quite so,' said Margot ironically. 'I thought it would be wiser if we saw each other alone first, so we could get our stories straight. You never know, someone might remember seeing us together at the Commem. Come to think of it, it might be a good idea to say we bumped into each other years ago at Oxford. Just in case.'

'Bumped into each other! We were lovers!'

'No one needs to know that.'

The revulsion rose from his stomach. As the room spun, he reached out blindly, grasping the arm of a chair for support. 'Did you know?'

She pretended not to understand. 'Did I know what?'

He had to force himself to speak the words. 'Did you know who I was? When we . . . '

Margot looked aggrieved. 'What a question!'

'Did you?' he insisted.

She pouted. 'You must think me terribly wicked.'

He shook his head, bewildered. 'I don't know what to think.'

'Darling Arthur.' Her eyes were languid and sensual. In a sudden change of mood she whirled around in front of him, hair flying, skirt riding high, revealing her thighs. 'How can you expect me to remember things like that after all this time? Who knows what I knew or didn't know?' A flurry of skirt and bare thighs as she spun again. 'What does it matter anyway?' She smiled coquettishly. 'I do remember one thing, though. I remember that fantastic night we spent together.'

His face was white. 'Don't even think about it.'

She frowned and pushed out her lips. 'Don't be such a spoilsport, Arthur. You take things far too seriously.'

'Aren't you ashamed of what we did?'

'What is there to be ashamed of?' she asked wide-eyed. 'It was wonderful. If you must know, I often think about it. It's better than any fix when I'm feeling miserable.' She smiled wickedly, relishing his discomfort. 'You were so good, lover.'

'Don't call me that.'

'Why not? You *were* my lover. It happened, didn't it? No use denying it.'

'I am your brother, Margot. Does that mean nothing to you?'

She came close, looking up at him seductively. 'Of course it does. It's the greatest turn-on ever. Just thinking about it gives me an orgasm.'

He stared at her, dumbfounded. His whole world had fallen about him, and all she could do was mock him.

'Now Arthur dear,' she said, her voice smooth as silk, slipping her hand through the crook of his arm and restraining him when he tried to draw away from her, 'don't look so guilty. There's nothing to feel guilty about. What did we do that was so terrible? Did we commit murder? Did we steal anything? Did we mug anyone? Of course not. We did no one any harm.'

'No one but ourselves.'

'Oh, phooey! We enjoyed every minute of it. I know I did.' Her hand tightened on his arm. 'Didn't you?'

He would not answer her.

'You did, didn't you?'

'Of course I did,' he agreed reluctantly. 'But what does that have to do with it?'

She nodded that mechanical doll-like nod of hers – once, twice, three times. 'Everything.'

'How can enjoying it make it right? For God's sake, Margot, we are talking about incest!'

'Darling Arthur,' she said reproachfully, 'how can you commit incest when you don't know you're doing it?' Her eyes wavered. 'What's so terrible about incest, anyway?' Before he could reply she added, 'Besides, I'm only your half-sister, so it was really only half incest.' Seeing the look of disgust on his face, she trilled with amusement.

'Incest is a sin.'

'Who says?'

'It's a sin against nature.'

'Really Arthur,' she said, pouting, 'you're beginning to sound like the most frightful prig. How can incest be a sin against nature? Doesn't the bible say "love thy brother"? Well, brother, that's exactly what I did. I loved you, I loved every bit of you. People do it all the time. It's been going on since Adam and Eve. The ones who call it a sin would be doing it if they had half a chance. Who makes these silly rules anyway? If it tastes good, it must be bad. The greatest sin is enjoying yourself.'

She was right about one thing, though it was precious little comfort to him. He had no reason to blame himself, no logical reason at all; but the truth was that logic had nothing to do with it. The shame he felt was not logical, it was instinctive. He most profoundly believed that what he had done was a sin, one of the greatest sins of all. Involuntarily he touched the scar on his cheek where the eagle clawed him.

To the end she taunted him. 'Such a looker you turned out to be, brother. You were stunning then, of course, but just a boy really, so sweet and innocent. Look at you now. A hunk. A real man.' She shook her head in admiration. 'And how about that divine uniform!' Moving close to him again, she ran the tips of her fingers down the shiny buttons of his jacket.

In spite of himself he was aroused. 'For God's sake, Margot.'

'You really are delicious,' she whispered. 'I could eat you.' Before he could stop her, she was standing on tiptoe and kissing him full on the lips, all the time smiling that enticing smile of hers.

Rushing out of the library he ran upstairs to his room. In the bathroom he rubbed his mouth raw with soap and water; but hard as he scrubbed, he could not wipe away the memory of that kiss. Hours later when he came downstairs for dinner, he could still feel the touch of her lips on his.

That night he lay sleepless, thinking about the unborn child. Would it have been a boy or a girl? How old would it have been now? Not much older than Mordred. She must have given birth to Mordred only a year or so after the abortion, perhaps as some kind of compensation. Grief and guilt in equal measure numbed his spirit. He was amazed that Margot should be so untouched by it all. Far from feeling shame, she seemed positively to take pleasure in what she had done. It was beyond his understanding. She had to be the most amoral person he had ever met, and for that he almost envied her. How much simpler life would be without the prickings of a conscience.

He searched his memory, recalling every second of the time they spent together. Again and again he tormented himself with the same question. Did she know? He remembered every word she said . . . *Fate makes us do bad things, and then it makes us suffer for them. There was nothing we could do about it. It was meant to happen* . . . The unspeakable now had a voice, and the voice a face, and the face a smile that mocked and shamed him.

He had tried to live a good life, and yet he was tainted by the primeval sin of incest. Surely he had not deserved that. But then, from deep down in his unconscious mind, his own voice rose up to condemn him. *Have we met before? Do I know you?* Why had he asked her that? Could he have known that Margot was his sister when he slept with her? Could Oedipus have known he was bedding his mother? No, that was impossible. Surely Oedipus was the victim of a malign fate?

The memory could never be erased, neither the guilt nor the shame of it. For the rest of his life he would have to confront what he had done. It made no difference that they were both guilty; shared guilt did not lighten the burden of the crime.

Twenty Seven

TWENTY-ONE TROOP under Major Pendragon crossed the border in darkness and trudged fifty miles, moving by night, holing up by day. The south-eastern corner of the Kingdom of the Euphrates was a barren desert, one of the hottest and most arid places on earth, known to the army as Kew Gardens. On the fourth day the fifteen man troop reached their objective. Jurassic Hill rose precipitously from the sand, the only significant elevation for miles, curiously alien to its surroundings. With its sloping body and jutting head, it reared menacingly above the desert like some great prehistoric creature. Here the troop set up camp and waited.

By day the temperature climbed to sixty degrees, the burning heat and relentless swarms of flies making it impossible to sleep. By night the temperature dropped below freezing. It was then that the men needed to be most alert, but despite the bitter cold they were sleepy. If there was a less hospitable place in the world, no one in the troop had been there.

On the afternoon of the eighth day the enemy arrived in a chaotic caravan of trucks and armoured cars, and camped a mile west of Jurassic Hill. They took their time, making not the slightest effort to conceal themselves. Clearly they had no idea they were being observed.

A few hundred yards to the east of Twenty-one Troop's position was Wadi Jahmah, a village of about a thousand inhabitants, eight hundred or so women and children, the rest elderly men; the young men of combat age were either hiding up in the hills or dead.

Two weeks ago Twenty-one Troop had located the rebel force by satellite, since when they had monitored their communications round the clock. It had not been difficult. So arrogantly confident were the rebels that they communicated openly by radio, neglecting to use even the most basic safeguards, frequency-hopping and encryption. By the time the enemy set up camp, Arthur knew everything he needed to know about them. The rebels planned to attack Wadi Jahmah the following morning. In the last twelve months several villages had been "cleansed". The methods were always the same. Every man and child was slaughtered, and the women raped before they too were brutally disposed of. Anyone who attempted to flee, worse still to resist, would be tortured and mutilated – men castrated, women's breasts cut off – and left to die in the desert.

Sergeant Bedivere had great respect for Arthur; to be a major at the age of twenty-four was good going in any regiment, remarkable in this one. It took two years to turn a man into a Special Operations soldier, and once he was trained he could operate anywhere in the world. He could parachute or hang-glide, climb ice and rock faces, fight in any conditions with a multitude of weapons. In his service with the regiment George Bedivere had come across many exceptional men, though none to compare with Major Pendragon. It was an honour to be part of the regiment, an even greater honour to serve under the major, a natural born leader.

The great vault of the desert sky was luminous, crammed with stars, awash with galaxies. Twenty-one-Troop's positions, however, were in deepest shadow. At fifteen minutes past eleven Arthur's headset beeped, and for a few seconds he listened intently. Then he nodded to the sergeant. 'It's on,' he confirmed. 'We move at four a.m. while it's still dark.'

Sergeant Bedivere was a cautious man. 'Let's hope they didn't get a fix on us.'

Arthur shook his head. 'They didn't spot us before. They're

not going to now.'

'All the same,' pointed out Bedivere, 'they outnumber us six to one.'

'That means the odds are in our favour.'

'How come?'

Arthur grinned. 'Man for man, we're ten times better than they are.'

Did it ever occur to the major that things could go wrong? Probably not. Sergeant Bedivere checked his automatic weapon for the umpteenth time, but his thoughts were far away. 'Ever think about death?'

'Sometimes,' admitted Arthur.

'It's not the dying that worries me,' said Bedivere, 'it's the bit that comes before.' He grinned wryly.

'You'll live to be a hundred and fifty, George,' said Arthur reassuringly, and focused his mind on the party to come.

There was an important job to be done. The so-called "coalition" had handed Iraq back to the Iraqi people in 2005. In 2007, at the insistence of the fledgling Iraqi government and the U.N., American and British troops were withdrawn. Less than a year later the country was torn apart by civil war – Sunni against Shiite, with the Kurds caught in the middle. The United States had been badly burned invading Iraq in 2003 and was reluctant to intervene again. Whilst the U.N. dithered, order was quickly and brutally restored by Sadiq el Shaeb (the People's Friend), well disposed to the west, and an enemy of international terrorism. Under his leadership a group of the most powerful tribes formed the K.O.E – the Kingdom of the Euphrates. But in the east of the K.O.E. there were still problems. The aim of the rebels, said Sadiq, was to destabilise the K.O.E., creating the kind of chaos in which international terrorists thrived. When Sadiq appealed to Britain, the government did not hesitate. A small contingent of special forces was sent out, their task to destroy the rebels and prevent the slaughter of innocents.

Three am. An hour to go. The sergeant was sleeping like a baby. Arthur moved silently down from the summit to the makeshift HQ. where, in a primitive shelter on a barren hill in the desert, all the paraphernalia of a high-tech war room was installed, computers and monitors, communications and radar, surveillance equipment, and the remote control of complex weapons systems.

'Any sign of movement?'

'Dead to the world, sir.'

Arthur was taking no chances. 'Lock on sensors.'

'Sensors locked.'

'Identify to scanner.'

'Scanning.'

Arthur studied the rebel camp through night vision glasses, referring all the time to the neat stack of screens and computers that monitored every movement, every sound, every variation of temperature. For days they had observed and analysed the advancing enemy by thermal imaging and sound and seismic sensors, while laser detectors picked up the minutest reflections from such things as gunsights and binoculars. The rebels were a small but formidable force: ninety-three soldiers, six trucks, two armoured cars. Their equipment was not sophisticated, but it was effective – automatic weapons, rocket launchers, missiles, some with high explosive, some with chemical, some with biological warheads. They could take on a battalion or destroy a sizeable city, not to mention a small, defenceless village. The irony was, as Arthur knew from experience, that they rarely used their devastating battery of weapons. What was the point of wasting precious ammunition when knives would do the job just as well? He was satisfied. It was clear the rebels had no idea that the British army was in the area. 'Thanks, John. I'll be giving you the signal to lock on weapons systems.'

'I'll be here. Nowhere else to go.'

Arthur nodded at the photograph by the computer. 'How's

Sally?'

'She's great, sir. We're starting a family.'

'You didn't tell me you were married.'

'We're not.'

'Ah,' said Arthur.

A bit square about things like that was the major; he got that look on his face sometimes, and you knew he didn't quite approve. All the same he was cool, he might not approve but he understood, and that was more important. He was one of the few officers who did, and the only one who knew all about the private life of every man in the squadron, who screwed around, who didn't, how many kids they had – in or out of matrimony – who they were sleeping with, who they'd like to sleep with, who was straight and who was gay. Men talked to him about their personal stuff. They trusted him, and they knew his interest in them was genuine.

'Is it going to be alright, sir?'

'Yes, John. It's going to be alright.'

Twenty minutes to go. Arthur made his way back up the hill, where George was snoring like a rhinoceros. The adrenaline was stirring, the saliva drying up in his mouth. Gently he shook the sergeant awake. 'Time to move, George.' In an instant Bedivere was alert. 'Here we go again.' They clasped hands. No need for words. The radio crackled in Arthur's headset. For a few moments he listened. 'I copy,' he said, his voice flat.

'What is it, sir?'

'The party's off.'

'Why, for God's sake?'

'Something about satisfactory assurances received,' said Arthur. 'No details.'

'You mean those bastards down there are not going to attack the village?'

'That's what they say.'

Arthur went down the hill to tell the men. After so many days of preparation, their reaction was naturally bad.

'What the hell do we do now, sir?'

'Sit tight. Our orders are not to engage the enemy. So we wait until they've gone. Whatever happens, they mustn't spot us.'

In the east the early morning sky was streaked with red. The camp below them stirred to life. Striking camp was as shambolic and undisciplined as setting up had been. A couple of hours later the trucks and armoured cars moved off in a westerly direction loaded with men and equipment.

'They kept their word,' said Bedivere.

Arthur nodded. 'Looks like it.' They watched the convoy disappear over the horizon, and they were still watching when the dust settled.

'What made them change their mind, sir?'

'Some kind of political solution. So in a way this party has been a success,' said Arthur, trying to sound convinced.

It was not yet eight a.m. The sun was low and the air still relatively cool. With the lifting of tension the men relaxed, allowing sleep to overwhelm their exhausted bodies. Arthur and Sergeant Bedivere climbed back up to the summit to keep watch. For a few minutes they fought sleep, but it was a losing battle.

Two hours later Arthur woke with a start, his heart pounding. Something was wrong. Suddenly the silence was broken by a scream of pain and terror and the sound of weeping. It came from the village. The rattle of automatic fire was followed by more screams. Every man in the troop grabbed his gun and leaped to his feet.

'Down!' cried Arthur, but he was too late. Automatic weapons opened up from every direction. In the first few seconds three men were killed and several wounded as the rest of the troop scrambled for cover behind rocks and scrub. For several minutes they were unable to move, not even to sight their guns, so heavy and accurate was the enemy fire. Arthur cursed himself for a fool; he had fallen into a classic trap.

Whilst his troop were asleep the rebels had sneaked back, some moving on to attack the village, the rest surrounding Jurassic Hill. Twenty-one Troop was pinned down.

'Fancy a quiet stroll, George?' whispered Arthur.

A wry smile. 'I think I'll wait till the bastards go home.'

'They're not going anywhere,' said Arthur grimly, 'not until their friends have slaughtered everyone in the village.'

George was a brave man, but he was also a realist. 'Nothing we can do about it.'

'Yes there is. We'll move down the east slope to the Wadi. That'll give us cover.'

George's eyes popped. 'In your dreams. The village is four hundred yards away. The Wadi can't be more than two hundred and fifty yards long.'

'More than enough,' said Arthur. 'When we run out of Wadi we'll make a break for it. I'll go first. You and the troop give me covering fire.' He was loading up with extra ammo.

Jesus, the man was serious! 'Forget it, sir,' urged Bedivere.

Arthur ignored him. 'Listen carefully, George. When I reach the Wadi, you, Rod, Harry, Ben and Elvis join me. Leave the rest of the lads here. They'll give you covering fire.'

'The rest of what lads?' asked George.

'They can still fire a gun even if they're wounded.'

'We'll be sitting ducks,' said George Bedivere gloomily.

Arthur grinned. 'See you down there.' He waved an arm in farewell as he moved off.

'You'll never make it, sir.'

But he did. And so did the rest of them.

The fire fight in the village was short and savage. When it was over, forty rebels lay dead. The rest of the gang fled. Of the six soldiers in the attack, only Arthur and George Bedivere were left standing. Two men took a direct hit from a mortar shell, one was blown to pieces when a bullet hit a grenade in the pack strapped to his waist, and one stepped on a mine, an American one as it happened. Sergeant Bedivere thought it was all over when a mercenary who was feigning dead jumped up and swung a long knife. As it flashed down on George's skull, Arthur fired a burst from his automatic rifle. The man was hurled back by the impact of the bullets, and the knife missed George's head by inches. But it sliced clean through his wrist, and there was his right hand lying in the sand. Of the thousand or so villagers, nine hundred survived unscathed, the rest were either shot or had their throats cut. A number were beheaded, perhaps because they had tried to resist the rebels.

It was unthinkable that those brutal murders should go unpunished. The instant the last casualty was helicoptered out, Arthur turned his attention to an armoured car abandoned by the rebels. Almost the entire chassis was exposed, most of the body having been ripped off by grenades and missiles. But the undercarriage and the engine were more or less intact. Miraculously, it started.

Taking with him two men, a mortar, a hand-held missile launcher, grenades, and a stack of automatic weapons and ammunition, he drove across the desert through the night. Just before sunrise he caught up with the main body of rebel soldiers. They had heard the armoured car in the distance, and knew it was heading for them. Recognising its peculiar engine hum, they prepared to greet their comrades; by the time they realised their mistake it was all over for them. Not a man was left alive.

PART TWO

Father and Son

One

A RTHUR stood stiffly to attention.

'You were given clear instructions to call off the operation,' said his Commanding Officer, a tall spare man with close-cropped greying hair.

'Yes, sir,' acknowledged Arthur.

'You disobeyed orders,' said the C.O. rapping his desk with his hand to emphasise each word.

'Yes, sir.' Arthur showed no sign of contrition.

Colonel Harcourt's voice was stern but his pale blue eyes surprisingly kindly. 'You're a fine soldier, Pendragon. I don't know that I ever came across a better officer.'

'Thank you, sir.'

'If you were to be court-martialled . . . ' – the C.O. shrugged – 'we all know what the verdict would be. Guilty. Dishonourable discharge. End of story.'

Not a muscle moved in Arthur's face. 'A brilliant career down the drain,' continued the colonel, 'reputation tarnished. I don't think you deserve that. Do you?'

'Not for me to say, sir,' intoned Arthur.

'For God's sake, man, the Foreign Office are after your blood. I'm trying to help you.' The colonel fiddled with the paper knife on his desk. 'They don't call us the Family for nothing,' he said quietly. 'A special bond and all that. Give me some ammo, Arthur.'

After a time, Arthur said, 'I was told to stand down the troop. When I asked for an explanation, they said a deal had been struck, the rebels had given an undertaking to leave the area. Obviously they never meant to keep their word and someone must have told them we were there. They set us up, made us think they really had withdrawn, and then they slipped back, surrounded our positions on Jurassic Hill and attacked the village.'

'You certainly had a right to defend yourself and your men,' agreed the colonel, 'but that's all.'

'We prevented a massacre, sir.'

The colonel prided himself on being diplomatic rather than confrontational. 'Could I tell the powers that be that there was some misunderstanding on your part?'

Arthur stared straight ahead. 'There was no misunderstanding.'

'Some confusion about the order itself?' The C.O. was inviting Arthur to help him find a compromise.

The invitation was firmly rejected. 'There was no confusion, sir.'

The colonel shrugged; there was nothing more he could do. It was hard to help a man who refused to help himself. 'They want to see you, Pendragon.'

'They, sir?'

'Some Under Secretary in the Foreign Office, I imagine. Whoever it is, take my advice and eat humble pie. You might just get off with a reprimand.'

It was not some Under Secretary who had summoned Arthur. It was the Foreign Secretary himself – his father, Uther Pendragon. Uther had played a key role in fashioning the New Millennium Party, the phoenix that rose from the ashes of the old Conservative Party. When they lost their fourth successive election by a landslide in 2009 the Tories were compelled to accept that they were looking extinction in the face. A palace revolution of young and ambitious M.P.'s led to the dumping of the Old Guard, Robert Marriott was elected leader and Uther Pendragon brought in as Party Chairman. Politics, Uther reminded his colleagues, had long ceased to be about ideology; it was about image and good management. Under his direction the old Conservative Party became the New Millennium Party, albeit a little late for the new millennium, its image restyled to appeal to a broader electorate. It was a heaven-sent opportunity for Uther who used all his P.R. skills, adapting many of Tony Blair's tactics in creating New Labour in the nineties. When, largely thanks to Uther, Robert Marriot became Prime Minister in 2013, he had shown Uther his gratitude with a seat in the cabinet, first as Secretary of State for Trade and Industry, more recently as Foreign Secretary.

'Normally I would not be handling this myself, but you're my son and you're in trouble. I should like to help.'

'Thank you, sir.'

'Sit down, and let's dispense with the formalities.' Uther placed a chair opposite Arthur, sat astride it, arms resting on the back, and regarded his son thoughtfully. 'This is a bad business, Arthur. It's been handled clumsily. Happens all too often when you delegate to petty officials. I know you're a man of integrity, I know you did what you thought was right. Trouble is, my people don't see it that way. They are setting you up as some kind of troublemaker. They say you had some sinister motive for what you did.'

'I would never do anything to embarrass the Regiment,' said Arthur.

'Nor His Majesty's Government, I imagine?'

No reply.

'No, of course not,' said Uther, answering for him. This was not going to be easy. 'I'll come straight to the point. You disobeyed an order, a particularly crucial one as it happens. What's more, you did it on the field of battle, or what passes for the field of battle these days.'

Arthur looked his father in the eye. 'You can have my resignation if it helps you, sir.'

'It isn't me who needs help,' said Uther acidly, abandoning

245

the laid-back approach and seating himself behind his massive mahogany desk. Was he pulling rank, Arthur wondered, or taking shelter?

'Soldiers, Arthur . . . they think they run the show, but they don't. A soldier is not required to express opinions, he's required to do what he's told. His job is to obey orders. Why? Because we live in a democracy. In a democracy the army does not run the country. The politicians do.'

'Hitler was a politician, sir,' Arthur pointed out.

Uther scowled. 'That is impertinent.'

'They hung men for obeying Hitler's orders.'

'Enough!'

Silence.

No, it was not going to be easy. 'I have the very greatest respect for the Special Forces, Arthur. For you too. I hear excellent things about you.'

'Good of you to say so, sir,' said Arthur stolidly.

'Don't waste it, my boy, I beg you. Don't throw it all away. You are young. Like all young people, you think everything you do is right and everything the older generation does is wrong.'

That was not how Arthur saw it. 'I like to understand the orders I'm given, that's all. I'm a soldier, not a robot.'

Uther smoothed the leather desktop. 'In that case, let me share a confidence with you. I dare say you have heard the expression *Realpolitik*?'

'I have.'

'Politics based on reality, Arthur – on reality, not on principles, not on morals, not on ideals. On reality.' Uther moved across to the window and looked out, a studied gesture that somehow seemed to imply that the world was a bigger and altogether more complex place than Arthur could possibly know. 'What I am about to tell you must not leave this room. Do I have your word?'

'Of course.'

Uther returned to his desk. 'The tribes in the east have

been a thorn in Sadiq's side for years. So he financed some mercenaries to "cleanse" the Eastern provinces for him – not wholesale slaughter, you understand, but enough to scare the eastern tribesmen out of the country. It was going pretty well . . . ' – He coughed – 'for Sadiq, I mean. But then the whole thing got out of hand. The mercenaries he hired were becoming too powerful. They were a threat to him. He invited us in, not because he wanted to stop the killing, and not because he feared a rebel uprising, but because he wanted to show the mercenaries who was boss.'

'Then why did you call off the operation?'

'Sadiq made a deal with the mercenaries,' said Uther.

Deal. A clandestine word, thought Arthur, the innocent-looking stone that covered the creepy crawlies. 'What sort of deal?'

'Sadiq is a shrewd politician. Knows how to divide and rule. That's why he's lasted so long. So what does he do? He gives the mercenaries a free hand in the East in exchange for their loyalty.'

'A free hand? Meaning they were free to continue slaughtering innocent people?'

'Those tribesmen have been at each others' throats for centuries,' said Uther imperturbably. 'Nothing we do will stop them killing each other.'

Arthur's blue eyes glittered. 'That is patronising, racist rubbish.'

A few stunned moments passed whilst Uther absorbed the rebuke, as a jousting knight absorbs the lance's thrust. The challenge could scarcely have been more direct or more powerful, and the insolence of it staggered him. How quickly the raw youth had become a man, and how ruthless in condemning his father. Uther was tempted to teach his son a lesson. A court martial was what he deserved, and a court martial was what he really ought to get; the problem, however, was the media. They would have the greatest sympathy for a hero of the Special Forces. It would not look good for the government if the truth came out. It would certainly not look good for the Foreign Secretary.

'I'm a generous soul, Arthur, as you know, so I'll overlook that comment. I am also prepared to overlook your indiscretion. On certain conditions. First, you tender a written apology; second, you give me your word that you will never disobey orders again; third, none of this will be discussed with the media, or anyone else for that matter. I can't say fairer than that, now can I?' Uther jumped up, hand extended. 'Come, my boy, let's shake on it. You are my son and a gutsy fellow. Let's bury the hatchet. Is it a deal?'

Deal. That furtive word again. 'There'll be no more killings?'

'I devoutly hope not. After all, we do have some influence with Sadiq.'

'What kind of influence?'

'We sell him arms, Arthur.' Uther spread his arms expansively. 'Rather a lot of arms in fact. Some people have their doubts, of course, but . . . ' A shrug.

'What sort of doubts?'

'Well . . . this is all highly confidential, Arthur . . . do I have your word . . . ?'

'I already gave it.'

A suspicious look. Uther trusted no one, not even his son. 'Iran is not the only player in the terrorist game, though they have always been a major one, even more so since they developed nuclear weapons. The fact is, the CIA, MI5 and Mossad believe that Sadiq finances and supports terror groups responsible for various bombings across the globe. Naturally we have had to be . . . discreet about that. The general public know nothing about it.'

Arthur could hardly believe what he was hearing. 'You are saying Sadiq is a terrorist?'

'In a way, dear boy. But,' a disarming smile, 'at least he's *our* terrorist.'

'What is that supposed to mean?'

'He might be responsible for the odd bombing here and there,' said Uther casually, 'but he would never bomb London or anything ungrateful like that. Why should he? He's in our pay. He's our man. That's why we had to help him out. You do see that, don't you?'

Arthur leaned forward in his chair. 'I want to be sure I understand you. Are you telling me it is now this government's policy to support mass murderers, just as long as they leave us alone?'

Uther spread his hands apologetically. 'I fear it's the only way to handle an intractable problem.'

'And you think that's the way to defeat the terrorists? Well sir, I don't. It's cowardly, it's short-sighted, and it's immoral.'

'Immoral!' echoed Uther derisively. 'What nonsense. Get real, Arthur. Come out of the woods. This is life, this is the world. What does morality have to do with the twenty-first Century? This is not about the Ten Commandments, this is about looking after number one – or Number 10, if you like.' Uther chuckled at his own witticism.

'There is still such a thing as right and wrong, truth and lies,' said Arthur. 'The lies of our leaders contaminate every man and woman in the country. They lose faith not just in politicians but in our way of life. How can we expect people to live an honest decent life if you set them such a dishonest example?'

Uther was unimpressed. 'Don't be so bloody naïve, Arthur. We're not talking right and wrong here; we're talking self-preservation. You think we're the only ones making deals with terrorists? Well I've got news for you. I could give you a list as long as your arm: China, Russia, America, Pakistan, India, Iran, France . . . dozens of countries. Quite apart from buying insurance, there's the arms trade to consider. It's hugely competitive. Frankly, we can't afford to be left out of it.'

'This is madness,' said Arthur. 'We are selling our enemies the weapons to destroy us. If you sow the wind, you reap the storm.'

Uther sighed. 'Do try not to preach, my boy. You are beginning to sound like Merlin.'

'You can jeer as much as you like, father,' said Arthur angrily. 'But the fact is, you have blood on your hands. Now I know what those men, women and children in the K.O.E. died for. They died for an arms deal. *Your* arms deal. That makes you as guilty as Sadiq.' He could hardly conceal his disgust.

Uther mangled a notepad, wishing it were his son's neck. 'Being a major in the army does not qualify you to pronounce on foreign policy,' he said coldly.

'Nor does it disqualify me from having an opinion.'

Uther was wondering what lay behind Arthur's protests. Being young, he was naturally a bit of an idealist, one of youth's more boring afflictions. Yet there had to be more to it than that, some hidden agenda. He thought he knew what it was. 'Best stick to things you understand, my boy. Politics is not for you.'

'I have no interest in politics,' Arthur assured his father, 'I'm a soldier.'

A hostile glare. 'If you want to continue being a soldier, you had better learn to do what you are told. If you had done so on this occasion, several men in your troop would still be alive.'

The blood rose in Arthur's face. 'If my troop had not intervened, a thousand innocent civilians would have been slaughtered. And you were willing to let that happen, something your constituents might be interested to know.'

Uther scorned the implied threat. 'Do you really think so? You know your problem, Arthur? You don't understand human nature. You think the man in the street gives a toss who lives or dies in the Kingdom of the Euphrates? Of course he doesn't. You want to know what he cares about? He cares about jobs, pay packets, mortgages, interest rates, vacations, the price of booze and cigarettes and petrol. Our arms trade with Sadiq is good for the economy. It's worth a few thousand jobs a year.'

'So tell me, father,' asked Arthur, stung by his father's cynicism, 'how many butchered men, women and children are the equivalent of one job? What's the going rate of exchange these days?'

'Easy for you to scoff, my boy. You don't have to make those calculations.'

'And you do?'

'I'm afraid I do,' said Uther, 'but if you quote me, I'll say you're a liar.'

It was wasted breath. If he and his father talked till doomsday they would never agree. 'Whatever happened to that ethical foreign policy you promised when they made you Foreign Secretary?'

Uther sat stiffly erect. 'It is a Foreign Secretary's duty to promote his country's interests overseas. That obligation is paramount.'

'Then why did you make the promise?' asked Arthur.

'Why?' Uther seemed surprised at the question. 'To impress the electorate, of course. Does that shock you? I see it does. Nevertheless, people understand politicians better than you think. No one takes that sort of statement seriously.'

'I do.'

'Then,' said Uther sadly, 'I fear you are extremely gullible.'

Arthur stood up to go. 'Permission to leave, sir?'

Uther's fingers drummed his desk nervously. If his son left now in this rebellious mood, he would most likely go straight to the tabloids. Uther drew a deep breath and forced his reluctant features into a smile.

'I fear the petty officials have handled this badly. What's more, I haven't done much better. Sit down, my boy. I owe you an apology. *Mea culpa*. Please forgive me.'

'Perhaps,' said Arthur, after a pause, 'I was too quick to condemn.'

'Think nothing of it,' said Uther jovially. 'Put it down to the Pendragon temperament.' He beamed at his son. 'You will make a fine leader of the regiment.'

'It's a long way from major to colonel.'

An insinuating smile and a wink. 'Indeed it is. But these things can be speeded up.'

It was distasteful to be offered such a blatant bribe by your own father. Arthur made no comment. To Uther's frustration his wretched son was adamant – no apology, not even a verbal one, and absolutely no commitment for the future. But furious as he was with Arthur for defying him, Uther was a realist. He knew when he was beaten. The truth was he didn't give a damn that Arthur had disobeyed orders, and just as long as he kept his mouth shut the government could spin that mini-disaster in the K.O.E into a triumph. A phone call to the Ministry of Defence ensured there would be no court martial. Believing he could count on his son's discretion, he had taken a calculated risk. What could Arthur possibly hope to gain by discrediting the government, still less his own father? Uther was satisfied he had read the situation correctly and handled it appropriately.

Even so, his son was becoming much too independent-minded for his liking.

Two

COLONEL HARCOURT had made it clear to Arthur that the 'slight hiccup over that K.O.E. incident' was well and truly forgotten. Moreover the Colonel had dropped a broad hint that he would shortly be taking early retirement, and that Arthur was being very seriously considered as his successor. The C.O. also stressed that the appointment would be made purely on merit, and that Arthur's father would have no influence whatever on the selection process. That unexpected news compelled Arthur to consider his future more seriously than ever. The conversation with his father had disturbed and confused him; he was not at all sure now that he wanted to make the army his career. He needed to think, and he needed to talk to the one person he trusted above all others.

'They tell me if I stay in the regiment I'll be in line for the top job,' said Arthur.

Merlin was impressed. 'C.O. of Special Forces. You've done well, Art. Outstandingly well.' Arthur flushed. A compliment from the magus was still something to be prized. 'But is it what you really want?'

'I'm not sure.'

'Well I am,' said Merlin positively. 'My advice is to leave the army as soon as possible.'

It was what Arthur needed to hear, although he had not admitted it to himself until this moment. Merlin was prodding him in the direction he wanted to go. He had loved being a soldier, it was exciting and it had taught him many things, not least about himself. Now it was time to move on.

'If I left the army what would I do?'

'Only you know the answer to that.'

'But I really don't know,' said Arthur. 'It's all so confusing.'

'Somewhere in the turmoil of your mind,' said Merlin, 'there is a spot where everything is calm.' The green eyes and the voice were both hypnotic. 'Let go, Arthur. Let your thoughts be taken by the whirlwind, and in the end you will find that quiet spot. Only then will you know what it is you really want to do.'

Arthur sat at the pine table in Merlin's kitchen, chin in hands, dreaming as he used to dream when he was a lad. His thoughts spun slowly at first, then faster and faster until, tossed and tumbled, they were flung by the whirlwind into a calm and restful place where, as Merlin had promised, Arthur's mind was at peace and he knew at last what it was he truly wanted. The trouble was it seemed so presumptuous. 'I would like to change the world,' said Arthur. 'Does that sound ridiculous?'

'It sounds like very good sense to me,' said Merlin.

'Perhaps,' suggested Arthur, that little mole of thought tunnelling in his forehead just underneath the skin, 'perhaps I could do something for poor and disadvantaged people.'

Merlin sat back in his chair, clasped his hands behind his neck and studied the wooden beams that supported the kitchen ceiling. 'If that's what you want, then you must do it. But don't deceive yourself, Arthur, you are not going to change the world by doing good work.' A searching look. 'Have you ever considered politics?

Arthur's only serious encounter with politics was one he would never forget, being carpeted by his father after that unhappy business in the K.O.E., and it had left a bad taste in his mouth. If all politicians were as cynical and disillusioned as his father, what was the point of going into politics? And anyway was it not a strange suggestion coming from Merlin? Did the magus not have other ideas for him?

'Only a stepping stone, of course,' said Merlin with a

knowing look.

A stepping stone to what? Arthur ignored the not so subtle hint. Merlin had not mentioned that troubling word 'destiny', but Arthur sensed it was in the air. 'My father says politicians can never change anything. If that's true, then what is the point of being a politician? I certainly wouldn't want to serve under him.'

'No need to,' said Merlin. From his perch on the mantelpiece Virgil nodded his head and hooh-hooed, as if agreeing with his master. 'There are other fiddlers and other tunes to play.'

Leo Grant was leader of the main opposition party in the House of Commons, formerly New Labour, renamed United Labour in 2012 following an eruption of bitter internecine strife. At Merlin's recommendation Arthur went to see Leo at his house in Bayswater.

Leo took to Arthur immediately. He knew something of his reputation – strong-minded, intelligent, responsible beyond his years, a young man who knew how to handle himself. 'Merlin tells me you are considering a career in politics.'

'Perhaps. It's his idea, really,' said Arthur. 'I'm certainly thinking of leaving the army.'

Leo had heard as much and wondered why. 'I understand you're in line for the top job in your regiment. If that's the case, why throw away such a wonderful opportunity?'

'I want to make a difference, sir,' said Arthur firmly. 'I want to change the world.'

Leo weighed up the young man. Coming from anyone else the response would have sounded pretentious, but somehow not from Arthur; he was unashamedly serious. 'If you feel that strongly, then I wouldn't hesitate,' said Leo. 'I'm sure your father would be delighted to have you in the New Millennium Party.' An innocent enough comment. There was nevertheless an implied question in it that was not lost on Arthur. Leo was challenging him to decide where his political loyalties lay.

'I know very little about politics, sir. One thing I have discovered though . . . ' Arthur looked round the room, untidy, comfortable, books on tables, books on the floor, books everywhere. He had heard that Leo Grant was a thinker, a man of principle and strong beliefs. For some reason he reminded him of Merlin – about ten years older perhaps – late fifties, Arthur guessed. 'My father is a clever man and a very successful politician, but . . . ' Arthur hesitated. 'He and I see the world very differently. I'm not sure I want to join New Millennium.'

'It could be in your best interest to do so,' said Leo Grant, playing the devil's advocate.

'With the greatest respect, sir,' said Arthur obstinately, 'the way I see it, my best interest is to be as independent as possible. I'm not sure how independent I can be working in my father's shadow.'

Interesting, thought Leo, here was a young man of conviction, someone he obviously needed to get to know better. Over the next few weeks Arthur visited Leo regularly, and from him he learned much about politics and also about the strengths and failings of politicians. Some of what Leo told him about his father confirmed what he already suspected: Uther's chief role as Foreign Secretary was to make secret deals with terror groups – 'buy them off' as Leo put it. 'Marriott and his cabinet decided long ago that the war against terrorists cannot be won,' he said. 'Islamist and other terrorists are too numerous, too well-organised and too highly motivated. The best you can hope for, they argue, is to contain them. To do that you have to make deals.'

'My father admitted to me that he made a deal with Sadiq. I thought that might be an exception to the rule. Are you saying that kind of arrangement is UK government policy?'

'I fear so,' said Leo. 'Unfortunately there are signs that this country is not alone. Other world leaders are trying to make their own deals with terror groups. Some of the extremists won't deal, but most terrorists will, if they can get what they want.'

'Do you think that's the way to counter the terrorist threat?'

Leo took time to answer. 'The problem is, the more you make deals with terrorists the more you encourage them to commit acts of terror. So no, it is not the right way, in my opinion. On the other hand, how else do you tackle the problem? The USA, the European Union, the UK, India, Pakistan, China, Japan, Russia, Australia and many other countries have virtually been at war with global terrorists for two decades. Where has it got them? I ask myself, is the world a safer place now than it was twenty years ago? My answer – no, it isn't. If this is a war, then clearly the terrorists are winning. Every year more and more people all over the world are killed and maimed in terrorist attacks – city bombings, kidnappings, missile attacks on trains, aircraft, ships, power plants.'

'So what's the answer?'

'Someone has to make a stand somewhere, somehow, or we shall all be lost.'

Over the next few months the two men became firm friends, and soon Arthur was a regular dinner guest at the older man's house. He learned that Leo's wife had died some years ago and that he had a thirteen year old daughter whom he obviously adored, yet it was not until his seventh or eighth visit that Arthur met her. It was early evening, and Arthur was waiting for Leo in the sitting room when the door opened and a young girl walked in. Arthur jumped up.

'Dad phoned. He said to tell you he's been delayed in the House. He's on his way home.'

'Thank you. You must be Guinevere.'

'Yes.'

'Arthur Pendragon.'

'I know.' She regarded him steadily. 'Dad talks a lot about you.'

'And about you too.'

'He still thinks I'm a little girl. He tells everyone I'm thirteen.' There was a note of disgust in her voice. 'Actually,' – a sharp look at Arthur – 'I shall be fourteen next month.'

'Is that all?'

'You mean I look older?'

'Much.'

A slight flush of pleasure coloured her cheeks. 'How old are you?' she enquired.

For some reason he found himself reluctant to answer the question. 'Twenty-three,' he said. 'Almost twenty-four.'

Head on one side, she considered him carefully. 'Twenty-four is a good age for a man,' she said, adding unexpectedly, 'You are very good-looking. But then I suppose you know that.'

This was certainly one of the most extraordinary conversations Arthur had ever had, and he felt strangely out of his depth. Was this the way thirteen year old girls talked, or was this one unusually outspoken? He considered returning the compliment but decided against it; she might think he was only trying to flatter her. Which would not have been true at all. The compliment would have been perfectly genuine, for she was indeed exceptionally pretty: dark eyes, black hair, wide mouth, long legs. A child, of course, though the emerging woman was already apparent in the way she carried herself, in her direct look, and in her feminine awareness. There was an oddly appealing blend of shyness and self-assurance about her, of awkwardness and grace, of childishness and maturity.

She considered him carefully. 'You have one sad eye and one happy eye. Did you know that?'

'Which is which?'

'You're teasing me,' she said reproachfully.

'I would never do that,' he assured her.

She was studying his face with the most concentrated attention. 'It's very unusual.'

'I imagine it must be,' he said.

When it came to saying good-bye, she held out her hand, and he took it gravely. Polite nods and smiles were exchanged, all in the most formal way imaginable. But if that miniature ceremony was conducted in a manner pointedly guarded, the look of admiration she flashed at him as she ran out of the room was anything but.

When Guinevere reached the privacy of her room, the first thing she did was tear down the photographs of pop idols and movie stars adorning the walls. It took her no more than a few days to find press cuttings and photographs of Arthur to put up in their place. When she returned to boarding school at the beginning of the following term, she immediately confided in her best friend, Gertrude Lancaster, a tall, fun-loving girl with huge eyes. 'Lanky' was thrilled at Guinevere's news, and gushed over a photograph of Arthur Pendragon in full army dress uniform.

'He's a major in the Special Forces,' said Guinevere casually.

Lanky's eyes grew big. 'Oh my God! Look at him. He's a dream! Didn't you just die when you saw him?'

'I thought he was nice,' said Guinevere, looking and sounding very composed.

That was too much for Lanky. 'What do you mean *nice*!' 'He's a *dish*. Did you tell him you liked him?'

Guinevere frowned her disapproval. 'I could never do anything like that.'

'Why not?'

'It would be totally immature. He would lose all respect for me.'

'I don't see what respect has to do with it.' Why, wondered Lanky, did Ginny always complicate the most simple things. 'Either you fancy him or you don't.'

'This isn't some schoolgirl crush,' said Guinevere in her most superior manner. 'I intend to marry Arthur one day.'

'Wow!' Lanky took a few moments to recover her breath.

'You don't think he's a bit old for you, do you?'

Guinevere smiled condescendingly. 'Young men bore me.'

'He's gorgeous,' said Lanky, ogling the photograph.

Guinevere snatched it away. 'Looks aren't everything. It's his character that's important. Arthur Pendragon is a man of consequence.' It was one of her father's favourite expressions, more an acknowledgement of a man's qualities as a human being than an appraisal of his success or celebrity.

'That's all very well,' said Lanky solemnly, 'but are you in love with him?'

'Oh you!' said Guinevere with a toss of her head and a flash of scorn in her eye. 'That's kids' stuff.'

Lanky was puzzled. What could possibly be more important than love? 'If you're not in love with him, how do you know he's the one for you?'

'Because,' explained Guinevere, 'we are compatible.'

Mischief glinted in Lanky's eyes. 'Compatible. That's when the man is twenty-four and the girl is thirteen, is it?'

'I shall be fourteen in a week,' said Guinevere severely.

In an abrupt change of mood, she pushed Lanky onto the bed and began pummelling her with a pillow, with every blow protesting fiercely, 'I'm not in love! I'm not in love!'

Though she worshipped her friend, there was still a great deal about Guinevere that Lanky found hard to understand: Ginny's cool, analytical mind was much to be admired, but what use was it when it came to feelings? Love was Lanky's absolute best thing. Hardly a day passed without her falling in love with someone or other, and she asked little enough in return. She would fall in love with a pop star for a signed photograph, or a classmate for a friendly glance, yes, even if they were not compatible and he was of no consequence at all. But understand her or not, oh, how Lanky wished she were half as mature, half as sensible and one tenth as beautiful as Guinevere. Most boys in the school were openly in love with her and the rest were too shy to admit it. Ginny, of course, was indifferent to all of them. A lot of girls thought her big-headed and vain for being so stand-offish, but not Lanky. Ginny deserved someone special; she had proved that, hadn't she? Only thirteen years old, and already she had a mature admirer, and not just any admirer, but dishy Arthur Pendragon. This was no teenage fantasy, this was the real thing.

One day, for sure, she would marry Arthur. For never for a single moment did Lanky doubt that what Ginny wanted, Ginny would get.

Three

2019

IT CAME AS A SURPRISE and something of a shock to Uther to hear that Arthur had resigned his commission in the army. His son's service career had been distinguished, and it was an open secret that he would have become Colonel of the Regiment. Even more disturbing to Uther was certain information he had recently obtained from his sources; Arthur was spending a great deal of time in the company of Leo Grant, Leader of the Opposition. Fraternising with the enemy? What could it mean? If, by any chance, Arthur was considering a political career, why had he not consulted his father who was in a better position to help him than anyone else? By nature suspicious, Uther tried to convince himself that his son's behaviour, though odd, was innocent enough. Arthur was, after all, a novice in the ways of the world. Neverthless the fact was, whether by accident or design, that his son's ship was heading the wrong way and needed a swift course correction. Who but Uther could do what was so obviously necessary? He invited his son to lunch at a smart Westminster restaurant much frequented by politicians. Being seen in Arthur's company would send the right message to M.P.s, journalists, and anyone else of influence who might be dining there.

There seemed little point in rushing things. Over starter and main course Uther chatted amiably about this and that, studiously avoiding anything contentious, confining himself to some chit-chat about the family, some choice Westminster gossip, and a couple of political jokes which Arthur laughed at politely. Over coffee Uther lit a cigar with some deliberation, leaned back, blew an aggressive stream of smoke at the ceiling and dangled the bait. 'A little bird told me you might be interested in becoming an M.P. Is that right?'

Arthur grinned. 'I have to be elected first.'

'We'll soon find you a suitable constituency,' said Uther confidently. 'Shouldn't take long. People die all the time.'

'How do you mean, suitable?' said Arthur warily.

'A *safe* seat,' Uther extended his arms in an expansive gesture. 'What else would be good enough for my son?' His cigar glowed red as he drew on it.

Arthur fiddled with a bread roll. 'That's good of you, father, but I would rather take my chances.'

'Of course, of course.' A shrewd look from under lowered brows. 'If that's how you prefer it,' said Uther, confident that his son would change his tune when he discovered how difficult it was to find a 'safe' seat without his old man's blessing. 'Just what the party needs. A man of principle.'

'Thank you, sir.'

'On the other hand . . . ' – Uther leaned back, eyes narrowed – 'you might like to consider short-circuiting the usual tedious procedure.' Another stream of smoke hit the ceiling and bellied out, sending long tendrils of smoke wriggling snake-like down the walls. A few diners coughed ostentatiously and looked indignantly in Uther's direction. Uther stared right through them. Arthur toyed with his starter and waited for his father to explain.

'I'm looking for a Parliamentary Private Secretary,' explained Uther. 'That way you would avoid all the hassle of getting yourself elected. Interested?' Why wouldn't he be, for God's sake?

'Isn't that a rather senior post for a new boy?' asked Arthur.

'Possibly. But . . . ' – Uther bared his teeth in a mirthless smile – 'it would be an excellent career move.'

A moment's hesitation, then Arthur said cautiously, 'I'm not sure I'm ready for such an exalted position. May I think about it?'

'Don't think too hard,' said Uther huffily, piqued at his son's guarded response, 'my offer may not be on the table for long.' Then, with a characteristically abrupt mood swing, his voice became seductive and his facial expression ingratiating. 'You would be surprised at the number of admirers you have in the House, my boy. And the absurd questions they ask! How many terrorists has your son killed? Who has he rescued lately? That sort of thing. Of course you never tell me anything, so I have to make it all up. I do a pretty good job, if I say so myself. You're a legend, I can tell you. I bask in the warm glow of your reflected glory.'

'Wild exaggeration, father,' said Arthur.

Uther leaned across the table conspiratorially. 'You are destined for great things, son. All I'm doing is offering you a chance to set your foot on the first rung of the ladder. What is there to think about? PPS to the Foreign Secretary. What! In a few years you could write your own ticket. How many newly elected MP's get a chance like that, d'you think?'

'Isn't that rather the point?'

Uther played dumb. 'I don't follow.'

'You don't think,' said Arthur, 'that it would raise a few eyebrows if I accepted such a plum job from my own father?'

A blank look. 'Why should it?'

It had to be said. 'Some people might say it smacked of nepotism.'

Uther feigned surprise. 'Nepotism! I doubt anyone would think such a vile thing of me – or of you,' he added hastily. 'If they did, it would only be sour grapes. And frankly, who gives a damn anyway? Politics isn't about soul-searching, Arthur. It's about ambition, it's about success.'

'I'm sorry, but that's not how I see politics.'

'No?' This time Uther was genuinely surprised. 'Really? How do you see it, then?'

'I see it as a way of helping people,' said Arthur.

'How very noble of you,' said Uther with heavy irony. 'I see it as a way of helping myself.'

Surely his father was joking? 'You don't mean that.'

'Oh, but I do,' said Uther.

'Then I'm afraid I can't accept your most generous offer.'

Uther's nose wrinkled as if it had been assaulted by a repugnant odour. 'I do hope you're not going to turn into one of those sanctimonious do-gooders.'

Arthur was accustomed to his father's swift mood transformations – one moment smiling like the Cheshire Cat, the next red in tooth and claw. 'I know I have a lot to learn but I intend to learn in my own way and in my own time. I prefer not to be beholden to anyone.' A moment's reflection. 'Above all not to you. Not to my own father.'

'I hear,' Uther remarked cattily, 'that you are palsy-walsy with Leo Grant.'

'He and I exchange views on world affairs from time to time,' said Arthur, trying not to sound defensive.

Uther's eyebrows arched. 'World affairs indeed! And what are your views on world affairs, if I may ask?' The tone of his voice suggested that Arthur's views on world affairs were of no consequence whatever.

Arthur refused to be riled. 'We have not discussed domestic issues like health care, education, pensions and so on. Obviously those are vital matters for most people. It seems to me, though, that Leo Grant is right when he says that the single most important issue in the world today is the one that affects the security of every citizen – terrorism, and how the free world is dealing with it, or rather failing to deal with it.'

Uther did not attempt to conceal his irritation. 'And what conclusions have you reached?'

'Leo thinks, and I agree with him,' said Arthur, 'that serious mistakes are being made.'

'No doubt he would handle it much better,' said Uther sarcastically.

'He says many world leaders secretly believe they are fighting a war they cannot win. He is convinced they are wrong.'

A sardonic smile. 'Well now,' said Uther, 'it's easy to criticize when you are in opposition. It is quite another thing to run the country.' Uther had a very shrewd idea what lay behind this, and he could have kicked himself for having come clean about Sadiq, a mistake he was paying for now. 'Let me ask you, Arthur, how would you tackle the problem of terrorism if you were in charge of the country? Remember they have the advantage of surprise, and their aim is to kill as many innocent people as possible. They want to destabilise the free world by spreading fear.' He considered his son. Should he be blunt? He lifted his shoulders. What did he have to lose? 'Ok, I admit it. Sadiq is no exception. Deals are done all the time. Not just here in the UK but all over the world governments are making compromises, paying huge ransoms, releasing convicted terrorists, trying to buy time and save lives. Maybe it's not such a great idea, but what else do you suggest we do?'

'Fight them,' said Arthur.

'We *are* fighting them.' Uther stubbed out his cigar savagely and lit another one. 'Our military resources are stretched to the limit and beyond. From time to time we invade someone. It never works.' Yet another funnel of cigar smoke flattened itself on the ceiling and billowed down the restaurant's walls. 'Iraq was a disaster and we are still living with the consequences. There's a limit to what tanks, bombs and missiles can do. Or the threat of nuclear weapons for that matter. Let's be realistic, there will always be terrorists and they will always have the advantage over us. We can contain them, perhaps, but we can never defeat them.'

'We can if we stand up to them,' insisted Arthur. 'If we don't, they'll destroy us in the end.'

'No they wont,' said Uther confidently. 'The fact is, when all is said and done, they're nothing but a nuisance.'

'A nuisance! You can't be serious, father.'

'Oh, but I am. Deadly serious. Look at the figures. Since

September eleventh 2001, terrorists have killed probably no more than ten or fifteen thousand people worldwide. Last year a hundred and twenty people died in the UK in terror attacks. The year before there was a bomb explosion at that nuclear power plant. Nasty, I'll grant you. Over three hundred dead, but the effects of radiation were not nearly as bad as we feared.'

'What is your point?' asked Arthur.

'Every year about three thousand people die in traffic accidents in the UK alone. In France it's nearly three times that number. In the USA it's over forty thousand. I don't speak of the maimed and injured. And then there are natural disasters: earthquakes, hurricanes, droughts, floods. How many died in the Tsunami of December 2004? A quarter of a million people? More? No one really knows. What about disease? Every year millions – no hundreds of millions – die of cancer, heart disease, AIDS and so on.' Uther paused for effect. 'I rest my case.'

'One thing has nothing to do with the other,' said Arthur. 'It's not a matter of statistics. Many terrorists are dedicated to a cause, and that cause is the overthrow of the free world. We are talking about a global threat to our civilisation.'

Uther snorted. 'A gross exaggeration.'

'So your policy is to allow terrorists to kill and maim innocent people with impunity,' said Arthur bitterly.

'That is a malicious simplification of what I just said.' Uther stubbed out his cigar, all the time casting venomous looks at his son. 'What I am saying is, because we can't eliminate the problem, we have adopted a policy of damage limitation. We let the terrorists make their point, knowing there's not a hell of a lot we can do about it anyway. Containment, Arthur, is the political buzzword of our time.'

'I acknowledge that sometimes compromises have to be made,' said Arthur.

'Very decent of you,' said his father with heavy irony.

'But not with terrorists. We are talking about sick evil men with no conscience and not a trace of human compassion. No, father, you don't make compromises with the devil. It can't be right. And morality aside, it's counter-productive. It only breeds more terrorism. The first duty of a government is to protect its citizens. If it doesn't do that, it is not doing what it was elected to do.' Arthur stood, thanked his father for lunch and left.

What a waste of a good meal thought Uther savagely, and a damned pricey one too, even if it was on expenses. He gulped down two large brandies, signed the bill and walked slowly out of the restaurant, doing a 'triumphal' tour of M.P.'s and media people on the way. On the drive back to the House Uther continued to think about Arthur. He had always seen his son as a rather quixotic figure, a knight on horseback tilting at windmills, certainly not someone who could ever be a serious contender. It seemed he had made a serious error of judgment. Arthur was developing a most unfortunate tendency to think for himself. Whatever next? It was all very worrying. As his PPS, Uther would have been able to keep a watchful eye on him, control him even, but now he would be a loose cannon, a menace to himself and everyone else. Uther's unease was heightened by the memory of that disturbing exchange with Merlin.

It is written that he will overthrow you.

Are you saying I should be afraid of my own son?

Many men are.

It was all nonsense of course, and Arthur would come round eventually. It was only a matter of time.

A few weeks later he learned that Arthur had been adopted as a prospective candidate by a United Labour constituency in the West Country; in another couple of months he took his seat as a backbencher in the House of Commons. Uther was mortified. What was that old saying about blood being thicker than water? Not in the Pendragon family it seemed. So be it; his son had thrown down the gauntlet. Uther would not hesitate to pick it up.

Four

2019

ARRAN GORE was dining at his club one evening when a voice boomed from the far end of the long centre table: 'Gore!' To shout from one end of the table to the other was considered bad form, especially offensive when the member was obviously the worse for drink. Arran did not respond. George Drummond, or Bulldog as he was known, was a habitual trouble-maker, stubborn and irascible. Being ignored only made Bulldog more aggressive. 'I'm talking to you, Gore!'

What concentrated the attention of everyone in the room, and charged the atmosphere with nervous expectation, was the well-known grudge Bulldog bore Arran: a close friend and business associate of his had recently been refused membership of the Club, and Drummond had somehow convinced himself that Arran, a member of the committee, had played a leading role in that decision. The dining room was suddenly eerily hushed, the sound of traffic outside on Piccadilly filtered through the windows, a police siren wailed in the distance.

Bulldog began to growl belligerently, resisting the vain attempts of his friends to shut him up; the more they tried to restrain him, the more angry and spiteful he became. 'Woshwrong with my friend, then? Woshwrong with him, Gore?' What was wrong with Bulldog's friend, as everyone in the club knew, was that he had dipped his hand into his company's pension fund, causing widespread hardship to his employees and their families. For that offence he had served a term in jail, a detail he had omitted to mention on his application form. The committee was constrained by Club Rules, and the vote to refuse the man membership had been unanimous.

'How's that lovely wife of yours?' Bulldog bounced on his chair, cackling. It was well known that Arran Gore's wife, Morgan, was no beauty. There was a sudden intake of breath in the room. An embarrassing situation had swiftly developed into a potentially explosive confrontation. Members at the far end of the table redoubled their efforts to silence the drunk, again without success. 'Taught anyone to fly lately, has she?' This second jibe was followed by another cackle of laughter.

Arran, who could stand Bulldog's jeering insults no longer, had to be held back. Bulldog, a powerful and thick-set individual, was dragged from the room by several friends. Outside in the hall Arran went up to him. 'You are drunk, George. When you are sober, I shall expect an apology.'

'Fat chance, Gore.' As Arran turned to walk away, Bulldog called after him, 'How is the crazy bitch, then?' Arran whirled round and let fly an accurate punch, drawing blood from Bulldog's nose.

The following day the two men met in the club bar, each flanked by friends ready to step between them should it become necessary. Arran repeated his demand for an apology. George Drummond, now sober, replied in characteristic fashion. 'Who's going to make me apologise?'

Arran sighed in frustration. 'If it's a fight you want, we can go a couple of rounds.' In the basement was a well equipped gymnasium where both men regularly worked out.

Bulldog touched his nose. 'I don't think so.'

Arran was smaller but quick on his feet, and for a man of his age still in excellent shape. 'Let's finish this business, George,' he said quietly. 'I simply want an acknowledgement that you were drunk and didn't mean what you said. That will be apology enough for me.'

'You want me to admit I was drunk? Fine. I was drunk. Now I'm sober.' Bulldog moved his face so close to Arran's that their noses were almost touching. 'And I still say your wife's a crazy bitch.'

Arran wanted to punch Drummond in the face but managed to restrain himself. 'If you refuse to apologise, I shall place the matter in the committee's hands and let them decide what to do.'

'Going to have me thrown out, are you?' jeered Drummond. 'Afraid to stand up for yourself? That makes you a coward, Gore.'

Arran Gore sighed. 'How do we settle this, then?'

A wicked grin. 'We fight a duel.'

'You can't be serious.'

'I am perfectly serious,' said George Drummond. 'Matter of fact I've read the Club rules on the subject. There's been an insult, so there has to be an apology. If there's no apology, then according to the rules there's a challenge, followed by a duel.'

The Out and About club had its origins in the seventeenth century when quarrels between members were commonly settled by duels. Over the years the Club Rules had been added to and amended but never rewritten. It was likely that for historical and traditional reasons no one had wanted to do anything quite so drastic. Arran was appalled: 'But that's absurd. Duelling has been illegal for centuries.'

'You can't have your cake and eat it, Gore. If the club rules apply to my friend, they apply to you as well.'

Arran was on the defensive now. 'I shall be happy to accept an apology.'

Drummond shook his head. 'You won't get one. So you have a choice: challenge me or resign from the club.'

'For God's sake, man,' protested Arran, 'this is the twenty-first century, not the seventeenth!'

'So what? I say a duel is the only way to settle this argument.' George Drummond folded his arms, signalling that, as far as he was concerned, that was the end of the discussion.

Arran was cornered. He glanced about him at his friends who looked as baffled as he felt. 'What kind of duel?'

'Something harmless.'

Sensing a light-hearted resolution of an unpleasant situation, Arran's friends nodded approvingly.

'Very well,' said Arran reluctantly.

'You have to challenge me.'

'Alright, I challenge you,' said Arran.

A triumphant smile. 'I accept your challenge.'

'What happens now?'

'We choose weapons. You are the challenger, so it's my choice.' Clearly Bulldog had done his homework.

'What do you choose?'

Drummond smirked. 'Bows and arrows.'

It was a relief to Arran, as to all the other members of the Out and About, to hear that the bows and arrows Drummond had in mind were obtainable at a toy store in Regent Street. Once this was established, Gore was ready to enter into the spirit of things. 'Very well. My, um, my seconds will attend you. That the form?'

'That's it.'

Seconds were despatched to make the necessary purchases, and the time and location of the duel agreed.

That evening Morgan phoned Arthur as she did from time-to-time. She trusted her half-brother, and he and Arran were good friends. Never one for small talk, she came straight to the point. 'He's going to fight a duel.'

'Who is?'

'Arran.'

Arthur knew Morgan was eccentric and claimed to have special powers. 'How do you know?'

'It came to me in a dream,' she explained.

'I see,' said Arthur, though he did not. It sounded as though Morgan had lost the plot. 'When is this duel taking place?'

'Tomorrow,' said Morgan. 'Something terrible is going to happen. I know it is.'

The poor woman sounded terrified. For her sake he decided it would be best to go along with her story. If he did not she would be mortally offended. 'What do you want me to do?'

'You must stop it.'

'Right.'

'Swear?'

A slight hesitation. 'I swear.'

'Bless you, Arthur. You can fly.' With that Morgan rang off.

It was just another one of Morgan's fantasies, of course, but even so he could not get that phone call out of his mind. He was as fond of his half-sister as she was of him, and admired her for being different and gutsy. People said she was mad, and perhaps she was, but she had a bigger heart than almost anyone he knew. He found himself tapping Arran's number.

'Arran, it's Arthur.'

'What's up?'

'Forgive me for asking,' said Arthur self-consciously, 'but . . . this is probably going to sound ridiculous . . . '

'Go on.' Arran guessed that this had something to do with Morgan.

Arthur ploughed on. 'You are not fighting a duel tomorrow, are you?'

A long silence. 'How on earth did you know?'

'Morgan phoned me.'

'Strange. I never told her.' Arran was embarrassed, not liking to admit that his wife had special powers.

'Morgan knows things,' said Arthur.

Arran chuckled. 'She claims she's a witch, bless her. Absolute nonsense, of course.'

Maybe, maybe not, thought Arthur. The fact was, she was right. 'So you are going to fight a duel?'

Arran explained.

'Isn't there a better way? Duelling went out aeons ago.'

'Bit of nonsense, that's all,' said Arran lightly.

'You're not duelling with weapons, then.'

'Good Lord, no,' said Arran. 'What do you take me for? We're using toys, bows and arrows actually. You're welcome to come along. It should be fun.'

An hour before dawn the following morning Arran Gore and George Drummond accompanied by their seconds met on Highgate Hill. It was still dark, but in the east the sky was faintly luminous. The two men and their seconds took up their positions a hundred yards from each other.

Arthur watched the preparations from a distance. He had promised Morgan he would stop the duel but he saw little point in getting heavy-handed with Arran; the whole thing was a charade, a child's game played by adults to ensure that honour was satisfied. The offence was real enough but the duel was not. Indeed he had the strange sense that these shadowy figures moving silently on the crest of the hill were not real people at all; or if they were, that they were actors performing some ancient rite. This was theatre, an imaginative solution to what might well have been a very nasty problem. Obviously there was nothing to be concerned about. It made no sense, then, to feel as troubled as he did. Doubtless his uneasiness was caused by the early hour and the morning chill.

With the most solemn and scrupulous care the toy kits were unpacked, the bows and arrows tested and handed to each protagonist. Both kits came complete with a target which was left in the box.

'What's the range of these things?' Arran enquired of one of his seconds who knew something about archery.

'They are small, but metal-tipped and well flighted, so they can travel quite a distance. With a level shot, I reckon the arrow can fly about fifty yards. If you shoot it up in the air, it might go a little further.'

'So we are well out of range.'

'We made sure of that.' The second winked. 'Mind you, if

anyone deserves an arrow in the rump, it's Bulldog.'

The two duellists and their seconds clapped their hands and stamped their feet to keep their circulation moving, their breath steaming in the cold air. Every now and then one of the seconds would look at the eastern sky and glance at his watch.

Arran Gore and George Drummond squared off. In the darkness they could barely make each other out but as the sky slowly lightened, the outline of each man became more distinct, especially that of Arran who faced the rising sun. As the rim of the sun nudged the horizon, Drummond's second spoke: 'Two shots each, remember. First shot to you, Bulldog. When you have fired, face your opponent full on and remain still'

Bulldog took the bow and arrow in his hand. 'Piece of junk. Give me the real thing and I'd make the bastard jump.' From the way he inserted the arrow, and weighed the bow in his hand, it was evident he was no stranger to archery.

Arran's second gave him the same instructions. As his opponent took aim, Arran stood unflinching. The arrow sped through the air with a distinctive hissing sound, falling to earth thirty yards or so from where he was standing. As his second had forecast, it lacked the momentum to carry the full hundred yards, though it had travelled further than its supposed range of fifty.

With some difficulty, Arran inserted the arrow, drew back the bowstring, aimed in the general direction of his opponent and fired. The arrow flew high into the air, hung poised for a second or two, and fell to earth barely ten yards from where Arran was standing. 'Oh,' he said.

A hundred yards away Bulldog wheezed with mirth. 'Try again!' he shouted mockingly.

'It's your turn,' Arran shouted back.

'Have one on me!'

'Right. I will.' Arran's lips compressed in a determined line. Taking the utmost care, he inserted a second arrow in the bow, pulled the bowstring back with all his strength until it seemed it must surely snap, took aim and released the arrow. This time it sped directly towards its target, and with such force that it landed only a few yards from Bulldog's feet. So accurate was the shot, that given another few yards momentum, it might well have struck him. 'Bastard!' yelled Bulldog. Narrowing his eyes, he flicked the arrow expertly into the bow, pulled back the bowstring with the full power of his massive arm, aimed high and released the arrow.

The ball of the sun sat on the horizon, setting ablaze the river Thames and the windows and rooftops of the City of London. In the distance Arran could just make out the shining dome of St. Paul's. It was the last thing he ever saw. As he shielded his eyes from the glare of the sun, the arrow tore through his hand and into his brain. His life was over before he hit the ground.

It was several moments before anyone could take in what had happened. Arthur was the first to move, rushing over to kneel by Arran. The steel tip of the toy arrow had penetrated his skull so far that only the flight and a few inches of shaft were visible. Arthur felt Arran's wrist and neck where his pulse should have been. There was nothing.

Bulldog stumbled across the grass and fell on his knees by the body. 'I don't believe it, I don't believe it,' he kept saying. He began to cry. 'It was a game, a silly game. This isn't happening. An ambulance! For God's sake get an ambulance someone!'

'I just phoned for one,' said Arthur quietly.

'He can't be. Tell me he isn't.'

'I'm afraid he's dead,' said Arthur.

'Oh God, what have I done? What have I done?' Bulldog sobbed violently, his whole body heaving.

One of his seconds touched him on the shoulder. 'Get a hold of yourself, Bulldog. The police will be here any moment.'

'The police! Why the police? You saw what happened, Pendragon. It was an accident. I fired to miss. I had no idea it would fly so far. It never should have done. I'll sue the makers, that's what I'll do. It's their fault, not mine. No one can say it was my fault.'

Arran's blind eyes stared up at the sky. Gently Arthur closed them. For a moment or two he stood looking down at his friend, then he took off his coat and covered him. George Drummond sat on the ground and held up his arms in appeal: 'Why doesn't somebody say something? You saw what happened. You can't say it was my fault. Don't try and pin this on me. You were all in on it, every one of you.'

Arthur broke the news to Morgan. Haltingly, he did his best to explain what had happened. It was the most difficult and painful thing he had ever had to do.

'It was an accident,' he said, 'a terrible accident.'

'Arran's tough,' said Morgan, 'he'll pull through, I know he will.' She put on her coat. 'Would you drive me to the hospital, please?'

Tears stung Arthur's eyes. 'Arran's dead, Morgan. I'm so very sorry.'

Morgan took off her coat, sat on the sofa and began to shiver. 'You said you would stop it.'

Head bowed, Arthur answered softly, 'I know.'

'You swore you would.'

'I'm so sorry.'

Morgan was observing Arthur with an odd look in her eye. 'Arran isn't in hospital?'

'No.'

'He's dead?'

'Yes.'

'He's not coming home?'

'No'. He tried to take her hand but she snatched it away.

'He's never coming home?'

Arthur shook his head. 'He's gone, Morgan.'

She leaped up, her face contorted with rage. Hurling herself at Arthur, she clawed at his face. 'I'll kill you!' she shouted again and again, 'I'll kill you! I swear I will!'

A week later Morgan phoned and asked if she could stop by to see Arthur at his flat that evening. Arthur was preparing drinks in the kitchen when he heard a soft 'Hooh-Hooh' in the sitting-room. Merlin was standing by the bookshelf with Virgil on his shoulder. As Arthur came in Virgil flew across the room, perched on his shoulder, nibbled his ear and went to sleep.

'He always did have a soft spot for you,' said Merlin, 'ever since you were a boy.' He embraced Arthur, taking care not to disturb the owl. 'Just like me.'

'I'm happy to see you, Merlin. I suppose you wouldn't care to tell me how you got in?'

'You wouldn't understand if I did,' said Merlin unkindly, helping himself from the plate of raw vegetables Arthur was carrying. 'Let's talk about Morgan,' said the magus, crunching a carrot, 'before she gets here.'

Arthur knew better than to ask how Merlin knew.

'Do you know why she's coming?' Merlin asked.

'To talk about poor Arran, I imagine. It's been a month already.'

Merlin shook his head.

'What does she want then?'

'To kill you,' said Merlin.

Arthur's eyes widened. 'Why on earth would she want to kill me?'

'Because she holds you responsible for Arran's death. Unreasonable of course.'

As unreasonable, thought Arthur, as the prickings of his own troubled conscience.

'Best be on your guard,' said Merlin, fading from view together with his voice. Seconds later he had disappeared, and so, with a nibble of Arthur's ear and a soft hooh-hooh, had Virgil.

Minutes later the doorbell rang. Morgan was dressed in black, accentuating the pallor of her face and her red-rimmed eyes. Under her arm was a large black handbag. She refused Arthur's offer of a drink. 'I'll try a few veggies,' she said, scooping up a handful and cramming them into her mouth. Within seconds she had emptied the plate. 'Good for the digestion,' she explained and belched loudly. The corners of Arthur's mouth twitched.

'How are you, Morgan?'

'Never better.'

Obviously that was not true. 'Is there anything I can do for you?'

Morgan opened her handbag and slipped her hand inside. For a long time she sat staring thoughtfully at Arthur, one hand in the bag, the other in her lap. One leg of her black tights was laddered, Arthur noticed, the other had a large hole through which the white flesh of her calf bulged. 'There is, actually,' she said. 'You can stand still.' From the bag she produced a long serrated bread knife and advanced on Arthur who watched her carefully, uncertain whether she only intended to scare him or whether she had something else in mind. When she spoke again it was as if she were explaining consequences to a small child. 'You killed my Bore,' she said, 'and so I'm going to kill you.'

'I never killed Arran,' said Arthur. 'He died because of an accident.'

A sudden convulsion of rage gouged Morgan's face. Clutching the knife in both hands she stabbed at Arthur's chest. Just in time he seized her wrist, prizing open her hand, and as the knife dropped to the floor kicked it under a chair. Morgan pounded his chest with her fists until she had no more strength in her arms. As suddenly as it erupted her rage subsided; Arthur watched her every move as she dipped into the bag again. A few seconds rummaging and she produced nothing more sinister than a clutch of grubby tissues.

'A Gore fought with Wellington at Waterloo,' she said, blowing her nose loudly and stuffing the sodden tissues back in

279

her handbag. 'Did you know that?'

'I don't believe I did,' said Arthur.

Without warning she threw her arms round his neck and kissed him on the lips. 'I love you,' she whispered fiercely, biting his lower lip so hard she drew blood. Arthur winced, gently disengaging himself. 'But I still want to kill you,' she added in the same fierce whisper.

None of it made sense, yet Arthur knew it was true. He had the feeling that Morgan could no longer distinguish love from hate, that in her heart the two emotions were interdependent, love feeding on hate like a parasite on its host. Merlin was right; he would have to be on his guard.

Five

AS A CHILD, Lancelot was introspective and sensitive. When people looked at the handsome boy a second time, as they invariably did, he would tuck his chin in his chest, or turn away in embarrassment. He and his father, Bertie Bancroft, a retired soldier, were touchingly protective of each other. Most men widowed after barely three years of marriage would have remarried but Bertie's wife was ever present in her husband's heart, an icon of womanhood that no woman of flesh and blood could hope to match. So all his love was lavished on his only child.

Lancelot was said to resemble Jane, his mother, a woman with darkly beautiful looks, who had drowned herself in a lake shortly after her son was born. As he grew older Lancelot learned to hide his vulnerability but was no less introspective. At university some found him proud and vain, some attributed his aloofness to shyness. He was much admired – by men for his sporting prowess, by women for his good looks and smouldering intensity. He was not one of the herd, partly because he was by nature a loner, partly because his fellow students found it hard to empathise with someone who seemed to take himself so seriously. His only close friend, Ian Duncan, was a sociable and fun-loving Scotsman, who on the face of it had little in common with Lancelot, aside from a mutual love of sport. Yet even this shared interest highlighted the differences in their characters. By the end of his first year Lancelot had already won a rowing and rugby blue, and but for the fact that there were only twenty-four hours in a day, would no doubt have won a blue for cricket, tennis and golf as well. Ian had enjoyed no comparable success, a fact that bothered him a great deal less than it bothered Lancelot who frequently criticised Ian for his laziness. 'You should have won a blue by now.'

A modest smile. 'I'm afraid I'm just not good enough.'

Two deep creases furrowed Lancelot's forehead. 'Why do you always talk yourself down?'

Ian thought about that. 'Perhaps it's because I'm more accepting than you are. I take life as it comes.'

For Lancelot that comment summed up everything that was wrong with Ian's attitude. 'But it's *your* life, Ian, don't you see that? Life is what you make of it.'

'I expect you're right,' said Ian doubtfully.

'Of course I am. You could easily get a blue for sprinting.'

'I suppose so'

'What's stopping you, then?'

Ian had no answer for that. 'I always do my best times in practice, I don't know why.'

'I do,' said Lancelot. 'You don't try hard enough.'

Ian wriggled his shoulders in embarrassment. 'To be honest, Lance, I don't enjoy competing. I really don't see the point of it.'

'The point,' said Lancelot, glaring at his friend, 'is to win.'

'But I run for fun.'

'For fun!' Lancelot was disgusted. 'Life isn't about fun, Ian. It's about using your talents, it's about being grateful you have them and making the most of them. When you are out there on the starting block, you have to close your eyes and see yourself winning. You have to tell yourself you want to win more than anything in the world.'

'But I don't. I'm quite happy to let other people win.'

Lance looked incredulously at his friend. 'What an extraordinary statement.'

'I know, I'm useless,' said Ian, smiling, 'and you're so good at everything.'

'Yes I am, aren't I?'

Ian had never come across anyone like Lancelot before. At first he had found his vanity disconcerting. Soon, however, he began to ask himself whether Lance was truly vain, or was it simply that he saw no point in pretending? He was either indifferent to or blissfully unaware of the offence he caused by being so uncompromisingly outspoken not only about himself but about everyone he met. Ian, the most agreeable man in the world, found his friend both exasperating and endearing. If only he could find a way of saying what he had to say without aggravating people. Yet was it not, after all, a rare and admirable quality in a man to speak the truth?

'Some people might think you were boasting,' said Ian mildly.

'I was not boasting. I was merely agreeing with you.'

'Wouldn't it be better if you left it to others to compliment you?' suggested Ian.

'I believe I am the best judge of my own capabilities,' said Lancelot haughtily, and then, seeing Ian raise his eyes to the ceiling, 'have I said something to offend you?'

'I just wish,' said Ian, 'you would try to be more sensitive to other people's feelings.'

'You want me to be dishonest?'

In this mood Lancelot was exasperating. 'All I want,' said Ian, 'is for people to like you as much as I do.'

'You think it important to be liked?'

'Of course I do.'

'That's why you don't win races,' said Lancelot severely. 'If you put as much effort into winning as you do into making yourself popular, you would have your blue by now.' Ian looked thoroughly depressed. 'I'm sorry,' said Lancelot gruffly, 'that was unkind.' He laid his arm on Ian's shoulder in a rare gesture of intimacy, then swiftly withdrew it. 'It's not that I don't want to be liked, Ian. I do. I get up in the morning and I look at myself in the mirror and I say, "Lance, this is your day

to be nice. Who knows, you might even make a friend or two."
And you know what? By mid-morning I am losing patience,
and by lunchtime I am beginning to despise myself. What can I
say? I find the price of popularity too high.' He looked almost
contrite. 'Does that sound arrogant?'

'Not really,' said Ian, reluctant to offend his friend.

'I can't change the way I am.'

'I wouldn't want you to change,' said Ian loyally.

Those qualities of Lancelot that most aggravated the
opposite sex were also the ones that most attracted them,
his introspection, his intensity, his proud manner. Never
indifferent, women either loved or professed to hate him, one
way or another their passion was always engaged. The more
aloof he held himself the more they crowded in on him, the less
responsive he was the harder they tried to gain his attention;
the worse he treated them the more they seemed to like it.

Lancelot was both a puzzle and a challenge: why, for
example, did he not have a girl-friend? Did he not like women?
Was he gay? There were various theories: he had been hurt in
love; he feared his own deeply passionate nature; his aloofness
was a masquerade to stimulate interest. The day came when
Ian was unable to contain his curiosity any longer. 'Tell me,
Lance,' he asked his friend, 'do you like women?'

Lancelot smiled. 'I'm not gay, if that's what you mean. Why
do you ask?'

'I see the way women look at you. But you never do anything
about it.'

'I don't have time for that sort of thing,' said Lancelot
dismissively.

'Are you saying you have never been to bed with a girl?'
It was a question he had wanted to ask his friend for a long
time.

'I have never been in love,' said Lancelot.

Ian's jaw dropped. 'What has love got to do with it? We are
talking about sex. Everyone does it these days. It's, well, it's

fun.'

Lancelot stared at Ian with those tormented eyes of his. 'This may sound strange to you but I am not interested in casual sex. Why does fun have to involve sex?'

What century was Lancelot living in? 'Is there something wrong with sex?'

Lancelot considered the question. 'It has never happened to me, but I believe that there is such a thing as being in love. I also imagine it must be something very special and precious.'

'It doesn't sound like fun.'

'Oh, fun!' said Lancelot contemptuously.

Ian was indignant. 'Is there something wrong with fun? I know running isn't supposed to be fun. But surely sex is?'

'Why must you have sex to have fun? To me sex without love would be meaningless, an abuse of my body, still more, of my emotions. I intend to keep myself pure for the woman I fall in love with. I believe in chastity.'

Lancelot had to be joking. But no, when Ian looked at him again, he realised his friend was perfectly serious. Besides, Lance did not make jokes. Had it not been for Ian's love of gossip, there the matter would have rested. But in hours the whole university knew not only that Lancelot did not "do" sex, but why he did not. The reaction was predictable. Acting hard to get was any man's prerogative. Cloaking such unfashionable behaviour in the guise of a moral imperative laid Lancelot open to ridicule and resentment.

Chastity was not a concept with which young people of the twenty-first century were in sympathy; many students had never even come across the word before, and those who understood its meaning could not begin to understand Lancelot. What could be said of such a man? That he was a prig? A male, macho bigot? Was he dysfunctional? A hypocrite? The general consensus was that he was all of those and more. With Ian's unwitting help, Lancelot had set himself up as a target; knocking him off his high horse became a crusade amongst the more sexually aggressive women in the university where the presence in their midst of a self-confessed virgin was taken as a slur on the good name of every female student.

But in spite of all their efforts, Lancelot was not unseated. He kept his principles and his virginity intact, though the successive assaults on his chastity created endless sport. Large sums were lost by those who bet against him. By all the laws of chance and averages he ought to have succumbed to temptation, yet he did not. He remained his customary aloof and disdainful self, and a virgin. As the weeks passed, with Lancelot still not unhorsed, the excitement died down, interest waned, and the final verdict was delivered; either he was asexual, or he was gay, or he was impotent. A line was drawn under the whole frustrating business, leaving the ladies free to concentrate on objects more worthy of their attention.

All but one. Lady Eleanor Shalott had a neat figure, a pertly pretty face, a wicked smile and an adventurous disposition. For weeks she had tried everything she knew to induce Lancelot to take notice of her, sitting next to him at lectures, frequenting the same libraries, going to the same movies, and making sure she was invited to the same parties. She became a clamorous rugby fan, sitting in the front row at every match he played in. She even took up golf. All in vain; he barely noticed her.

At first it was only a bit of harmless fun, as her heart was not engaged and her pursuit of Lancelot nothing more than a diversion; luring a reluctant man into bed presented her with a unique challenge, one she could not resist. Certainly Lancelot's attractions were a bonus. What drove her on, however, was more the thrill of the hunt than the prospect of the kill. As time passed, however, something strange and unaccustomed began to happen to her. The image of Lancelot's dark good looks and burning eyes occupied her mind. She had difficulty sleeping, and when she did, was tormented by variations of the same dream in which she followed a man who walked alone, his face turned away from her. He led her down blind alleys, and invariably, just as she was reaching out to touch him, disappeared into thin air. After a sleepless night she would wake in the morning feeling depressed and frustrated.

Presumably it was simply wounded pride that was making her unhappy. But why, she asked herself, was she losing sleep over such a trivial thing? What did it matter if Lancelot was a virgin? What was it to her if the silly man took pleasure in manipulating the female population of the university for his own satisfaction? Coming to her senses, she decided to abandon the chase before it became an obsession. But then one day she literally bumped into Lancelot as he was leaving a lecture, and to her astonishment he spoke to her. In her confusion she was quite unable to reply. What exactly he had said she was not sure, probably some passing reference to the lecture. Lancelot rarely spoke to anyone other than Ian Duncan, and virtually never to a woman, so it was hardly surprising that his words had been banal. What else was to be expected? The crucial point, she concluded, was not what he had said to her, but that he had said anything at all.

The more she thought about it, the more certain she became that, in his awkward fashion, Lancelot had been trying to express interest. Reaching that conclusion she was lost. So grateful was she for his attention that she now allowed herself to admit what she had never admitted before; she had fallen for the wretched man. It was obvious she would have to make the first move, or wait till kingdom come. Fortunately, Lady Eleanor was not retiring by nature. So that when Lancelot opened the door of his college digs the following evening, there on the sofa of the sitting room lay Lady Eleanor Shalott, wearing a charm bracelet. To find a woman in his digs was bad enough, to find a naked woman there, was intolerable.

'What do you think you're doing?' he enquired loftily.

'What does it look like, darling?' She wiggled her way to the bedroom, followed closely by Lancelot.

'Please leave.' He demonstrated his seriousness by retrieving her clothes, some from the bed, some from the floor, handing them to her and retiring to the sitting room to wait. Minutes later she emerged dressed and weeping, though in truth less damage was done to her heart than to her pride. She would be the laughing stock of the university, of that she was certain, and Lancelot would dine out on the story for weeks. Had she understood his character better, she would have known she need have no fear for her reputation. But she did not understand him at all, and so her reaction was to attempt to defend her reputation by destroying his. Within hours the word had spread that Lancelot had tried to rape the Lady Eleanor Shalott in his college rooms, and was being questioned by the police.

Ian rushed over to give his friend moral support. 'Everyone says she's a liar. They all know you would never do anything like that.'

'Do they?'

'How can you doubt it?' said Ian earnestly.

'Forgive me, Ian, but I don't share your rose-coloured view of human nature,' said Lancelot. 'People love to gossip. It's something of a national pastime, isn't it, destroying people's reputations? Never believe the best of anyone if you can possibly believe the worst, especially if they don't conform to the dreary, politically-correct norm. They hate me, Ian. They hate me because I'm not one of them. Wouldn't they just love it if Lancelot the virgin turned out to be Lancelot the rapist.'

'I can't say I blame you for feeling bitter. The whole thing is so unfair. The worst of it is, none of this would have happened if it hadn't been for me.'

'I certainly wish you had kept our discussion confidential,' said Lancelot, 'but there it is. You were not to foresee the consequences.' He shook his head in bewilderment. 'Why does she hate me so much? I never showed the slightest interest in her.'

Ian was about to make the obvious reply but thought better of it. Lance would never understand.

Two days later Lady Eleanor was fished out of the river Cam and rushed to the local hospital where she was detained for a few hours before being released. The apparent suicide attempt won her much sympathy. Until now, most students had been inclined to give Lancelot the benefit of the doubt. Eleanor's desperate act convinced many that she was telling the truth. The students' mood changed abruptly, and feeling against Lancelot ran dangerously high.

In college an angry crowd gathered round the old well in the centre of the quadrangle. Some students had obviously drunk too much. From the window of his rooms Lancelot looked down on them with disdain. 'Look at the lynch mob. Nothing less than a hanging will satisfy them.' As he spoke, someone shouted and threw a stone at the window, cracking it. Another followed, and another and another, until finally a brick smashed through the glass, and dropped on the floor. Lancelot did not move a muscle.

Ian Duncan jumped back. 'Get away from the window. Things are getting out of hand, Lance. Let's get the hell out of here before someone is hurt. We can climb out of the bedroom window, across the back quad and over the wall. Hurry!'

'I refuse to run away,' said Lancelot proudly.

'What do you suggest we do then?'

'I'm going down to talk to them.' Lancelot moved to the door.

Ian grabbed his arm. 'Don't do that. They wont listen to you.'

The foot of the spiral staircase leading to Lancelot's rooms was blocked by a group of young men. As he walked slowly down the stairs, however, they backed away and let him through. Out in the quad the students cleared a path for him. There was some belligerent muttering, and a cry of "rapist" from one female student, but no one tried to stop him. Head held high Lancelot walked through them,. By the well stood a giant of a man, the Hon. Daniel Shalott, Lady Eleanor's brother. As Lancelot appeared, Daniel's face distorted with rage. 'You're a coward and a rapist. I'm going to break every bone in your body, starting with that beautiful nose.' He spat in Lancelot's face.

The blood surged in Lancelot's head. His eyes misted over, his nails scored the palms of his hands as he struggled to control himself. It was not just that he wanted to hit the man; he wanted to kill him.

Daniel Shalott's punch had the whole weight of his body behind it. Lancelot ducked, and the huge fist flew over his head. The force of the blow swung Daniel round, throwing him off-balance. He tripped and fell, and the back of his head smashed against the cobbled surround of the well. The big man lay motionless. In the stunned silence Lancelot knelt at his side and felt his pulse. 'Call an ambulance.'

As the ambulance drove off, the crowd in the quadrangle quickly dispersed, with hardly a look or a word exchanged. For the next few days a strange inertia took hold of the university, as if the very life and soul of the place had been extinguished. Students went about their business as before, but now they were joyless and subdued. Few spoke of Lancelot or Eleanor, and no one mentioned the alleged rape. Theirs was a communal grief and a communal guilt, a sense that all were suffering, and all were responsible.

Daniel Shalott fought for his life in intensive care, his parents and Lady Eleanor constantly by his bedside. For two days he lay in a coma. On the morning of the third day his condition rapidly deteriorated. The neuro-surgeon could do no more: 'We must pray for a miracle,' he said. In the late afternoon the situation became very grave as Daniel's condition worsened. Whilst they waited for the end, a nurse brought word that Lancelot was outside, insisting on seeing the dying man. 'Tell him to go away,' said Daniel's father. His wife shook her head. 'We must let him say goodbye.'

Lancelot nodded stiffly as he came in. Sitting on the bed,

he clasped Daniel's hands. 'Daniel,' he said, 'I know how tired you must be but you must not give up. For your parents' sake. For your sister's sake. For my sake.' The lids of Daniel's eyes were ringed with blue, his face white as the sheet on his bed. Lancelot bent over him, tears streaming down his face. 'Don't leave us, I beg you.' One of his tears fell on Daniel's cheek and lay there glistening in the light of the bedside lamp.

Lancelot closed his eyes and prayed to the God he was not sure he believed in. 'Grant me a miracle, God. Don't take Daniel now. Bring him back to us.' Then he kissed the dying man on the forehead and left without a word.

'Who does he think he is?' said Eleanor, when he had gone. 'Jesus Christ? The arrogance of the man!'

Five minutes later Daniel opened his eyes and announced that he was ravenous. When they told him what had happened, he insisted on seeing Lancelot. Lancelot sent word that he was delighted to hear the good news but asked to be excused since unfortunately he had an essay to write.

The police asked Eleanor whether she wanted to press charges. She said that on reflection she may have been mistaken. In her own mind she now doubted that Lancelot had actually tried to rape her. Asked to explain her sudden change of heart, she said she could only think she had been suffering from premenstrual tension.

No one asked Lancelot, nor did he attempt to explain, what happened in the hospital that day. It was, everyone agreed, a remarkable coincidence that the dying Daniel Shalott should so miraculously have recovered after Lancelot's visit. From that day on Lancelot was something of a hero in the university.

Lancelot tried to dismiss the episode from his mind. It had been good fortune, nothing more. No other explanation was possible. He wished with all his heart that people would just forget the whole thing, and stop treating him as if he were some kind of freak.

Six

Four months before the spring general election Robert Marriott stood down as leader of the New Millennium Party and Prime Minister. His resignation was a shock to the public but came as no surprise to his colleagues who had known for some time that he had cancer. Marriott had quit without leaving a footprint in the sands of international affairs, nor in truth had he done much for the country. His chief contribution was to his own Party where, with Uther's help, he had restyled the old Conservative Party and made them electable after many years in opposition.

There were several would-be successors, though probably only one serious contender. Having been for years a fixer at the highest level, Uther Pendragon was in a position to call in many favours. If a Party grandee or a sympathetic businessman needed a favour – a stock exchange tip, a box at Ascot, a dirty weekend in the south of France – Uther was their man. It did not seem to matter that he enthused no one; he was considered competent and unflappable, qualities much in demand in a world in turmoil.

Despite the change in leadership the polls indicated that the New Millennium Party would be re-elected for a third term. The grim inevitability of yet another election defeat weighed heavily on the leader of United Labour, Leo Grant, who could do little but mull over with Thomas Winnington, Chairman of the Party, the prospect of another four years in the wilderness.

'What are our chances?' asked Leo.

Winnington gave a rueful smile. 'The truth?'

'The truth, Thomas.'

'My feeling is that New Millennium will get in again, but with a reduced majority – probably around fifty seats,' said Winnington.

'If Uther Pendragon succeeds Marriott, how will that affect us?' asked Leo.

'He has serious flaws, no doubt about it, both as a politician and as a man,' said Winnington. 'But he's plausible, and there's always a honeymoon period, so by the time people discover how incompetent he is, it'll be too late. He'll be Prime Minister.'

'I'm not so sure,' said Leo. 'There are rumours in Westminster that Pendragon's on the take in a big way. We could make things very hot for him.'

Winnington shook his head. 'That might rebound on us. Where's the proof?'

Leo had no answer to that.

'We should stick to a political agenda,' Winnnington cautioned. 'God knows we have enough ammunition. The government's record is poor. Every year that passes the UK is more and more divided – rich and poor, north and south, town and country. Terrorist incidents are on the increase. Under Blair our Party made hundreds of promises and kept very few; now it's the turn of New Millennium to do the same thing. They talk strong and act weak, they promise gold and deliver dross. That's their Achilles' heel, and that's what we should concentrate on, not on Uther Pendragon.'

Leo Grant nodded thoughtfully. 'I have another idea, Thomas. 'I'm getting on.' A grimace. 'Sixty-one already. I can hardly believe it.'

Thomas Winnington frowned. 'Who cares about age? You are the best man for the job. That's all that matters.'

Leo acknowledged the compliment with a smile and a small inclination of the head. 'Uther is how old? Fifty-nine?'

'About. So?'

'We should find a young man to take him on. New blood, Thomas, would galvanise the electorate. People have been disillusioned with politicians for years, we all know that. Fresh faces and a youthful approach, that's what we need to win this election.'

'I don't agree,' said Winnington. 'What we need is experience and a safe pair of hands.'

Leo Grant looked unconvinced.

'What's on your mind, Leo?'

'Arthur Pendragon.'

'You want to bring Arthur into the shadow cabinet?' Thomas Winnington was an experienced campaigner. He neither accepted nor rejected anything until he had given it his careful consideration. 'It's a thought. A bit young for the cabinet, though, isn't he?'

'I want him to succeed me.'

If Winnington was surprised he didn't show it. 'Who knows? He might well do that one day. He's a talented young man.'

'Not one day, Thomas. Now. I want to stand down. I want Arthur Pendragon to succeed me.'

'Let me get this straight,' said Winnington slowly, 'you are proposing that a man of – how old is he exactly . . . ?'

'Twenty-six,' said Leo calmly.

' . . . that a man of twenty-six should become leader of United Labour?'

'That's right.'

Thomas Winnington shook his head, tut-tutting his disapproval. 'I'm sorry, Leo, but it simply doesn't make sense. We have a perfectly good leader. Give me one good reason why we should change horses in mid-stream.'

'I'm tired, Thomas, tired of being in opposition, tired of lies and broken promises, tired of what used to be this great country going downhill year by year, tired of living in fear, and tired as hell of not being able to do anything about it. You want more reasons?'

Winnington's shoulders slumped. The burden of depression bore down on him. He had never known Leo talk so negatively. 'Very well. Tell me why you think Arthur Pendragon can win the election for us.'

'Because, Thomas, he's a man of principle. Because he means what he says. Because he's strong. Because he has vision. Because, young as he is, people have enormous respect for him. And because he's not afraid of taking on his father.' Leo could see he was making some impression on Winnington. 'In only two years look how Arthur's star has risen in the Party and in the House. I tell you, Thomas, the man's a natural born leader.'

'You could be right,' said Winnington. 'I just don't think he's ready for the job.'

They agreed to talk further. In the event, however, the decision was made for them. That night Leo invited Arthur home, told him what he had in mind and insisted he go away and think about it. The next evening Arthur gave him his answer. 'I'm more than flattered by the offer,' he said, 'but the answer is no.'

Leo hung on doggedly. 'You understand that I intend to stand down as leader soon whatever happens.'

'Not before the election, surely?'

'No. I shall see the election through, lead the Party for a year or so, and then . . . ' – emphasising his commitment to the idea, Leo punched his right fist hard into the palm of his left hand – 'then you will be a leading candidate for the succession.'

Arthur did not answer Leo directly. 'You agree that my father will almost certainly be elected leader of New Millennium?'

'Who knows? Your father has enemies. He's ambitious, some would say ruthless. The road to the summit is littered with the bodies he has stepped over.'

'The chances are, though, that he will take New Millennium into the election,' insisted Arthur.

'Let's say he does,' said Leo. 'What then?'

'In my opinion he has the qualities that could make an excellent Prime Minister.'

'You really believe that?' asked Leo, astonished.

'I do. I know what people say about him but he has the experience. I don't. In any case . . . ' – Arthur hesitated – 'I'm not sure I want to be a leader. I was born to be a backbencher.'

Leo laughed. 'That's rich! You have told me more than once that you want to make a difference, that you want to change the world. Well let me tell you, Arthur, you can't change the world from the back benches. One day you will have to throw your hat in the ring.'

'Maybe so,' said Arthur, 'but at this moment in time I believe I'm too young for high office.'

'Age has nothing to do with it. Please think again.'

Arthur shook his head. 'I am greatly honoured by your confidence in me, sir, but no. I have made up my mind.'

'And if we win the election?'

'Then I will think about your offer again – if it still stands, that is.'

'It will,' Leo Grant assured him.

Uther was returned unopposed. He had achieved his ambition, just as Merlin said he would all those years ago. Leaving his celebrating supporters, he drove to Brackett Hall, brushing away tears of joy, and relishing the police escort that accompanied his new exalted status. This was the greatest day of his life and he wanted to share it with his wife.

It was Uther's misfortune that this day also happened to be the day Igraine decided it was time to leave her husband. For weeks now she had been reflecting on her marriage, wondering where it had gone wrong. Had she expected too much of Uther? Perhaps. But he had changed; he was not that glamorous and exciting man she had danced with on that memorable New Year's Eve when they first met. Then she had been the willing centre of his universe; now, like some dead planet, she orbited his sun. That very morning Igraine had finally confronted the painful truth; it was no use denying any longer that her marriage had foundered. There was nothing to be salvaged but the truth. Even as Uther burst into the sitting room, she said it: 'I want a divorce.'

Uther was so shocked that for a few moments he could neither move nor speak. 'Come again?' he muttered weakly.

'I want a divorce,' she repeated.

At first he thought she must be drunk or drugged. Looking at her more carefully he realised she was neither. This was no sudden declaration made in the grip of some noxious substance, nor even in the heat of anger. 'How long has this been brewing?'

'Twenty-five years.'

'I see,' he said, although he didn't. He paced the room aimlessly, casting anxious looks at her. 'You can't be serious, Igraine. I may not have been a perfect husband but I haven't been such an ogre, have I? I've tried to be a good father to your children. I have given you security and a beautiful home. What is so wrong with that? Damn it, I've given you just about everything a man can give a woman.'

Tears filled Igraine's eyes. 'Except love.'

'Not true.'

'Why pretend?'

'Really, Igraine,' he protested, 'this is all very distressing. Tonight, of all nights.'

'I am sorry,' she said bitterly. 'Is the timing inconvenient for you?'

He could hold back no longer. 'I have great news.' A dramatic pause. Then, arms flung wide – 'You are looking at the new Prime Minister.'

'Congratulations.' She could not have sounded less interested.

'Is that all you have to say?'

'What were you expecting?'

'Something a bit more fulsome perhaps?' he suggested.

'I am not in a fulsome mood.'

He switched into reproachful mode. 'You are being very unkind, duchess. And very unjust.'

She smiled sweetly. 'And how is May Middleton? Well, I hope?'

He raised his arms in mock surrender. 'So that's it.'

'Not all of it, by any means, but part of it, yes.'

Oddly enough, though things were not exactly going well, he felt relieved. Jealousy was something he understood. 'If I give you my word never to see her again?'

'It's a matter of total indifference to me whether you see her again or not,' she responded coldly.

'Then why do you want a divorce?'

'Because I don't love you anymore.'

His mouth opened and shut but no sound came out, his face was drained of colour, his eyes wounded. But then, with one of those rapid mood changes of his, he assumed that sham expression of contrition that she knew so well, and that infantile voice that she found so demeaning to his dignity as a man, and so insulting to her intelligence as a woman.

'Duchess,' he crooned, 'why must you be so cruel? Alright, I have sinned. *Mea culpa*. There, I confess.' He shook his head in self-reproach. 'I am a child compared with you, a naughty little boy, that's what I am.'

'You flatter yourself. You are a liar and a hypocrite.'

'Don't be like that, duchess. Give your old man a kiss and let's make up.' He bent his head towards her.

It was so grossly patronising and insensitive that suddenly she was enraged. 'Damn you, you bastard! Damn you!' She knew only that she wanted to wipe that inane smile off his face. Before he could stop her she had reached out and dragged her nails down his cheeks.

'Bitch!' He drew back his fist to strike her. She flinched, and his arm dropped to his side. In all the years there had never been any physical violence between them before. They were both in shock. She was the first to speak. 'I shouldn't have done that.'

'I deserved it.'

'Forgive me,' she said.

'I should ask forgiveness, not you. Give me another chance, Igraine. You were always the one, you know. You always will be. I love you.'

Could it be, she wondered, that he was being sincere? Certainly he looked it. He was still a fine looking man. In an unconscious gesture of affection, she touched his hair; it was greying now but she could still remember when it was jet black. Quickly she pulled her hand away. What was she doing? She had witnessed this same performance so many times, yet here she was again, almost believing he meant what he said.

'Do you really?' she found herself asking.

'You know I do.'

Worn out with quarrelling, they leaned against each other, like two ancient columns in a ruined temple. How was it possible, she asked herself, to feel anything for him, after all he had done to her? But she did. Was it what people called love? Or was it something else, something that had bonded them together over the years almost without their knowing it?

As they separated, he said, softly, 'twenty-five years, duchess. Surely they count for something?'

That brought a response from deep within her. It seemed he felt much as she did. Perhaps they really did have something worth saving after all. But then he spoiled everything by adding, 'I need you, duchess. If you leave me now, I'm done for. I'll have to resign before I've even moved into Number 10. What a scandal it would be. What a disgrace. Don't walk out on me, please.'

Oh God, he would never change. Never. 'It's always about you, isn't it? Always what *you* need.' Her eyes filled with tears.

He knelt by her. 'Please, duchess. I'll do anything you want.'

'It's too late.'

'I'm begging you.'

'For God's sake, Uther.'

'Give me another chance,' he pleaded. 'I'll make it up to you, I swear I will. '

'You really are impossible,' she said crossly. What a fool she was, what a weak, gullible fool.

He beamed, sensing she had relented. 'I adore you, duchess.'

In the bathroom he studied his reflection in the mirror, dabbing his face with tissues, examining each one for traces of blood, and murmuring sardonically, 'She loves me . . . she loves me not . . . ' It had been a close call, the closest yet.

In the spring election New Millennium was duly re-elected, their majority down to twenty-two seats. As the results were announced and it became clear that the Party was heading for a narrow victory, Uther gloated with the Party faithfuls in Central Office. Later he declared for the cameras outside Number 10: 'The country can now look forward to another five years of stability and prosperity.' There were those, even is his own party, who did not share his confidence.

Seven

2021

THE PARTY Sir Leo Grant gave for his daughter, Guinevere, was ostensibly for her eighteenth birthday. In his mind it was also for what in former times would have been called her "Coming Out". Although Leo was far from anxious to marry off his daughter, the guest list included some of the most eligible young men in town. In his opinion she was much too young to marry, and secretly he dreaded the thought of parting with her. Still, her happiness came first. The more men she met, he reasoned, the more discriminating she would become, and the better her chances of finding the right one.

Watching the young men compete for her attention, and how charmingly and graciously she handled them, he thanked God for blessing him with a sensible daughter. Not only was she sensible, she was beautiful as well; and that was not just a proud father's opinion, everyone said so. Sooner or later she would fall in love and marry. Would it, he wondered, be that laughing young man dancing with her now? Or perhaps one of that group leaning against the bar eyeing her with such interest? He knew them all, and all of them perfectly decent specimens of manhood. But oh, they were so young! At that age it was difficult to know who you were, let alone what you wanted in a lifelong partner. Whomever she married, he reasoned, it really ought to be someone a few years older than her. The girl had a strong character and a mind of her own. She would need a loving hand, yes, but a firm hand too.

When Arthur arrived Leo greeted him affectionately. By now he had a very soft spot for this young man. 'I have some news for you,' he told Arthur.

'Good news I hope.'

'Depends on your point of view.' Leo lowered his voice. 'I've reached a decision. I'm going to resign as leader of United Labour. It's the right thing to do.'

'No it isn't,' said Arthur. 'No one could possibly take your place.'

Leo was a determined man, he never gave up. 'I have someone in mind,' he said slyly.

'You know my feelings on that subject.'

'Won't you change your mind?'

'I'm sorry, Leo,' said Arthur and wandered off to mingle with the other guests. Waiting for a drink at the bar he tried to talk to a young fellow more or less his age, or perhaps about five years younger, he guessed. It was like wading through treacle. 'Arthur Pendragon,' he said, extending his hand in greeting. 'Glad to meet you.'

'Lancelot Bancroft,' came the stiff reply a few seconds later.

After another long and awkward pause, Arthur tried again. 'Friend of Guinevere, are you?'

A blank look. 'Guinevere?'

More silence.

'You must be a friend of Sir Leo, then.'

'No.' The seconds dragged on. 'Ban is,' said Bancroft addressing his drink.

'Ban?'

'My father.'

'I see,' said Arthur, wondering what to say next. This was certainly a most difficult and unrewarding conversation, hardly worth the struggle. Now that he had his drink he was tempted to excuse himself and walk away; for some reason he did not. Despite this young man's distant, not to say superior manner, there was something rather forlorn and vulnerable about him that appealed to Arthur and made him want to breach those formidable defences. A few more false starts and it emerged

302

that Arthur was a member of Parliament. To say that Lancelot was unimpressed would have been a gross understatement; he made it brutally plain that in his opinion all MP's were on the make, and every politician either an incompetent or a liar or both. Where did they go from here, wondered Arthur, feeling a touch bruised. Not one to give up easily, he let drop that he had been a major in the Special Forces, and was gratified by the reception he received; Lancelot was clearly impressed. A breakthrough! Disarmed by Arthur's quiet charm and genuine modesty, Lancelot was soon talking to a man he had known only a few minutes, an entirely new experience for him.

He told Arthur that his father was an ex-army man and that he himself was thinking of making the army his career. Arthur immediately offered his help. 'I hope this doesn't sound patronising,' he said, 'but if you do decide to join the army, why don't you get in touch? I have some pretty good contacts.' Lancelot reacted with a look of such disdain that for a moment Arthur was irritated, until he remembered his own reaction when Uther offered him help with his career. 'Look, I'm not proposing to pull any strings for you. I know you wouldn't want that. It's just that sometimes it helps to know the right people.'

'I'm sure it does,' was Lancelot's stiff response.

Lancelot's father, Bertie Bancroft, friend of Leo Grant and a great admirer of Guinevere, wandered up to Leo and without any preliminaries let fly his customary staccato burst of words, betraying his army credentials: 'That daughter of yours. Absolute stunner. She and Lance. What do you think?'

'Believe me, Ban, she could do a lot worse,'

Ban surveyed the crowd of youngsters at the bar and on the dance floor. 'Expect they'll meet.'

'He's a fine chap, Lancelot, no question about it,' said Leo Grant. 'A bit young for Ginny, perhaps. Somehow I have the feeling she'll go for an older man. One thing for sure, though, whatever I think, she'll do exactly what she wants.'

Ban rattled off again. 'Tall girl. Jumping about. Skirt up her thighs. Who is she?'

'Gertrude Lancaster. Friend of Guinevere. Her closest friend, I would say. Good-natured, if a little wild. Heart's in the right place, though.'

Whilst Lanky galloped round the floor, Guinevere came over and chatted with her father, politely warding off several young men who asked her to dance.

'Where's Ban?' she asked.

'Gone to get a drink. Why?'

'I just met that son of his.'

'Lancelot. What do you think of him?' asked Leo.

Guinevere raised a supercilious eyebrow. 'He's the most arrogant, patronising bore I ever met.'

Leo winced. 'Best not mention that to Ban.'

Talking to her father, Guinevere seemed preoccupied, surveying the dance floor with a frown on her face.

'Anything wrong, Ginny?'

'Nothing, dad. It's a wonderful party and you're a poppet.'

'Gertrude can be a little over-exuberant at times,' he ventured.

That apparently innocuous observation drove the colour into her cheeks and released a torrent of condemnation. 'It's embarrassing the way she behaves. Throwing herself at men, it's . . . shameless. Women should have more respect for themselves if they want to be treated like women and not sex objects.'

Leo looked at his daughter in astonishment. He had never seen her so angry. Her cheeks were flushed, her eyes bright with tears of rage. Tears? This was not his Ginny, not like her at all. Was it really Gertrude's behaviour that was distressing her?

'I wonder if things have changed all that much in the last thousand years,' he said. 'When it comes to the mating game, I mean.'

'Oh dad, how would you know?' said Guinevere, giving her father a withering look.

Leo winced. His daughter had a sharp tongue and knew how to use it. Yet an instant later he was totally disarmed. She put her arms round Leo's neck and kissed him. 'Forgive me. I'm a beast.'

'Nothing to forgive. Off you go and enjoy yourself. This is no time to be sitting with your father.'

'There's not a man in the room who can hold a candle to you.'

'Come now, Ginny. Not one of those fine young men? I don't believe it.'

'They're all so – immature.'

'Not all of them, surely.' He sneaked a sidelong glance at her. 'That's a fine man over there. And judging by that bevy of beauties round him, I should say I'm not the only one who thinks so. Wouldn't you know it?' Another keen look at his daughter. 'There's Gertrude chatting him up.'

'Who?'

'Arthur.'

Guinevere lifted her chin in a characteristic gesture. 'Arthur?' It was as if she had never heard the name before.

'Arthur Pendragon, the MP. You met him once, I'm sure you did. Probably years ago, though. You were always away at school when he came to dinner.'

'Arthur,' she mused. 'Yes, I do vaguely remember him.'

Vaguely? Had Leo not seen his daughter looking rather intently at Arthur earlier in the evening? Perhaps not, he could have been mistaken. More important, he was disappointed that Arthur had not asked Ginny to dance. Obviously he had other things on his mind. Quite the ladies' man these days.

'Just look at that. Dragged onto the dance floor, and by Gertrude, wouldn't you know?'

'Really, father,' Guinevere's colour was high again, 'why should I care what Mr. Pendragon does? It's of no interest to

305

me. He's your friend, not mine.'

So that was the way the wind blew, was it? He managed not to smile, and just as well, he thought, or he would never have heard the end of it.

'Indeed he is. A very good friend, and a quite outstanding man. I like him very much.' He began to whistle under his breath, and was unable to resist another quick look in his daughter's direction. 'Gertrude seems to have taken quite a fancy to him . . . and he to her,' he added, innocently. 'What do you think, Ginny?'

A proud tilt of the chin. 'I really couldn't say.' Then, abandoning the mask of indifference, she added tartly, 'Just look at her. How could she? I'd rather die than throw myself at a man like that.'

'How fortunate I am to have such a sensible daughter.'

Guinevere directed a suspicious look at her father but his face was inscrutable. He appeared to be wholly absorbed in sniffing his glass of burgundy.

As she got up to leave, there, unexpectedly, was Arthur.

'I rushed over when I saw you weren't surrounded by men. I've been wanting to dance with you all evening but the youngsters have beaten me to it every time. Wont you please put me out of my misery?'

Guinevere hesitated. For a moment it seemed she was about to excuse herself, but then she smiled with obvious pleasure. 'I'd be delighted.' Taking Arthur's arm, she walked off with him to the dance floor.

'I do vaguely remember him,' murmured Leo to himself, relaxing his facial muscles in a quiet smile. Leaning back in his chair with a sigh of contentment, he sipped his wine, and fondly observed, in the discreetest imaginable way, the two people he loved most in all the world.

'I'm afraid I'm not much good at the latest dances,' said Arthur apologetically. 'No match for these youngsters.'

'Are you so old, then?'

Arthur laughed. 'Perhaps youngsters is the wrong word. I suppose I meant people of your sort of age.'

'And what age might that be?' she asked coyly.

'I know you are just about eighteen because of this party. I would have known anyway.'

'How?' She could feel her heart thumping at her breast.

'You won't remember but we met once years ago. I have never forgotten it. You told me you were an almost fourteen year old. That means you are now an almost eighteen year old.'

So he did remember, then. 'Fancy your remembering that. Such a very trivial thing.'

'I remember something else you said. You said twenty-four was a good age for a man.'

Guinevere blushed. 'Did I say that?'

'You did.' Arthur smiled.

'You must have thought me a precocious brat.'

'I thought you were enchanting.'

She lowered her eyes and said nothing.

He was afraid he might have offended her. 'It was so delightfully unexpected coming from a thirteen year old – I beg your pardon, an almost fourteen year old.'

When she looked up at him again, she was smiling. 'So that means you are now an almost twenty-seven year old.'

Absurd but it sounded old. 'Afraid so.'

Thinking of another thing she had said five years ago, she blushed again. Unless her memory was playing tricks on her, she had told him how good looking he was. No, her memory was not playing tricks. She remembered it quite clearly. Horror of horrors! It was the sort of outrageously flirtatious thing Lanky might have said. Hopefully he was too chivalrous to mention it, even if he too remembered. She prayed he would change the subject.

'You like dancing?' he asked, as if in answer to her prayer.

'I love it.'

'I do too.' He cleared his throat. 'If only I had the chance to practice more.'

It was obvious what he was getting at, though she pretended not to understand, looking about her with keen interest at the other dancers on the floor. Seeing Lanky prancing about, her mood darkened and she was suddenly uncertain of herself.

Arthur mistakenly concluded from her silence that another hint was needed. 'I don't suppose you know anyone who could give me dancing lessons?'

'Indeed I do,' said Guinevere sweetly. 'You should talk to Gertrude. She is an excellent dancer, as of course you know. I am sure she would be more than happy to give you as many lessons as you like.'

Eight

A T TWENTY-THREE, Lancelot was already a captain in the Grenadier Guards. A natural soldier, smart and enthusiastic, he knew how to give and take orders. Despite being a stern disciplinarian he was respected by his men as a fair-minded officer, and valued by his superiors for his conscientiousness and dedication.

Ian Duncan was stationed at the same army camp up north. No one, himself included, understood what he was doing there, for no man could have been less suited to military life. The fact was, that after coming down from university, he had no idea what to do with himself, and until something better came his way, he decided to follow the friend to whom he was devoted. Despite being scruffy, lazy and unfit, Ian had managed to reach the rank of first lieutenant by being agreeable to everyone. The general view, though, was that he would still be a first lieutenant when Lancelot was a general.

There were times when even Ian found Lance difficult to be around. Super-critical, finding fault with his men when more senior officers found none, he hated bad language, loathed slovenliness, and above all despised what he perceived to be lack of commitment. If only, thought Ian, if only Lance would take life just a little less seriously, if only he would have a drink with the boys now and then. The sad truth was that being one of the boys was not in Lancelot's nature.

Despite his misgivings, Ian had never altered his view that his friend was an exceptional human being, a big man in every way, a man of strongly-held principles. Was there not, moreover, something heroic in his refusal to compromise? Certainly there was nothing mean-spirited about him; he had none of the petty imperfections that flawed the characters of lesser men. In an inconstant world, Lance was constant; you always knew where you were with him.

The parade ground incident, therefore, came as a particular shock. It began when Ian was shaken from a deep sleep by the platoon sergeant. He reached for the watch by his bed. 'What time is it?'

'Past two, sir.'

'What's up?' He was still half asleep.

'Best come and see, sir.' Ian threw on a dressing gown and followed the sergeant to the parade ground.

It was mid-winter and a bitterly cold night, the moon was full, intermittently obscured by clouds. That very morning there had been a parade of honour for the Minister of Defence and it had not gone well. Instead of giving their usual perfectly co-ordinated display, the men had marched raggedly, like raw recruits. It was one of those unfortunate things that happen from time to time, even in the best of regiments, and the Colonel had made no comment afterwards. Nor did anyone else. But Captain Bancroft who led the parade had felt humiliated, and typically had assumed the full burden of responsibility.

In the darkness a voice rang out from the other side of the parade ground. It seemed to come from the platform known as the dais on which the Colonel took the salute at regimental parades, and it was so loud that at first Ian thought the commands were directed at him: 'Get those arms up! Straighten those backs! Left! Left! Left, right, left!' As his eyes adjusted to the dark he could just make out a dim figure standing on the dais.

'Who is that?' Ian asked the sergeant.

'Captain Bancroft, sir.'

The clouds parted to reveal the full moon, and suddenly the parade ground was lit up as if it were day. There on the dais was Lancelot in his pyjamas, standing rigidly to attention. 'You there! What d'you think you're doing! Ranks three and four, you're a shambles! Get back in step! Left! Left! Left, right, left!' Ian and the sergeant exchanged glances, then without a word they ran across the parade ground to the dais. Ian looked up at his friend. 'Lance! What do you think you're playing at? You'll wake the whole camp.'

'You down there, get back in line! Get back, or I'll have you court-martialled!'

'It's me, Lance. It's Ian. Come down, man.'

'By the right, quick march! Eyes right! You there, get your head round! Stay in line! You're wandering all over the place! Chin over your right shoulder! Swing those arms!'

In the still night air the echoes of his voice rebounded from the camp buildings, creating such a confusion of sound that there might have been a dozen men shouting orders. One by one, the lights came on in windows around the camp.

'Lance! Come down! You'll catch pneumonia.' But Ian might as well have been talking to the moon.

'You there in the second row! Get in step! You too, Mathews! And you, MacPherson! Jones, hold your rifle steady. It's not a toy! Steady on your shoulder!'

'I'm coming up to get you, Lance.'

'That man in the front there – Captain Bancroft! What kind of salute is that? Straighten your upper arm! Hand parallel with your shoulder! Look at you! Your position's all wrong. You're supposed to be leading the parade. You should be setting an example. You're a disgrace to the army! Damned disgrace, I say!'

They ran up the steps of the dais. The sergeant was about to grab Lancelot when Ian stopped him. 'No. His eyes are shut. He's sleep-walking. He can't see us. I don't think he knows we're here.' Taking Lancelot by the arm, they guided him down the steps and onto the parade ground. 'Gently does it. Mustn't wake him.' Crossing the tarmac Lancelot was quiet. As they approached the camp he threw back his head and bawled at the top of his voice, 'You're a disgrace, Bancroft! Damned disgrace! Have you on a charge!'

Aroused by all the noise, a huddled group of pyjama-clad officers and other ranks watched curiously as the three figures approached. Ian muttered something about sleep-walking and hurried Lancelot passed them. By the time they got him back to his quarters he had calmed down. They rolled him into bed and tucked him in mumbling again and again, 'Disgrace, Bancroft. Have you on a charge.' A few minutes later he was sleeping peacefully.

The next morning Ian knew he had to tell Lancelot what had happened. If he did not tell him, someone else would. When he had finished, Lancelot put his head in his hands. 'What a humiliation.'

'Nonsense,' said Ian, making light of it. Lots of people sleep-walk. Could have happened to anyone.'

'What will they think of me?' moaned Lancelot.

A grin. 'Since when has that ever worried you?'

'This is the army, Ian. If you lose the respect of your men . . . ' Lancelot threw up his arms in despair. 'You might as well give up.'

'It will all be forgotten in a day or two.' For all his reassuring words, Ian looked uncomfortable. 'There is one thing . . . '

'Well?'

'You might want to see – well, a shrink . . . or someone,' he ended lamely, conscious that Lance was watching him intently.

'You think I'm crazy,' said Lancelot. 'That's it, isn't it?'

'Be reasonable, Lance. There are plenty of other reasons for seeing a shrink.'

Lancelot was in no mood to be reasonable. 'What are you saying, then?'

'Something may be troubling you?' suggested Ian.

Lancelot thumped the wall in frustration. 'Nothing is

troubling me.'

'Fine, then. Fine. Don't see a shrink.' Ian wished he had never mentioned the word.

Later that morning the Colonel called Lancelot to his office.

'What shall I say?' he asked Ian.

'Tell him the truth; you were sleep-walking and you didn't know what you were doing. You weren't responsible.'

Lancelot seized on the word. 'Not responsible? What is that supposed to mean?'

Ian sighed. For his friend's sake he had to stay calm. 'It means what it says. You were not responsible for your actions. Nothing he can do about that. Nothing anyone can do.'

Lancelot paced the room restlessly. 'I shall have to resign.'

'Nonsense! You'll be a general one day, everyone says so. Where would the army find another man like you?'

'Where would I find another friend like you?' To Ian's astonishment Lancelot put his arms round his shoulders and hugged him. It was so unexpected that he had to turn away his head to hide the tears.

Colonel Marsden was sympathetic, almost too sympathetic, which was hardly reassuring for Lancelot. Anger would have been easier to deal with. 'Sit down, Bancroft.' For a few moments the C.O. fiddled with a paper knife. 'That incident last night on the parade ground. What's the story?'

'I have no recollection of it. I'm told I was sleep-walking.'

'So I understand.' The C.O. looked concerned. 'You're a fine officer, Bancroft. I hope you will make the army your career. We need men like you.'

'Thank you, sir.'

'This business, though. I think you should take it seriously.'

'I do. I'm ashamed of myself.' Lancelot looked down at the floor.

'No need to be,' the C.O. assured him. 'It was not your fault.

No blame can possibly be attached to you. What happened was obviously entirely beyond your control.'

Lancelot studied his boots. *Beyond his control.* The last thing he wanted to hear.

The C.O. shifted uneasily in his chair. 'I'm no doctor, but, er . . . ' – A diffident cough – 'may I suggest you have a medical check-up?'

That meant a doctor, not a shrink. Something of a relief. 'I'll do that, sir.'

'Excellent.'

With his hand on the doorknob, the C.O. added, 'Mind you, sometimes these sort of things . . . it might not actually be a physical problem. Could be some kind of, well, not mental disturbance exactly, but that sort of thing . . . if you know what I mean.' He extended his hand. 'Alright, Bancroft?' Lancelot nodded dumbly. 'I am not very well up on these matters,' the C.O. continued, shaking Lancelot's hand vigorously. 'Very sympathetic, though, I assure you, very sympathetic indeed. Today's army is most understanding about these things, as I'm sure you know.'

Lancelot took a week's leave and had a check-up. In a couple of days the results came through: there was nothing wrong with him. The doctor gave him a reassuring smile: 'As perfect a specimen of manhood as ever I've seen. I'm happy to give you a clean bill of health.'

A clean bill of health. What should have been a reason for celebration was, on the contrary, cause for profound concern. Nothing was wrong with him. Nothing physical, that is. He went back to his flat and tried to think . . . *not mental disturbance exactly* . . . his father had told him so little about his mother. He looked like her, that much he knew. He had her brown eyes, her long face, her high forehead. Physically they were apparently much alike; and in one other respect too; they were both what Ban called 'highly-strung'. He had hinted as much without going into details. What kind of inner torment made someone take their life? Why was his father always so reluctant to talk about his wife, more especially the circumstances leading to her death? It wasn't what his father had told him that troubled him, it was what he hadn't told him.

Lancelot had never been frightened of anything before but he was now; so frightened that he could not sleep for worrying – not that night, nor the next, nor the next. There were endless questions and no answers. How could there be? In the end rational thought was overwhelmed by fatigue, leaving him drained and without the will to resist. The following day Lancelot was due back at camp. He had planned to take the train.

By chance Ian Duncan had driven up to London for a friend's party. Sleeping until noon after a late night, Ian guessed Lancelot would already be on his way to camp, but decided to pass by his flat anyway. There was no answer when he buzzed the street door intercom. He had missed him. But as he was walking back to his car, something caught his eye – an unexpected glimmer of light from the second floor – Lancelot's flat. It was two o'clock on a sunny winter's afternoon and the lights were on in the front rooms. Lancelot must have forgotten to switch them off before he went out.

Ian got in his car and for a few moments sat staring ahead. It didn't make sense, Lance was one of the most meticulous and organised people he knew. Would he leave the flat and forget to turn the lights off? One light, perhaps, but all of them? He went back and buzzed the intercom a second and a third time, long, insistent rings. Still no answer. He was about to give up when a middle-aged lady opened the door.

'May I help you?'

'I was ringing Captain Bancroft's bell. He must have gone out.'

'Lancelot?' She shook her head. 'I don't think so. At least he was up there a few minutes ago. I heard him walking about.'

'He doesn't answer.'

'The intercom is always giving trouble. Why don't you go up and knock on his door.'

Upstairs Ian knocked twice. No answer. He rang the doorbell. Again no answer. He was just turning away when he thought he heard a voice inside Lancelot's flat. He knocked again. Silence. He left his finger on the bell for a full thirty seconds. Again he thought he heard a voice, and this time he was certain that it came from Lance's flat. He made up his mind. One of the useful things he had learned in the army was how to pick a lock, though until now he had never had the occasion to test his skill. The lock clicked. He pushed the door open. Lancelot was lying on the floor, deathly pale, muttering incoherently. By his side was an empty box of sleeping pills and a half-empty bottle of whisky.

When he recovered consciousness a few hours later, Ian was at his bedside; but it was a couple of days before Lancelot was willing to talk. The doctors accepted that the overdose had been accidental. Ian knew differently.

'That sleep-walking business preyed on my mind.' Lancelot stared ahead, addressing his comments to the wall of his room. 'I made a fool of myself. I let down the army. I let everyone down.'

'That was no reason to try and kill yourself,' Ian said angrily. He could not understand why his friend had done such a stupid and selfish thing. Yet at the same time he also blamed himself. He had not been there for Lancelot.

'Put it down to hubris and ego,' said Lancelot humbly.

'That all?' Ian badly needed to understand what had driven his friend to attempt suicide.

Lancelot folded down his top sheet and smoothed it carefully. 'Not entirely.'

'Want to talk about it?'

Did he? How much did he want to tell Ian? He decided on a partial explanation, without going into details. 'You were the one who said it first.'

'Said what?'

'That I didn't know what I was doing. That I was not responsible for my actions.'

'Forgive me, Lance.' He should never have said such a thing. 'That was grossly clumsy of me. I didn't mean that at all.'

'Yes, you did,' insisted Lancelot. 'And you were right. I was out of control. That's the one thing that has always scared me – ever since that business at University. I wanted to kill that man. I nearly did.'

Ian was beginning to understand. 'Absolute nonsense! That was a freak accident.'

'It's not what I did,' said Lancelot, 'it's what was in my mind that scares me.'

'You never touched him. That's all that matters,' said Ian reassuringly.

'I wish it was.'

'You are the sanest person I know.'

In that moment Lancelot realised that Ian understood him far better than he had ever given him credit for. 'Thank you for that.'

As he stood up to go, Ian patted his friend on the shoulder. The gesture was minimal but it said everything there was to say about their relationship. 'The world wouldn't be the same without you,' he said warmly. 'Not for me, not for a lot of people. I wish you would remember that.'

'Bless you, Ian.'

Ian had been in the right place at the right time. A happy coincidence? Was that all there was to it? The more Lancelot thought about it, the more convinced he became that it was more than just coincidence. He had wanted to end his life, but for some reason he had not been allowed to. Could it be that that some divine power had intervened, using his friend as its instrument?

Nine

2022

H AVE I EVER shown you around the facilities?'
Arthur's heart beat faster. Facilities – a neutral word –
but for him it still conjured up the secret world that all those
years ago had been so tantalisingly off-bounds to boys and staff
alike. When he was a boy at Glastonbury school, Arthur and
his friends had often tried to locate Merlin's famous "facilities".
They knew exactly where they ought to be – somewhere
behind the sports hall – but somehow, when they went to look
for them, there was nothing there but fields. Their carefully
planned midnight expeditions had proved equally frustrating,
for they invariably ended up back where they started, as if their
legs were playing tricks on them.

'I don't believe you have.'

'You don't mean it!' Merlin's eyebrows lifted in mock
astonishment, the feathers on Virgil's head standing erect in
sympathy. 'How very remiss of me.' He strode ahead of Arthur,
tut-tutting and scolding himself all the while.

It was shameless play-acting, as Arthur well knew. He had
never seen Merlin's facilities, not because Merlin was absent-
minded but because he had not wanted him to see them. Now
suddenly, out of the blue, he had received from the magus an
apparently casual invitation that he knew he could not refuse.
Merlin sped along somewhere behind the sports hall heading
who knew where, his white robes flowing behind him in the
breeze, Virgil perching precariously on his shoulder. It seemed
that, for some reason known only to himself, Merlin had finally
decided that Arthur should see his secret place. But why now,

after all these years? How they got there, Arthur had no idea, but suddenly a door opened and shut and 'here we are,' said Merlin, a touch of drama in his voice.

At first Arthur was disappointed. He had no clear idea what he was expecting but whatever it was, it was more than this. One dreary laboratory led to another, each crammed, it seemed, with the kind of experiments Arthur used to conduct when he was a lad – row upon row of bottles and test tubes filled with liquids all colours of the rainbow. True, there were inexplicable eruptions of smoke from cupboards and dark corners, and mysterious winking lights, and strange looking engines – one with such a high-pitched scream that it made poor Virgil squawk loudly and hide his head under his wing. But on the whole it was pretty disappointing. Where were the inventions of the once world-renowned inventor? Where was the magic of the magus?

As the tour progressed (with no commentary from Merlin), it became apparent to Arthur that the impression created by the first few laboratories was a false one, quite possibly deliberately so. He understood enough of science and technology to know that some serious research was going on. But what exactly? It was time for Merlin to come up with some explanations. 'What are you up to?' Merlin contrived to look innocent. 'Don't be coy, Merlin. You brought me here for a reason.'

Merlin grinned, happy that his protégé was intrigued. 'Well now,' he said, 'in this laboratory we are conducting experiments into some rather advanced forms of communication. Another lab through that door there is dedicated to surveillance techniques. We are also playing around with a few weapons of different categories and uses.'

Playing around was good, thought Arthur, and so typical of Merlin.

'I should mention,' added Merlin, 'that there are a couple of laboratories you cannot see – for various reasons.'

Did the magus not trust him, Arthur was wondering.

Merlin read his thoughts. 'It's not that, Arthur. I trust you completely.'

'Why can't I see those laboratories, then?'

'Take the lab devoted to nano-technology,' said Merlin. 'The air has to be permanently controlled. Human intrusion would contaminate it.'

Arthur was highly intrigued. 'Why are you experimenting with nano-technology?'

'Our goal is to insert nano-chips into some rather small devices,' Merlin explained.

'Small? How small?'

'Two or three microns.' A sharp look. 'Does that mean anything to you?'

'Not a lot,' admitted Arthur.

'A human hair is a hundred microns thick. Does that give you some idea?' Arthur nodded mutely. What could he say? It was all too incredible for words. 'These little fellows,' continued Merlin, 'can be injected into the blood, or sprayed into the air to be inhaled. Once they are in place, they could be activated from thousands of miles away.'

Arthur hardly dared ask. 'To do what?'

'To kill – amongst other things,' said Merlin almost casually.

'My God.' Arthur was now seriously concerned. He knew that scientists in the R and D special unit in Beaconsfield where Merlin had once worked were continually developing advanced weapons and technology. But Merlin was no longer working for the British Government. Who was he working for now? Had the magus sold himself to the highest bidder? And if so, for what? Money? Knowing Merlin as he did, that seemed to Arthur highly unlikely.

Merlin tried to reassure Arthur. 'It need not always be that absolute. Micro-organisms have many different uses. In medicine, for example, they have enormous potential to cure disease. In warfare their controlled use could greatly limit the number of deaths and life-threatening injuries. They could slow down or speed up reactions. They could contaminate or decontaminate. They could confuse. They could put a man to sleep. They could be used to send or receive messages, or simply as spies.'

Arthur's head felt like cotton wool. It was hard to take all this in. 'Spies?'

Merlin was enjoying himself. 'Imagine a microscopic spy in your bloodstream sending messages via satellite on your vital functions and on your every movement – or your every thought, for that matter – though I must admit we are not quite there yet.'

'Why are you doing all this?' Arthur had to ask the question, though knowing Merlin he very much doubted he would get a straight answer.

'For one thing, we know that some very dangerous terrorists may one day have access to nano-technology,' said Merlin grimly. 'It pays to stay ahead of the game.'

"We" know, Merlin had said. Who was "we"? Again there was an implicit acknowledgement that Merlin was not working alone. Obviously he had helpers. Not even the magus could do all this himself. So who was helping him?

Yet again Merlin read Arthur's thoughts. 'The answer to your question is yes, I do have helpers, men and women who will one day be actively involved . . . somewhere else. They are people who share my beliefs and are dedicated to the cause.'

Cause? What cause was Merlin talking about?

'Before I answer that,' said Merlin, as if Arthur had spoken, 'I want to show you an important experiment, perhaps the most important of all. Come.'

Merlin led Arthur to a laboratory at the heart of the whole complex and was immediately challenged by the door monitor to give the codeword of the day. Much to Arthur's astonishment, the codeword was Arthur. Obviously Merlin had planned the visit. Next Merlin was asked for his palm print. Finally he was told to look directly at the screen.

'They don't trust even you?'

'The computer trusts no one, or not until it has identified them.'

'What about me?'

'It accepts you because you are with me. Without me you would not get through this door.'

The door slid smoothly open and they walked in. Arthur paused while his eyes adjusted to the dim light. Gradually he became aware of a silver globe that seemed to float in the air at the far end of the room. As he watched, fascinated, the globe was suddenly illuminated so that it shone as brightly as a miniature moon. He could see now that it stood on a thin metal rod.

'That globe is made of titanium-hardened steel,' said Merlin, 'about as strong a metal as it is possible to produce with the resources of modern technology. By the way, it is thirty centimetres in diameter. Now look over there.'

About ten feet away, at the other end of the table, was a black box no more than ten centimetres square. In the side of the box facing the silver globe was a small hole.

'Let's go into the next lab,' said Merlin. 'No, wait. I want you to feel the globe first.'

Arthur ran his fingers over it, then clasped it in both hands testing its weight; it was very heavy. As Merlin said, it was about thirty centimetres in diameter, and solid as solid could be.

'Let's go,' said Merlin briskly.

The adjoining room was in darkness. The whole of one wall was a window.

'Sit here, facing the window.'

Arthur did as he was told.

Merlin tapped the glass. 'Anti-UV and shatter-proof.'

On the table in front of them was a panel with illuminated dials, switches and knobs. 'Watch carefully,' said Merlin as he flipped two switches, waited a few seconds, then, one by one, slowly turned three dials a half circle clockwise, and one a half circle anti-clockwise. The dials registered what Arthur assumed was some kind of power surge. He had no idea what to expect but felt the tension of anticipation. The palms of his hands were sweating, his heart pounded against his ribs.

'What am I watching?'

'The globe. The black box.'

For a few seconds nothing happened. Then, quite suddenly, the hole in the black box glowed white, and the silver globe at the end of the table was no longer there. Merlin turned to Arthur with a grin. 'What do you think of that?'

'Some kind of illusion.'

'What if I told you that your eyes did not deceive you?'

It was one of the magus's illusions. It had to be. 'No, Merlin, you can't fool me. The globe could have melted I suppose, but then I would have seen something.'

'It did not melt, I assure you,' said Merlin.

Then what else could it have been but some kind of magic trick? 'You are saying it was not an illusion, and it didn't melt?' Arthur was determined to pin the magus down.

'Correct.'

'I'm sorry,' said Arthur, shaking his head, 'but that's impossible.'

'There are more things in heaven and earth . . . '

'So I've heard.'

Merlin waved through the window at the laboratory they had just left. 'Go and see for yourself. I'll stay here.'

The metal stand was there. Arthur reached for the globe that rested on it, the globe he knew must still be there, even though he could not see it. But where it had been less than a minute ago there was nothing. Again and again his hands passed though thin air. But what his hands had already accepted, his brain could not. Painstakingly, inch by inch, he scoured the whole laboratory, every surface, every nook and cranny, even dropping to his knees to examine the floor. Nothing. He tried to think but his brain was numb. It was impossible but it had happened. It was no illusion. The silver globe had not simply disappeared. It had ceased to exist.

Merlin's voice boomed on the intercom: 'Come back, Arthur. The experiment is not over yet.'

Merlin's fingers moved quickly over the panel, once again adjusting switches and dials.

'Watch.'

'What am I looking at now?'

'The black box. And where the globe was.'

Once more the hole in the box glowed white, only now it seemed a hundred times brighter than before. So intense was the light that even with the window's special protection, Arthur was momentarily blinded.

'Open your eyes, Arthur.'

He looked, looked again in disbelief, closed his eyes, and looked a third time. The silver globe had reappeared. This time he needed no invitation. He ran into the lab next door, but could only stand and stare at the globe, fearing to touch it.

Merlin's voice echoed jovially over the intercom. 'It won't bite you.' Reaching out, Arthur ran his hands over the cold steel. The globe was thirty centimetres in diameter, and as solid as solid could be.

'Explain,' Arthur demanded later over a cup of tea.

'What you have just seen, the greatest scientific minds in the world have been trying to accomplish for years,' claimed Merlin, with his customary lack of modesty. 'Billions of dollars have been poured into research. But no one has ever succeeded in doing it.'

'Doing what?' asked Arthur.

'Dematerialising matter.'

'I thought that was just a theoretical concept, something that only happens in science-fiction movies.'

'It's a great deal more than that,' said Merlin. 'Scientists at CERN in Geneva actually succeeded in producing a single atom of matter more than thirty years ago. But that's as far as it got.'

'Why?'

'Because even to materialise that single atom cost billions of dollars. The world economy could not possibly sustain such a programme.'

When would the magus cease to amaze him? 'So you have done what no one else has done, or perhaps ever will do.'

'Not for many years to come, quite possibly for centuries, perhaps never. Clever of me, don't you think?' Merlin looked unashamedly smug, and Virgil puffed up his feathers proudly so that he looked twice his normal size.

Now that Arthur had recovered from the initial shock, his mind focused on what to him was the most inexplicable aspect of the demonstration. 'That globe, like every other material thing, is composed of matter. But if matter is destroyed, how can it reappear again?'

'It can't,' said Merlin.

'But it did. I saw it. I touched it.'

'That is because the globe was not destroyed,' said Merlin. 'It was deconstructed, which meant it could be reassembled again. The two modes are linked. I call them Demat and Remat. There is also a third mode.'

The hairs tingled on the back of Arthur's neck. 'What is that?'

'Elimat.'

'When matter is eliminated?'

'Correct.'

'In other words, destroyed.'

'Yes.'

'For ever.'

'For ever.'

'My God.' Now Arthur was beginning to understand the significance of what Merlin was telling him.

'Quite so,' said Merlin calmly. 'The potential is unlimited.'

Later, over a coffee, Arthur asked the questions that were troubling him. 'These experiments you do, and the laboratories and so on. It must all cost a great deal of money. Where does it come from?'

'I prefer not to answer that question,' said Merlin.

Arthur was dismayed. Merlin seemed to be confirming his worst suspicions. 'Why not?'

'You suspect me of taking bribes – or something else in kind – from some government? Or perhaps from big-time criminals?'

'I didn't say that,' said Arthur, his voice low.

'Nevertheless it is what you thought.'

Arthur could not deny it.

'I am disappointed, Arthur,' said Merlin. 'I thought you had more faith in me.' He raised his hand to silence Arthur's protest. 'I will tell you only this, and you will have to be satisfied with it.' It did not help to allay Arthur's suspicions that Merlin looked so very uncomfortable. 'The project on which I am working does indeed require money, a great deal of money, as you say. No one in the world would finance me, that I have always known. Even if some individual or government were willing to, I should lose the most precious and important of all things – my independence to act as I see fit. So . . . because there was no other way to get the money I needed for my project . . . ' Merlin mumbled the words. 'I stole it.'

'You what!'

'That's right, Arthur,' said Merlin calmly. 'I stole it. How, I will not tell you. All I will say is that those from whom I stole are the very worst kind of criminals. Their money does as much harm to the world as the terrorists. More, perhaps.'

Arthur had some idea what Merlin was talking about. 'You mean – ?'

Merlin lifted a hand to silence Arthur. 'I mean no one. I mean nothing. My only justification is the vital importance of the cause.'

That word again. 'What cause, Merlin?'

'Oh, you know,' said Merlin casually. 'Saving the world.'

For a long time Arthur was too overwhelmed to speak. 'These experiments,' he said at last, 'they are not just experiments, are they. I mean, this is not the end of it.'

'No, Arthur,' said Merlin, 'this is not the end. This is the beginning. Of course, not all experiments work out. But the successful ones are developed, first on a small, then on a large scale. Some exist only as prototypes. Some are already in full production.'

'Where?'

'Far from here,' said Merlin vaguely.

No one could be more infuriating than the magus. 'Can't you tell me more?'

Merlin threw Arthur a crumb of information. 'On an island.'

'May I see it?'

'Soon.'

And that apparently was that. He could get no more out of the magus. The more Arthur reflected on what he had seen and heard, the more anxious he became. Not for the first time he asked himself a painful question. Was Merlin sane? If he were not, thought Arthur . . . such power in the hands of a madman . . .

Ten

2023

LEO GRANT was still trying to persuade anyone who cared to listen that he intended to stand down as leader of the United Labour Party. The problem was that he had cried wolf so often that no one took him seriously any more. In his desperation to move things along, he now made it known to a few selected members in the House and to some key party activists that his resignation would be 'in the very near future.' What exactly he meant by that was not clear, neither to the Party nor to him. The fact was that Leo had left the date of his departure open for a very good reason; he had no intention of handing over the reigns to anyone but Arthur, and he had not yet convinced Arthur to stand as his successor.

In the spring of 2023, however, something happened that made Arthur think again. A mystery figure calling himself Lord Mark proclaimed the independence of the counties of Herefordshire and Worcestershire. That evening, television newscasters featured the proclamation as their lead story, focusing on the identity of Lord Mark. Who was he? Should he be taken seriously, or was he just some crackpot? No one seemed to know.

The following morning the story was headline news in every newspaper in the country with most carrying the full text of Lord Mark's statement. Journalists were divided between those convinced it was a hoax and those who believed that the long anticipated break-up of the United Kingdom had begun.

The message was as follows:

We, the LandLords, can no longer tolerate the inhumane and divisive policies of Westminster.

Your record speaks for itself. You have turned our cities into fortresses of privilege and wealth. In so doing you have ignored the needs of the underprivileged. You have cut welfare to the bone, targeting the poor, the homeless, single parent families, the sick and the elderly. You have made the rich richer and the poor poorer.

We country dwellers have been deprived of the basic amenities that are the right of every citizen. Our shires and counties are supposed to be autonomous, but what use is that when council budgets are cut by Westminster every year? Our mail is not delivered, our trash is not collected, our shops have disappeared, our transportation system has broken down, our police force is understaffed, our schools are underfunded, our hospitals are a sick joke.

From this day forward we reject the authority of Westminster. In due time we shall implement the expropriation of the land the capitalists have stolen from us over the centuries. God gave us the land. It is our land, the people's land. It belongs to us by right. We shall never surrender it. We – not you – are the law. We – not you – are the government. We – not you – will make all decisions relating to our Kingdom – who lives, who works and who travels here.

We, the wronged people of Herefordshire and Worcestershire, this day proclaim our independence, and call on our persecuted brothers the length and breadth of the land to follow our example. A new era has begun.

Lord Mark of Cornwall,
The LandLords.

When after several days no further statements were issued by the self-styled LandLords, the press and the general public began to lose interest. A Downing Street spokesman said that in his view the whole thing was an elaborate hoax, unworthy of serious consideration. Arthur did not agree. At Prime Minister's question time a few days after the release of Lord Mark's statement, Arthur rose in a packed and silent House to put a question to the Prime Minister. Expectation was high, for although it was by no means the first time the Prime Minister had been challenged by Arthur Pendragon, the exchanges between father and son had invariably been sharp, and were becoming sharper with each successive confrontation.

Arthur wasted not a moment. 'In the view of the potential seriousness of the subject I would like to put a number of questions to the Prime Minister – all relating to the same matter.'

'If the Prime Minister has no objection,' said the Speaker.

Uther inclined his head graciously.

'Very well,' continued Arthur. 'My questions are these. Who exactly is Lord Mark? Who are the Landlords? What are their aims and objectives? On what basis has the Prime Minister assured the House that Lord Mark's ultimatum is nothing but a hoax? Where is the evidence for this assertion?'

From the government backbenches there were shouts of 'Sit down!' Arthur had asked too many awkward questions for their liking.

'Many members,' continued Arthur, who had no intention of sitting down until he had finished, 'are deeply concerned at the Prime Minister's casual handling of this matter – some of them, I dare say, on his own side of the House.' This jibe was greeted with laughter, loud cries of protest and counter protest and shouts of 'withdraw!' Waiting for the House to quieten down, Arthur raised his right hand and pointed directly at his father. 'I cannot help suspecting that we are not being given the whole story by the Prime Minister. It would not be the first time,' he shouted above the uproar as he sat down.

Uther gave a forceful reply justifying the government's position, succeeding at least in satisfying his own Party. Lord Mark, he said, was a social misfit, a drunk and a drug addict;

his so-called followers were united only be their hatred of what they termed 'capitalists', a term that in their view included anyone who owned land. They clung to Lord Mark because they too were malcontents, people on the fringes of society. There was no rebel movement, no substance to the breakaway threat, no truth in Lord Mark's claim that the budgets of Worcestershire and Herefordshire had been slashed, no truth in the wild accusations relating to hospitals, the transport system, the police and so on. 'It is self-evident,' Uther concluded, 'that the law of the land upholds any man or woman's right to own land. Anyone who tries to take it from them by illegal means will be dealt with the full force of the law.' In answer to a question about Lord Mark, he amused the House by informing them that Lord Mark was not a lord at all. *Lord* was apparently his first name, one he had taken by Deed Poll, an indication of the unseriousness and vanity of the man. In the Prime Minister's view *Mister* Mark (more laughter in the House) saw himself as some kind of latter-day Robin Hood. The government did not intend to waste any more time on this deluded individual.

Whoever else Uther had satisfied, he had not satisfied Arthur. A few days later Arthur requested, and was granted, an interview with his father in 10 Downing Street.

'I believe Lord Mark could one day pose a real threat to the stability of this country,' he began. 'I am told he already has a following – a not insignificant one.'

Uther was not in the least perturbed. 'I don't deny it. He's a kind of cult leader, wouldn't you say?'

Arthur shook his head. 'More than that. An increasing number of disaffected citizens feel no loyalty to our country, indeed hardly any sense of belonging to it. They are the ones he is targeting. Lord Mark is no fool. He sees the trend, and he's taking advantage of it.'

Uther drummed impatient fingers on his desk. 'What trend?'

'Town against country,' said Arthur, 'North against South,

East against West, the haves against the have-nots, ethnic and religious differences creating social and geographical divisions. I believe that far from being a deluded individual Lord Mark is a very clever, very dangerous man. My information is that he is secretly training bands of vigilantes in remote areas of the countryside.'

Disbelief rode the steep arch of the Prime Minister's eyebrows. '*Your* information?'

Arthur had seen his father's play-acting before. It was obvious that the Prime Minister had access to the same intelligence Arthur had seen. Why then did Uther insist that Lord Mark was not to be taken seriously? It did not make sense. 'One day he might lead a full-scale revolution,' he warned. 'We could be talking not just civil strife but civil war.'

Uther regarded his son thoughtfully. 'There are wheels within wheels,' he observed mysteriously.

Arthur awaited an explanation, but none was forthcoming. 'What wheels within what wheels, father?' he asked. 'Why are you making light of a clear threat to national security?'

Uther smiled – a bland smile that left his eyes cold. 'Government policy,' he observed.

'Are you saying,' said Arthur, 'that it is government policy to bury its head in the sand?'

'It is government policy not to create needless panic. Do me a favour, Arthur,' said Uther wearily, 'call off the dogs. You are making political capital out of this business.'

'And you are trying to silence the opposition,' retorted Arthur. 'It won't work. A lot of people are genuinely concerned, and you know it.

Uther removed a file from his 'in' tray, dropped it in his 'out' tray, and taking his time, re-aligned it with compulsive care. Arthur's eyes followed it. 'Listen to me,' said Uther, his voice low, as if he were afraid of being overheard even here in the secure confines of Number 10. 'And listen carefully, because I shan't repeat it.' He jumped up and began to pace the room.

'You talk of revolution. Well how's this for a revolutionary thought?' Uther paused for dramatic effect. 'What if you are right? What if there really is a growing rift between town and country? Does it really matter?'

What kind of question was that? 'What are you saying, father?'

Uther grasped the arms of Arthur's chair and loomed over him, his face inches from his son's. 'What I am saying,' he said, enunciating his words with exaggerated clarity, 'what I am saying is who gives a damn if a few deprived areas of the country decide to go it alone? You want to know something? It's what many people have been hoping for a very long time.'

This was a new and startling thought for Arthur. 'What people? Who are these people?'

'People like me, Arthur, people who see how strong and prosperous we are in London and in the other great cities of the United Kingdom. People like me who believe our poor deprived country cousins are a millstone round our necks. They want schools? They can have them. They want transport? They can have that too. Hospitals and police, post offices and garbage collectors? Theirs for the asking. Welfare? As much as they like – from cradle to grave, if that's what turns them on. All those good things they can have, as long as they don't expect us to pay for them. We have better things to do with our hard-earned money. Let them break away. Good luck to them, say I. Good riddance too,' he added provocatively.

So that was it. Uther was ignoring the Landlords' threat because he hoped they would do his dirty work for him. 'I cannot believe I am hearing this from the Prime Minister of the United Kingdom.'

'Believe it, Arthur,' said Uther. 'Just don't quote me.'

'Have you forgotten that you were elected by all the people of this country?' said Arthur. 'That means *all* the people, wherever they are, including the deprived and the underprivileged.'

A tired smile. 'Spare me the clichés.'

333

Arthur stood up to go. 'You are even more dangerous than Lord Mark, father. Power has gone to your head.'

'Power?' Uther chuckled. 'What power is that, pray? You think politicians have power, do you? Dear me, no. Not any more. Not in the twenty-first century. The multi-nationals have power, the drug barons have power. The arms dealers, the crime syndicates, the media moguls – they have power. What power do politicians have?'

'The power to change things,' said Arthur.

Uther opened the door to show his son out. 'How very naïve of you. Let me tell you something, Arthur. We politicians can do a lot, but the one thing we can never do is change things. Take my advice, forget all this idealistic claptrap of yours. You are living in Never-Never Land. Get real, or you won't last long in this business.'

Eleven

2023

THE CONFRONTATION with his father gave Arthur a sleepless night. The next morning he called Leo Grant.

'I'm on board,' he said without elaboration.

Leo understood. 'You'll stand?'

'Yes.'

Leo laid aside his mobile, sat back in his chair and let out a long contented sigh. This was a memorable day.

The Party grandees all agreed that the matter of the succession needed to be handled with discretion. Arthur was much admired but still only twenty-nine. Few in the country, or indeed in United Labour, thought of him as a candidate for leadership of the Party, or at least not yet. It would take a while to smooth the way, a few weeks, perhaps, a few months at most, so in the meantime it was vital that the mass media knew nothing. There were backbenchers to be sounded out, party faithfuls to be prepared. Assuming all went according to plan, one or two well-disposed journalists would plant a suggestion here and drop a hint there that Leo Grant might stand down as leader of United Labour, and that one of the candidates for the succession could be Arthur Pendragon.

Uther had his spies everywhere, recognising as he did that having the right information at the right time was crucial to success in politics. It was not long before a mole in the ranks of United Labour passed on to him some interesting and extremely disturbing gossip. If it were based on fact, and Uther thought it must be, then Arthur was being groomed as the future leader of United Labour. It was a sobering thought, for his son was already a thorn in his side, and seemed destined to become much more powerful and influential. He had both the charisma and the intelligence to galvanise the opposition. Yes, he could be a problem.

It is written that he will overthrow you. He could not get those ridiculous words of Merlin out of his head. Not that his son would ever succeed in bringing him down. New Millennium was still the people's choice, even if their majority had been rather drastically cut in the last election. And He? Uther Pendragon? Was he not a popular Prime Minister? Of course he was! Everyone said so. Arthur didn't stand a chance. Nevertheless something had to be done. What was the use of having information if you didn't make use of it? Uther called a journalist friend and gave him an exclusive. The following day the story appeared in one of the biggest-selling London tabloids. It began:

A secret plot has been hatched by United Labour frontbenchers to topple leader Leo Grant who, they believe, is no longer up to the job. My inside source tells me that the young and inexperienced backbencher, Arthur Pendragon, has the support of the plotters whose intention is to crown him heir apparent.

The next day Leo Grant attacked the Prime Minister in the House for spreading malicious rumours, but it was too late, the damage was done. United Labour backbenchers, most of whom had not yet been consulted about the succession, were incensed. As for the electorate, polls indicated that if an election were called, New Millennium would be back with an increased majority. Leo Grant was bitterly disappointed but there was nothing he could do. The rumours had well and truly spread and continuing to deny them would only give them the oxygen of publicity. He would just have to bide his time. Meanwhile he would stay on as Party Leader. Told that his father had leaked the story to the Press, Arthur shrugged the whole thing off. He was content to remain a backbencher as long as he could express his views in the House, and no one, not even his father, could stop him doing that.

The truth was that ever since Guinevere's party about a year ago, Arthur had become increasingly preoccupied with other, more personal matters. His concentration was not what it used to be. He remembered how he used to day-dream when he was a boy. At twenty-nine, though, was he not a little old for that sort of thing? Adults were meant to dream at night while they slept, not during the day when they were wide awake and had more important things to do. It was disconcerting, not to say downright worrying. One moment he would be absorbed in answering a letter to a constituent, the next he was staring out of the window, thinking thoughts that had nothing at all to do with politics.

Yesterday, for example, he looked out of his office window and saw a couple walking down the street. Now and then they touched hands, nothing more than that. They were not even looking at each other. Yet it was obvious. Love was a strange and disturbing thing. It came at you from nowhere, and for no apparent reason. Not that reason had anything to do with it. For was not love a kind of temporary madness, a chemical imbalance in the brain? It changed everything, or so they said. Certainly it made it hard to concentrate.

Arthur had been inundated with invitations – invitations to smart dinners in private homes and restaurants, invitations to theatre and the opera, to country weekends and gallery openings, fashion shows and charity evenings. Never had his social life been so active. As a result there had been attachments but none of the girls, attractive and charming though they were, had come close to disturbing the chemical balance of his brain. It was obvious, moreover, that the invitations were planned and co-ordinated by the mothers of all these eligible young ladies in a systematic campaign of frightening efficiency. Astonishingly, he had, over a period of a few weeks, been out with every unattached girl at the dance. Or not quite every girl.

One of them he had not seen again. He had thought of phoning her. In truth he thought of little else. But what would be the point? Obviously she was not interested in him.

Why should she be? For one thing she was far too young for him. Twenty-nine and eighteen did not walk the street together, let alone touch hands. He would be wasting his time. Though she was, he had to admit, exceedingly mature for her age. On an impulse he phoned Leo Grant to invite him out to dinner. As fate would have it, it was Guinevere who answered the phone. They began to go out, and the more time she spent with Arthur, the more Guinevere liked him. She was reassured by his strength, touched by his gentleness, and impressed by his insight. No man but her father had ever understood her as well.

As the days and weeks passed, something was happening to Guinevere. Lanky detected, and found remarkable, a certain softening of her friend's manner, and a tender look in her eyes that she remembered seeing for the first time that night of the party. Fleeting then, the look now seemed more settled, as if it were content to be where it was and was contemplating taking up residence. Despite the most vehement protestations to the contrary, Lanky was convinced that her friend was falling in love.

Arthur was relaxing in the sitting room of his flat when Merlin's illuminated holographic head gradually materialised in the bookcase in a gap between a book on astronomy and the complete works of William Shakespeare.

'I hope you don't mind my mentioning it,' said Arthur carefully, not wishing to offend his friend and mentor, 'but I find magic and technology a confusing mix.'

Merlin sighed. 'What am I doing wrong this time?'

'I would like to see the whole of you.'

'I don't think you appreciate just how tiring all this materialising and de-materialising is.'

'Then please don't trouble yourself,' said Arthur quickly.

'Your head will do fine.'

'Too late,' said Merlin, manifesting all of himself in an armchair. Virgil, perched on his shoulder, ruffled his feathers and hoo-hooed a greeting.

'She's not the one for you,' said Merlin in a sing-song voice.

Is this what the magus had come for – to interfere with his private life? He had never done that before. 'How can you say that? She is perfection.'

'Perfection is not the word I would use to describe Guinevere.'

Arthur was offended. 'You obviously don't like her.'

'On the contrary, I like her very much. She is highly intelligent and quite remarkably beautiful. Still I fear she is not your cup of tea – or your glass of champagne for that matter. Find someone else, that girl will bring you pain. You will get over this infatuation.'

Infatuation? No, that was not the word to describe how he felt about Guinevere. He had been infatuated with women before, seeing only what was on the outside; this was surely different. True, it was Guinevere's beauty that had first entranced him. Was that not always the way of a man and a woman? Love had entered through his eyes, but it had quickly captured his heart and soul. His whole being was filled with Guinevere and nothing could ever change that. Life without her would be unthinkable. Merlin would never understand. How could he? What did he know about love? Still less, about being in love.

'A great deal more than you suppose,' said Merlin, responding to the unspoken question. 'I was in love myself once. Still am, if you must know.'

This was a new and startling thought for Arthur, revealing a very human side of Merlin that he would never have suspected. Who was the lady, he wondered.

'Her name is Nimue,' said Merlin, answering once again the question that had not been asked.

'Tell me about her,' said Arthur.

From the legs up Merlin's body began to fade. 'One day, one day, one day,' his voice echoed.

Arthur wanted to know more but he would have to wait for a better time to question Merlin about his love life. Meanwhile the magus had got it wrong, he was certain of that; Guinevere was most assuredly the girl for him. An entrancing face filled his mind's eye, a radiant smile lit up dark eyes, and then, in a sudden change of mood, a proud tilt of the head and a toss of black hair accompanied a scornful glance and a sharp rebuke. The blood jetted in his veins, his heart double-somersaulted in his chest. Find someone else? Who could possibly compare with Guinevere? No one. She was unique. There was no one like her in the whole wide, wondrous, love-smitten world.

Nothing was left of Merlin now but a wistful smile and a glow of green orbs, and just above where his shoulder had been, there was Virgil's heart-shaped face. A few moments later they had both disappeared, leaving only the voice of the magus. 'Testosterone – is often prone – to mislead or suborn you. A bad rhyme but good advice. Don't say I didn't warn you.'

Lanky waited impatiently. Guinevere had phoned with something important to tell her. The suspense was unbearable. The instant the bell rang, she rushed to the door and flung it open. Grabbing Guinevere by the hand, she pulled her into the sitting room. 'Sit!' Guinevere did as she was told. 'Now tell!' Guinevere fiddled with the ring finger of her left hand. 'He asked you, didn't he?'

Guinevere nodded.

Throwing her arms round her friend, Lanky shrieked with joy. 'It's too much! I can't take it in. You and Arthur! It's a dream come true. Now darling,' – sitting on the sofa next to Guinevere she wriggled bum and shoulders ecstatically and settled down for a long, luscious listen – 'I want all the details. Everything. Nothing left out, you understand. How he proposed. How you accepted. What he said. What you said.

Word for word. The lot.'

'He was very sweet.' Guinevere hesitated. 'It wouldn't be fair to . . . '

'Come on, Ginny, don't clam up on me. Give!' begged Lanky.

Guinevere looked uncomfortable. Lanky could see she would have a hard time getting it out of her. It was too aggravating for words. In Guinevere's place she would have recited the proposal syllable for syllable, forwards, backwards and sideways, up and down and inside out, and what's more, fleshed it out with an exhaustive description of voice inflexions and facial expressions. 'What's the point of coming here,' she complained, 'if you're not going to tell me anything?'

'But I am,' said Guinevere.

Lanky was on the edge of the sofa. 'Well, go on.'

'He asked me to marry him.'

'Ye-es?'

'And I said no.'

Lanky rolled her eyes in exasperation. 'Be serious, Ginny.' She looked at Guinevere again. 'You are serious.'

'Yes.'

'You turned him down?'

'Yes.'

'You actually turned him down.'

'Yes.'

'We are talking about the same man, are we?' said Lanky incredulously. 'Arthur . . . ? Arthur Pendragon?'

'Yes.' It was little more than a whisper.

Lanky put her head in her hands. 'Tell me it isn't true.' Her muffled voice was anguished.

Silence.

Lanky looked in horror at her friend and saw what she had overlooked before. Guinevere's face was pale, her eyes circled with dark shadows.

'Well Ginny, you finally lost it. I always knew you would

sooner or later. Congratulations! You are now one hundred percent certifiable.'

'I knew you'd say that.'

'What else is there to say? You have just thrown back the catch of the season. Or any other season.'

Guinevere lifted her chin and said nothing.

'Do you mind telling me why?'

Guinevere looked down at her hands. 'I don't know. I wish I did. I suppose I funked it. He's so bloody distinguished and important. Ex-army. Rising star in the House. Dad says he's sure to be Prime Minister one day. It's more than I can handle. I don't deserve him.'

'If we all got what we deserved,' observed Lanky darkly, 'we would die spinsters. Try again.'

The tears welled in Guinevere's eyes, overflowed and rolled down her cheeks. 'I didn't sleep a wink for thinking about it. I only know I don't feel the way I ought to feel. I don't light up when he comes into the room. I don't feel that special excitement they talk about. And anyway,' – she wiped the tears from her face – 'I'm not even sure I want to feel like that. The thought of losing control scares me. I think I must be too selfish to fall in love.'

Lanky simply could not understand how a bright girl like Ginny could be so stupid. But her disappointment and frustration were as nothing compared to Leo's. He had never made any secret of his admiration for Arthur. When Guinevere broke the news to him, he was shocked. He begged her to reconsider, but Guinevere would not be budged. Arthur was not for her, she said, and Leo had no choice but to accept the inevitable. He knew his daughter, and once she had made up her mind, no words of his could sway her.

No words. But circumstances perhaps. Though Guinevere still lived with her father, she did not normally attend his dinner parties. She was curious, then, when he invited her to one.

'Any special reason?'

'I need some young blood. Too many old fogies, most of them the wrong side of sixty. Will you come?'

'If you want me to. Will there be anyone I know?'

'Could be,' he said non-commitally.

Drinks were being served, and most of the other guests had arrived when in walked Arthur Pendragon. Guinevere did not know which way to look. What was he doing here? She could only imagine that her father was promoting Arthur's political career by inviting a few influential politicians and businessmen to dinner to meet him. Her dad had told her he was thinking of standing down as leader, and she had heard talk of Arthur taking over. All very well, but why was she invited? This was not her scene at all. She had little interest in politics, as her father well knew. She tried to lose herself in earnest conversation with an elderly judge whom she had never met before. Then with a murmured apology she excused herself and rushed blindly into the arms of the very man she was trying so hard to avoid.

'Guinevere! What a marvellous surprise. I didn't expect to see you here. How are you?'

'I am well, as you see,' she said, her head in a spin. 'Quite well. Fine, thank you. Very well, in fact. And you?'

'Excellent.' Arthur lowered his voice discreetly. 'Who are all these old codgers? This isn't Leo's usual sort of dinner party. We seem to be the only ones under seventy. What's he up to?'

'I was just wondering the same thing myself.'

For a moment or two they searched each other's face for an answer, and then, as the light dawned, they both began to laugh.

It was alright as long as they were laughing but when they were serious again she was too embarrassed to look at him. She could not think of anything to say, so she stood with head bowed, tracing patterns on the carpet with the tips of her shoes like an awkward teenager. How immature she must seem to him. What must he think of her? Across the room she directed at her father a look of such concentrated hostility, it would have bored a hole in an iceberg. Adding insult to injury, he smiled back at her and waved. She could have killed him. How dare he! How dare he interfere in her life like this! It was unforgivable. How could he be so insensitive, so sly? If he had any concern for her feelings, any concern at all, he would at least have had the decency to prepare her for what was bound to be the most excruciatingly uncomfortable experience of her whole life.

To her great surprise though, it was nothing of the kind. Once started, she could hardly stop talking, and barely addressed a word all evening to anyone but Arthur, forgetting completely that the man to whom she was so cordially chattering was the same one whose proposal she had turned down only a month before.

After dinner they had taken a stroll in the garden, at his suggestion. It had been pleasant, very pleasant. Indeed if she had found anything in him to criticise, it was his excessively cheerful manner and lively conversation. Where was the pale and wan lover? Where the downcast eyes and gloomy expression?

'It's so good to see you again, Guinevere,' said Arthur as she blushed. Oh Lord, what a ninny she was. 'You too.' Here she had taken the opportunity of re-establishing their relationship on a correct footing, just in case he might be under any misapprehension. 'I wouldn't want to lose your friendship.'

'Nor I yours,' he responded.

When all the guests had left she did not even have the heart to scold her father. What was there to complain of? Arthur's conduct had been beyond reproach, he had handled himself like the gentleman he most assuredly was. That night, being so stimulated, she found it difficult to sleep. There were, aside from pleasant memories, some rather puzzling aspects of Arthur's behaviour that needed thinking about – his whole attitude towards her, for one thing; he had acted more like a close friend than a rejected suitor. A lesser man than he might have displayed some resentment, or at the very least feigned indifference to show how little he cared. But Arthur had gone out of his way to demonstrate how much he enjoyed her company, which she found pleasing but at the same time disconcerting.

All in all he had behaved impeccably, perhaps a shade too impeccably. Did he have to take quite so readily the hand of friendship she had offered him? Should he not have been just a trifle listless and melancholy, rather than so very joyful and animated? Why had he not toyed with his food at the dinner table, instead of eating like a horse? Could he have fallen out of love so quickly? There was not even the tiniest hint that he was pining for her. How could he be so fickle! What could it mean? Should a man as gallant as Arthur not have taken some pains at least to hint of a broken heart? That at any rate was how it seemed to her. The only reasonable assumption was that he was not heartbroken at all, and that, being rejected, he had all too casually abandoned his love for her.

It was, to say the least, disappointing. How could men be trusted when even the best of them, it seemed, was so capricious? She could not help questioning whether he had ever loved her at all, whether indeed at this very minute he might not be complimenting himself on a lucky escape. In which case, should she not be doing the same?

Twelve

LANCELOT AND HELENA had been childhood friends but had long gone their separate ways, he to the army, she into modelling. So Helena's phone-call came out of the blue.

She found it weird to be sitting across a table from Lance. How long had it been? Eight years? Nine? He had been a young teenager – fourteen or fifteen – when she last saw him. Now he was a man, and a very good-looking one. What else about him had changed, she wondered. Not a lot, it seemed; there was still that aura of melancholy about him, those brooding eyes, that reluctance to communicate. He had hardly said a word since they took their seats in the restaurant. Yet Helena knew instinctively that Lance's aloof manner was a pose to protect a shy and vulnerable man.

Whilst they were waiting for the first course she sipped a glass of wine, and Lancelot, who neither smoked nor drank alcohol, moved his knife and fork around. She could see he was searching for something to say.

'I was ten when we met,' she said, prompting him. 'You must have been twelve.'

'Were we really that young?'

She smiled. 'Afraid so.'

She sensed that he was doing much the same as she was, weighing her up, comparing what she was now and what he remembered of her. 'You were pretty good at climbing trees – for a girl.' Now it was his turn to smile, and when he did, she noticed particularly that his brown eyes remained strangely sad.

'As good as you any day.' They had always been competitive.

'You were a real tomboy.' He made it sound like a compliment. Was there a hint of affection too?

Helena remembered wishing she had been born a boy, so she could always be Lance's friend. 'I suppose I was.'

'Happy days,' said Lancelot, for though he would never admit it he had missed Helena dreadfully when her parents moved from the country to London.

'Yes, they were.'

He smiled at her, and this time his eyes lit up. They both relaxed and the ice was finally broken.

'You mentioned something about a spot of hot water?' Lancelot remarked casually over coffee.

She was tempted to run out of the restaurant. But when she looked up, those dark eyes of his were filled with such concern that she opened her heart to him. 'His name is Lambert Harford,' she began haltingly. 'I – well, I fell for him.' She flashed a glance at Lancelot over her wine glass, but his face was impassive. 'He took me everywhere and I was flattered. He introduced me to pot.' She caught the fleeting look of disgust on Lancelot's face. 'I had never smoked a joint before,' she said quickly. It seemed important for Lancelot to know that. 'I thought what the hell, everyone does it, don't they?' She sipped her wine. What must he think of her? Nothing good, that was for sure.

'Go on,' he said. 'I'm listening.' He spoke gently, not sounding at all judgmental. She was grateful for that.

'It wasn't long before my head stopped working. Oh yes, I forgot to mention, he's a photographer – professional. I let him take photographs. Nude ones.' She avoided Lance's eyes, her hands tightly clasped on the table. 'It was stupid of me, of course. Somehow or other he convinced me it would help my career. No, to be honest, it wasn't even that. Half the time I was so stoned I didn't give a damn what I was doing.' She blushed. 'The photographs were what you might call uninhibited, not

347

pornographic, or anything like that, but not how a girl wants to see herself in the tabloids either.'

Lancelot could feel the anger gathering in his chest. 'Has he sold them to a newspaper?'

'He says he will if I don't pay him twenty-thousand pounds. I haven't got that sort of money.'

'Tell him to publish the photos and be damned.'

She shook her head. 'I can't do that. It would be embarrassing for me, and even more for mum and dad. They would be the ones to suffer most, especially my dad. I would lose modelling work but that's the least of it.' She thumped the table in frustration. 'I've been such a fool.'

'I'd like to help if you'll let me,' said Lancelot quietly. He watched her lips set in a stubborn line. That brought back memories, it was the way she looked when he would try to stop her climbing a tree.

'I'm not asking for your help. It's just advice I need,' she insisted. 'It's my problem. I'll deal with it.' She could see from the way he looked at her that he didn't believe she could. 'My credit's good,' she explained. 'I'm sure I can borrow what I need.'

He could have told her it would be a waste of time and money, because you could never pay off blackmailers; they always came back for more. What was the use though? It would be a waste of time arguing with her, she was as obstinate as he was.

So obstinate that it was not easy to persuade her to go out with him again. He waited for her in the restaurant. As she sat down, there on the table in front of her was a large manila envelope. 'What's this?' she asked.

'Prints. Negatives. End of story.' Lancelot busied himself with the menu.

Quickly she flipped through the contents. She knew she ought to be thanking him, when instead she was tormenting herself with the thought that he must have looked at the photos. Her face flushed redder by the second.

He cleared his throat self-consciously. 'He assured me they were all there.'

She could not look at him. 'They are.' He had seen them. He must have done.

'I had no idea how many he took,' he said, reading the menu with the keenest attention, 'so there was no point in checking them.'

He was telling her he hadn't looked at them. Could it be true? She would not have believed most men but Lancelot she did, he wouldn't lie, he would scorn to. She was so grateful she wanted to throw her arms round him and kiss him. 'I don't know how to thank you. I'm just so relieved. I'm quite overwhelmed. I don't know what to say. How did you get them back?'

'It wasn't too difficult,' he said, making light of it. 'I phoned Lambert's studio and said I was coming round for a chat. He was waiting for me with two friends of his. When I say friends, I think they were actually professional bouncers. They certainly looked it. Naturally I warned them I had boxed at Oxford, but for some reason they seemed to find that amusing, I don't know why. They became quite aggressive.'

Her hands were clenched so tight the knuckles were white. 'Oh no, Lance. What did you do?'

'I knocked them out,' he said, consulting the wine list.

'What, all three of them?'

'Only the two bouncers,' said Lancelot. 'I'm afraid I had to hit them quite hard. Lambert was very co-operative after that. He produced the photographs almost immediately. Of course he tried to keep the negatives, but I managed to make him see reason.'

It was all too thrilling and too wonderful and, yes, too embarrassing for words. She touched his bandaged hand.

'A couple of broken fingers,' he said, drawing his hand away. 'I never fought without gloves before. Those men had the hardest jaws.'

It was unbelievable. To think he had done all this for her! It

349

was so brave of him, so daring, so gallant. It was like having your very own knight in shining armour! Chivalry was still alive and well. Who would have thought it in this cynical and disillusioned age? Bending her head, she kissed his bandaged hand. Impulsively he reached out and touched her face, though whether it was a sign of affection or a simple acknowledgement of the kiss was not clear; whichever it was, in the sweet confusion of the moment she was overcome by an emotion entirely new to her.

Lancelot wanted to ask her out again, but the incident had left him deeply troubled. Not for the first time in his young life he had committed the unpardonable sin; he had lost control. The two men had attacked him without warning, one with a table lamp, the other with a flick knife. Nevertheless the damage he had inflicted on them worried him. It was only later he learned that both men had spent several days in hospital with badly bruised faces, broken jaws and noses, and fractured ribs. No wonder he had hurt his hand. It shocked him to discover he was capable of such extreme violence. Even more shocking, he remembered nothing about it. One moment the two men were advancing on him, the next they were lying unconscious on the floor, the time between a blank.

Had his mind blocked out an unpleasant memory? Or was there a more sinister explanation? Was there some malfunction in his brain creating a rift between thought and action? Again he asked himself the question that had troubled him so long. Had he inherited some weakness from his mother? *It might not actually be a physical problem. Could be some kind of, well, not mental disturbance exactly, but that sort of thing.* He had so many questions about his mother, and only his father's stunted answers. Why had she taken her own life? Everyone who knew them said that she and dad adored each other. The closest his father had come to an explanation was to hint that pregnancy sometimes had strange effects on women. Was that the real reason, or was he hiding something? Was the delicate balance of her mind disturbed, not temporarily, but permanently? Did that explain those uncontrollable fits of anger that convulsed him from time to time?

Helena now knew for certain that she had found the only man she would ever love, and was determined not to let him get away. Had he not, like the traditional valorous knight of story books, ridden to the aid of the damsel in distress and rescued her from the wicked ogre? Such a man was worthy of special effort, and she would not allow pride to stand in her way. If she wanted to see him again, it was up to her to make the running. If the knight would not come to the damsel, then the damsel would have to go to the knight. And so she did. For a time they were inseparable companions, though nothing more than that.

Ban was delighted. The hooded, world-weary eyes of Helena's father, Harold Pemberton, assumed a gentler look. With what he imagined were subtle hints, he recommended his daughter to find a nice young fellow and settle down. Helena was only too happy to oblige, if the right man came along. On that subject, however, there could be no compromise, for there was now only one right man.

Though it pleased her to think of Lancelot as the hero of her girlish fantasies, she was not by inclination a romantic spirit, nor did she aspire – as so many women of her generation did – to success in some business or profession. To marry, settle down and have children was what she wanted above all else. A semi-detached in Battersea would comfortably accommodate her dreams for the future. But what about Lancelot's dreams? Would he feel trapped in her vacuum-packed life? Would he warm to her dull friends? Would he eat dinner on his knees watching television? Would he walk the dog in the park? Would he kick a soccer ball with the kids on a Saturday morning? How would he earn a living? Would he make the army his career, or if not, be a lawyer or an accountant, or take a job in the city trading equities?

Hard to imagine. Somehow a collar and tie, a nine-to-five routine and a houseful of children did not seem to be Lancelot's cup of tea. She asked herself, could a knight in shining armour ever be Battersea man? Time alone would tell. Meanwhile, resolved to press matters, she made it clear to Lancelot that she wanted to go to bed with him.

His reaction took her by surprise. 'It may sound silly to you,' he said, 'but I don't think a man and woman should sleep together until they are married.'

Helena's eyes grew large. Was he ending their relationship? Or could it be Lancelot's way of proposing? 'Fine,' she said, a determined look in her eye, 'let's get married.'

That he had not expected. 'I don't think I'm ready for marriage just yet,' he said, having the grace to look apologetic.

'When will you be?' She knew it was foolish to try and put him in a corner but she could not help herself.

Lancelot mumbled something inaudible.

'What did you say?'

'In a couple of years . . . or so . . . is what I said.'

Was he serious? 'You expect me to wait two years for sex!'

She made him sound unreasonable, priggish even. It was, he thought, very unfair of her. What was he to do? He was trapped between Scylla and Charybdis, either to be drowned in the whirlpool of sex, or swallowed by the monster of marriage, both terrifying prospects. Yet for all his reservations and misgivings the inevitable happened. An excellent Italian meal, a little more red wine than usual, Helena more beautiful than he had ever seen her, and the two of them fell into bed. The next morning both were thoughtful and subdued. Everything that had seemed so simple to Helena the night before was infinitely more complicated the morning after. Last night she had given herself to the man of her dreams; the question was, whom had she woken up with? Was this man lying in bed beside her still the man of her dreams? Or was he just a man she had spent the night with? How could you feel close to someone when you were not at all sure who they were? This was not remotely how she had expected to feel.

Lancelot too was far from happy. Why, lying next to this lovely girl, did he feel intimacy and estrangement in equal measure? Why was he feeling ashamed of himself? Was it because he had taken advantage of Helena's unconditional love? Was it that he did not appear to feel what a man in love was supposed to feel? Or was it that he had betrayed his own long-held principles?

It had certainly been pleasurable, if not the mind-expanding experience he had hoped it would be. In the morning the mysteries of the universe were still mysteries, and life every bit as inexplicable as it had been the night before. More depressing still, in the intimacy of their sexual union he had never felt more isolated. What was he afraid of? Of feeling too much? Or too little? Lancelot was beginning to fear that he was destined never to love anyone, or worse, that he was incapable of loving. Lying next to Helena, the image came to him of another woman, a woman he would always worship, but had never known. Through a veil of water, his mother gazed at him with sad eyes.

Helena's mother, Francesca, was the first to suspect what had happened. 'What's wrong, darling?'

The tears streamed down Helena's face. 'Nothing.'

Francesca put her arm round her daughter. 'I've never known you to cry about nothing.'

'I don't know how to tell you,' wailed Helena.

'Try saying, I'm pregnant,' said her mother briskly.

Helena wiped her eyes.'How did you know?'

'Is it Lancelot?'

'Yes.' Somehow mothers always knew.

'What are you going to do?'

'Have the child, of course,' said Helena firmly.

Francesca took that for granted. She had something else in

mind. 'Are going to tell him?'

That question had already given Helena many a sleepless night. 'I haven't decided yet.'

Though she would never say so, Lancelot, in Francesca's opinion, was a poor marriage prospect. For one thing he was far too self-involved, and for another he was altogether too attractive. Any woman who married him would spend her life fighting off the predators. Besides, he had the look of a wanderer, and she doubted he would ever settle down to family life. Her conclusion was that Helena would be better off saying nothing about the baby, at least for the time being. This was, in any case, 2023, not 1923; the world had changed, there were plenty of single mothers these days, and precious few marriages. Why did Helena have to marry Lancelot? Why did she have to marry anyone? The child could be raised by her mother, with her grandmother's help, and would have all the love and security in the world.

From there it was only a small leap of faith to convincing herself that this pregnancy was no accident; it was His will, a heaven-sent opportunity for her to shape her grandchild's mind and instil in it humility and a proper love of God. Francesca was a born-again believer. When first married she had been, like Harold, an atheist, or at least an agnostic. Later she had seen the light, and had chosen to follow the path that led to redemption and everlasting life. So during the weeks that followed she tried, though not too hard, to persuade Helena to break the news to Lancelot. That much she saw as her Christian duty; she wanted nothing on her conscience. Much to her relief, Helena stubbornly refused. She never doubted for a moment that Lance would marry her if she were to tell him she was pregnant; but she had her pride; she would have him on her terms or not at all. Better to stay single than lure a man into marriage.

When the army posted Lancelot overseas, it came as a shock to Helena. Still she said nothing.

Harold was puzzled. Why had his daughter given up modelling? Why did she spend most of her time moping around the house? It was not like her at all. She was an active and lively young woman, normally never at home. What was going on? Francesca offered no explanation. Not the most observant of men, he could not help noticing, around the fifth month of her pregnancy, that Helena was putting on weight.

'Does she have some woman's – um – condition?' he enquired tentatively of his wife.

'So you've noticed,' said Francesca in her condescending way.

'What exactly is wrong with her?'

'Nothing. She's pregnant.'

Poor Harold took it badly. The unthinkable, the thing that only happened in other families, had happened in his. For a long time he raged against the man responsible for his daughter's predicament. When he had calmed down, he insisted on knowing who the father was.

Francesca's lips were sealed. 'You had better ask Helena.'

'Where is he?' he demanded. 'Why isn't the bastard here? He'll do the right thing, or I'll know the reason why.'

Francesca pursed her lips in disapproval. 'The right thing, Harold? And what might that be?'

Francesca had a way of ignoring the obvious when it suited her. 'He's going to marry her, the piece of shit.'

'You want your daughter to marry a piece of shit?'

'For God's sake, woman, you know what I mean. Anything's better than being a single mother, isn't it?' Harold was an old-fashioned man with old-fashioned views.

Francesca lifted her head and looked down her nose at her husband. 'That, Harold, is a typical male macho comment. I find it grossly offensive.'

'I only want what's best for my daughter. I intend to see she gets it.' He flattered himself that he still had some influence with Helena.

'Who is he, darling?' he asked Helena.

'Dad, it doesn't matter who he is. He just happens to be the father of my child. I'm not going to marry him.'

'It all seems very irresponsible to me,' said Harold unhappily.

Helena slipped her arms round her father's neck. 'Have I let you down?'

'Of course you haven't.' He kissed her. 'I couldn't have wished for a better daughter.'

'Then please don't worry about me, dad.'

'Is it anyone I know?' He could not resist asking.

Helena shook her head. She didn't want to lie but she didn't want to tell him the truth either.

Harold was close to tears. This was not what he had planned for his only child. A girl like Helena could have married anyone, anyone at all. Why did she have to get involved with some useless layabout? She was obviously ashamed of him, or she would have told him who he was. Silly child. How could she think so little of herself? 'You may think I'm an interfering old fool,' he said, 'and I dare say you are right. But why you dropped Lancelot I shall never know. He's an exceptional young man. One thing I do know, if he was the father of your child, he would never walk away.'

Helena was silent.

'I always hoped that you two . . . ' Harold bit his lip hard, determined not to break down in front of his daughter. Everything was topsy-turvy these days. Men behaved like girls and girls behaved like men. The trouble was, when girls got themselves pregnant they were the ones left holding the baby. He bared his soul to his friend, Ban.

'Instead of finding God, my wife would have done better to find her daughter a husband. You don't suppose,' he asked hesitantly, 'that Helena and Lancelot might still . . . you know?'

'No idea,' said Ban. The last thing he would ever speak to

his son about was women. 'Keen on the army. In his father's footsteps. More's the pity. Brighter than me. Much. Ready to take the plunge? Wouldn't know. Know nothing about his love-life.' Ban directed a shrewd look at his old friend. 'Whip off an e-mail? Helena preggers. That sort of thing?'

Harold shuddered. 'Don't do that. She would never forgive me. Besides, it really isn't Lance's business, is it? Why should he pick up the tab for another man's dinner?'

'Whatever you say.'

'You know, Ban, old chap, I used to dream of walking my daughter up the aisle. Always wanted to send her off in style. Nothing too fancy, just something to remember. They say her wedding day is the happiest day in a girl's life. Isn't that what they say? It'll never happen now.' A lone tear rolled down Harold Pemberton's face. Ban was distressed for his friend. He wished he could think of something to say to comfort him.

It was a boy. When Lancelot returned home with his regiment, the baby was six months old. 'Why didn't you tell me? We'll get married right away.'

After all these months of self-doubt and torment, Helena's moment of truth had arrived. How many times had she enacted this scene in her mind, imagining every word, every expression, every nuance of meaning, hidden and concealed. Everything would depend on Lancelot's reaction. She had always known he would offer to marry her. The question she asked herself: was he doing it out of a sense of duty, or because he loved her? So direct and searching was her look that his eyes faltered; that was already significant she told herself. Words were unnecessary when you loved someone as much as she loved Lancelot. Avidly she searched for some indication in his expression, his voice, his manner – anything that might give the tiniest clue to what he was thinking.

She tested him. 'What if I were to tell you it isn't yours?'

He could not hide his shock and dismay.

'Would you marry me if you were not the father?' All too

357

aware she was pushing him into a corner, she could think of no alternative. For her it was the all-important question, and she had to ask it.

Lancelot hesitated. 'Well, that would be different, of course. I would have to think about it . . . even so . . . '

She said flatly, 'It isn't your problem. It's mine.'

'Who is the man?'

And with that question it was all over.

'Do I know him?'

'Perhaps you do, perhaps you don't.' A bright smile. 'Who knows anyone?'

'When are you getting married?'

She looked away. 'We are not getting married.'

'How can that be? It's his child. It's his duty to marry you.'

'His duty? You make it sound like a penance.'

He shifted uneasily. 'What I mean is, I'm sure he wants to marry you. I'm sure he loves you.'

'I told you, Lance, it's not your problem.' She could see he was badly hurt; he had tried to hide it but it was obvious from his manner. He thought ill of her for going to bed with another man. She was bitterly disappointed in him. It was unreasonable of her but she could not help herself. How could he believe her capable of sleeping with another man? How could he think that of her? Didn't he know he was everything to her? Didn't he know there never had been, never could be, anyone but him? All she said was, 'Don't be angry with me.'

'I was fond of you,' he said. 'I thought you knew that.'

Tears filled her eyes and she turned away to hide her face. The reproach was more than she could bear.

There was, he thought, nothing more to be said. What right did he have to say anything? It was not as if they had sworn to be faithful to each other, though somehow he had assumed they would be; he had expected better of her. She was not the girl he took her for. What was worse, she seemed to treat it all so lightly, as if it were something of a joke. He wondered about the man. He hated him, and his hatred was like a physical pain. If ever he met him, he might not be able to control himself. If he saw him now, he would kill him.

'Can I see the little one?' he asked.

'Of course.' She left the room and came back holding the baby.

Gently he touched a plump cheek. 'What do you call him?'

'Galahad.'

He held out his forefinger, and the baby squeezed it in its tiny hand. Lancelot smiled.

Helena smiled back. Her heart was being wrenched in two. 'You like children, Lance?'

'I should like to have a son.' Not that he had given it much thought until now. 'Some day I hope I shall.'

'Some day?' Not today, not tomorrow, not the day after, not ever.

'It's perhaps a little soon for me,' he said, uncomfortable with the subject. 'I still have things to do.'

'What sort of things?'

'Oh, you know.'

'Saving the world?'

'Something like that.'

When they said good-bye, her courage almost failed her. She wanted to cry out, 'It's yours! Galahad is your son!' But she did not. What would have been the point when his plans so obviously did not include her? Still, the temptation was there, and no doubt always would be. After all, he had a right to know he was a father, she told herself. Was that not sufficient reason to be honest with him? It might have been if she were not so angry and disillusioned. She hardened her heart. He deserved to be punished for doubting her, he deserved to be punished for not loving her enough.

It was a long time before she saw Lancelot again and she missed him desperately. She began to neglect herself, not bothering to dress, often not bothering to eat. This Helena was a very different woman from that bright-eyed, self-possessed young model who once went briskly about her business, happy with whom she was. Strong enough for both of them, Francesca took care of Galahad, and scolded her daughter back to health. 'A mother doesn't have the luxury of being weak. Your son needs you. Without a husband, you will have to be more of a mother, not less.' She was right, of course, though that did not make it any easier for Helena. She resented her mother for always being right.

'I'm going to tell Lance,' she said defiantly.

It was the last thing Francesca wanted. Yet knowing how stubborn her daughter could be, she did not argue with her. 'It's your decision, not mine, darling,' she said dutifully. 'I'm only here to help.'

'I can't tell him,' said Helena, backing down immediately. 'You know I can't. I just wish I wasn't so alone.' She knelt down, laid her head in her mother's lap and sobbed.

'You are not alone, darling.' Francesca stroked Helena's hair. 'You have me. As long as God lets me live, I shall be here for you and Galahad.'

'It's Lancelot I want.'

'I know, I know,' said Francesca soothingly. 'I'm afraid you will just have to get used to doing without him. Believe me, child, he isn't worthy of you.'

Helena shook her head. She knew differently. It was she who was not worthy of him.

Every day, morning and evening, Francesca fell on her knees and gave thanks for this gift from heaven. The boy would be as much her son as Helena's, more so in fact. For she, not Helena, would be the one who would see to it that Galahad dedicated his life to God. And Galahad would be the perfect man, a man whose power came not from this world, but from his Father in heaven.

Thirteen

2023

ARTHUR STRAPPED himself in. Somewhere in the dim light of the cabin was Merlin, words leaping from his mouth, eyes shining like two moons. As the craft took off Arthur was thrust back in his seat. A loud roaring assaulted his ears and a light as brilliant as ten thousand suns stabbed his eyes. His lips splayed on his teeth, monstrous hands gouged his cheeks, and a cruel vice clamped his limbs as he sped like a bullet through the dark tunnel that links this life with the next. Suddenly there was light. The roaring stopped, and his body was floating free, tumbling in slow motion in a void of silence. Voices showered down on him like space dust. 'Open your eyes, we're here. Open your eyes, we're here. Open your eyes, your eyes, your eyes.' As his head cleared, the scatter of voices merged into three, then two, then one voice. And that voice said, 'Open your eyes, Arthur.'

The next world was even more breathtaking than the one he had just left. But then he realised, with something like a pang of disappointment, that he was still alive, and that the voice was Merlin's voice telling him to look down.

'Where are we?'

The magus did not answer directly. 'What do you think of it?'

Arthur looked down and marvelled at what he saw. 'Incredible.'

'I thought you might like it,' said Merlin smugly.

Far below, in the middle of the blue Atlantic ocean, shimmering in the sunlight like a pearl, was an island, and on the island was a great city, a vision of some future age, the embodiment of a dream. What astonished Arthur, apart from its amazing beauty, was the perfect symmetry of its layout. Obviously it had been planned with the greatest care, and for some specific purpose.

As they approached the ground, he saw that all the buildings were white and geometrical in shape, pyramids and squares, rectangles and spheres. The sole exception was what appeared to be the ruins of an ancient castle; a corner tower, crumbling walls, and the remains of an entrance gateway. At regular intervals around the perimeter of the island stood clusters of white columns, tall and slender, each crowned with a halo of antennae moving silently and purposefully, like the feelers of a giant insect probing the sky. As he watched, a silver sphere flashed in the sunlight, hovered in the still air, and accelerated away. In an instant it was gone.

'What was that?' asked Arthur.

'A Nimble. Like ours.'

'Which is?'

'A fighter aircraft,' explained Merlin. 'The acrobat of the sky, as the name implies, and fast, very fast.'

'How fast is fast?'

'About Mach seven,' said Merlin sneaking a sideways glance to observe Arthur's reaction.

Arthur knew something about force 'G' and the pull of gravity. Surely that sort of speed would tear a man apart. 'How can a pilot survive at Mach seven?'

An airy wave of the hand. 'All in good time.'

The moment they touched down, the belly of the Nimble gaped. Arthur followed Merlin down the short ladder. Merlin beamed. 'Welcome to Camelot.'

Arthur felt a surge of excitement unlike anything he had known before. So this was Camelot! The tall white buildings seemed to hover over him like benevolent spirits, the grass was greener and the flowers more beautiful than any he had ever seen, an avenue of trees inclined gently in the breeze as though bowing to him, and in the distance the sea whispered his name. They climbed into the only visible means of transport, the Hovercart, a compact buggy with huge wheels moving on land, or, depending on the terrain, a few feet above it. As they passed the buildings, Merlin murmured from time to time what Arthur assumed was a reference to their functions: 'Command Control . . . Robot Centre . . . Naval HQ . . . Airforce HQ . . . Computer Network . . . Satellite Control . . . Bunkers' . . . and finally, a name that sounded like NIWIS.

They were outside a building shaped like a perfect pyramid. Arthur was hoping Merlin would stop, but he drove on. 'Aren't you going to show me round?'

'That's what I'm doing,' said Merlin evasively.

They passed a spherical building. 'I would have liked to see what goes on in there,' said Arthur.'

'All in good time,' said Merlin, intoning the phrase like a mantra.

So frustrated was Arthur that he was tempted to jump from the vehicle and take a look for himself. The problem was choosing the right moment to jump. Merlin was an erratic driver, and Arthur could never be sure when the Hovercart would lift off and when it would touch down. He decided it was too risky, so he had to be content with asking, 'When will the time be good?' to which Merlin replied enigmatically, 'You will be the one to decide that.'

'That rectangular building over there.' Arthur pointed. 'It says NIWIS over the entrance. What does NIWIS mean?'

'Nothing Is What It Seems,' said Merlin, as if it were the most obvious thing in the world.

Arthur was intrigued. 'What happens in there?'

Merlin muttered something rude under his breath and put down the Hovercart with a thump. 'I find it difficult to drive this thing and talk at the same time. I'm not saying it's your fault,' he added hastily. 'The fact is, even when I'm not talking,

I'm a poor driver. Always thinking of something else.' He stared accusingly at Arthur. 'You were asking me something. Ah yes. NIWIS. Well, the technology is new, but the idea is as old as warfare itself. The aim is to make the enemy believe whatever we want him to believe, to see what we want him to see, to hear what we want him to hear, and of course not to see or hear what we don't want him to. Deception is a deadly weapon and NIWIS has developed it to a fine art.'

Arthur's attention was distracted by a group of short squat people several hundred yards away. 'Who are they?'

'Robots,' said Merlin casually.

Arthur peered at the magus suspiciously. Was he joking? 'Did you say *robots*?'

'I did.'

'What exactly do they do?'

'Pretty much everything,' said Merlin. 'They have many different functions. For example there are maintenance robots, surveillance robots, land robots, sea robots, pilot robots, tracking robots, destroyer robots, pilot robots . . . ' His forehead ridged in thought. 'Who else now . . . ?'

Arthur was not sure he had heard right. 'Pilot robots!'

'That's right.' Merlin blinked innocently. 'It's no joke, I assure you.'

'No, of course not,' said Arthur, a touch embarrassed for having thought it might be. Something clicked into place in his head. 'Just now I asked you how human pilots could withstand Mach Seven. Are you saying that . . .?'

'I am,' said Merlin. 'In any military operation requiring high speed flight, a robot pilot would fly the Nimble.'

For a while Arthur was silent, absorbing what he had learned in his short time on Camelot. Whatever Merlin was up to, it was certainly extraordinary, as he might have expected of the magus; it was also disturbing. Ahead of the Hovercraft now was a building perched on one short, thick pillar, then another exactly the same, and another and another – a whole cluster of buildings that looked like a field of huge white mushrooms. 'Those low spherical shapes,' said Arthur. 'What are they?'

'The entrances to underground bunkers and pens,' said Merlin.

'What's in them?'

'Scuttles,' said Merlin. 'Nimbles. Eclipse.' The shadow of a smile crossed the face of the magus as he watched Arthur wrestling with the strange names. 'And last, but not least, the Kraken.'

'I already know that Nimbles are your fighter aircraft,' said Arthur. 'What about the others?'

'Scuttles are basically transport aircraft, very versatile and highly manoeuvrable, designed to operate in difficult terrain – mountains, forests, deserts, you name it. Eclipse is a giant cigar-shaped aircraft. It has a huge range and can carry a small army together with its weapons and transport. It also has highly accurate long and short-range missiles, satellites and various UAV's, and serves as a flying observation and communications HQ. Incidentally,' said Merlin, who was obviously thoroughly enjoying himself, 'all our aircraft are capable of vertical take-off and landing. The Kraken is another giant, a sea craft, basically the equivalent of Eclipse. Its weapons systems are as potent as an armada of battleships, and it has the advantage of being able to operate both on the surface and underwater.'

Arthur's brain felt as though it had been sliced into thin onion-like layers, all expanding rapidly in concentric circles. But where the centre of the onion was, and when the circles would stop expanding, he had no idea. 'Is this all your doing, Merlin?' he heard someone say, someone with a voice very like his.

'With a little help from my friends,' said Merlin, with a wink. The Hovercart landed with a thump outside a low, white building. 'Command Control,' Merlin volunteered. 'Come and have a cup of tea.' The lighting inside the building was dim with a bluish tinge. Arthur followed Merlin down a long, bare corridor into a room that he assumed must be his office – a small desk, several computers and wall monitors, books and papers, a sink, a few plates, mugs, a kettle, a fridge. All very sparse and functional, yet somehow radiating energy, the energy of the magus.

Merlin bustled about making tea while Arthur tried to regroup the moving parts of his brain. From the Hovercart he had seen numerous people either walking along paths or chatting outside buildings and guessed there were a lot more of them inside those buildings, probably also in Command Control where he and Merlin were now. What was it Merlin had said when he first showed him round his 'facilities' at Glastonbury? *Yes, I do have helpers, men and women who will one day be actively involved somewhere else. People who share my beliefs and are dedicated to the cause.* What exactly, Arthur wondered, was this island? Where was it? Who lived on it?

'A lot of questions,' responded Merlin, though Arthur had not asked them. 'First let me tell you something about the island.' He handed Arthur his tea. 'It was deserted for centuries. Later, much later, a man lived here alone, a man who had inherited the island. He lived and died here.' Merlin sipped his tea, his green eyes staring fixedly at Arthur over the rim of his mug. 'Once, they say, this island was a kingdom ruled by a great king.' A sly look. 'Do I need to tell you who that was?'

Arthur ignored the bait. 'Those ruins that I saw when we were landing . . . was that his castle?'

'So they say.'

'It's just a coincidence,' murmured Arthur to himself. 'It has to be.'

Merlin made no comment.

'Surely someone must have spotted what was going on here?'

'No,' said Merlin.

'Not from the air?'

'No.'

'From the sea, then?'

'No.'

'It seems you have had the most incredible luck,' said Arthur mischievously, knowing full well that Merlin did not believe in luck.

The magus was clearly stung by the suggestion. 'Luck has nothing whatever to do with it.'

'Explain then,' said Arthur.

The magus sat proudly erect. 'No one can see the island, unless I choose to let them see it.'

Even coming from the magus that sounded like an empty boast. 'Why not?' said Arthur.

'Because,' said Merlin tantalisingly, 'it is mantled.'

Arthur sighed. Yet more riddles. 'What does that mean?'

'It means the island cannot be detected, either visually or any other way.'

'What if a ship ran into it?'

'That couldn't happen,' Merlin assured him. 'It would be diverted without even knowing it. I have taken care of that.'

'I don't see how you can hide the island from satellites,' said Arthur.

'Oh but I can and I do,' said Merlin smugly. 'No prying eyes, wherever they are, can penetrate the island's mantle.' It was a simple statement of fact, and knowing the magus, Arthur had no doubt it was true.

Was there nothing the magus had overlooked? 'Who knows about this island?'

'I do. You do. My friends do.'

Arthur was curious. 'Friends?'

'The people who work here. There are not many of them yet, but there will be more – scientists and researchers, doctors and surgeons, teachers, engineers, constructions workers, architects and others. All experts in their field.' The *crème de la crème* as they say.' Merlin's huge eyes shone. 'Not only are they the best,

Arthur, these men and women believe in what we are doing. Otherwise they would not be here. They are convinced that Camelot is the only hope for the world.'

'You say there will be more,' said Arthur. 'When?'

'When the time comes.'

'When will that be?'

An apologetic shrug. 'I'm afraid I can't answer that.'

'Why not?'

'Because, Arthur, it depends on you.'

Frustration piled on frustration. It was as if Merlin were standing on the far side of a deep chasm beckoning him. He was tempted, but he was also fearful. How could he get across without plunging into the abyss?

A thought occurred. Politics had taught Arthur caution. 'These friends – are they confined to the island.'

'They are free to come and go as they please.'

Strange that Merlin should be so relaxed about it. 'Are you not afraid someone might give the game away? Either deliberately or accidentally.'

Merlin nodded his head in approval at the question. 'We have taken care of that too. No one can leave Camelot until they deposit the relevant part of their memory in the memory bank. The bank decides what they take with them and what they leave behind. Once they have done that, they are free to go, and of course to return.'

Arthur's lively mind launched him in another direction. 'You said there was a kingdom here long ago.'

'I did.'

He had him now. Even Merlin couldn't think of everything. 'Then,' said Arthur, 'the island must be recorded on old maps and charts.'

'It was,' conceded Merlin, 'until quite recently.'

'I don't understand.'

'Some years ago there was a disturbance in the Atlantic. Ships and planes reported seeing strange lights and explosions in the area. Quite a show it was, apparently but no one knows exactly what happened. It was a mystery; some said it was a huge volcanic eruption, others were convinced it was an earthquake, some even thought it was caused by the impact of a meteor. Scientific opinion was divided. Only one thing was certain: the island disappeared without trace. No, I lie. They did spot some debris floating in the ocean fifty miles west of its original location: fragments of rock, vegetable matter, that kind of thing.'

Arthur saluted the master. 'You think of everything, Merlin.'

Merlin grinned happily. 'Good of you to say so.'

Now came the most important question of all. 'What are you doing here, Merlin? What is it all for?'

Merlin took Arthur's empty mug and set it down with his own. Fastidiously, concentrating on the small task, he washed the mugs and laid them upside down to dry. 'There,' he said, satisfied with his work. 'Now what was the question?' Arthur had the strong impression that all this was a performance contrived to heighten tension. 'Ah, yes. What's it all for? I was wondering when you were going to ask me that.' The magus took Arthur by the hand. 'Come, I have something to show you.'

The control room was flanked by rows of monitors. Moving slowly down the long lines of screens Arthur was sickened and horrified to find himself confronted by images of suffering and misery on a massive scale; skeletonic children, sharp bones thrusting at their skin, starving to death somewhere in North Africa; hundreds of dead and injured people littering the streets after a suicide bombing in South East Asia; a Russian hospital, wards and corridors crammed with men, women and children suffering from radiation sickness; mutilated bodies in a Middle East desert; unarmed civilians being battered to death by men in camouflage gear somewhere in South America. The walls of the control room were covered with scene upon heart-rending scene of brutality, torture and murder.

For a full minute Arthur was in shock. 'When did all this happen?' he asked, turning away, unable to stomach the horror any longer.

'What you are looking at,' said Merlin, 'is happening now as we speak. All these pictures are being transmitted live.

'How is that possible?'

Merlin perched on a stool and signalled Arthur to do the same. 'The basic technology is quite simple, it is the extent and efficiency of the coverage that is unique. The pictures are beamed back to us in various ways – by satellite dishes, unmanned air vehicles, miniature robots and many other devices, some large, some microscopic. Some of our electronic 'spies' are detected and destroyed, but there are always others to take their place. We know where to look, and what to look for. Very little escapes our attention as we scan the world, and our coverage is infinitely more comprehensive than anyone else's. We are not the only ones of course. The USA, Russia, China, Japan, the United Kingdom and some other European countries all have highly sophisticated observation and tracking systems. They know pretty much what is going on, though they do very little about it.'

Arthur knew that was true, and not just about his father but about many world leaders. 'Why do you think that is?' he asked.

'Many reasons,' said Merlin. 'Inaccurate intelligence, the wrong weapons, incorrect strategy and a shortage of appropriate personnel all make it difficult, if not impossible, to deal effectively with terrorists. But there are other, even more serious problems.'

'Such as?'

'The ones you know of, Arthur. Lack of unity, lack of will, and a tendency to make shabby and cynical deals with terrorists instead of confronting them.'

Arthur nodded. This was familiar territory. 'Surely it's not all doom and gloom? The United States, our own country, Russia – they are all trying to fight terrorism in their way. And they have their successes from time to time.'

Merlin looked at the monitors. 'From time to time isn't good enough, is it? This is a war, and we are losing it. The world is in mortal danger.'

'You really believe that?'

'I am certain of it,' said Merlin solemnly.

'Even if that is true,' said Arthur, 'how can we defeat the terrorists? They have the advantage of surprise. They strike when and where they choose, and they have the most powerful and sophisticated weapons.'

'The answer to your question is here, Arthur,' said Merlin. 'On Camelot we have what it takes to destroy those who threaten the very existence of the free world. When they talk, we shall hear them. When they move, we shall track them. When they hide, we shall find them.'

That word again. 'We?'

'There will be no more than a hundred and fifty of us – excluding the robots.' Arthur expected a smile, but the magus was serious. 'On this small island will be based the most highly-trained and motivated military force on the planet. They will confront the forces of darkness, all those who threaten the peace of the world and the future of mankind.' The green eyes glowed. 'Of course they would need a leader, and not just any leader but a man of integrity, a man of heart and soul, a man of cunning who knows how to outsmart the enemy, a man of courage who fears no one but God himself, a man, in short, much like that ancient king we were speaking of just now. Can't you see them, Arthur?' said Merlin, his eyes shining like green moons, 'can't you see them riding out to do battle, just like King Arthur and his knights of old? But instead of horses they will ride air and sea craft, Nimbles and Scuttles, Eclipse and Kraken, and the weapons they wield – one in particular – will be far ahead of their time.'

'Can force really solve the problems of the world?' asked Arthur.

'Sometimes force is the only way,' said Merlin. 'History has shown that appeasing the wicked invariably ends in disaster. Evil men must be confronted, or the good will be destroyed. But being more powerful than your enemies is not enough. The greatest power does not come from armies and weapons.' The green eyes glowed brighter and brighter as the magus was inspired by a vision of things to come. 'Imagine, Arthur, imagine a kingdom founded on love and respect and justice, imagine a small, dedicated band of men and women ready if necessary to sacrifice their lives, not from envy or hatred, not for a country, not for a religion, but to create a peaceful world, a just and happy world, a world that the meek truly can inherit. What a cause, what a noble cause that would be.'

Tears stung Arthur's eyes. For a long time he said nothing. 'This weapon you speak of. Can you tell me more about it?'

'Come with me,' said Merlin. Outside Command Control he faced Arthur, 'Describe something you see. Now, at this moment.'

'Anything?'

'Anything.'

Arthur looked around. 'I see a tall, white building, some kind of office block it looks like.'

'Where exactly?'

'About two hundred metres away, there at three o'clock.' Arthur pointed and turned back to face the magus.

Merlin looked in the direction Arthur had indicated and shook his head. 'I don't see it,' he said.

'Stop playing games, Merlin. It's over there.' Arthur swung round and pointed, frowned and looked again. 'I don't see it either. It was there just now. Where has it gone?'

'Where indeed?' said Merlin, his face expressionless. Even as he spoke the office block reappeared. 'Why there it is,' he cried. 'It must have been there all the time. Or was it?' he mused.

'What do you think, Arthur?' asked Merlin, eyes wide and innocent as a child's.

Suddenly Arthur understood. This was no game, this was not one of Merlin's illusions. 'The silver sphere,' he murmured.

'Quite so,' said Merlin.

'Demat, Remat, Elimat.' This had to be the ultimate weapon.

Merlin nodded, his expression solemn. 'We call it Excalibur.'

'Terrifying,' said Arthur. 'The very thought that someone might use it scares me. Excalibur could destroy the world.'

'Every weapon developed by man from the beginning of time has had the power to destroy, to a lesser or greater extent,' said Merlin. 'Some, like nuclear or chemical or biological weapons, are as destructive to the environment as they are to man. Excalibur is different, not just in degree but in kind. It has infinitely more destructive power than any weapon ever invented, yet it can also immobilise life in order to preserve it.'

'I'm not sure I understand,' said Arthur.

'It's really quite simple,' said Merlin. 'Let me explain. And please pay attention,' he added sternly, as if Arthur were still his pupil at Glastonbury School. 'It is true that Excalibur destroys matter – whether people or things – but only in Elimat mode. In Demat mode Excalibur merely suspends matter; it does not destroy it. The proof of that is Remat, the mode in which the suspended matter is rematerialised. You have seen both Demat and Remat in operation.'

Arthur nodded. 'The silver sphere disappeared and reappeared. So did the building just now.'

'Correct,' said Merlin. 'You said Excalibur could destroy the world. I say that on the contrary, it could prevent the world being destroyed by the most deadly weapon of all.'

A weapon more powerful than Excalibur! How could that be? 'What weapon is that?'

'Man,' said Merlin. 'In the right hands, Excalibur could save the world from mankind for mankind.'

'The right hands?'

'Your hands.'

Arthur shook his head. 'No, Merlin, not me. I am not the man you think I am. I am a man like other men. I have the same hopes, the same fears, the same desires. The same sun warms my back, the same wind blows in my face. I am just an ordinary man.'

'That you are not,' said Merlin positively.

'I have seen men die,' said Arthur. 'I want no more deaths on my conscience.'

The tour of Camelot over, Arthur stood by the Hovercart and gazed across the island at the elegant white buildings radiant in the sunlight, and at the slender columns waving their hands at the sky. Here was a city built for the benefit of generations yet unborn, a space-station that was not in space. Here it was in the middle of an ocean on planet earth, the most thrilling, the most incredible, the most magical sight he had ever seen.

And the most frightening. He had known fear on the battlefield, and he knew fear now. This, though, was a different kind of fear, the fear that he was being led down the wrong path. Merlin had spoken the truth. To be more powerful than your enemies was not enough. You had to be better than they were. But if he fought fire with fire, would he be any different from his enemies? Would not his face become the monster's face?

Without knowing he was doing it he touched the scar on his left cheek where the eagle scratched him when he was a boy. 'Let me go, magus. Find someone else.'

'There is no one else – you are the one. It is your destiny. Listen to me, Arthur. In the long history of the world there have been many times when mankind was in mortal danger. By some quirk of fate, or if you like, by divine intervention, a saviour was always there to pull us back from the brink – a soldier or a saint, a humble peasant, or a supernatural being. But in whatever guise the saviours came, they all had one thing in common. They believed in themselves. That belief was what gave them the courage to confront the wicked.'

For a moment Arthur was almost convinced. 'Help me, magus. Help me to believe.'

'Only you can do that,' said Merlin.

That night Arthur slept fitfully. In the small hours he was suddenly wide awake; he got up, opened the window and looked out into the night. A soft breeze touched his face bringing music the like of which he had never heard before, played on instruments fashioned in an age long gone. In the distance he could hear the muffled beat of a solitary drum. Here and there in the darkness, as if the countryside were rousing itself from sleep, sparks flashed and flared to fires, filling his nostrils with the acrid smell of burning wood.

He could hear voices now, at first a confused murmur, growing more distinct the nearer they approached, until they slipped through the window into his head, and it seemed that every man and woman in the world was repeating over and over again, "Arthur! Arthur! Arthur!"

In the darkness appeared a great castle with towering turrets and buttressed walls, lit by a forest of torches. On the ramparts soldiers stood by great pyramids of rocks and steaming vats of hot oil, preparing to repel the enemy. In the courtyards below, horses neighed, shifting nervously on the cobblestones, held on tight reign by squires, as a hundred and fifty knights, their armour winking red and gold in the torchlight, assembled to do battle. On the battlements there was a sudden agitation of soldiers, swords drawn for battle, or no, swords drawn not for battle, but in salute. A knight appeared, his golden armour shining so brightly that for an instant Arthur was dazzled; and in that instant, the hubbub of noise ceased.

In the silence the knight turned his head in Arthur's direction. Something about him seemed familiar. A moment later and he had turned away again. Drawing his sword he raised it high, and from the walls and ramparts, from the courtyards and corridors and stairways, from every door and window of the castle, cheer upon cheer erupted, every cheer answered and overwhelmed by a defiant and much louder cheer from the huge army drawn up a few hundred yards beyond the castle. For as the first light of dawn appeared, there, silhouetted against the sky, were a thousand knights on horseback and fifteen thousand or more foot soldiers. The enemy outnumbered the small band of knights in the castle's courtyard by more than a hundred to one.

As the sun touched the horizon, the drums of the two opposing armies tapped in dreadful counterpoint. The portcullis was raised, and the knight in golden armour clattered through the castle gates and across the drawbridge followed by his men. Signalling them to halt, he bowed his head, and after a few moments of silent prayer, kissed the hilt of his sword and lowered the visor of his helmet. Then spurring his horse, he galloped directly at the enemy. In seconds he and his men were surrounded.

The breeze brought to Arthur the grim clang of steel on steel. Many a knight crashed to the hard ground, mortally wounded by sword or lance; many more, thrown by their mounts, lay helpless, unable to move, weighed down by their armour, waiting to be trampled to death or skewered through the visor. Horses reared up to the sky, dripping saliva and blood, screaming their agony. Thousands of footsoldiers were slaughtered; those who survived scattered and ran in terror from the battlefield.

Through all the chaos and confusion of battle the knight in golden armour galloped back and forth on his white horse, and no man could withstand him. At the day's end, when only the faint cries of the dying disturbed the silence, he rode up and down the field of battle, his sword flashing red in the light of the setting sun.

Around him lay thousands of the dead and dying, both knights and footsoldiers. From the far corners of the field his men galloped to him, having suffered miraculously few casualties. Removing his helmet, he bowed his head and thanked God for the victory. Then brandishing his sword in triumph, he led his knights back to the castle. Reigning in his horse as he approached the drawbridge, he looked back at the battlefield strewn with bodies, and on his face was a look of such profound sadness that Arthur was moved to tears.

There had to be another way, a better way than Merlin's.

Fourteen

As the weeks and months passed, Uther's malicious leak to the Press was gradually forgotten, and Arthur's star was once more on the rise. A man of integrity and principle had appeared on the political horizon, an excellent performer in the House, respected by his own Party on both back and front benches, popular with the British public, indeed everything a politician ought to be.

In the spring of 2024 Leo Grant finally stood down as leader of United Labour. Arthur Pendragon offered himself as the new leader and was elected by unanimous vote.

The following day the Prime Minister, his father, Uther Pendragon, rose in the House of Commons. 'We have not always seen eye to eye,' he began, 'however I would be failing in my duty as Prime Minister if I did not wish the right honourable gentleman otherwise known as my son, much luck and success as leader of the opposition.' A pause for effect, and he added, to laughter and applause, 'Long may he continue to hold that office.'

Arthur responded gracefully. 'I thank the gentleman whose name I bear for his kind words, and can only assure him that I intend to pay him the greatest compliment a son can pay his father – by stepping into his shoes at the earliest opportunity.'

Members, many on the government benches, appreciated the joke. Uther did not. After the debate he caught up with Arthur in a Westminster corridor. 'Stepping into my shoes,' he hissed scornfully. 'Stepping into my shoes!' he repeated loudly, his voice trembling with anger. 'Let me tell you, Arthur, these shoes are a few sizes too big for you. You know your trouble? You are so blinded by your own arrogance and conceit, you think yourself a match for me. Stepping into my shoes! Think again. Without me you *were* nothing, you *are* nothing, you always will be nothing.' And with that final insult, Uther stalked off.

For a moment or two Arthur stood there, shaking his head like a boxer who has walked into a heavy punch. Such venom, and voiced in public. What on earth had got into his father? He and Uther were political opponents but this was something else; this was personal. He could only think Uther must feel seriously threatened by him to react so furiously to such a routine exchange of banter in the House.

As it happened it was the last time laughter was heard in the House for a long time. The remainder of the year saw a dramatic increase in the number of terrorist incidents across the globe. May saw the hijacking of an American passenger liner in the Caribbean. The release of nearly a hundred convicted and suspected terrorists was demanded, and although about half that number of prisoners were quickly released, the liner was blown up by suicide bombers with the loss of almost all passengers and crew. In early June huge bombs were exploded at both ends of the Eurotunnel, and simultaneously on a train under the English Channel, causing massive destruction and the loss of many lives. The Eurotunnel link was closed indefinitely. In the same month a missile struck a nuclear power station in Illinois resulting in substantial damage and loss of life. The resulting radiation, experts predicted, would take several years to clean up, creating severe health problems for many thousands of people. On the 22nd July a tanker anchored off an East Coast UK refinery exploded with a full cargo of LNG – Liquid Natural Gas – destroying not only the port and the refinery but a large part of the adjoining town. An east wind carried the cloud of contamination over the city and the adjoining countryside. By the time the wind dropped the next day at least fifty square miles of the country had been affected.

It was immediately confirmed that the explosion had not been an accident but a terrorist act.

In the House of Commons, Uther Pendragon expressed his deepest condolences to the victims, promising that all those affected would receive every possible assistance the government could provide, both now and in the future. He also gave his word that 'the perpetrators of this vile act will be hunted down and brought to justice.'

At such a time, criticism of the government over its inadequate handling of the terrorist problem would, Arthur felt, be inappropriate. He therefore contented himself with adding his and his Party's condolences to those of the Prime Minister and assuring him of his full support in difficult times. In private, however, it was a different story. For Arthur this was a terrorist incident too far and he was determined to have a showdown with his father. An attack of this kind had long been predicted by experts, despite which very little had been done by the government either to protect 'high-profile' targets such as nuclear power plants and refineries, or to safeguard people living in adjoining areas. Another fiery confrontation in Number 10 between Arthur and Uther spilled over yet again into ill-tempered exchanges in the corridors of Westminster.

There was no doubt that the New Millennium Party had been damaged by this latest terrorist incident. The media and the public were asking why more was not being done to hunt down and destroy terrorist cells who, it seemed, continued to carry out such attacks with relative impunity. The increasing audacity, ruthlessness and efficiency of Islamist and other terrorist groups, and the failure of the security services and politicians to deal with them, created a sense of instability and foreboding, not just in the United Kingdom but throughout the world.

On the Fourteenth of July, 2024 – the anniversary of Bastille day – a French terrorist group calling itself the Children of the Revolution kidnapped the French President, killing three policemen and two bodyguards in the process, and demanded a ransom of ten billion Euros. No one, not even the French security services, had ever heard of the Children of the Revolution. It was surmised that the group might be a front for a Middle Eastern country, possibly the Kingdom of the Euphrates. That this outrage was perpetrated on Bastille Day was regarded as a sick joke, an insult to a nation that embraced the ideals of Liberty, Equality and Fraternity, a blow at the very heart of French pride and self-esteem. When the French government refused to negotiate with the terrorists, they sent them the little finger of the President's left hand, threatening to cut off one finger a day until the ransom was paid. A deal was swiftly struck – for approximately half the amount demanded, it was widely rumoured – and the French President was duly released.

As Leader of the Opposition, Arthur spoke up for punitive action. Terrorism, he argued, was not a national but an international problem, and as such had to be dealt with by joint international action. Only a united free world could defeat the terrorists. If this government could not do the job, let it resign and leave it to those who could.

Uther insisted, and many in the House agreed with him, that this was an internal French matter. 'France, some might say regrettably, has not been ruled by this country for several centuries.' This sally was greeted with cries of 'hear, hear!' and much laughter on both sides of the House. 'France is a sovereign state, and must deal with terrorist acts as it sees fit.'

Later father and son met in an ante-room. 'You may have won the debate, father,' said Arthur, 'but you lost the argument.'

'Nonsense,' said Uther, 'you're a bad loser.'

'Kidnapping the French President is not just a national issue,' said Arthur, ignoring the dig, 'it is one that affects every democratic country in the world. It could happen here. It could happen to you.'

'If it does,' said Uther dryly, 'I count on you to pay the

ransom.'

'For God's sake, father, be serious. You can't make the problem go away by pretending it doesn't exist.'

'Let's assume for a moment that you might have a point,' said Uther. 'Mind you,' he added hastily, 'I'm not saying you have. What would you do in my place?'

'Persuade the French to join an international task force to hunt down the Children of the Revolution and bring them to justice. It's essential we show the terrorists we mean business. If we don't, we shall live to regret it.'

'I don't share your pessimism, Arthur,' said Uther. 'Terrorist incidents are unpleasant, certainly, but don't let's exaggerate their significance. Throw your microscope away. Take the macrocosmic view. From time to time there are earthquakes, the tectonic plates move. This is one of those times. We have to expect a few tremors now and then.'

'These tremors, as you call them,' said Arthur, 'could be the precursors of a cataclysmic upheaval that one day will tear the planet apart.'

'Relax,' said Uther, flashing an ingratiating beam of a smile at Arthur, 'let's not quarrel about this, my boy. Fighting terrorism ought not to be a political issue.' Uther's expression changed abruptly from amiable to funereal. 'You think my heart doesn't bleed when innocent people are killed and maimed by these bastards? Of course it does. I'm a feeling man, as everyone knows.' Uther struck his breast to emphasise how feeling he was. 'Make no mistake, Arthur, the fight against terrorism is at the top of my agenda. I eat it, breathe it, sleep it.' Sensing perhaps that he had overstated his case, and that Arthur was far from convinced, Uther offered what sounded like a truce. 'Look here,' he said, with an abrupt display of geniality, 'why don't you and I sit down with the boys from MI6 and the anti-terror branch and discuss tactics. Put a bomb under them.' An apologetic grin. 'Metaphorically speaking, of course.' His brows arched. 'How would that be?'

'I'd like that,' said Arthur.

'Then we'll do it. Mind you,' said Uther, 'I'm not committing myself to any change in government policy, or anything like that.' A genial smile. 'You wouldn't expect that, now would you?'

No change meant no progress. His father had thrown him nothing more than a sop. 'Is it still government policy to do deals with terrorists?'

'I don't mind telling you what government policy is, Arthur. Between ourselves, that is. Of course if you quote me, I'll deny it.' Uther lowered his voice to a conspiratorial blur. 'The way I look at it, the bad guys – terrorists to you – they are bound to notch up a success or two here and there. Let's face it, we can't stop them every time. They'll win a few battles, but there's no way they're going to win the war. Whenever they get seriously out of line, we give them a bloody nose, just to let them know who's boss. But if we over-react, they might get the idea we're afraid of them. They might even start to believe they're the ones running the world.'

Arthur shook his head despairingly. To think that this man was Prime Minister of the United Kingdom. He wondered how many world leaders like him there were out there. 'That may have been true thirty years ago but it certainly isn't now. The bad guys are not satisfied with pickings any more. They don't want our left-over scraps. They want everything. And if we're not careful they'll get it. The world has never been such a dangerous place. These days you can make weapons of mass destruction in a bath tub, or on a kitchen table – a nuclear bomb, deadly biological agents like anthrax and botulism, gangrene and cancer and plague, not to speak of chemical killers like sarin and nerve gas. Today it's the French President. Tomorrow? Who knows? It could be a city. Or a country. My God, they could hold the world to ransom.'

Uther clapped his hands in ironic applause. 'Great stuff, Arthur. Apocalyptic talk. Whatever next? Doomsday?

Ragnarok? Twilight of the Gods?'

In his heart Arthur knew he was wasting his time. Still he refused to give up. Somehow or other there had to be a way of making his father see reason. 'You can mock, but is it really so fantastic? Think, father, think. The terrorists have the weapons and the technology to destroy us. They also have the will, which is more than we seem to have.'

Arthur gave his son a patronising pat on the arm. 'You worry too much. Everything is going to be alright. Trust me.'

Within a few days of this latest confrontation between father and son, rumours about Arthur began to circulate in Westminster and the news media, rumours that were difficult to scotch because they had no substance, and appeared to be mere expressions of opinion. Where they originated no one would or could say. When the Downing Street Press Office came under suspicion, they issued a vehement denial. The essence of the rumours was simple. Arthur, it was said, could not be trusted, either by his colleagues or by the electorate – not because he was not a man of principle, but because he was a man of too many principles – in other words a zealot, one of those passionately dedicated idealogues who start wars without meaning to. Principles blindly adhered to were dangerous things. Terrorists murdered people in the name of principles. The sad truth was that Arthur Pendragon was misplaced in politics. He should take the cloth, or become a professor of some abstrusely theoretical subject at some remote place of learning. Practical matters like running the country should be left to others.

The final, and perhaps most damaging rumour of all, insinuated that Arthur's motives were suspect. What did he really mean when he spoke of uniting the free world? Such arrogance! Such presumption! Who was going to lead this united world of his? Why, Arthur Pendragon of course! Was the leader of the opposition a would-be dictator parading in a freedom fighter's clothes, a latter-day fascist, posing as the planet's saviour?

One minute Arthur was alone in his office, the next, Merlin was there. So accustomed was Arthur to these sudden manifestations that he no longer bothered to comment on them. Virgil hopped on Arthur's left shoulder and gently nibbled the lobe of his ear.

'How wonderful,' said Arthur gratefully. 'He never forgets me.'

'He never forgets people he loves.'

Arthur looked every bit as flattered as he felt. Merlin relaxed in an armchair whilst Virgil settled down on his master's shoulder and closed his eyes.

Arthur pulled a face. 'I'm not doing very well, am I?'

Merlin stroked Virgil's chest. 'Politics is a rough game.'

'So it seems,' said Arthur ruefully. However rough it was, though, he had to see it through, despite the damaging rumours, despite being disillusioned with Uther and the government, despite his frustration with world leaders, despite all his doubts. 'There has to be a political solution to the world's problems,' he said.

Merlin raised a delicately dubious eyebrow. 'Has to be?'

'Ought to be, then.'

'In case there is not, Camelot is ready for you,' said Merlin enticingly.

Arthur's eyes dreamed as he half remembered. 'We visited an island, you and I . . . '

'Did we?'

'You spoke of knights riding out to do battle against the forces of darkness . . . ' Arthur's eyes were clouded with pain.

'Go on,' said Merlin.

'In whose name will they ride?'

'In the name of every decent man, woman and child in the world,' said Merlin quietly. 'In the name of those whose only desire is to live in peace. In the name of the meek who will one day inherit the earth.'

'In the name of what government, what international body, what court of law?'

'If mankind self-destructs,' said Merlin, 'where will your governments be then? Or your international bodies, or your courts of law?'

Even if Merlin was right . . . 'Justice must be done,' said Arthur. 'The rule of law is paramount.'

'The first law of the universe is order,' said Merlin. 'When chaos threatens, order must be restored, if necessary, imposed.'

Arthur flinched.

'I know the thought of fighting fire with fire troubles you,' said Merlin. 'It troubles me too, Arthur. But like that great king of old, you have no choice. Not if mankind is to be saved.'

'The wicked take the law into their own hands,' said Arthur. 'If we do the same, are we any better than they?'

Merlin leaped up. Startled, Virgil hooh-hooed grouchily and fluttered about the room before settling on the mantlepiece. As Merlin paced, his white robe brushed the carpet. 'It's the story of Athene and Perseus.'

'Explain, magus.'

'Medusa, the Gorgon, turned her enemies to stone by looking at them. Athene gave Perseus her shield to use as a mirror so that he could overcome the monster without looking at her directly.' Merlin stopped dead in the centre of the room and directed his penetrating gaze at his beloved protégé. 'You don't have to become your enemy, Arthur. The face of the monster is not your face. It is the monster who is responsible for his actions, not you. You are good, he is wicked, he uses his power to achieve his own selfish ends, you use yours for the good of humanity, he is cruel and immoral, you are merciful and just.'

'You have such faith in me,' said Arthur.

Merlin's eyes glowed tenderly. 'I know you, Arthur. I know you better than you know yourself.'

Head in hands, Arthur pondered until the storm in his head subsided. 'I still believe my way is the right way,' he said at last.

'Your way?'

'The democratic way. I believe it is possible to use political power and influence to solve the problems of the world. I also believe it is possible to convince the leaders of the free world to unite in the fight against the powers of darkness.'

Merlin began to fade. 'The time may come,' he said, as he and Virgil disappeared, 'when you will change your mind. If that should ever happen, I shall be there for you.'

Fifteen

2024

ARTHUR KNEW something was wrong the moment he saw George Bedivere's face. George was the most unflappable man he knew, but for once he looked harassed.

'Read this,' he said, laying a file in front of Arthur. 'Phone me. I'll be with Leo and Thomas.'

'What's up, George?'

George Bedivere shook his head. 'Read it,' he said, and hurried out.

The file was stamped MOST SECRET and it made grim reading. For several years Uther Pendragon had been under the surveillance of MI5, and the evidence they had gathered was damning. It seemed that when he was Minister of Foreign Affairs he had accepted huge sums of money from Sadiq el Shaeb of the Kingdom of the Euphrates. It was obviously no coincidence that during that same period a substantial quantity of light and heavy arms, tanks, aircraft, missiles and high tech equipment had been secretly delivered to the K.O.E., even though it was at the time on Britain's list of arms-embargoed countries. If that were not shameful enough, there was evidence of secret arms-for-cash transactions with Colombian drug producers, and with two rogue states – one in South-East Asia, one in the Middle East – known to support active terrorist groups.

For a few minutes Arthur sat staring blankly at the wall, trying to come to terms with what he had read. He had not believed the rumours about his father, or perhaps he had not wanted to. To see them now confirmed in black and white was devastating. Swivelling his chair, he looked out of the window of his sixth floor office. Across the road was Big Ben and the gothic-revival mass of the Palace of Westminster. Below lay Parliament Square, flanked by the statues of famous statesmen – Palmerston and Peel, Canning, Disraeli and Churchill – great men all, men of vision and foresight, men of courage and initiative. Men of integrity. Around the corner, Whitehall and Downing Street were out of his line of sight; Arthur presumed his father would be at his desk in Number 10 attending to affairs of state, unaware of the deadly danger he was in. He tapped into a secure line. After a brief pause George Bedivere, once Arthur's platoon sergeant, now shadow Defence Secretary, Leo Grant and Thomas Winnington appeared on the wall screen.

'How did you get hold of this?' asked Arthur.

'A contact in MI5 gave it to me,' said Thomas Winnington. 'He said he would be in deep trouble if his bosses found out. I'm not so sure about that.'

Arthur nodded. 'You think it was an authorised leak?'

'I think MI5 are testing the waters,' said Winnington.

Arthur rocked gently in his chair. 'Why would they want to do that?'

'Speaking as a lawyer,' said Leo, 'I would say a great deal of their evidence might be inadmissible in a court of law. Some of the surveillance tactics they used were pretty unorthodox. As you know there are strict legal guidelines about that sort of thing. My guess is that MI5 decided it would be a waste of time sending the report to the CPS. But there's more than one way of skinning a cat.'

George Bedivere grunted. 'They want us to do their dirty work for them.'

'Where do you stand on this, Arthur?' They all knew what Thomas Winnington was asking. Blood was thicker than water, wasn't it?

'He has to go,' said Arthur. 'One way or another.'

Leo nodded. 'That's what we hoped you'd say. We have to confront him with the evidence and demand his resignation.'

'Knowing my father, he might feel he has nothing to gain by resigning.'

'We've thought of that,' said George Bedivere. 'We suggest offering him immunity from prosecution; only if he resigns, of course.'

'I don't like it,' said Arthur. 'It smells of a cover-up.'

'What choice do we have?' said Leo. 'In this case the end justifies the means.'

'Dragging your father through the courts is not going to help anyone,' said Winnington. 'Everyone involved will be damaged – the security services, politicians on both sides of the House, above all the country. Let him resign on the grounds of ill health. No one will ask any questions, and we'll make sure the report is never published.'

Whilst Arthur pondered, they watched him anxiously. After a while he nodded his head in agreement and the three men breathed a sigh of relief. 'Who is going to wield the knife?' he asked.

They were all looking down at him from the screen.

'Forget it,' said Arthur. 'Don't ask me to bring down my own father.'

'It has to be you,' said George Bedivere. 'He knows that if you make a deal, you'll stick to it. He trusts you. You are probably the only man in the world he does.'

Arthur took a seat on the other side of the Prime Minister's desk.

'Coffee?'

Arthur shook his head.

'No?' Uther sipped his coffee and sighed contentedly. 'They make an excellent cup of coffee in Number 10.' A grin. 'One of the perks of the office.'

'This is not a social call, father.'

'So I gather. You look like Banquo's ghost.'

'You read MI5's report?'

390

'I did.' Uther left a void of silence for Arthur to fill.

'Any comments?'

Uther poured himself another coffee. 'I found it enormously entertaining. Always did have a weakness for spy fiction.'

'So none of it is fact?'

'Lies from beginning to end,' Uther assured him. 'A crude attempt by my enemies to discredit me. They won't succeed.'

'Then,' said Arthur, 'you would not object if the report were made public?' It was bluff, but worth a try.

Uther toyed with a lump of sugar. He nodded his head firmly as if he had reached a decision. 'No sense in playing games; it's all true. Every word of it. For once MI5 have got it right. So what? So I made deals with some unsavoury characters. You know how it started? Years ago the Party was heavily in debt, we had been on the opposition benches for ten years and we looked like being there another ten. I told the PM I would put the Party in the black within a year, and that's exactly what I did. He asked no questions, he was very grateful. Before I knew it I was in the cabinet.'

Uther had not addressed the most distasteful accusation in the MI5 dossier. Reluctantly, Arthur wielded the knife. 'MI5 say you transferred money to numbered bank accounts in Switzerland.'

Uther thought for a long time before replying. To lie or not to lie? That was the question. For him it was not a moral issue, he told lies every day. Damn it, he would not be Prime Minister if he didn't. The real issue was simple: which would serve him best, a lie or the truth? He decided that the truth would put more pressure on his son. 'What if I did? I had a wife and children to support. Before you judge me, Arthur, let me remind you of something. From the day I became an M.P. I devoted all my time to the Party, and none of it to my property business. The result was I lost a fortune – in the service of the Party, Arthur, in the service of the Party. Remember that. What's more, when I asked my own son to help me rescue my

391

business, he turned me down. Had you done your filial duty, things might have been different. There would have been no need for me to take desperate measures.'

Arthur's feelings for his father were complex. The one certain thing was that he loved him, and nothing Uther had done, or probably ever would do, would change that. He was acutely and embarrassingly aware of his father's shortcomings, but he had learned to live with them, as one lives with the imperfections of an old house, or, for that matter, of old friends. As for respect . . . ? Had he ever truly respected his father? How could you respect a man whose natural inclination was to distort and manipulate the truth, and what's more, do it so utterly plausibly? 'Some people would call it a gift,' said Arthur.

Uther brightened. 'A gift?' he echoed hopefully.

'This talent you have for misrepresenting facts and rewriting history. It is ludicrous and cowardly of you to try to shift the blame for your corruption onto me. If you were so concerned for your family, you should have quit politics and looked after the business yourself. The truth is, the only person you ever really cared about is Uther Pendragon. You wanted to get to the top, and you wanted it at any price. You and no one else are responsible for your actions. It's time to go, father. For God's sake go with dignity. It's the very least you can do.'

Uther trembled with anger. Never had his son, never had anyone spoken to him like this before. How dare he! He should not have allowed him back into his life. He should not have made that deal with Merlin. 'I shall never resign, if that is what you are suggesting. Never! You don't fool me, Arthur. You wouldn't dare publish the MI5 report. You know damn well what would happen. The scandal would destroy the New Millennium Party. We would be unelectable for years to come. As for United Labour, do you really think they would walk away from the devastation unscathed? I don't think so. And now I come to think of it, let's talk about you, Arthur. Is anyone going to believe you knew nothing about my little peccadillos?

My own son? I don't think so, my boy, do you? You would have to kiss goodbye to your political career.'

After this harangue Uther fell back in his chair panting. He was so short of breath that Arthur feared he was about to have a heart attack. He waited for his father to calm down. 'None of us will look good, that's true, father,' he agreed. 'But that's a risk we are ready to take. No one but you took bribes. No one else was involved. The MI5 report makes that clear.'

Uther laughed like a man enjoying a good joke. That he could laugh at such a time was something Arthur marvelled at. If his father was a rogue, he was a gutsy one. 'Who believes MI5?' said Uther witheringly. 'Lying and deception is their business. No, they'll believe me. I'll make sure every member of the cabinet, every spin doctor, every secretary, every under-secretary, every frontbencher and backbencher in the Party is tainted. I'll throw so much mud, some of it is bound to stick. Go back to your friends, Arthur, and tell them this. They can cut off Samson's hair, but if they do, he'll bring the house down on all of them, every last one. There'll be nothing left but dust. Tell them that, will you.'

Arthur, George Bedivere, Leo Grant and Thomas Winnington talked into the small hours. Everyone knew what had to be done but no one knew how to do it. Uther was right: bring him down, and he would bring the house down with him. Finally Arthur said, 'If that's the price we have to pay, perhaps we should pay it.'

Silence.

Leo shook his head. 'I'm sorry, but no. I am not prepared to take the risk, I fear the consequences would be catastrophic. Uther knows what he's talking about; it's not just New Millennium, it's the whole works that would be damaged. The people of this country would be even more disillusioned with politics and politicians than they are already; it would take years to regain their respect.'

'I agree,' said Thomas Winnington. 'There's too much at

stake.'

Arthur focused bleary eyes on Bedivere. 'George?'

'I'm with Leo and Thomas,' said George bluntly.

Leo was the last to leave. 'You said it yourself. Your father has to go. The question is, how do we force him to resign?'

Arthur raised his arms and let them drop helplessly by his side. 'I really don't know. The report is the only weapon we have, and Uther knows we dare not publish. So what's the answer?'

Leo shrugged. 'It's up to you now.'

Up to him. Was that what it meant to be a leader? People relied on you to perform miracles. For some reason he thought of Merlin.

Sixteen

2024

IN HIS FLAT Arthur dialled the evening news. Instead of the news, what came up on the wallscreen were two intensely bright green orbs. 'Merlin?' Around the orbs, bits of Merlin's face materialised like pieces of a jigsaw – eyebrows, mouth, cheeks, ears, forehead and hair, chin and nose, until finally the whole face was assembled. The last thing to appear was the smile.

'What's to be done, Merlin?'

The mouth formed the words 'Come with me.' No sooner had it done so than the face receded into darkness. Under a starry sky lay an island in a moonlit sea, on the island a glimmer of white buildings. A fast zoom, and the camera focused on one of them. There stood Merlin pointing at a sign over the entrance – the one word, NIWIS. 'Mean anything to you?'

Arthur shook his head, puzzled. 'No.'

Reaching up, Merlin dabbled his fingers in the heavens and drew down a handful of stars. For a few moments they chased each other round and round his head, then broke away and streaked towards Arthur, seeming to burst in his face, dazzling him. When he opened his eyes again, there onscreen was the full-length magus, white robe, linen jacket, shoulder-length blond hair. 'Remember now?'

Arthur's eyes dreamed. 'Yes . . . NIWIS . . . Nothing Is What It Seems.'

'Suggest anything to you?'

The words came back to him. *'We make our enemies see what isn't there. And not see – what is.'*

Merlin spread his hands. 'Precisely.'

'How does that help me?' asked Arthur.

'Simple. Make Uther see what you want him to see, even though what you want him to see is not there.'

'Riddles, Merlin,' complained Arthur. 'Why is it always riddles?'

'You want your bread sliced and buttered on both sides,' said Merlin tetchily, his image fading from the screen.

For hours Arthur's thoughts ran here and there chasing elusive ideas with no hope of catching them, like a friendly dog half-heartedly chasing a rabbit. At the end of every blind alley stood Merlin shaking his head and pointing in the opposite direction. Mentally exhausted and thoroughly exasperated, Arthur fell into a deep sleep.

When he woke the following morning, there it was – the solution – bright and shining and clear as a full moon. Yet around the solution was a dark ring. Arthur was troubled. His father had to be brought down, and he was the one to do it. But by deception and cunning? Was Leo right? Did the end justify the means? By the time he had shaved and dressed, he had convinced himself that he was being over-sensitive. Corruption was a disease. If it were not rooted out, the whole system would become infected.

He laid the text on Uther's desk.

'What's this?'

'Your letter of resignation.'

Uther sighed wearily. 'We've been through this before. You're wasting my time.'

'If you refuse to sign it,' said Arthur, 'I shall e-mail your MI5 file to the *Daily Telegraph*.'

Uther leaned back in his chair and considered Arthur through narrowed eyes. 'And see our whole political system tainted and your father disgraced?' He shook his head. 'Somehow I don't think so. You see, Arthur, you are one of that rare breed, a good man, and like all good men, you have a conscience. You care what happens to people.'

Arthur produced his palm computer and sent a signal to the computer on Uther's desk. The wallscreen flickered, and on it was the text of a letter signed by Arthur.

Uther frowned. 'What the hell is that?'

'My covering letter to the editor. And now . . . ' Slowly Arthur scrolled down several more pages, allowing Uther plenty of time to read them. 'Your MI5 file.'

'You'd never dare send it.' Uther was less confident than he sounded. Being confronted by that damned file up there on the screen was a little unnerving. If this was poker, then Arthur had certainly raised the stakes. Was he bluffing? Most probably, though there was a resolute look about him that Uther found disquieting.

A few more taps on the palm computer, and there on the screen was Charles Meadows, editor of the *Daily Telegraph*. It was clear to Uther from Arthur's greeting that he and Meadows had already discussed this. 'Morning, Charles. You'll have the story in the next few minutes.'

'Can I have an exclusive?'

'No guarantees,' said Arthur.

'At least give me a clue what it's all about,' pleaded Meadows.

Uther was studying every nuance of expression, every word and every inflexion. Never for a second did he take his eyes off the screen.

'It will be of great interest to your readers,' promised Arthur.

Though it was less than Meadows had hoped for, he would take whatever he could get. 'Is that all you can tell me?'

'For the moment,' said Arthur.

'Why am I onscreen in Number 10?' Surely the story must have something to do with the PM. But what? And why, Meadows asked himself, was Arthur Pendragon involved? Was it personal? A family problem? Ill health, perhaps? Or . . . wait a minute . . . could it be divorce! Was that it? Was Uther's wife leaving him? There had been rumours over the years. Was this an exercise in damage limitation?

'That would be telling,' said Arthur, giving nothing away.

For a journalist this was more than frustrating. 'If it was anyone but you, Arthur . . . ' And with that the screen went blank. Charles Meadows knew he had all he was going to get – for the moment, at least.

Uther was trying to read the expression on his son's face, but it was impenetrable.

'Which is it to be?' asked Arthur, 'resignation or exposure?'

Uther was beginning to feel the pressure. 'I can't believe you'd be such a fool – you, Westminster's golden boy.' Uther smiled ruefully. 'As you know, I'm a realist. You have to be in this business. I hate to admit it, but next time round the chances are that United Labour will win the election. And then . . . think of it, Arthur. You will be Prime Minister of the United Kingdom. Are you ready to throw all that away?'

'With great reluctance,' admitted Arthur. 'But if I have to . . . ' He shrugged. 'There comes a time when a stand has to be made.'

My God, thought Uther, he isn't bluffing. He really means it. He had heard of such men, men who were willing to sacrifice everything for a point of principle, though this was the first time he had had the misfortune to meet one. And to think it had to be his own son! 'Don't do this to me, Arthur,' he begged, making his plea shamelessly personal. 'Whatever our differences, you're the one man in the whole world I can trust, the only friend I have. Don't abandon me when I need you most.'

'That's what you did to me,' said Arthur quietly.

Uther sat with head bowed. 'So that's what this is all about. Getting even.' Though Arthur wanted to deny it, in his heart of hearts he wasn't sure. Abruptly Uther switched to ingratiating mode. 'Come now, my boy,' he said, beaming benevolently, 'why quarrel when we can work together? Leave United Labour. Cross the floor of the House. Join me in the great crusade. Think what a team we would make. You would be my trusted lieutenant. I would give you anything you wanted – a knighthood, a peerage, a cabinet post, anything at all. No terms. No strings. I offer you an Aladdin's cave of choices. Take what you want.'

'Nice try, father.'

A reproachful look. 'There must be something you want.'

'There is,' said Arthur.

A glimmer of hope in Uther's eyes. 'Name it.'

'Your resignation.'

Uther could not conceal his disappointment. 'That's one thing you'll never get.'

A tap on the palm computer, and the first page of MI5's file on Uther was onscreen. Fingertip resting lightly on the send key, Arthur looked at Uther. 'This is it, father. The moment of truth. When I tap this key, Meadows will have the file in seconds, and nothing you or I do can stop it going to press. There'll be no going back.'

Uther's mouth set in a stubborn line. 'You wouldn't dare.'

All Arthur had to do now was pull the trigger, and it would all be over. If only it were as easy as that, he was thinking. It was painful enough when you had the enemy in your sights but when it was your own flesh and blood you were about to consign to oblivion . . . 'Last chance, father.'

'You haven't got the guts.'

A tap on the send key and Uther watched in horror and disbelief as the story of his treachery scrolled swiftly to its end. Onscreen now was the *Daily Telegraph* answer back, confirming receipt of the text.

'Jesus Christ, what have you done?' Head in hands Uther repeated over and over again, 'What have you done? What have you done?' He looked up, his eyes wild. 'Phone Meadows. Now! For God's sake phone him! Tell him it's all lies. Tell him it's a forgery. Tell him anything you like but get that report back while there's still time.'

Arthur did not stir.

'What the hell are you waiting for? You don't think he'll believe you? Is that it? Offer the man a peerage then. He'll sell his soul for a peerage. I know these journalist types.'

'It's no use, father.'

'Don't say that.' Uther looked pleadingly at his son. 'For God's sake help me, Arthur. There must be something you can do.'

Arthur shook his head. 'It's too late.'

Such was the tension in his mind and body that for several seconds Uther actually stopped breathing. Then he lay back in his chair and gave a sigh so profound that it seemed to draw the very soul out of him, and with it all his hopes and dreams. He was beaten and he knew it. He had gambled and lost. 'Dear God, Arthur, you've ruined me.'

Arthur shrugged. 'I'm sorry it had to be like this.'

'What happens now?'

'You must sign the letter,' said Arthur.

Uther summoned up all his courage. 'Ah, but should I sign it now, or should I sign it tomorrow? Or should I not sign it at all?' As he toyed with his predicament Arthur watched him, half in astonishment, half in admiration: Nero fiddling while Rome burned. How typical of his father. 'Will I? Won't I? Will I join the dance?' Sliding open the left-hand bottom drawer of his desk, Uther produced a bottle of cognac and a glass. 'You know something, Arthur, I don't think I will. At least not now. I'll wait until the story hits the headlines.' Uther looked at his watch. 'They deliver the morning papers at six a.m.' he said. 'Did you know that, Arthur?' Arthur shook his head. 'No? Well, we all live and learn in politics, isn't that so?' He poured himself a triple brandy. 'Cheers! I shall celebrate my last twelve hours as Prime Minister in an alcoholic stupor.'

'If you don't jump now, you'll be pushed in the morning,' said Arthur, trying to sound casual. 'Wouldn't it look better if you did the honourable thing?' This was the moment on which everything turned. How would his father respond? If he refused to resign now, all would be lost. There would be no reason for him to resign in the morning.

'The honourable thing?' Uther poured himself a large cognac and downed it in one gulp. 'Why not? It'll be a new experience.' He shrugged, took out his pen and signed the resignation letter. Arthur scanned the letter onto his palm computer and transmitted it to the Web Channel's News Service. Seconds later every newspaper in the country had the full text of the Prime Minister's resignation.

A number blinked on Arthur's palm computer. He transferred the editor of the *Daily Telegraph* to the wallscreen. 'I have your story, Arthur,' said Charles Meadows, 'or I presume that's what it is. I need the key code to unscramble it.'

'Forget it,' said Arthur, 'it's a non-starter. There's a bigger story on the Web Channel.'

'What's that?' asked Meadows.

'The Prime Minister has resigned.'

'Jesus!' The screen went blank.

Uther looked uncomprehendingly from Arthur to the screen and back again. And then the penny dropped. 'You bastard! You scheming bastard! You tricked me!'

Arthur said nothing. What could he say? The cat was out of the bag. He would rather his father had not found him out but now that he had, he was not going to lie about it.

'You put the text onscreen to bamboozle me. I assumed that because I could read it, Meadows could too, but he couldn't. You sent it to him alright, but you sent it encrypted. You conned me into resigning.'

'I'm afraid I did, father,' said Arthur. '*Mea culpa*,' he added mischievously. He expected another outburst, but to his astonishment a hint of a smile disturbed Uther's features.

'Damn me,' he murmured, 'damn me if you aren't a chip off the old block.'

It was dusk. Uther poured himself yet another drink from a near empty bottle of cognac, and staggered across the room to the window. In the street below a tabby cat licked his paw with great concentration. He watched it, fascinated. To that cat nothing else in the world mattered. Prime Ministers could come and go, and what the hell was it to him? He would go on licking his paw. He envied it. My God how he envied it.

The heat of the summer's evening was oppressive. Apart from the cat, Downing Street was deserted, as were many other streets up and down the country. At this very moment millions would be watching the late news, though did anyone really care what they were looking at? Of course not. Why should they? They had no say, no influence, no real involvement in what was happening in the world. For them the news was just another game show, only without prizes. A new millennium had dawned, but what was really new about it? Nothing. Democracy was a sham. People never had any control over their lives, and they still hadn't.

One thing was certain, his story would sell a hell of a lot of newspapers. As for the telly, he shuddered to think what they would do with it. What would it be – Soap or Reality TV? A bit of each? What did it matter? No one could distinguish fantasy from reality any more. All those channel-hoppers looking for a real life experience wouldn't recognise one if they had a head-on crash with it. Tomorrow's Reality Celebrity show would be the Prime Minister – da dum – in – wait for it – *The Crucifixion of Uther Pendragon!* with repeats at hourly intervals from breakfast to midnight, and from midnight to dawn for the benefit of shift workers. To enhance the illusion, real nails and actual blood would be used. His torment promised to be first class reality entertainment, like all the other news the great British public so enjoyed watching – floods, fires, earthquakes, tornadoes, famines, plagues, surgical procedures, rape, murder, torture, massacres, sexual abuse, executions, crimes of greed and passion, wars and terrorist incidents.

There was a crack of thunder. In a way it was a relief. The storm had been brewing for a long time, ever since they made him Foreign Secretary in fact. The cat jumped and ran for shelter. The few pedestrians in Whitehall disappeared as the merciless rain lashed tarmac and paving stones. Rats leaving the sinking ship, thought Uther. Everyone runs for cover when the rains come.

One more drink left in the bottle. As he tossed it back the sweat was already streaming down his face. A sharp pain stabbed the inside of his left arm, the glass fell from his hand. Throwing back his head he fought for breath, gulping in air. His throat seized up and he started to choke as the room spun round him. A vice-like pain gripped his chest, squeezing the life out of him. Folding to his knees he laid his forehead on the carpet and drifted into unconsciousness.

Seventeen

2024

THE RESIGNATION of the Prime Minister was banner
headlines in the morning papers, prompting endless
speculation. Journalists, by nature sceptical, had difficulty
taking so sudden and dramatic an announcement at its face
value. The PM's letter mentioned health problems but gave
no details. Some columnists suspected that the real problem
was not the PM's health but powerful enemies in the New
Millennium Party. Had there been a palace revolution? More
titillatingly newsworthy, he was rumoured to be fond of the
ladies. Was this a pre-emptive move to head off a sex scandal?

But when, a few hours later, the news of Uther's heart attack
broke, the doubters were silenced. Uther was popular with the
electorate, and there was considerable interest in the details.
How soon would he recover? Would he recover at all? At
first the cardiac infarction was reported to have been a mild
one. But as the day wore on and the doctors' bulletins grew
more cautious, press and TV reports assumed an increasingly
valedictory note, as if they were premature obituaries.

For the political hacks there was only one issue. If it came to
it, who would step into Uther Pendragon's shoes? Candidates
for the succession rushed into TV studios. Their message was
invariably the same. First, they expressed earnest regret that
the Prime Minister's health had compelled him to resign.
Second, they professed total optimism that he would make a
full recovery. Third, they stressed their unequivocal disinterest
in succeeding him. And fourth and last, they hinted how
eminently qualified they were should they be compelled to

answer the call.

Towards evening Uther waved Igraine and his step-daughters out of the hospital room. He wanted to be alone with Arthur.

'The doctors say you're doing fine,' said Arthur.

'Doctors are even bigger liars than politicians.' Uther reached out and patted his son on the arm. 'Thank you for your concern.'

'I blame myself for this.'

'You did what you had to do. You were not to know my ticker was going to give out.'

'A few weeks rest and you'll be back to normal.'

A wicked smile. 'Normal is one thing I shall never be.'

Uther lay back on his pillow and closed his eyes. Arthur could scarcely believe the change in his father. Yesterday he was a man in his prime, still fighting, still seeing off his critics with disdain, still answering questions on the floor of the House with his customary confidence and flair. Under attack he had stood tall and proud, as he always did, his colour high, his voice strong and vibrant. Now his face was ashen, his voice weak. Twenty-four hours ago his hair had been charcoal grey. Now suddenly it was white. In one day Uther Pendragon had become an old man.

'Cigar,' demanded Uther.

'You really think you should?'

Uther snorted irritably. 'Of course I bloody shouldn't. Inside jacket pocket and be quick about it.'

Arthur grinned. 'I can see you'll be giving the nurses trouble.' He clipped the end of a huge cigar and put it carefully in his father's mouth.

As the match flared, Uther's nostrils twitched. 'Always liked the smell of sulphur.' He winked at Arthur. 'Something to look forward to.'

For a while he lay puffing contentedly, then thrust the cigar at Arthur to dispose of. 'Last cigar I shall ever smoke, and I can't even finish it. Sod it!'

'You'll be Cuba's best customer for years to come,' said Arthur confidently.

In the corner of the room was a TV set, switched on, but with the sound turned down. The appearance of a man he loathed threw Uther into a sudden rage. 'Anthony Jarvis, the obsequious turd, the devious scumbag!'

'You want me to turn up the volume, father?'

'What for? I know exactly what he's saying. He's saying he can't wait for me to get better. Lie! The truth is he can't wait for me to die. He's denying he's a candidate for the succession. Lie! He would sell his kids, his wife and mother too for a shot at Number 10. Look at that nauseating smile.' Pushing himself up, Uther shouted at the screen, 'They're yellow, Tony! Get them capped!' and fell back, panting. Moments later he was directing his rage at the screen again. 'Who gave you your first job? Whatever happened to loyalty, arsehole?'

He began to cough uncontrollably, a rasping, pitiful sound. Arthur held the cup of water to his lips. Uther took a couple of sips and lay back, exhausted. 'That man claims to be my friend. I have no friends.'

'You have many friends,' Arthur assured him.

'The Prime Minister has many friends. Uther Pendragon has none. Watch out, Arthur. The House of Commons is a dangerous place. It's not your enemies you need to worry about, it's your friends. Your enemies sit opposite you where you can keep an eye on them. Your friends sit behind you and stab you in the back. Take a tip from me, be on your guard. It's always the ones you trust most who betray you.'

The words were not aimed at Arthur, though they might well have been. He had done what had to be done, but that did not make it any easier to live with. A chip off the old block, Uther had said, and he was right. His father's mind was wandering, his thoughts far away now. 'I have done such things, Arthur . . . bad things.'

'I doubt if anyone can look back on their lives without some regrets,' said Arthur consolingly.

'True, very true.' Uther leaned towards him and whispered hoarsely, 'Do you believe in Judgement Day?'

'In a way.'

'This is mine.'

'You mustn't think like that. You must concentrate on getting better.' Right or wrong, his father had always seemed so unassailable to Arthur. And here he was so vulnerable, so ill, so desperately ill, his skull protruding through the flesh. It was almost too much to bear, the more so since it was he who had put him here. He wanted to put his arms round him and tell him that everything was going to be alright. 'I love you, father.'

Uther chuckled, 'Thank God for that. Think what you might have done if you had hated me.'

Arthur gave a wry smile.

'Where did it go?' asked Uther. 'Life. Where did it go? I want it back. Just as I'm beginning to understand what it's all about, it's over. Absurd, isn't it? I never dreamt this would happen to me. All those years that old man with the scythe was trailing me without my knowing it. And now he's finally caught up with me.' A wheezy laugh. Uther's eyes were suddenly fiercely focused. What was he thinking of? 'I have something to confess.'

'Yes, father?'

'Your mother's first husband . . . '

'Godfrey Whittaker.'

'They say he shot himself.' Uther's voice was stronger now, his eyes feverishly intense. Trembling fingers dug into his temples as if he were trying to root out a painful cancer.

'Shall I send for someone, father?'

'Who?'

Arthur hesitated. 'A priest?'

'A priest!' Uther was outraged. 'Why would I want a damned priest?'

'I don't know what your religious beliefs are,' said Arthur. 'We never talked about things like that. I just thought you might want to . . . ' How to put it?

'Might want to what?' asked Uther suspiciously.

'Ask God's forgiveness.'

'God? God! It's none of his bloody business! It's my son's forgiveness I'm asking for.' Uther grasped Arthur's hand in a surprisingly powerful grip. 'Godfrey wouldn't give your mother a divorce. He would have dragged us through the courts. It would have been a huge scandal. He wanted to blacken your mother's name. And mine.'

'I don't have to hear this.'

'But I have to tell you.'

Arthur shook his head. 'No, father, you don't.'

'Won't you forgive a dying man?'

'It's not for me to forgive you,' said Arthur.

'Who can forgive me, then?' asked Uther plaintively.

'Igraine, your wife.'

Uther's grip tightened. 'If you won't forgive me, at least listen to me. Hear my confession.'

Arthur knew what his father was about to tell him. He had known it since first he met him, though until this moment he had never been able to admit it to himself.

'Godfrey didn't commit suicide. I killed him. I shot him. There was a bang, and he dropped dead. The most amazing thing. That's all there is to a man's life. Bang. And it's over.' He peered anxiously at his son. 'You can't forgive me, I can see it in your eyes. No one can.' Uther's attention now seemed concentrated on the sheet covering his bed. Over its surface his frail hands wandered, flattening out the creases compulsively. But for every crease he smoothed away, another one appeared.

Arthur was reluctant to ask the question, though it was one that needed answering. 'Did she know? Did Mother know?'

Uther gave no sign of having heard him. 'It was soon after we married,' he said, his eyes wandering, his trembling fingers scrabbling at the sheet. 'We were in a restaurant in the South of France. This young fellow stopped at our table and handed her a rose, a red rose. Then he gave a little bow and walked on. She was so happy, and I was so jealous. How I loved her.'

'Did she know, father?' asked Arthur again.

'Know what?'

'That you killed Godfrey.'

A long silence. 'I never asked her.'

For a time the only sound in the room was the steady beep of the heart monitor.

'*Peccavi*,' said Uther. 'I have sinned. How many times have I said that? First time I ever meant it.' They had all sinned, thought Arthur. His sister's sin was his sin; his father's sin was his sin. Could anyone escape their destiny? 'I was always an ambitious man, Arthur. Ruthless too. Anyone who stood in my way was my enemy. Before you were born, Merlin told me I would have a son. He made a prophecy. One day, he said, your son will overthrow you.'

Arthur stared at his father. 'So *that's* why you wanted me adopted.'

'I never wanted you adopted,' said Uther remorsefully, 'I wanted you dead. I was afraid of my own son. It was your mother who saved your life. Don't ever forget that. When you came back to me years later I was happy to see you, but I was still afraid of you. I was certain that sooner or later Merlin's prophecy would be fulfilled. And now it has been. It was written, Arthur.' Something in the corner of the room drew Uther's attention. In his father's eyes Arthur saw what he had never thought to see – a look of terror. Summoning his last reserves of strength, the dying man raised himself up, staring intently at the television monitor.

'What is it, father?'

'There!'

'I don't see anything.'

'He's come for me!'

409

'Who? Who is it?'

'For God's sake, man, don't you see!' Uther pointed a trembling finger. 'Look there!'

'There's no one there.'

'Is it you, Godfrey? God forgive me.' As the pain erupted in Uther's chest he opened his mouth to cry out, but no sound came. In the final moment of agony his body arched up from the bed and his eyes rolled in their sockets. Falling back, the last of his life slipped away in a long shuddering sigh.

Eighteen

THE MAN who had lived so long in the public eye was buried privately in the churchyard of Brackett village. Igraine stood by the graveside, her face obscured by a veil; Margot, elegantly beautiful in a black couture dress, was flanked by her husband, Lennox, and their five sons; Arthur stood a little apart amongst a group of friends and a sprinkling of politicians. Where were Elaine and Morgan he wondered.

As Arthur left at the end of the short service, a policeman was waiting for him by the entrance to the cemetery. 'Good afternoon, sir.' The policeman saluted.

'Good afternoon. Can I help you?'

'It won't take a moment, sir.' The policeman beckoned Arthur to follow him.

'What's it all about?' said Arthur as the policeman hurried off. One or two friends and several politicians were looking at him curiously. 'Caught up with you at last, have they, Arthur?' a member of New Millennium's cabinet shouted, to the amusement of several guests.

In the police car a plain-clothes policeman in the back seat leaned across, opened the door and gave an awkward salute. 'Jump in, sir.' As Arthur shut the door behind him the car moved off slowly. 'Won't keep you a minute, sir.' The policeman held out a hand. 'Detective Inspector Warren.' Leaning back he ordered the driver to drive somewhere quiet. As the car drew into a lay-by Arthur waited for an explanation

'I'm afraid I have some bad news for you, Mr. Pendragon. It

concerns one of your sisters, or half-sisters, I believe.'

Arthur's heart missed a beat.

'I'm sorry to have to tell you,' said the D.I., 'that Elaine Pendragon is dead. My sincere condolences.'

Arthur's first thought was for his mother. 'Does Mrs Pendragon know?'

'Not yet, sir. I am talking to you first, because the Chief Constable would like you to be the one to break the sad news to Mrs. Pendragon before the press gets hold of it.'

'When did this happen?'

'Last night, sir,' said the D.I.

Strange.'Why haven't we heard about it before?'

The policeman chose his words carefully. 'There are unusual circumstances, sir.'

Arthur was rapidly losing patience. 'Get to the point, man.'

'As you probably know, Miss Pendragon was playing Peter Pan in Huddersfield.' Arthur nodded. Morgan had suggested they go up to see Elaine, but he had not been able to find the time. 'She was flying across the stage on the wire when she fell.' The D.I. lowered his voice discreetly. 'She broke her neck. Died instantly.'

'My God. What a tragedy,' said Arthur, 'what a terrible accident.'

Detective Inspector Warren studied a herd of grazing cows. 'It wasn't an accident, sir.'

It took a moment for Arthur to take that in. 'What was it, then?'

The policeman did not answer the question directly. 'Elaine's sister, Morgan, she was in the theatre at the time. In the wings, to be precise.'

Arthur was torn. Still impatient for the policeman to get to the point, he now dreaded to think what that might be. 'Surely you are not suggesting that Morgan was somehow involved in Elaine's death, inspector?'

'Apparently there'd been a running feud with the producer,'

said Warren, 'all through rehearsals.'

'What about?'

The Inspector did not know where to look. 'Morgan wanted Elaine to play Peter Pan without a wire.'

Oh, no. Not that. Poor Elaine, thought Arthur. Poor Elaine, poor demented Morgan.

'She went on and on about it. Wouldn't give up. Obviously the producer refused to play ball.' The Inspector lit a cigarette and inhaled deeply, smoke trickling from each side of his mouth. 'He knew Morgan was upset, of course, but as far as he was concerned that was all there was to it. Never thought for a second she would do anything bad.'

'So the police think that Morgan . . . ' Arthur left the rest unsaid.

'There's no think about it, sir. The harness was tampered with.'

'How can you be sure it was her?' asked Arthur, though he knew it had to be.

'All the evidence points that way. And anyway, she confessed. Said she was convinced Elaine could fly, so she didn't need a wire.'

'What will happen?'

'Obviously there was no intent to kill, so it isn't murder. Technically it's manslaughter. But under the circumstances . . . ' The inspector left the rest unsaid. He and Arthur stared at each other.

'She'll be referred for psychiatric examination,' said Arthur.

'I think that's the likely outcome, sir.' The policeman tapped the driver on the shoulder and the car moved off. 'Drop you anywhere?'

'The cemetery, please. I left my car there.'

'You'll be telling Mrs. Pendragon?'

Arthur nodded. Dear God. As if his mother hadn't had enough for one day. 'Yes.'

After the funeral service Igraine stood at the sitting room window staring with blank eyes, seeing neither the gardens, nor the tree-lined driveway, nor the crowd at the end of it. All she could see in her mind's eye was the gaping grave and the black figures clustered round. All she could hear was the silken voice of the vicar and the dreadful thud of earth on coffin. Uther was dead. Yet so powerful was her sense of his presence, that standing there in her widow's weeds, she half expected him to slip his arm through hers and whisper in her ear, 'You don't really think I'm dead, do you, duchess? It was all a game, you know, one of my little tricks. I shall never be able to forgive myself. What a thoughtless piggy I am. My fault entirely. *Mea culpa.*'

She pictured him smiling that charming smile of his, gazing at her adoringly, making her feel, if only for a moment, that she was the only woman in the world. She wanted to kiss him, and she wanted to scratch his eyes out. With a start she remembered where she was, becoming aware of the crowd still assembled at the gates to pay her husband homage. How ironic, she thought, that Uther's best friends were the ones who scarcely knew him at all.

Silence enveloped her . . . It was that bitter-sweet summer of '93. Uther had invited her down for the weekend to see his grand new house. He confessed he had bought it, furnished and decorated it all for her, and that in fact Brackett Hall was hers, as he was too, and always would be. He had known how to do things in the grand manner. If she would not be his wife, he had said, he would never marry. *Brackett Hall will be my Xanadu. I shall be a solitary old bachelor and dine alone every night at the head of a long empty table.*

But it was her, not him, who would be dining alone now. She had lost two husbands, Godfrey and Uther, so alike in looks, so different in temperament and character. Godfrey had loved her, though she had never loved him. She had loved Uther, though he had never loved her. In the end, though, it had made no difference, for he was still the most exciting man she had ever met. *And with my dying breath I shall whisper one word – not Rosebud but Igraine.* And now he was gone. Never again would he make her pulse race with anger or desire. He had murmured his last words of love, paid his last compliment, told his last lie, smiled his last dissembling smile.

She had tried not to love him, she had wanted not to love him. She had told herself that if you didn't feel, you could never be hurt, so that all she had to do was not allow herself to feel. That had proved impossible. The truth was, she could hardly remember a time when marriage to Uther had been anything but painful. Life, she thought, was hard for everyone, but harder, much harder for the ones who feel.

Leaning back on the sofa she dozed, dreaming that Uther was alive. Half asleep, half awake, she heard that domineering voice in the hall outside telling one of the servants off. He was coming this way. In a moment he would be here, filling the room with his powerful presence. There was a knock on the door. She jumped up, her heart beating fast. Was it him? Was it really him?

Arthur came into the room and gently took her hand. 'Can we talk, mother.'

On his way out, the library door was open. Arthur looked in and saw Margot standing by the bay window on the same spot and in the same pose as the first time they had met as brother and sister. The evening sun lit her face with a soft, golden light. The years had been kind to her, thought Arthur; she was as beautiful as ever she was. Turning as he entered she looked at her brother, a suggestion of a smile disturbing her lovely mouth. 'I shall put this moment in a cupboard and lock it up,' she said softly. 'And when I'm old and grey, I shall take it out and look at it.'

'What is it you want, Margot?' he asked her.

The familiar pout. 'Darling Arthur. You've been neglecting

415

me.'

'I know all your tricks. You're wasting your time.'

She turned on him that reproachful look he knew so well. 'Please don't scold me, darling. I do so hate being scolded.' Moving close, she brushed a piece of cotton from his shoulder, an assumption of intimacy that he found disturbing. 'You loved me once.'

'We have been through all that a long time ago. Why bring it up now?'

'Because it's true.'

'I thought I loved you,' he said. 'But it wasn't you I loved. It was someone who didn't exist.'

'Oh, but I do exist, Arthur,' she said, with a mischievous smile. 'What must I do to prove it?'

'I have to go.'

'You are being tiresome. Who cares about your silly politics? I haven't seen you for ages.' He could feel the warmth of her body against his. 'I've missed you so terribly. Have you missed me? No? Not even just a little, Arthur? Just the teensiest bit?'

'Margot, forgive me. I have to get back to town.' He tried to move to the door but she took his hand in both of hers. 'I adore your hands.'

'Behave yourself,' he said sternly.

'My God,' she said, 'you sound just like Lennox. You can't imagine what a bore he is, boring, boring, boring. If they handed out Oscars for the borer of the year that man would have a houseful by now. Can't imagine what I ever saw in him. And now that his business is going down the drain he's even more boring than ever. He walks round the house with those pleading puppy-dog eyes of his. What does he want of me?'

'Sympathy? Moral support?' suggested Arthur.

A peevish twitch of the mouth. 'More scolding? Really, Arthur, you should have been a schoolmaster.' Again he made to leave. 'Please don't go.' She laid her hand on his arm in gentle appeal. 'Did you make your peace with my stepfather?'

'Yes.'

'I didn't,' she said lightly, turning a pirouette.

'I'm sorry.'

'Don't be.' She stamped her foot. 'I loathed him. He was a pig.'

'This is hardly the time, Margot,' said Arthur. 'We just buried him.'

A disdainful look. 'Blessed relief.'

'He was our father.'

'Yours, precious, not mine. He was my stepfather.' She smiled a coquettish smile. 'More's the pity.'

He took the bait. 'What does that mean?'

'Think of it, my darling,' she cooed. 'If he had been my father, you would have been my brother, not just my half-brother.' Margot shivered with excitement. 'How piquant, how delicious.' The tip of her tongue moistened her lips. 'Think what fun we might have had.' Her dark eyes engaged his provocatively.

He turned away. 'You're too much, Margot.'

It was as if she had not heard him. 'Dear Uther,' she said dreamily, 'how he adored little girls. He certainly adored me. Always called me his own little angel.'

Arthur frowned. 'What are you suggesting?'

'It was not my wings he was interested in.'

'Uther would never harm a child,' said Arthur dismissively.

Margot smiled sweetly. 'I never said he did, now did I? No, he was much too clever for that. He had other ways of getting his kicks.'

'I refuse to listen to this,' said Arthur, angry now. But he could not bring himself to leave.

'When I was a little girl,' continued Margot dreamily, 'my step-father would invite men round to the house and make me sit on their knees; young men, old men, good-looking men, ugly men, fat men, thin men, all sorts of men. But they all had one thing in common; they were randy bastards. He liked to

417

watch when they put their hands up my skirt and did things to me. He would get very excited. Very excited indeed, if you know what I mean.'

Arthur shook his head in disbelief. 'Why have you never mentioned this before?'

'I was afraid of him. Now he's dead, he can't scare me any more.'

'He can't defend himself either.'

'There was this gardener,' said Margot, ignoring the comment. 'His name was Martin. One day Uther fired him, no one knew why. The very next day he hired a young man. Tom, his name was. Martin was getting on but he was still a good gardener. Tom knew nothing about gardens.'

'I don't want to hear this, Margot.'

She went on taunting him. 'Don't you want to know what sort of man your father really was? He *was* your father, after all. You might be more like him than you know,' she said with an insinuating smile.

'Say what you have to say and let me go.'

'I must have been ten or eleven. One day when I was walking in the garden, Tom dragged me into a shed and raped me. When I told Uther, he warned me not to say a word to anyone. If I did, he would back Tom, and everyone would know I was a liar. Mother would die of shame, and the family would be disgraced. What was I to do? I kept quiet. I stayed away from the garden. For a time nothing happened. Then Tom came looking for me. After that he raped me dozens of times. And every time he did, Uther watched.'

'Dear God!'

'Have I shocked you, darling?' Arthur couldn't look at her. 'Do you believe me now?'

'I – I suppose so.'

'Do you really and truly?'

'Yes.'

Margot threw back her head and laughed delightedly. 'Then

418

you are even more naïve than I took you for!'

He shook his head in confusion. 'Are you saying it was all lies?'

Margot thrust out her lips.'I do so hate that word. It's so gross. Not lies, Arthur – fibs. Call it porkies, if you like. Uther always did.'

He was bewildered. 'I'll never understand you. Why put me through all this torment?'

Margot clapped her hands. 'Did I do that? Darling heart, how wonderful! You're jealous! So you do love me after all.' Before he could stop her, she was standing on tiptoe, arms round his neck, whispering in his ear, 'Take me, Arthur. I want you, I want you. Let's do it now. I'll sit astride you.'

He could only stare at her in horror.

'Any way you want. Quickly, quickly.' She seized his hand and tried to pull him to the sofa.

'In the name of God, Margot,' he cried, 'I could never touch you again. Don't you know that?'

She shrank from him as if he had struck her. Her eyes narrowed angrily. 'It's not about me at all, is it? It's about that tart Guinevere. She's got to you. What a fool you are! What a gullible fool! You have no idea what she's like. She puts herself about all over town. Fucks anything that moves.'

Arthur shook his head incredulously.

'You didn't know?' Margot was screeching now. 'Don't tell me you thought that mealy-mouthed bitch was for real? All that mincing and simpering? You're not that naïve, surely?'

'Good-bye, Margot.'

She reached out her arms to him. 'Don't go. Don't leave me now.'

But he was gone.

Through the window she watched the car headlights sweep round the cobbled courtyard, down the avenue of plane trees and out into the main road. Long after the sound of the engine died away, she was still standing there.

In the darkened drawing room Igraine sat smoking a cigarette. The dim light from the night sky filtered through the net curtains. A few moments earlier, as Arthur's car drove off, its headlights roving the façade of Brackett Hall, the room had lit up for a second or two, then plunged into darkness again. She had listened intently to the hum of the engine as it faded into the night. That sound, dying into silence, had left her feeling inexpressibly alone. If only he did not have to go; if only he could have stayed. If only things had been different. In her desperation she convinced herself that she would never see her son again, that he would be as dead to her as Elaine was now.

She switched on the table lamp by the sofa. This would never do. She could not sit in the dark forever. She would have to face the world, live her life, see people, make journeys. She had loved and hated a man. But then love and hate were Siamese twins, bound heart and heart, head and head, body and soul. One could not survive without the other.

What would her future be? It was ironic. When she was married there were so many things she dreamt of doing and never could, so many times she had longed to have her life back. Yet now that she had, she had not the least idea what to do with it.

PART THREE

Destiny Fulfilled

One

2024

UTHER'S DEATH had left the New Millennium Party in disarray, partly because there was no obvious successor, partly because details of his corrupt dealings were inevitably leaked to the Press. The fallout affected all parties to some extent, though chiefly New Millennium who had been in power more than fourteen years. *Four Years Too Long* and *Time For A Change* were the buzz-phrases of the day. The last general election had been in 2020. Had he lived, Uther would no-doubt have called an election sometime in 2025, but any delay was now unthinkable. Both opposition and electorate demanded an immediate election which was duly called for the earliest possible date, September 2024.

Arthur spent the morning of the election with his aides and helpers at Party Headquarters. As the early results came in things were looking good, the polls forecasting a landslide victory for United Labour. Around mid-morning Arthur felt a slight prickling sensation in the palms of his hands, and as he scratched them, the prickling became progressively more intense. Quickly he excused himself and rushed down the corridor to his office.

Perched in Arthur's 'in' tray, Virgil opened an enquiring eye as Arthur entered the room, hooh-hooed a soft greeting and went back to sleep. Merlin was standing by the window admiring the view. 'The Palace of Westminster, Big Ben, Parliament Square, Westminster Bridge.' The magus considered Arthur, a hint of mischief in his bright eyes. 'You are going to miss this view. From Number 10 all you can see is Downing Street.'

Arthur sat at his desk and scratched Virgil's chest. 'I'm not there yet,' he said.

Merlin took a seat facing him and beamed fondly. 'Ever the cautious one.'

'You think I'm making a mistake, don't you?'

'You must go where your conscience leads you,' said Merlin quietly.

Arthur swivelled his chair and looked across at the soaring towers and turrets of the Palace of Westminster. 'If we win the election, I shall be Prime Minister of the country where parliamentary democracy was born. I should dearly like to see a truly United Kingdom again. And then . . . ', his eyes dreamed over, 'a united world.' He turned back to face his mentor. 'Is that so impossible?'

'Nothing is impossible if good men do what must be done,' said Merlin, green orbs glowing.

A rueful smile from Arthur. 'I know what you expect of me Merlin, but I still believe my way is the right way. I agree with you that the world is in mortal danger; what we don't agree on is what to do about it. It is still my hope that all our problems can be solved by peaceful means.'

'And if they can't?'

'If force has to be used,' said Arthur, 'then it must be used in the name of all the democratic countries of the world.'

For a long time the faint hum of traffic in Parliament Square disturbed the silence. 'I doubt that will ever happen,' said Merlin. 'Ask yourself why, more than twenty years after the trauma of 9/11, the terrorists are still winning the war.'

'In my opinion there are two explanations,' said Arthur. 'Firstly, instead of being united, the democracies are divided by self-interest.'

'And you think you can persuade them to work together?'

'I really think I can,' said Arthur confidently.

Merlin looked unconvinced. 'Secondly?'

'Secondly,' continued Arthur, 'politicians make promises

they know they can't keep. Why? To impress the electorate and win votes. And with an eye on those same votes they pay terrorists to kill someone else in some other country, any country but in their own. Sometimes, in the short term, it works, sometimes it doesn't; in the long-term it never does.' Arthur swivelled his chair and looked down at the statues lining the square. 'We are now paying a heavy price for the selfishness and shortsightedness of yesterday's world leaders.' He turned back to Merlin. 'Unless things change, tomorrow's world leaders will pay an even heavier price.'

'That, I fear,' said Merlin, 'is a condition, like human nature, that no one can change – not even you.'

'It has to change,' said Arthur. 'We cannot afford to fail. Fortunately I shall not be working alone.'

The raised eyebrows of the magus asked the unspoken question.

'If I do become Prime Minister,' said Arthur, 'I shall be far more supportive of the United Nations than my predecessors.'

Merlin looked deeply sceptical. 'If the nations are divided,' he said, 'how can the organisation that represents them be united? The UN can only be as effective as the world allows it to be. In practice it is manipulated by hundreds of special interests, each with their own ideologies, religious beliefs and agendas.'

'What alternative is there?' asked Arthur.

Merlin reached out a hand. Virgil hopped onto it, and from there to Merlin's shoulder. 'I think you know the answer to that.'

'Camelot?'

The magus gave the slightest of nods.

'In a democratic world people ought not to take the law into their own hands,' insisted Arthur.

'If they don't,' said Merlin, 'there will soon be no democratic world.'

'Perhaps you are right,' said Arthur. 'I don't know. I only

know there ought to be a better way.'

Merlin bowed his head in defeat. He had tried and lost again. 'I pray you find it,' he said as he and Virgil faded.

By evening it was clear that United Labour had won the election by a huge majority – over a hundred and fifty seats. At the age of twenty-nine Arthur Pendragon had become the country's youngest Prime Minister since William Pitt.

Barely two months after the election the world was shocked by horrific satellite pictures of thousands of men, women and children massacred in the eastern region of the Kingdom of the Euphrates, formerly Iraq. With its huge oil resources and geographically strategic location, the K.O.E. was again one of the foremost powers in the Middle East, its ruler, Sadiq el Shaeb, even more brutal and ruthless than Saddam Hussein.

In the days following the massacre, its full horror was exposed by the world's media; exact figures were impossible to obtain but it was estimated that between fifty and a hundred thousand people had died, struck down by some kind of chemical or biological attack. Suspicion naturally fell on Sadiq as the tribes inhabiting the eastern regions of the country had never accepted him as their leader.

The United Nations deplored the massacre. There was almost unanimous condemnation by world leaders, and a general consensus that something ought to be done. Unfortunately no one could agree who was responsible, nor how they should be punished, nor who would punish them. Arthur talked by Satellink with Winslow Marsden, the President of the United States, arguing that the democracies would have to agree on joint action.

'And get dragged into another quagmire?' said Marsden. 'No thank you, Arthur. Bar Israel, we don't have a real friend left in the Middle East, now that most of the old feudal families have been overthrown by the Islamists. The mullahs might not like Sadiq, but if it comes to a showdown with the west they'll support him. If we interfere, we'll get our ass kicked, just like we did when we invaded Iraq in 2003.'

'We have a moral obligation to help the oppressed,' said Arthur, 'whoever and wherever they are. We go to the aid of the sick and the starving, why not the victims of brutal dictators? If the democracies ignore mass murder, what kind of future is there for the world?'

Winslow Marsden was not overly impressed by appeals to his conscience. It was not that he didn't have one, he liked to do the right thing whenever he could. It was just that doing the right thing meant doing what was best for his country. 'Frankly, Arthur, I have more immediate concerns than the future of the world. My first duty is to protect the people of the United States of America. Face facts. We attacked Iraq in the nineties . . . half a million men and Christ knows how many tanks and aircraft. And what happened? He was still there at the end of it, and stronger than ever.

'Ten years later we attacked him again. OK, he wasn't as much of a threat as we thought, but at the time we were convinced we were doing the right thing. What happened? The Iraqis turned against us. We lost American lives, and we lost our moral standing in the world. Was it worth it? Was it hell! Two years after we pulled out, Iraq was run by another dictator. No, Arthur, we've learned our lesson, and by God we've learned it the hard way. There's a limit to what even the greatest power on earth can do.'

Arthur was resolute. 'We can't let Sadiq get away with mass murder.'

'What do you suggest we do?'

'Take control of his airspace, fly in a small, high-tech military force, secure the eastern region and take Sadiq, dead or alive. Then we send in an international team to set up field hospitals, take care of the wounded and help get the area back on its feet. The vital thing is for the free world to take joint action.'

The President gave the suggestion some thought. Then he

shook his head. 'Sorry, Arthur, the American public would never go along with it. They've seen their boys come home in body bags once too often. I have an election to fight next year.'

'We all have elections to fight,' said Arthur. 'We also have to fight for what we believe in.'

Winslow Marsden did not appreciate being told where his duty lay. 'Look here, Arthur, I don't like this situation any more than you do. It's a mess but it isn't our mess. Let's leave it to the people of the K.O.E. to deal with.'

The President would not be swayed. Arthur had lost the argument, and he knew it. He spoke to more than twenty world leaders in Europe, Asia, North and South America and Africa, whose reaction was much like the President's. Everyone was shocked by the massacre and no one could agree what to do about it. Again and again the same comment was made; fighting terrorism was one thing, invading another country was something else. Arthur vented his frustration on his cabinet. 'What sort of future do our children have if we turn a blind eye to such a horrific crime?'

Thomas Winnington sighed. 'It may seem short-sighted to you, Prime Minister, but the electorate is more concerned with taxes and jobs and pensions than they are with the K.O.E.'s problems.'

'My father used to say things like that,' said Arthur. 'Since when did you become so cynical, Thomas? You were one of those who criticised Uther for his weak foreign policy, weren't you?'

'I was,' conceded Winnington.

'Then what has changed your mind?'

'I can't speak for the others,' said Winnington, 'but I was a backbencher then. Now that I'm a cabinet minister, I have to be a realist.'

Arthur struggled to control his impatience. 'But don't you see, Thomas, that's exactly it. Being a realist means confronting men like Sadiq.'

'With respect, Prime Minister,' said Leo Grant, Chairman of the Party and Arthur's greatest friend and supporter in the cabinet, 'it is a first principle of international law that no one has the right to interfere in the internal affairs of another country. Even leaving aside such legal considerations, Thomas is right – we have to be realistic. If we launch a strike against Sadiq, we risk starting a war in the Middle East, perhaps even a world war. Is that what you want?'

Arthur was close to despair; if his own colleagues were against him, who would be for him? 'For God's sake, Leo, don't you see? The greatest risk is doing nothing. If we do nothing we'll be telling all the terrorists and terror states in the world that it's alright to kidnap and hijack and bomb. Taking them on involves risks, of course it does, but ignoring them will make a third World War inevitable. And the next war will be a global war, more devastating than any war in history. There will be no borders, and no distinction between friends and enemies – only mass destruction and millions of deaths – billions perhaps. It will be Armageddon.'

There was a meaningful rustling and shifting of paper, and a number of knowing glances exchanged around the table. Even George Bedivere, his old friend and comrade, would not look Arthur in the eye as he summarised the cabinet's view. 'I think you are exaggerating the actual risk posed by terrorists, Prime Minister. Of course they make life difficult for us, but do they actually threaten the stability of the state? I don't think so. At least they haven't done so yet. Our job is to find practical solutions to practical problems.'

'Then,' said Arthur, 'in the name of our suffering fellow men, women and children across the globe let's do it.'

For a while no one spoke. Then Thomas Winnington said, to nods of approval, 'We were not elected to put the world to rights.'

The following day the K.O.E. Foreign Minister gave the

United Nations his country's official explanation of the massacre: the warlike tribesmen in the East had long planned an attack on the peace-loving Kingdom of the Euphrates. In preparation for this attack they had stockpiled huge quantities of biological and chemical agents. A fire had broken out in their secret depot, releasing deadly poisons into the atmosphere. The rebels had been killed by their own weapons.

Despite the world's scepticism, the story could not be disproved. Sanctions were debated in the UN after a peace-keeping initiative was voted down by the Security Council, but even on this topic no agreement was reached. A few countries offered the surviving victims humanitarian aid which was immediately refused by the K.O.E.. There were the customary vehement protests by Human Rights groups, and soon the world had forgotten what had happened. But not Arthur. 'The man is literally getting away with murder. Mass murder.'

George Bedivere heaved his big shoulders in embarrassment.

'And we sit back and do nothing?' Surely George would stand by him? 'It can't be right.'

Bedivere shrugged. 'What can we do? Let's face it, the UK is not a world power anymore. Hasn't been for years. Our armed forces have been cut to the bone by successive governments. There's no way we can go it alone. Not even the Yanks can do that. They stopped being the world's policemen after the Iraq debacle. No more foreign adventures for them, no more talk of bringing democracy to the world. They'll only act if they feel their vital interests are threatened.'

'Surely that's the case here?' said Arthur. 'You do see that, George, don't you?' He was pleading with his Defence Minister.

George Bedivere's massive chin jutted obstinately. 'What I see is what I'm paid to see. Oil is losing its strategic importance as an energy source. No, I'm sorry, Arthur, there's no vital interest involved. Not for the U.S., not for us.'

From the window of the Prime Minister's office Arthur looked out at Downing Street. A couple of fat pigeons pecked here and there, some tourists peered curiously through the wrought iron gates that separated the street from Whitehall, a policeman stood outside Number 10, hands clasped behind him in the manner of a prince or a clergyman; a tranquil, reassuring scene, a scene familiar to every Londoner, a vignette of a peaceful and secure way of life that people took for granted because they lived in a democracy.

'A hundred thousand men, women and children brutally massacred. Not in our vital interest, George?'

George studied the carpet. 'I'm afraid not, Prime Minister.'

'Then God help the human race.'

Arthur tried to dismiss the horror from his mind but he could not. The satellite images of the victims were still fresh in his memory. He doubted they would ever fade.

Two

Across the fields the two men strode, Arthur breaking into a run every few yards to catch up with Merlin who set so fast a pace that his white robe trailed behind him, as if it too had difficulty keeping up.

Virgil clutched his master's shoulder anxiously. A moment before the wind had gusted so strongly that it hurled the owl backwards off his perch in a whirling ball of flying feathers. In that moment of panic he flapped his wings frantically in order to gain height, all the time shrieking his rage. When the wind dropped as suddenly as it rose, he settled again on Merlin's shoulder, grumbling in the back of his throat.

'Alright, old chap?' Merlin soothed the owl's ruffled feathers, and Virgil nibbled his master's fingers to show how much he appreciated his concern.

Yesterday Arthur had presided over a meeting of the cabinet called to discuss London's readiness, or otherwise, for a possible major terrorist attack. There had been a lot of talk and no decisions, except to leave things as they were. The *status quo* was agreed by a show of hands, even though Arthur had made it clear that for him, at least, the *status quo* was entirely inadequate. Angry and disheartened, he had been only too glad to accept Merlin's sudden invitation to stay overnight at his cottage on 'important business'. As an ex-Special Forces man it had not been too difficult for Arthur to throw off his body-guards. A call to his PPS from the car reassured him that the PM was away on an 'urgent personal matter', and would be back in Downing Street the next afternoon. A high speed drive to Somerset was followed by a light supper in Merlin's kitchen, a game of Monopoly and a good night's sleep. The two men were up at dawn and off on a trip to only Merlin knew where. Arthur asked no questions, though he had his suspicions.

It all appealed to his sense of the absurd. Here was the Prime Minister of the United Kingdom stumbling across the countryside, chasing after a wild figure with shoulder-length hair, flowing robes and a furious barn owl on his shoulder.

'How much further?' panted Arthur.

A grunt. 'Not far.'

Arthur knew better than to waste breath asking any more questions. The instant they reached the stream bordering the wood, the gusting wind calmed. Merlin sat on the grass by the water's edge, signalling Arthur to join him. Virgil flew into an oak tree and settled himself down, his eyelids blinking, rapidly at first, then slower and slower, until finally his black eyes were shuttered. Seconds later he opened one enquiring eye to check that Merlin was still there. Reassured, he ruffled his feathers, inflating his body to twice its normal size, and drifted into sleep, deflating as he did.

In the stream a few sleepy fish moved with the ebb and flow of the water. Two or three of them gently nuzzled Arthur's hand.

'The salmon is an extraordinary fish,' Merlin mused inconsequently, 'all that swimming against the current, all that battling against the odds. Is he not much to be admired? A noble creature, independent of spirit, brimful of courage' A sly look at Arthur. 'Why does he swim against the stream, negotiating rapids, climbing cataracts, leaping falls, when it would be so much easier to go with the flow?' A wondering shake of the head. 'Is it his destiny? Has he perhaps been specially chosen to save his race from extinction? It makes you wonder, doesn't it?'

Arthur said nothing, though Merlin's meaning was by no means lost on him.

'In everyone's life,' continued the magus, looking everywhere but at Arthur, 'there comes a defining moment, a moment when they must choose between the easy solution and the difficult one. The moment passes quickly, so quickly that most people miss it, either because they are too short-sighted to recognise it for what it is, or because they recognise it and are afraid to do anything about it.'

For a few moments neither man spoke. Something made Arthur look up, and there through the trees was the great mound of Glastonbury Tor with St. Michael's tower on its summit. The hairs rose on the back of Arthur's neck. His spine tingled.

'Years ago when you were a boy we climbed the Tor, you and I,' Merlin reminded him.

'I remember.' Arthur was lost in the green moons now, hearing nothing but Merlin's voice, seeing only the images he conjured up.

'What do you see?' asked the magus.

Arthur stared into the distance. 'I see two figures on the summit.'

'Who are they, Arthur?'

Arthur shielded his eyes from the early morning sun. 'A man and a boy. That's odd. Before when I looked . . . '

The magus prompted him. 'Yes?'

' . . . it was all a blur . . . like a picture in two dimensions, one too far away, the other too close.' Arthur peered through cupped hands as though he were looking through a telescope.

'And now?' asked Merlin.

'The two images are in focus,' said Arthur excitedly.

'Time past and time future have merged, then?'

'Yes.'

The magus gave a long, satisfied sigh. 'They are now time present.'

'Yes.' Arthur lowered his hands. He was looking at the magus now.

'So the man . . . ?'

'Was you, Merlin . . . will be you . . . *is* you.'

'And the boy?'

For a long moment Arthur hesitated. 'The boy is me.'

The eyes of the magus glowed with a sudden blinding light. When the light died, Arthur was himself again. Beside him sat Merlin, chin on chest, snoring like a warthog. His body relaxed, his mind at peace, Arthur was filled with the joy of living. The stream shimmered in the dappled sunlight, the warmth of the sun caressed his face, the soft rush of the wind stirred the trees.

After lunch the two men sat quietly and peered into the kitchen fire. Merlin had withdrawn into his head, leaving Arthur to reminisce about the past; his thoughts drifted back to his childhood and to those high summer days at Ponterlally when he and Keir would sit for hours on the riverbank by the stone bridge.

'There are bigger fish for you to catch,' said Merlin suddenly, apropos of nothing.

Silence broken only by the crackling of burning logs.

Then Merlin began to speak, conjuring up images of things beyond the borders of belief. Yet extraordinary as they were, Arthur had the feeling they were real, and that in some other place, some other time, he had seen them all before . . . Eclipse and Kraken, Nimbles and Scuttles, rectangles and squares, pyramids and spheres, slender towers waving at the heavens, all on a shining white island set in a grey green sea. When exactly he had seen these things he could not remember, though he guessed it must have been before time past and future merged into time present.

'The time for dreaming is over,' said Merlin. 'And the time for doubt has passed.'

'You have been my friend and mentor since I was a child. Don't desert me now,' begged Arthur.

'I shall never desert you,' said Merlin. He stared into the fire.

'But you are the one who must bear the burden.'

'If I should fail?'

'Fail!' Merlin smoothed the air with his hands as if to erase the word. 'Why talk of failure? Remember, you will have more power than the world has ever known, the power you need to fight the forces of darkness. Imagine, Arthur.'

For a moment Arthur's eyes dreamed, as they used to when he was a boy. But then, like those two figures on the Tor, the dream and the reality became one, and it was as if a door had opened and he had walked through it and entered the world of his imaginings.

'Imagine a man,' said Merlin, 'a man who lived many centuries ago. This man is the only one on the planet to possess, let us say, a sword, a sword so magical that it made him invulnerable. Imagine that, Arthur. Such a man would have the power to save the world, would he not?'

'Perhaps,' said Arthur uncertainly.

'A gentle man,' continued Merlin, 'a man of conscience with a heart and a soul, a man of peace who against his will becomes a man of war, compelled to impose order on chaos, doing it reluctantly, only because he believes there is no other way.' He looked intently at Arthur. 'Someone once said that the meek would inherit the earth, but only if the strong helped them do it.'

'I am trying to remember,' said Arthur. 'When was it?' His eyes clouded as he roamed his memory. 'It was on Glastonbury Tor. I was eleven years old, and . . . yes, I remember now. It was you who said it, and you were talking about King Arthur.'

'I was talking about you,' said the magus.

In the long silence that followed everything became clear to Arthur, all the things that he had known or almost known but had never allowed to enter his conscious mind. Above all he understood that he had been given the choice to accept or reject his destiny. Now at last he knew what Merlin meant by that word. Destiny was not a trap set by a malign fate for a man to fall into; it was the product of all the choices he made in his life.

As the flames of the kitchen fire died down, Merlin put Arthur into a deep sleep. At first it seemed to him that he was entering the world of his dreams, as he had so often done when he was a boy. Yet in his sleep he understood that these were not dreams but reality, the reality of his own future. He saw great battles in the sky and on the sea, he saw the destruction of evil and the death of tyrants, he saw the wicked perish and the good prosper. And he saw himself seated at a round table surrounded by friends and comrades some of whom he knew, some whom he would know in the future – proud Lancelot and noble Galahad, Ian Duncan, George Bedivere and Leo Grant, Gawain, Agravaine, Gaheris, Mordred and Gareth. He saw acts of love and hate, acts of meanness and generosity, acts of friendship and acts of treachery. He saw the first battle and the last.

When he awoke he felt overwhelmed by the responsibility of it all. Merlin was right, it was his burden and his alone. Was he strong enough to bear it? His fingers touched the scar where the eagle's talons had slashed his cheek when he was a boy.

'We are all flawed,' said Merlin, 'none of us is perfect. Nothing is in this universe. If there were such a thing as perfection, the universe would be symmetrical. But if it were, if matter and anti-matter were perfectly balanced, there would be no matter, only energy, and we would not be here, we would not be anywhere. Now there's a mystery for you. We owe our very existence to the imperfection of the universe.'

Suddenly Arthur knew that everything in his life had led him to this moment. 'When the time comes, if it comes, will you be with me? On Camelot, I mean.'

'If she will let me,' said Merlin wistfully.

Arthur could not hide his astonishment. 'Who?

'Nimue. The one who casts a spell on me.'

Arthur remembered now that Merlin had mentioned her

before. Could Merlin be playing one of his games? No. One look at his face told Arthur this was no joke. He was concerned for his friend and wanted to know more. Wherever Merlin was in the byways of his mind he read Arthur's thoughts. 'We met at university,' he said. 'We fell in love. For a time we lived together. Then one day she left me.'

'So it's all over,' said Arthur.

Merlin shook his head. 'It will never be over,' he said. 'Nimue's passion is devouring. It is less about love than about possessing. She wants to shut me in a cave and roll a stone over me so that I will be hers forever.'

'Then she must be very stupid.'

'Why so?'

'To imagine she can trap the magus.'

Merlin smiled. 'You have a great deal to learn about women.'

When it was time to drive back to London, Arthur said goodbye to Merlin who handed him a small urn. 'A long time ago I made a promise,' he said. 'Now it is you who must keep it for me. I told you once that the island of Camelot was given to me not for any material thing, but for love. In this urn are the ashes of Robbie, beloved by the Lord of Camelot, and in turn by you and me. Robbie is dead, but love never dies. When you bury his ashes on the island it will be a sign that Camelot is founded on honour and respect, on justice and mercy, and on love, Arthur, above all, on love. These are the principles by which you and your followers must live. Abandon them and you will lose your power, and Camelot will be doomed. Hold fast to them, and you might even save the world.'

'I shall try not to disappoint you.'

'You will never do that, not if you remember the meaning of Pendragon.'

Arthur's face was blank.

'You don't know?'

438

Arthur shook his head. For some reason he could not explain, his heart was beating fast.

'Hmm. A serious gap in your knowledge,' said Merlin, looking suspiciously pleased, happy to have found something that he could still teach his protégé. 'Hundreds of years ago the word "pen" meant a chief, and the word "dragon", a leader. So there you are, Arthur. It is in the blood. You were born to be a leader of men.'

'How shall I know?' asked Arthur.

'There is a legend that the Round Table appears at the full moon,' said the magus.

'Where?'

'At Bossiney Castle.'

Arthur was trying to puzzle out that conundrum when, much to his embarrassment, Merlin dropped on one knee and kissed his hand. 'I have served you as best I could,' he said humbly. 'The rest is up to you.'

Three

ARTHUR PASSED a few hours in Ponterlally with Hector and Elizabeth and tried to pretend it was just like any other visit. But Elizabeth knew better. Her beloved son was not his usual cheerful self, and something about the way he looked at her had the feel of goodbye about it. 'When shall I see you again,' she asked, trying not to sound anxious.

'As soon as I possibly can,' said Arthur cheerfully, wishing he could tell her more. The truth was that he did not know himself when, if ever, they would meet again. 'Don't worry mother, We'll talk regularly.'

None of this made sense to Hector. He knew what was in Elizabeth's mind but she had got it all wrong. Arthur was not going anywhere. How could he? Was he not the Prime Minister?

Arthur had not met Keir since that traumatic night climb at Oxford. It was time, he decided, to pay him a visit. Nothing had changed; he was still the same old Keir, still living alone, still alternately defensive and aggressive, still expecting imminently, or so he insisted, to be appointed a director of the internet provider he had worked for since leaving school, still – and this was hardest of all to take – still jealous and esentful of Arthur. After only a few minutes awkward conversation Arthur was wondering why he was there. Was it nostalgia for his childhood? Was it guilt? Could it be, despite everything, affection? Whatever the reason, he was reluctant to lose touch with Keir, though he had nothing to offer him; not yet. But all hints that Arthur might wish Keir to join him at some time in the not too distant future were scorned. 'You'll have to come up with something more concrete than that, my dear chap. Something bloody attractive too. This is Keir you're talking to. I'm a highly saleable commodity in the city. Everyone in the world wants me.'

When he said goodbye, Arthur tried to hug his adoptive brother. It was like trying to hug a wooden board.

If Igraine registered Arthur's hints that he might not be around for a while, she did not respond to them, being far too pre-occupied with her own problems; in a short space of time she had lost her husband and her eldest daughter, and poor Morgan had ended up in what Igraine referred to as a 'sanatorium', though she and everyone else knew that it was really a secure psychiatric ward. Arthur, whom she once so dearly loved, she now held responsible for the death of her husband. Uther's lies, his hypocrisy, his cheating, his fraudulent activities, his chronic adultery were all forgotten. Igraine had sanitised his memory, loving him in death far more than she had ever done in life.

'Uther was a good man,' she insisted, flashing a defiant look at Arthur. 'I adored him. And he adored me.'

What he could he say? Like so many things about his father it was partly true. Unfortunately the part that was not true contaminated the part that was.

'I wish he were here now.' Igraine burst into tears.

Arthur tried to hug her but she was unresponsive, standing stiffly in his embrace. 'I'm sorry, truly sorry. I never dreamed it would end the way it did.'

'Didn't you?' Igraine dried her eyes. 'You were cruel, Arthur. Your father welcomed you back into the family and into his heart. He deserved your gratitude. Not your . . . ' She searched for the right word but could not find it.

Nor could Arthur. What was the word that described what

he had done to his father? Deception? Treachery? Betrayal? Whatever it was, he would have to live with it. Even though he had no cause to feel guilty his conscience would trouble him for the rest of his life.

Then there was Guinevere. What was he to say to her? And where was he to say it? Certainly he had no intention of subjecting her to the attentions of the *papparazzi*, who would be far more difficult to shake off than his bodyguards. If the two of them were seen together he could imagine what the tabloids would make of it.

It was four years, almost to the day, since Guinevere had rejected Arthur's proposal of marriage, and in that time there had, of course, been men friends, though none of them serious involvements. Arthur was still a bachelor. Like her, he had obviously not yet found the 'right one', though it would surely not be long before he did, now that he was an even bigger catch than ever . . . Prime Minister of the United Kingdom, young – well, relatively young – macho, charming, intelligent, entertaining, and as good-looking as any man had a right to be. Incredible that no one had managed to catch him, when it seemed as if the whole world was trying to marry him off. The gossip columnists were always linking his name with some girl or other, and it was rumoured that the Party grandees would like him to settle down sooner rather than later.

From time to time she bumped into him, and whenever they met, she was reminded what an exceptionally kind and caring person he was. He actually listened to what you were saying, a rare attribute these days when everyone was so intimately involved with mobile phones and computer monitors. She told herself that her feelings for him were entirely rational and nothing at all to do with love. It was simply that she enjoyed his company; he made her feel so relaxed and secure that whenever she saw him it was a bit like coming home. How old must he be now? Thirty? No, thirty-one. And she was twenty-one. No doubt he found women of her age very immature, certainly far too young to be married to the most important man in the country. Oddly enough, she could scarcely remember now why she had turned him down.

A couple of weeks ago he had made a brief appearance at a charity dinner at Grosvenor House. There had been much whispering and turning of heads as the Prime Minister walked all the way across the Great Room to her table and sat between her and her father. To her surprise it was not her father he wanted to talk to, it was her. Their conversation was still running in her head as if it had been recorded. First there was the usual exchange of platitudes.

'Good to see you, Guinevere.'

'You too.'

'How are you?'

'I'm fine.'

'Good, good.'

This was hardly typical of the relaxed conversationalist she knew. Altogether he seemed ill-at-ease. There had then been some rumblings in his throat, impossible to interpret.

'I'm sorry?' she enquired diffidently.

'I was – um . . . ' – the clearing of his throat was followed by more rumblings – ' . . . I was trying to say how much I have . . . missed having you around, and that, um . . . ' He was eyeing the podium. Was he about to rush back to his table for the speeches?

'Yes?' Her heart was racing.

' . . . I wanted to tell you . . . that if anything should . . . that is to say, if there would be a . . . change in my situation, or . . . if I were not able to be with you . . . for an indefinite time, let's say . . . I would be . . . I would be . . . sad not to see such a . . . dear friend again. Very sad,' he ended lamely.

What was all that about? Then suddenly she understood what he was trying to tell her in his halting fashion. *A change in my situation . . . not able to be with you for an indefinite time* . . . It could hardly be clearer. He was getting engaged, and he wanted her to know. *Sad not to see such a dear friend.* A dear friend! That was telling her, wasn't it? He might have loved her once but all that was over. She was nothing more to him now than a dear friend. As for *an indefinite time*, well that was simply another way of saying forever.

But why, she asked herself, had he broken the news in such a roundabout way? Why had he not just come straight out with it? The more she thought about it, the angrier she became. Could he possibly imagine she was carrying a torch for him? Surely not. Did he expect her to be heartbroken just because he was getting married? Did he think she would make a scene? Run screaming into the street? Throw herself under a bus? It made her blood boil. The presumption of it! The arrogance of the man! Why would she care if she didn't see him for an indefinite time! She wouldn't care if she never saw him ever again! After a sleepless night she could not wait to tell her father about this aggravating conversation, expecting him to be as outraged as she was. To her chagrin, Leo did not at all react as she had expected. Instead, listening to what Arthur had said, he looked thoughtful, even a little anxious.

'You don't think you might have misunderstood him, do you, darling?' he asked.

'No, I do not,' she said fiercely. 'That man thinks he's God's gift to women.'

'Hmm.' Leo decided that saying nothing was by far the most prudent reaction.

'I'm quite sure he thinks me shallow and trivial and quite unworthy of him,' said Guinevere bitterly. 'Well, that doesn't bother me in the least,' she asserted, looking very bothered indeed, her father thought. 'I don't give a hoot for his opinion. I'm completely indifferent to it,' she said loftily. 'I only wish he would not make his contempt for me quite so obvious.'

There was on her father's face that non-committal look he assumed when he did not agree with her. She found it intensely irritating, insufferably coy; what was worse, it made her wonder whether he had known all along that Arthur was getting married. If so, he had hidden it from her. Why would he do that? Of course! He was trying to protect her. The notion was deeply offensive. Surely he could not for one moment believe that she would be affected by anything Arthur did? He was being just as presumptuous and condescending as Arthur – more so, in fact. It was all too annoying for words. 'I don't care if he is the Prime Minister. He's a vain and self-important man,' she concluded.

Leo's eyebrows lifted steeply. 'Oh, do you think so?'

How it infuriated her – that *oh, do you think so*? It was so sly, so damned patronising. Of course she bloody well thought so! She would not have said it otherwise, would she? Why couldn't he just say he disagreed with her? Because he was a coward, that was why. A fine thing when you couldn't rely on your own father for moral support. 'Men always stick together, don't they? Such devious creatures!' Delivering that final insult she ran out of the room, slamming the door so hard that the walls shook.

Guinevere was hurt and angry. She could not even confide in Lanky. What would be the point? She would only tell her what a fool she had been, and that she didn't need to hear from anyone. Normally hard-working and social, she took time off from her job in the estate agent's office, and passed most of her days taking lonely walks round London's parks, enjoying the sights and scents of spring.

Nature had never much appealed to her before, or rather she had never really noticed it, but now she became consciously and acutely aware of the natural phenomena she had always taken for granted – sunshine and cloud, the shifting patterns of light and shade on grass, the song of birds, the riffling of water in a wayward breeze, the opening and closing of a flower. For the first time in her adult life she looked about her with eyes as honest and direct as a child's, seeing things she had never seen before. On her long solitary walks she discovered a new world.

In that world, moreover, she was also re-examining her own feelings and finding that when she looked at them honestly and directly, they too opened up to her as miraculously as flowers to the sun. Suddenly it was blindingly obvious; she had made a terrible mistake, indeed may have ruined her life. For she had turned down a man who had all the qualifications of a perfect husband, a genuinely remarkable and talented man who loved her, or who had loved her once. What could be more foolish than that? Unless it was to turn down the man she loved?

She became an avid reader of *The Times*, expecting daily to see the announcement of the Prime Minister's forthcoming marriage. Strangely enough it did not appear.

Four

2026

Addressed to the Prime Minister of the United Kingdom, the ultimatum was delivered to 10 Downing Street shortly before nine a.m., London time, Friday, the 24th October, 2026. Two hours later the cabinet met. On the table in front of every minister was the text of the message. Arthur read it aloud:

A number of devices containing fissionable and biological material have been concealed in your capital city. These devices will be detonated at nine a.m. on Tuesday, the 28th October, should you fail to meet the following demands:

1.   One hundred and twenty-five billion United States dollars are to be wired to us. You will be given the relevant account details on your confirmation of the availability of the necessary funds.

2.   Our freedom fighters listed separately are to be released immediately and unconditionally from your prisons and delivered at the times and to the places which will be indicated by us.

3.   The Prime Minister of the United Kingdom will publicly acknowledge that he and his government is responsible for the murder of thousands of our blessed martyrs, falsely accusing them of terrorist activities. He will announce to the General Assembly of the United Nations that Britain has renounced its so-called war on terrorism and ceased all aggressive activities outside its borders.

4.   As a consequence of these criminal activities, the British Prime Minister, Foreign Minister and Minister of Defence will

*surrender themselves for trial by an International Court of
Justice whose members will be appointed by us.*

'The message is signed by a group calling itself "The Angels
of Mercy".'

Everyone was talking at once. Arthur raised a hand and
immediately the cabinet room was quiet. 'One at a time please,
ladies and gentlemen. You will all have your say.' He nodded at
Thomas Winnington, the Foreign Secretary. 'Thomas?'

'Are we the only country targeted?'

'The same ultimatum has been received in eight capital cities,'
said Arthur. 'London, Washington, Beijing, Tokyo, Moscow,
Berlin, Paris, and the European Commission in Brussels.'

There were murmurs of incredulity around the table. 'Eight
countries! Unbelievable! Who are these maniacs?'

Arthur turned to his old army comrade. 'The Minister of
Defence has prepared a few facts for us. George.'

'Thank you, Prime Minister.' George Bedivere consulted
his notes. 'The Angels of Mercy first surfaced about ten
years ago. Like many terrorist organisations in the Middle
East, Central Europe, Asia and South America, they began
financing their operations by dealing drugs. They have always
had conventional weapons and bomb-making capacity. More
recently we think they may have laid their hands on some real
nasties, chemical and biological weapons, and perhaps some
small nuclear weapons too, though as far as we know they
have never used them. Over the years they have developed links
with various anti-Western terror groups, especially Islamist
extremists. They are totally ruthless and highly professional.'

'They want us to release prisoners,' said Thomas Winnington.
'Have they given us a list of names?'

George Bedivere nodded. 'Yes.'

'How many are we holding?' asked Winnington.

John Aitkinson, Home Secretary, answered the question.
'We have five of them in high security prisons in this country.

The Americans and the French have locked up a few – I'd say about twenty in all.'

'Has this group actually carried out any terrorist acts?' The question came from Diana Partridge, Secretary of State for Trade and Industry.

'Depends what you mean by terrorist,' said Bedivere. 'Their activities could be categorised as criminal, though they use tried and tested terrorist techniques. So far their speciality has been kidnapping for money. They have a nasty habit of torturing their victims on camera and releasing the videos to various TV stations in the Middle East.'

There were exclamations of horror around the table.

'If they don't get what they want,' continued Bedivere grimly, 'they don't hesitate to kill. They do that on camera too. As you can imagine, people tend to agree to their demands. All in all they have extorted huge sums of money – I'm talking many millions.'

'Were they behind the kidnapping of the French President two years ago?' asked Leo Grant, who, as Chairman of the Party, was a member of the cabinet as a Minister without Portfolio

George Bedivere shook his head. 'That was another Islamist group, the Children of the Revolution. No direct links as far as we know. Although . . . ' He shrugged. 'We can never be sure. The scenario gets rewritten every day.'

'If their speciality is extorting money,' said Aitkinson, 'couldn't this just be a huge bluff?'

'It could,' said Bedivere. 'What makes me doubt its seriousness is the fact that this ultimatum is a major departure in a number of ways. First, to my knowledge, they have never before used the threat of nuclear or biological weapons. Second, until now they have targeted wealthy companies and individuals, not governments. And third, there's the sheer scale and arrogance of the ultimatum.'

'I've just realised,' said Lionel Gottfried, Chancellor of

the Exchequer, 'that we are talking eight times a hundred and twenty-five billion dollars. A trillion dollars! The mind boggles!'

Thomas Winnington expressed what they were all thinking. 'Surely they must know their demands are unrealistic?'

'To me that indicates that either it's a bluff,' said George Bedivere, 'or that they have no intention of negotiating.'

'Let's not jump to conclusions,' cautioned Arthur.

'Do we have any idea what they do with the money they extort?' asked John Aitkinson.

'What they claim to do,' said Bedivere, 'is redress social wrongs world-wide. Hence the name Angels of Mercy. They say they help the poor, the starving, the sick, the victims of war, that sort of thing. We see absolutely no evidence of that.'

'What are they trying to achieve?' asked Aitkinson.

George Bedivere deferred to Arthur. 'We are not sure,' said Arthur. 'So far they have said very little about their ultimate goal. It could be a worldwide Islamic State. Or the overthrow of Western style democracy. The chances are there's a hidden agenda somewhere.'

'And what might that be?'

'They claim to act in the name of Islam,' said Arthur, 'though many Muslim leaders disown them. We don't have conclusive proof but we suspect they are the terrorist arm of one of the countries in the Middle East. If that's true, then with this sort of money that country could change the balance of power in the Middle East – in the world, for that matter.'

Angela Furnival, Secretary of State for Employment, asked, 'Are you talking about Iran?'

Arthur hesitated. 'I'll get to that in a moment.'

'Where do they get their weapons from?' Thomas Winnington wanted to know.

'Many came from the break-up of the old Soviet Union, of course. But believe it or not,' said Arthur, 'they also came from Europe and America. It's an old story. On a number of occasions government stockpiles of radio-active waste in the USA and Sweden were broken into. It was always hushed up, but quite a lot of "dirty" uranium has gone missing over the years.'

'Quite a lot?' echoed Angela Furnival. 'How much is that?'

'I wish I knew,' said Arthur frankly. 'The fact is no one does. It's hard to credit, but neither the Americans nor the Swedes ever kept proper records of their stockpiles. We do know that some terror groups have significant quantities of the stuff. In the last twenty-five years there have been a number of incidents involving the use, or the threatened use, of uranium, both dirty and enriched.'

'Which is this?' asked Leo Grant.

'Hard to say,' admitted Arthur. 'The ultimatum talks of fissionable material. It could be enriched but it might not be. Nevertheless dirty uranium is still deadly. A simple mechanism does the trick. The bomb is detonated by remote control – a signal from a mobile phone, for example. Each bomb would probably be about a third of the size of the Hiroshima type, or it could be smaller.'

There were a lot of worried faces in the room as it began to dawn on every member of the cabinet that this was potentially the most serious global terrorist threat ever.

'They also talk about biological material,' John Aitkinson reminded them. 'You think they have biological weapons?'

'We have to assume they do,' said Arthur. 'In the last three decades there have been at least fifty relatively minor terrorist incidents worldwide involving biological weapons. We all know how easy these things are to produce and conceal. They could be freeze-dried and packed in small containers – nerve gas, anthrax, smallpox, plague, botulinum toxin, aflotoxin, clostridium, plus a whole new generation of deadly poisons.'

Angela Furnival raised her hand. Arthur nodded in her direction. 'Prime Minister, you referred to a possible change in the balance of power in the Middle East. You seemed to be talking about Iran. Who exactly are the political masters of the Angels of Mercy?'

Arthur nodded. 'An absolutely crucial question. To kill the monster you must go for the head. When bin Laden was alive we used to think all Islamist terror groups took their orders from Al Qa'eda. But then we discovered that Al Qa'eda weren't the only players in town. Recently we have noticed a change in terrorists' geo-political strategy.'

'Can you explain?'

'These days,' continued Arthur, 'terror groups are targeting not just Europe and The United States, but many other countries, including Russia, China and Japan. In other words they are confronting all the developed nations. Setting the poor against the rich could be a good way of destabilising the planet and creating chaos.'

'With what aim?' asked Angela Furnival.

'Out of the ashes of the old world a new Empire would arise.'

'An Islamic Empire – is that what you mean?' asked Leo Grant.

Arthur considered the question carefully. 'We all know that Al Qa'eda orchestrated the Islamist revolutions of the second decade that overthrew the old Arab feudal regimes. We also know that the financial and logistical backing came from the Iranian mullahs. There is no escaping the fact that since then Iran has been dominant in the Middle East, its power contained to some extent by the West, aided by Israel. The CIA, our own MI6 and Mossad are picking up more and more talk of a Second Persian Empire, an Empire that would control not just the Middle East but the whole world.'

'If these devices really exist,' said Julian Petherbridge, Secretary of State for the Environment, 'what are the chances of finding them before the deadline expires?'

It was the question on everyone's mind, and every cabinet member was looking to the Prime Minister for reassurance.

Arthur could read it in their eyes. He had no intention of handing out placebos. The cabinet had a vital job to do; it was important that no one underestimated the gravity of the situation. 'All we know at this moment,' said Arthur, 'is what the Angels of Mercy tell us, and that may or may not be true. If the devices are planted in London, they could be very difficult to locate. It's a huge area to search. We shall have a better idea in a day or so.'

'Let's get to it,' said George Bedivere who could not wait to do something, anything, just as long as they didn't have to sit around talking any longer. 'We only have four days.'

'And if we don't find them?' asked Thomas Winnington. It was the doomsday prognosis. 'What happens if the devices are detonated? How many casualties? How much damage?'

Arthur nodded at the Defence Secretary. 'George?'

'Obviously any assessment depends on the number of devices, how powerful they are, and where they are planted. Right now, we don't have the answers to those questions, so we can only make assumptions.' Encased in a black leather glove George Bedivere's right hand was tempered steel. He thumped it on the table, and a large map of central London appeared on a wall screen. 'OK . . . first let's talk about the explosive effect of the nuclear devices, and let's assume they are all somewhere in the city centre. If that's the case, I'm afraid we can expect a very significant number of casualties and huge destruction of property and amenities.' With his left hand he tapped the keyboard in front of him. 'Note the circles on the map. The smallest circle indicates the area of more or less total destruction – radius, one to two thousand yards. Could be somewhat greater. The next circle extends the area by a further two to four thousand yards – that's the area of medium destruction. Some buildings may survive relatively unscathed but not many. Most will be significantly damaged. The third circle shows the area of lesser damage – another five thousand yards or so.'

He looked up and down the big table, anticipating questions, but there were none. No one moved or made a sound. The atmosphere was tense. 'Apart from the destruction of property,' he went on, 'which would of course be instantaneous, huge areas of London would be seriously contaminated by radiation – buildings, transport systems, water, food, schools, hospitals, the River Thames, canals and so on – the list is endless.'

'How long would that take to clean up?' Thomas Winnington asked.

Jean Morton, the Health Minister, responded. 'The contamination could last for years. It doesn't bear thinking about. We believe our medical and civil defence services are well prepared, but if contamination were widespread, they would have difficulty coping with the sheer scale of it. There are adequate stocks of anti-radiation pills but the problem will be distributing them.'

If the devices really existed, and if they were detonated, London would be devastated. The enormity of the threat that confronted them was beginning to sink in. It would take years to recover. The only hope was to find and neutralise all the devices, and that, in the short time available, and despite the sophisticated detection equipment at the disposal of the armed forces, would be a huge challenge.

'Now we come to casualties,' said George Bedivere. 'I left that till last because obviously the estimate depends largely on the success of our evacuation plans. I have to tell you, though, that there could be as many as a hundred thousand immediate deaths, and perhaps a million serious injuries from the blast, burns and so on.'

'And I suppose,' said Thomas Winnington, 'the story would be much the same in all the other targeted cities?'

'More or less,' Bedivere confirmed, 'except that in Beijing and Tokyo where the population concentration is much greater, I would expect the number of casualties to be correspondingly higher.'

John Aitkinson, Home Secretary, shifted in his chair and suggested hopefully, 'Surely that's a worst case scenario?'

George Bedivere shook his head firmly. 'It's a realistic one. What's more, it doesn't take into account the biological threat which is hard to assess in terms of casualties. No, ladies and gentlemen, I'm afraid what we are facing is not just a catastrophe in the making for this generation, it could well affect generations to come.' He spoke gravely and with emphasis. 'I am talking about the possibility of many deaths, horrible, lingering deaths, a plague of diseases associated with nuclear and biological contamination affecting all sections of the population, including millions still unborn.'

No one spoke. In the silence every member of the cabinet was looking at Arthur. He spoke quietly, directing his eyes at each member of the cabinet in turn, emphasising their personal involvement. 'Since the beginning of this century we have witnessed many terrorist acts. But nothing to compare with this. Each of you has a vital role to play. We have less than four days – ninety-three hours, to be precise – to find a solution. If we remain calm and focused we shall succeed.'

George Bedivere nodded his agreement. 'The cabinet is a hundred percent behind you, sir.'

There were emphatic nods and murmurs of agreement.

Arthur spoke crisply and decisively. 'There will be another meeting of the cabinet at three this afternoon. George, I shall want a report on military options. Jean, you will report on measures taken by civil defence, fire and ambulance services, hospitals and other emergency medical services. John, you will update us on the latest intelligence from MI5 and MI6. We need any information we can get, and we need it now – any possible leads on the location of the devices, or on the Angels of Mercy. You and George will also co-ordinate the activities of the Metropolitan police and the Chiefs of Staff. I also want an immediate twenty-four hour link set up with Interpol and with the police and intelligence and security services of the seven other countries involved.'

The Chancellor spoke hesitantly. 'I hate to mention it, sir, but do you want me to prepare a report on the availability of funds, should it become necessary?' His voice caught in his throat. 'Should all else fail?'

Arthur's response was uncompromising. 'Surrender is not an option. There is no question of giving in to extortion and blackmail. It would be a disaster for the world if we did. What we need is to establish a link with the Angels of Mercy, and to gain time by talking to them, time to trace the devices and time to track down the terrorists and deal with them.'

George Bedivere nodded. He was in full agreement with Arthur. Nevertheless, he prided himself on being a realist. 'What if they refuse to talk?'

'I am not interested in what-ifs,' said Arthur curtly. 'You all know what has to be done. Let's do it.'

Now that they had an action plan, the atmosphere in the cabinet room was considerably less despondent. The Prime Minister may not have offered any easy solutions, but he had at least shown decisiveness. 'A few final words, ladies and gentlemen,' said Arthur. 'As you know, we have declared a state of emergency under the Emergency Powers Act. This allows us to call in the armed forces, not only to maintain essential services, but also, should it become necessary, to requisition property. Fifteen minutes from now I shall be speaking to the nation, and after that to the House. The evacuation of London will begin shortly. It will be a daunting task. If we include those who travel into town to work or shop, we are talking about ten to twelve million people. We need to act fast, but remember, whatever we do we must avoid panicking the population. The Secretary of State for Transport is working urgently on the logistics. That's why he isn't here now.'

Immediately after the cabinet meeting broke up, Arthur was onscreen with Winslow Marsden, the US President. 'With the greatest respect to your illustrious twentieth century predecessor,' said the President grimly, 'there are times when 'war war' is better than 'jaw jaw'. This is one of them.'

'I don't disagree with you,' said Arthur, 'but it is essential that any action we take be co-ordinated with all eight countries.'

The caution did nothing to improve the President's mood. 'See here, Arthur, when it comes to action, we'll do what we need to do. We are still the most powerful nation on this planet.'

'Power alone will not locate the devices,' warned Arthur, 'nor will it track down the terrorists.'

'Don't you believe it. We have eyes in the sky that can read the print on a can of beans,' the President boasted. 'We have ears on the ground that can pick up a grasshopper's cough. Not a mouse craps on this planet without our knowing it.'

There was no point in taking issue with Marsden, especially when the issue was theoretical. 'Let's concentrate on identifying and locating the Angels of Mercy,' said Arthur.

'Iran is behind this. Or the K.O.E.. Or both.'

'Probably. But where's the evidence?'

The blood rose swiftly to the President's face. 'Evidence! Who gives a fuck about evidence! This is war, man, not a trial in some goddam court of law! I'll show the mother fuckers they can't mess with the USA. We've taken all we intend to take from these bastards. If it comes right down to it I won't hesitate to nuke them. And I won't be asking the UN's permission either.'

But without a target to strike, there was little the United States or anyone else could do. Unleashing nuclear missiles would result in millions of innocent deaths, and would almost certainly plunge the world into nuclear war. Every developed country now had a substantial stockpile of nuclear weapons and long-range missiles. A few so-called 'rogue' states were also known to possess some nuclear capability. Nuking was not a realistic option for dealing with terrorists, and Winslow Marsden knew that as well as Arthur. But then what *were* their options?

457

Minutes later Arthur was on TV addressing the nation. Immediately after the broadcast he was driven to the House of Commons where he made a further statement. He took pains to reassure the House and the country, sounding confident that the devices would be located and neutralised. However, as a sensible precaution, and to ensure that the army, the police, firemen, ambulances and other vital services had complete freedom of movement, he urged everyone who lived or worked in London to leave the city as soon as possible.

There was ample time, he said, for a total evacuation, and no need to panic. Public transport was being geared up to cope with the increased flow of people, and temporary accommodation erected on the outskirts of the city for those who had nowhere else to go. No private cars were to be used for the evacuation. It was essential that roads were kept open, more especially the main arteries in and out of London, so that key transport and other vital services were able to do their job efficiently.

As the Prime Minister began his speech the House was packed. By the time he sat down, a mere handful of MP's remained. Arthur could not help wondering where they had all gone. If even MP's were starting to panic, how would the general public react to the crisis?

By Friday afternoon the evacuation of London was under way, and with some isolated exceptions the population remained calm. It was clear, however, that the transport system would have difficulty coping with the huge numbers already thronging the streets. Crowds had gathered at bus stops and underground stations across the city. Though they were orderly enough, it was soon impossible to tell where one queue began and the next ended.

By nine a.m. Saturday morning, a million people had left London. It was good but not good enough. There were three days to go, a mere seventy-two hours. The evacuation would have to be speeded up, or millions would be stranded in the city when the deadline expired on Saturday morning.

In Beijing and Tokyo, Paris, Berlin and Brussels, the scene was much the same as in London. Tension was building but no serious incidents had so far been reported. In Moscow and Washington sporadic fighting and some rioting and looting had already broken out. People were beginning to ignore the regular broadcasts appealing for a calm and orderly response to the crisis.

By mid-afternoon the situation had deteriorated further. Outbreaks of violence were no longer confined to Washington and Moscow. From Berlin and Paris, Beijing, Tokyo and Brussels, the news was grim. Street fighting had broken out, resulting in deaths and widespread vandalism – the overturning and burning of buses, cars and trucks, and widespread looting of shops, stores and private houses. People fought to hire taxis at usurious rates, or attempted, despite warnings, to escape in their own cars; but scarcely any made it, the majority being dragged from their vehicles and attacked by angry mobs desperate to escape the city.

It was feared that if the devices were not found soon, mobs would take over the streets. The threat posed by panic and chaos was now as great as that posed by the devices themselves. Positive news was desperately needed.

Winslow Marsden appeared on television to tell the people of the United States and the whole world what he thought they needed to hear. The Administration, he said, had information that would shortly lead to the arrest of the terrorists and the destruction of the devices. It was not so much an exaggeration as a blatant lie, for neither the whereabouts of the terrorists nor that of the devices was known, and no one had even succeeded in establishing contact with The Angels of Mercy. Yet for the moment the lie was believed and the President's words, relayed across the globe, offered the reassurance people were looking for.

At five p.m. Washington time, ten p.m. London time, the eight nations held an onscreen conference linking Zhongnanhai in Beijing, the Prime Minister's residence in Tokyo, the Federal Chancellery in Berlin, the Kremlin in Moscow, the Elysée in Paris, the offices of the European Commission in Brussels, the White House in Washington and 10 Downing Street in London. The world leaders, together with their aides, were projected in 3D on wrap-around screens, creating the illusion that they were sitting together in one conference room.

Winslow Marsden now seemed more relaxed. 'The CIA is convinced it's a bluff, a clumsy attempt at blackmail.'

'Is it then so clumsy?' enquired the German Chancellor. 'They have us running round like – *wie heiss das auf Englisch*? – ya, hot cats.'

'We'll be making a big mistake if we let them call the shots,' said the US President. 'Look at their ultimatum. Who could take it seriously? A hundred and twenty-five billion dollars! What am I saying? A thousand billion dollars! A trillion dollars! They know we could never hand over that kind of money.'

The German Chancellor coughed. 'This depends on how they think we value a human life.'

'Or a thousand lives,' said the French President.

'Or a million,' said the President of the European Commission glumly.

'There are no devices,' said Winslow Marsden scornfully. 'It's all bullshit. I refuse to authorise one cent of taxpayers' money, and I'm not letting any of those murdering bastards out of jail. Even if I wanted to, I don't have the authority. Congress would never allow it. And what about their other demands? We have to admit we are murderers and face prosecution! How about that! Can you see the President of the United States of America standing trial in some goddamn kangaroo court!'

A shadow of a smile crossed the face of the Russian President. 'Maybe is not such bad idea.'

'Now see here . . . ' The US President bit his tongue. 'Very amusing,' he conceded.

'Is not joke,' said the Russian President.

The President of China contributed a subtle offering. 'This is the day of the fox, not the bull.' After some puzzled looks, this apparently obscure observation was tacitly interpreted as a word of caution.

'France will act to protect its own interests,' said the French President. 'In case of need, we shall be ready to discuss terms.'

'That,' said the US President sardonically, 'comes as no surprise to anyone.'

A Gallic shrug and a 'pouff' of disdain was the only reaction.

'I beg you,' said Arthur, 'let us concentrate on finding common ground. I see this crisis as an acid test of the courage and resolve of the free world. We have to demonstrate that we can speak with one voice and act together firmly and decisively. If we fight amongst ourselves, we are lost. Our greatest strength is our unity. They will try to divide us in order to weaken us. We must not let that happen.'

The US President was in favour of calling the evacuations off and telling everyone to go home. 'If we don't, we'll have a bloodbath on the streets of our cities.' The Prime Minister of Japan considered that far too risky. The President of the European Commission thought it irresponsible. The Russian President favoured sending troops to the Kingdom of the Euphrates who his intelligence services were convinced had engineered the crisis. The President of China was against using force under any circumstances. The French President refused to commit himself to joint action. The German President suggested offering the terrorists a smaller ransom. Arthur watched and listened, frustration welling up in him like a physical pain.

As tempers flared it became clear that no decisive action would result from the conference call. It was agreed that nothing would be said or done until they consulted again the following day. Ironically, it was the only point on which agreement had been reached. Contrary to the spirit of that agreement, however, sources close to the White House hinted that there was "strong evidence" that the ultimatum was a hoax. The news flashed round the world and was greeted with relief. In all eight capitals hundreds of thousands now tried to make their way home, though movement in the streets was painfully slow in any direction.

But then on Sunday morning, nine a.m. London time, an e-mail was posted on the internet. No sooner had Arthur finished reading it than Winslow Marsden was onscreen. 'They say they've concealed two unarmed devices in the White House.' Arthur nodded. 'They claim there are two unarmed devices in Downing Street. They have given us the co-ordinates so that we can . . . ' He broke off. 'As we speak, I'm being told a similar message has been received by the other six countries.'

'So am I,' the President confirmed. 'I don't get it. What are they up to?'

'It's their reaction to last night's news release from Washington,' said Arthur. 'Your people said it was a hoax. If my guess is right, the Angels of Mercy are about to prove it isn't. They obviously anticipated we might think they were bluffing, so they prepared themselves in advance. There can be no other explanation. They must have planted unarmed devices with that in mind. It shows we are dealing with extremely intelligent and highly professional people.'

The President did not believe a word of it. 'I don't buy that. There are no devices. We called their bluff, and now they're getting desperate. That's all there is to it.'

The President was being irrational in Arthur's view. But once again, what was the point in arguing? 'We'll know soon enough,' he said.

Within a short time reports began to come in from around the world. Unarmed devices had been located in Beijing, Tokyo, Berlin, Brussels, Paris, Moscow, in the White House, and in Numbers 10 and 11 Downing Street. In each capital there were two devices – one nuclear, one biological – sixteen in all.

Minutes later the eight leaders were again on the wrap-around screen. 'According to our experts,' said the French President sombrely, 'if the two devices we found had been armed and detonated, the centre of Paris would have suffered severe contamination and massive damage. I don't wish to speak of casualties, but the estimates are frightening. One device was a small but powerful nuclear bomb, the other a cocktail of biological poisons. This is no hoax, *messieurs*.'

'The Angels have made their point,' agreed Arthur. 'Whatever doubts we may have had, we now know we have to take them seriously.'

'Ok, so I underestimated the bastards,' said the US President, 'but that doesn't change a goddam thing. No one is going to push the United States around. We will never give in to terrorist blackmail.' Arthur nodded vigorous approval. 'Are we all agreed on that?' he asked. The response was unanimous. No surrender. No compromise.

'Then,' proposed Arthur, 'we carry on with the evacuations, and pray we get everyone out of danger in time. Meanwhile we keep trying to open communications with the terrorists. Our immediate objective must be to get an extension of the deadline.'

The Prime Minister of Japan was disconsolate. 'What if not successful?'

It was the 'what if' scenario that Arthur always refused to discuss. 'We can't even think of that,' he said. 'One thing for sure, delaying the deadline will save lives.'

The German Chancellor rubbed his tired eyes and unshaven face. 'And is giving us more time to catch the terrorists.'

Winslow Marsden flipped through the pages of a memo in front of him. 'The CIA are certain Iran is behind the Angels.'

'Is not infallible, the CIA,' remarked the Russian President dryly.

'Maybe not, but a couple of neutron bombs on Tehran would solve a lot of problems,' snapped the President angrily.

'Why only two?' enquired the French President with heavy

irony.

The President of the European Commission was incensed. '*Non, non.* I will not listen to such talk! The Commission will never sanction the use of nuclear weapons.'

'What will you sanction, then?' enquired the US President disdainfully. 'Food parcels?'

'I am also not agreeing to the use of nuclear weapons,' said the German Chancellor, 'under any circumstances.'

A heated discussion followed, in the middle of which the US President disappeared from the screen, followed shortly by the others. Once again, no course of action had been agreed. One thing was clear, if the Angels of Mercy could plant unarmed devices in supposedly secure Government buildings, they were certainly capable of planting the real thing more or less wherever they chose. It had to be assumed that the devices existed, and that they were armed. But despite the most intensive searches, not a single one had been found.

Five

Sunday, 26th October

AT NINE A.M. Washington time on Sunday, Winslow Marsden spoke once again to the American people, this time making no reference to any arrests but expressing confidence that a solution to the problem was imminent, and hinting at ongoing negotiations. The truth was, that for all his reassuring words, there were no negotiations and no prospect of a solution, imminent or otherwise. On the contrary, police and security forces were losing hope of finding the devices. The search area was enormous and time was running out.

In London, operating around the clock, thousands of troops and police combed government offices, private houses and apartments, business premises, museums, railway stations, factories, depots, theatres, concert halls, shops and warehouses. Below the city, the underground and the huge network of sewers were searched. Above it flew dozens of helicopters crammed with the latest detection sensors.

Compounding all the other problems, the search was hampered by the swiftly deteriorating situation on the streets. The information about the unarmed devices had been posted on the internet by the Angels of Mercy. Any lingering hope that this might be a cruel hoax had evaporated. Those sceptics who had remained in their homes, and those who had left and had then returned, now took to the streets to swell the ever-growing crowds.

By Sunday afternoon the evacuation of London had slowed almost to a halt. Moreover there was now a new and dangerous development. A million or more people were defying the ban on the use of private cars, frustrated by the enormous queues at underground stations and bus stops. North, south, east and west, every road out of London was hopelessly blocked by cars and taxis.

In the morning, and again in the afternoon, Arthur appeared on nationwide television to appeal for calm. But all that people really wanted to hear was that the devices had been located and disarmed. Since he was not able to tell them that, nothing he said had any effect. Later that morning the cabinet met yet again, their fourth meeting since the crisis broke. At the long table were two empty chairs. On their way to Downing Street John Aitkinson, Home Secretary, and Angela Furnival, Secretary of State for Employment, had been attacked by a mob of drunken youths in Whitehall and beaten senseless.

'It grieves me to bring you this terrible news,' Arthur told his shocked colleagues. 'We are witnessing the breakdown of law and order, and I fear things can only get worse. London is on the verge of mob rule. Until the crisis is resolved, I am asking you all to remain in Number 10. I cannot guarantee your safety. You are at least safer here than on the streets. Sadly the news from the other capitals is much the same, or worse. We are all of us dealing with widespread panic and hysteria.'

George Bedivere protested. 'What about our families? We can't just desert them.'

'Give them whatever guidance and reassurance you can,' said Arthur. 'But I'm sorry, you are all vital to the success of our efforts, and your safety is paramount. The people depend on us. Our first duty is to them.'

The news from overseas was increasingly worrying. From Beijing there were reports of dozens of rioters shot dead by troops in Tiananmen Square. In Moscow, the police had melted away, and the army was nowhere to be seen. The city was in the hands of looters and vandals. Every store on Kutuzovsky Prospekt had been ransacked, several public buildings had been set on fire by arsonists, and mobs were attacking the Kremlin.

In Berlin, police were battling angry, violent mobs on the Kurfurstendamm, the Unterdenlinden and Strasse des 17 June. By now nearly half the population of Tokyo and Brussels had been evacuated. Of those who remained, many had barricaded themselves in their houses, the rest had joined the mobs to loot shops and stores, or roamed the streets looking for victims to mug.

In Paris, not only shops but art galleries and museums had been looted. The Champs Elysées, the Rue de Rivoli, the Avenue de l'Opera and the streets and boulevards on both banks of the Seine were blocked with the wrecks of crashed and burned-out vehicles. In the Place de la Concorde, in the Jardins des Tuileries, around the Tour Eiffel, and in the Place Charles de Gaulle at the base of the Arc de Triomphe, rival mobs battled. Already there had been many injuries and several deaths resulting from incidents of road rage, and more than a million vehicles paralysed the city centre in one massive traffic jam. The incessant wail of car horns was like the cry of some giant primeval creature in the agony of its death throes.

Hundreds of private boats and public ferries had been seized. Those who resisted the hijackers were thrown into the river. Crowds thronged the banks and bridges of the Seine, waiting for a chance to jump onto a passing boat. As a result many capsized, sinking almost instantly, taking their terrified passengers down with them. Bodies drifted in the turbulent waters. Even strong swimmers were helpless in the powerful currents, waving their arms in desperation as they screamed for the help no one could give them. The few boats still afloat swept by, their passengers averting their eyes from the wretched souls drowning in the water.

In Washington people lay on the streets and sidewalks, some with knife or gunshot wounds, others run down by cars and trucks in the blind panic to escape the city. Many were dragged from their cars and beaten, those who beat them frequently attacked in their turn by others. A car, it seemed, was worth more than a life, or several lives, even a car that could make no progress through the blocked streets. In one tragic incident an oil tanker turned on its side and exploded, incinerating more than eighty cars and buses packed with screaming men, women and children. Traffic backed up miles from the city centre. Every road was blocked: Pennsylvania and Constitution Avenues, Wisconsin and Massachusetts, where the embassies had all been vandalised or petrol-bombed.

By late afternoon street-fighting had broken out in London. In Oxford Street, the Cromwell Road, Finchley Road, and on every bridge across the Thames, people lay exhausted or badly hurt, passers-by stepping over them with scarcely a second glance. There were no ambulances to be seen anywhere, no doctors or nurses. In the traffic jams emergency services were unable to operate; even if they had been, the hospitals were too full to cope with any more casualties. Mugged for valuables or money, or knocked down by cars, the wounded, the dead and the dying lay on trollies in corridors, on the floors of reception areas, on the pavements outside.

Across the city huge fires burned unchecked. Harrods, petrol-bombed, was a mass of flames, as was Harvey Nichols and Selfridges in Oxford Street. Virtually every shop and store in the centre of London had been looted, in Regent Street and Bond Street, Knightsbridge and Sloane Street, the King's Road, the Fulham Road and Kensington High Street. Over Buckingham Palace and the Houses of Parliament hung a great pall of smoke.

Amidst the chaos and terror on the streets, some oases of calm remained, a sign that English phlegm was not entirely a thing of the past. A few ancient and elite London clubs remained open, their members studiously oblivious to what was happening outside. In the Garrick, a case of the finest vintage claret was being sampled in the bar. In the Athenaeum, a lively dispute raged on the subject of whether Elizabeth the First was indeed a virgin Queen. In Whites, a few senior members languidly discussed the comparative merits of the legs and breasts of the two young waitresses serving their drinks. In Grays, two dozen bottles of malt whisky were lined up on the bar, the blindfolded contestants wagering fortunes on their ability to identify them by taste.

In the dim interiors of St Paul's and Westminster Abbey, so far untouched by vandals, a few elderly people sat quietly, heads bowed, eyes closed, praying to a God their children and grandchildren no longer believed in.

At six p.m. London time, one p.m. Washington time, the government of Iran released a statement on television and the Internet condemning all degenerate, cowardly and corrupt leaders of suffering peoples. They were, the statement said, paying the price for their godlessness, and for the contempt they had shown the Arab nations, and in particular the people of Iran. The Angels of Mercy, the statement claimed, had been driven to desperate acts by the barbarity and injustice of their treatment at the hands of the eight sons of Satan. Whilst Iran did not condone terrorism, it wished to make clear that any attack on its sovereignty would result in a terrible and appropriate response.

This carefully worded bulletin was interpreted as confirming that the Angels of Mercy were controlled by the Iranian government, or were at least operating with their full knowledge and approval. As expected the US Administration reacted strongly. If the Iranians were supporting a bunch of ruthless terrorists they would have to take the consequences. What those consequences might be was not specified, though there was naturally much speculation. Some commentators forecast a nuclear attack on Iran.

Whilst the eight leaders watched helplessly as their capital cities plunged into mayhem and chaos, a second statement released by the Iranian government less than an hour later confirmed their willingness to 'facilitate negotiations' with the Angels of Mercy. Within seconds, a jubilant American President was onscreen in Number 10. 'They're backing off, Arthur. What did I tell you? All we had to do was tough it out.' For the first time it did indeed seem that there were grounds for hope. In the circumstances, and after consultation between all eight leaders, it was agreed, though with considerable reluctance on the part of the American President, to transmit a conciliatory message to Tehran expressing confidence that they would assist in resolving the crisis.

In response, the Iranians indicated through their overseas embassies the nature of a major concession they claimed to have negotiated. The timing of the explosions would depend on the "attitude" of each government involved.

Yet another onscreen conference was hastily arranged. Whilst the Iranian announcement was vague, no doubt intentionally so, it appeared that the terrorists were now willing to negotiate separately with each country. It was what Arthur had feared. He urged his fellow world leaders not to be deceived. 'It's nothing but a trap. Divide and rule. If we fall into it, they'll play one against the other, and we shall all be the losers. I repeat, our strongest weapon – perhaps our only weapon – is our unity. If we surrender that, we are all done for.'

'Mr. Pendragon right,' said the Chinese President. 'We must stand shoulder to shoulder, for the sake of future generations.'

Winslow Marsden was unimpressed. 'It's this generation I'm accountable to. They are the ones who put me in the White House. It's their lives at risk. If I have to make a deal to save thousands of American lives – maybe hundreds of thousands – then I'll sure as hell make a deal.'

'Only a few hours ago,' said Arthur, 'you assured me the United States would never negotiate with terrorists. We were all agreed. No surrender, no compromise.'

'That was a few hours ago. This is now, and we're that much closer to a major catastrophe. The way I see it, this is a tactical withdrawal, not a retreat, and most certainly not a surrender. We'll go after those terrorist bastards when we're good and ready. But we're the ones who'll choose the time and place, not them. Meanwhile we have no option. We have to negotiate.'

The French President agreed. 'France too is ready to negotiate. We shall release their comrades from our prisons. We are also prepared to discuss money. I am certain they will accept much less than they have demanded. We would even, for the sake of the glory of France and to save lives, be ready to discuss some foreign policy adjustments, perhaps even some government resignations.'

The Prime Minister of Japan nodded. 'If settlement possible for less than full demands, we are also ready to talk.'

Arthur refused to give up, though in his heart he knew he was losing the argument. 'I beg you, all of you, think what you are doing. These people are ruthless. They cannot be trusted. Any deal they make, they will break – if not now, then in a few weeks, a few months, a few years. What will they demand next time? Our lives? Our women and children? Our countries? Our only hope is to remain united. We must show them that we speak as one, act as one. We dare not surrender to blackmail. We all have one thing in common – our belief in democracy. But what good is democracy if we are not willing to fight for it?'

'Admirable sentiments, Monsieur Pendragon,' said the President of the European Commission. 'I salute an idealist. Regretfully this is a time for being practical.' The Russian President scowled. 'When gun is pointed at head, is luxury, idealism.' The President of China had swiftly changed his mind. 'Democracy, fantasy. Survival, reality.' Arthur looked at the German Chancellor, his last remaining hope. 'I respect your views, Mr. Pendragon,' said the Chancellor. 'What is more, I fear you may be right. But I have not your courage. I too am for negotiating.' The videolink was cut, and Arthur was alone.

The terrorists' third communication came at eight p.m., London time. Like the first and second message it was posted simultaneously in all eight capitals. The sting was in the last sentence. 'This is our final communiqué. We inform you that we are ready to negotiate with your country separately from the seven others. But we warn you that we shall explode three devices in each capital in turn in a sequence to be determined by us, *unless and until we have concluded a satisfactory settlement with all eight of you.*'

Within seconds, the US President was on the secure line to Arthur. 'You have the Angels' message?'

'Yes.'

The stubborn bastard would have to see reason now. 'You agree it changes everything.'

'It changes nothing,' said Arthur.

'You mean you still refuse to negotiate?'

'I do,' said Arthur.

Winslow Marsden's blood pressure soared dangerously. 'You can't be serious!'

'I am absolutely serious.'

The President's voice leaped an octave. 'I don't believe this!' he shrieked. 'What kind of man are you? How many good people have to die because you are too goddam arrogant to talk to terrorists?'

'That is a gross distortion of the facts,' said Arthur quietly.

A long silence.

'I apologise.' The President sounded contrite. 'I shouldn't have said that. Look . . . ' Winslow Marsden faltered, searching for the right words to persuade Arthur. 'Do this for me, my friend. Do it for all of us. You believe in democracy, don't you?'

'Of course.'

'In a democracy, the majority rules. Right?' said the President. Surely he had him now.

'Even in a democracy bad decisions can be made,' said Arthur.

'It's one against seven,' said the President, trying desperately to control his anger. 'Who are you to say this is a bad decision?'

'Surrendering to terrorist blackmail is always a bad decision,' said Arthur bluntly.

The President tried flattery. He had tried everything else and failed. 'We need your advice, Arthur. We need your brains. We need your guts. You can be there in the background helping all of us get the best possible deal.'

Arthur shook his head. 'If we surrender, it will be the end of the free world. It will be the beginning of chaos.'

The President's voice climbed to a hysterical shriek. 'You don't get it, do you, Pendragon? If we don't make a deal with those mother fuckers, they're gonna blow us all to hell! And that includes you! Well, let me tell you something, if they don't destroy London, I will. I'll nuke you fucking Limeys! Do I make myself clear?'

'What is clear, Winslow,' said Arthur calmly, 'is that their tactics are succeeding. We're at each others' throats when it's them we should be fighting.'

Winslow Marsden shook his head in frustration. 'For the love of God,' he said wearily, 'how the hell do we fight them? We don't know where they are. We don't know where the damn devices are. Time is running out. I'm asking you – no, I'm begging you – to co-operate.'

For a few moments Arthur was silent. 'What exactly do you want from me?'

'In three minutes from now,' said the President, 'I'll be online to the boss man of The Angels of Mercy. He is waiting for my assurance that we're willing to negotiate. That means all eight of us. If not, there's no deal. Seven of us are ready to talk. What do I tell him about you, Arthur?'

There flashed through Arthur's mind the images of those men, women and children brutally slaughtered in Wadi Jahmah. What had changed since then? The so-called Free World had always made squalid, self-serving, cynical deals with dictators and terrorists. What made them do it? Self-interest? The illusion of power? Fear? Greed? Stupidity? All those and more. And now the politicians were about to make yet another cowardly compromise, just as they had at Jurassic Hill. Only this time it was not a village but the whole world that would suffer the terrible consequences. What had changed? Nothing. And nothing ever would until someone had the courage to take on the murderers.

'For chrissake, Arthur,' the President pleaded, 'what do I tell him?'

'Tell him,' said Arthur, 'tell him he'll be hearing from me.'

Six

Sunday, 26th October

THE MEETING in the cabinet room had been called for ten p.m. Sunday evening. Ministers sat grim faced and silent, waiting impatiently for the Prime Minister to appear. The minutes ticked by . . . five, ten, fifteen minutes past ten.

'He did say ten, didn't he?' The Foreign Secretary looked up and down the table seeking confirmation.

Heads nodded. No one spoke. They were all hoping that the Prime Minister would rush in at any second, apologising profusely for being later. More minutes passed.

George Bedivere shifted uneasily in his chair. 'Not like him at all,' he muttered. 'He's never late for cabinet meetings.'

Finally they were tired of waiting. Arthur's PPS was summoned and questioned. 'He was here about an hour ago. Spoke to the US President. Then he said something about going out.'

'Going out? Where?' asked the astonished Bedivere.

'He didn't say.'

George Bedivere was now very concerned. 'Are you sure? Where would he go at this time of night? The mobs are out there. The streets aren't safe. Anyway, why would he want to leave Number 10 at a time like this? Think, man, think!'

The PPS tried to recall every detail of his last conversation with the PM – what he said, how he looked, how he sounded. 'He gave me the impression he had an urgent appointment to keep. He seemed to be in a hurry.'

'Maybe he just forgot about the meeting,' suggested Lionel Gottfried.

'The PM doesn't forget things like that,' said Leo Grant looking deeply concerned. 'Besides, he was the one who called it.'

Julian Petherbridge suggested a more reasonable explanation. 'You don't suppose he has fallen asleep?'

George Bedivere thumped the table with his steel hand. 'Of course! That's it! I doubt he has slept more than a couple of hours since the crisis broke. That has to be the answer.'

But it was not. A room by room search proved unsuccessful, the PM was nowhere to be found. As the PPS left the cabinet room, the panic was rising in their throats. George Bedivere looked about him uncertainly. 'As Defence Secretary, are there any objections if I chair the meeting?'

There were none. George did his best, but although he commanded considerable respect, even he was unable to concentrate the attention of the cabinet. They felt badly let down by the Prime Minister. How could he desert them at a time like this? Without his leadership and guidance they found it hard to think rationally. In the hour of mortal danger he had been so strong, so confident, so undaunted. What could they hope to achieve without him?

Now that he was no longer there to strengthen their resolve, they were suddenly convinced that a deal had to be made with the terrorists. But what sort of deal? No one had given it any thought. Why should they? Until now any deal had been unthinkable.

George Bedivere spoke in a low voice, as if he were far from happy with himself. 'Look, I frankly admit I'm out of my depth. Why don't I ask the US President to negotiate for us? I don't like handing over our sovereignty to the Americans, but what choice do we have? We're almost out of time, and none of us is properly prepared.' He looked at his watch. 'It's eleven p.m., thirty-four hours to the deadline. All those lives at stake . . . Do I have your agreement? Those in favour?'

Up and down the table hands were slowly raised. The vote

was unanimous. If ever they had the will to fight, they had lost it now. The meeting broke up in silence and the cabinet members filed out with heads down, avoiding each other's eyes. The Prime Minister's PPS was waiting for George Bedivere in the corridor. 'For what it's worth, the two policemen on duty in Downing Street both say they saw the PM leaving Number 10.'

'Are they quite sure it was him?'

'Absolutely positive.'

'When did he leave?'

'Shortly after he spoke to the US President, so it must have been between eight-thirty and eight-forty-five. I questioned them separately and their stories are identical. They saw him heading up Downing Street in the direction of Horse Guards Parade. He was walking fast, they say, and he seemed very focused, as if he knew exactly what he was up to. To me that sounds like a man in full control of himself, if you understand my meaning.'

The corners of George Bedivere's mouth drooped. He understood the PPS's meaning only too well. So Arthur had not panicked, then. What he had done, he had done deliberately. Who would have thought it of him? The PM had abandoned ship. And after all his brave talk. *Our duty is to the people. They depend on us.* Nothing could excuse this final, shameful act of treachery.

It was hard to take in. 'He was the most level-headed man I ever met.' George Bedivere shook his head in disbelief. 'A deep thinker. He did nothing on impulse. What he did could only have been pre-meditated. That means he knew the situation was hopeless, so he decided to save himself.' Bedivere looked about him furtively to be sure they were not overheard. 'Though how the hell he expects to get away, I can't imagine. Every road is blocked. Frankly I don't fancy his chances. If the mobs catch him, they'll tear him to pieces.'

'Um.' There was obviously something else on the PPS's mind,

though he seemed reluctant to say what it was.

'Out with it.'

'Both policemen swear they saw some flying object swoop down somewhere close to Number 10, probably on Horse Guards Parade. It was out of sight for a short time, and then they saw it rise up over the rooftops and hover for a second or two. And then . . . '

'Get on with it.'

' . . . it disappeared. Anyway that's how they described it. It's probably complete nonsense. They are both tired and overwrought.'

'Must have been a helicopter.'

'They were adamant. This craft, whatever it was, made no noise. And it was round.'

George Bedivere's eyes widened, his shoulders heaving as he broke into a derisive guffaw. 'So are my balls,' he said.

A disc-shaped object hovered silently over Bossiney Castle. Slowly it sank to earth and disappeared in the shadows. With sunset came the night sounds. An owl hooted, a fox barked. Here and there bats squeaked, taking their high frequency soundings. An occasional flurry of wind disturbed the trees, and in the distance white horses raced across the Atlantic waves.

On a ridge overlooking Bossiney Mound stood a man, silhouetted against the dying light. So still was he that he might have been a statue of an ancient god, or a solitary column surviving from some pagan temple. After a while a white-robed figure joined him, and the two men waited there, silent, motionless, linking earth and heaven, time past and time future.

High up the west winds blew. Clouds raced across the night sky, filtering the moonlight. It was eleven p.m., Sunday, October the 26th, and the moon was full. Bossiney Castle glowed with an eerie light. A cloud moved across the moon, land and sky merging in one dark mass. Inside Bossiney Mound a dim light glowed, illuminating first the base, then inching higher, growing brighter as it rose.

When it broke the surface of the mound, there in the darkness, bathed in shimmering silver, lay the Round Table.

Seven

Monday, 27th October

By NINE A.M. MONDAY, London time, all eight capitals were in the grip of the mobs. Gangs drifted through the streets, lacking any obvious leadership, driven, it seemed, by some sinister collective subconscious, looting, burning, raising and tearing down barricades, battling rival mobs, and sometimes, for no obvious reason, erupting in savage fighting amongst themselves. Rumour and counter-rumour flared, died down and erupted again spontaneously, like rampant bush fires . . . the terrorists were defiant . . . they had surrendered . . . a deal had been struck . . . negotiations had broken down . . . the devices were located . . . the search had been called off . . . helicopters were evacuating the seriously sick and wounded . . . they were ferrying to safety political leaders, the rich and privileged.

By mid-afternoon, not even a cat could have found its way out of London. Every surface road was blocked. In the labyrinthine tunnels and corridors of the underground system that had offered the last hope of escape, all was mayhem and chaos. Lifts, escalators, platforms, even the lines themselves were crammed with the dead and dying, some electrocuted, others suffocated or trampled to death. Outside every underground station in London thousands of screaming, panic-stricken men and women fought to get in, battling with thousands equally desperate to get out.

Frustration and fear, the conviction that the politicians had betrayed them, and a growing sense of impotence in the face of a ruthless and invisible enemy, created not just mass hysteria, but a frenzied need for revenge – revenge not on the Angels of Mercy who were beyond anyone's reach, but on whatever scapegoat could be found. Any representative of officialdom unfortunate enough to be out on the streets – the police, the armed forces, fire and ambulance services, postmen, traffic wardens, even trash collectors, no matter who or what they were – if they wore a uniform, they were seized by the crowds and beaten mercilessly. From time to time, if a length of rope was available, some poor wretch was strung from the nearest lamp-post to wild cheers and applause, murder being the mobs' sole entertainment now, killing the only focus of their anger, distracting their attention, however momentarily, from their hopeless plight.

As night fell, several huge crowds, each more than fifty thousand people, moved slowly but inexorably, like a many-headed monster, east along the Thames Embankment and north across the Thames bridges – Vauxhall and Lambeth, Westminster and Waterloo – destroying everything and everyone in their path, massing finally in Parliament Square, chanting, jeering, fighting, lobbing petrol bombs at the Houses of Parliament, toppling and smashing to pieces the statues of soldiers and statesmen lining the square.

While about half of the mob encamped in the square, the rest drifted up Whitehall and Victoria Street, shouting anti-government slogans, and hurling missiles at the few windows still unbroken. Lamp-posts uprooted along the way were used to batter down the massive doors of the Home Office, New Scotland Yard (the police had long since fled), the Ministry of Defence, the War Office, the Department of Transport and Environment. Every government building was stormed by the rampaging mobs, and chairs, desks, tables, filing cabinets, carpets, mirrors, chandeliers, statues and paintings hurled from windows and balconies onto the massive bonfires burning on the streets below. From time to time a building was torched, a great ball of flame bursting through its roof with a noise like a thunderclap. The screams of their own comrades trapped inside were greeted by some of the mob with cheers and cries of derision, and by others with shamed silence. By three a.m., half of Whitehall and Victoria Street were ablaze. Across the city, far into the distance – east, north, south and west – huge fires burned, casting a sinister red glow on the underbelly of the dust cloud that hung over London. As they gazed up at that fearsome and impressive sight, with their white faces, twisted mouths and frenzied eyes, the savage cries of the people were like those of anguished spirits begging to be released from the torments of hell.

At about four a.m. Tuesday morning the crowds began to gather outside the great iron gates barring the entrance to Downing Street. Inside, a dozen armed police waited, automatic weapons at the ready. For a time the mob was content to taunt them but when they refused to open the gates, they became enraged. Vehicle parts, door knockers, iron railings and scaffolding bars were hurled over the top of the gates, knocking two policemen unconscious. The remaining policemen retreated to a safe distance. The mob began to push the gates, chanting, 'Heave! Heave! Heave!' Pressed against the gates those in front cried out in pain and terror, but their cries were ignored, the collective decision was to break down the gates, and nothing could change it. Dozens were trapped, arms, legs, chests, faces thrust against the bars, their screams muffled by the shouts and cries of the mob.

Nothing could withstand the power of the advancing mass of people. The great gates bent and buckled, then with a loud crack, the locks, chains and padlocks that secured them burst. Over the crushed and broken bodies of their comrades and of the two fallen policemen, the mob surged into Downing Street, screaming for blood. As they did so, the police opened fire, and the front two or three rows fell, mortally wounded. For a moment the crowd stopped in its tracks; then, pushed inexorably from the rear, regained its forward momentum. Again and again the police fired, until finally, their ammunition exhausted, they threw away their weapons and backed away in terror from the mob. There was no escape. Despite their pleas for mercy, they were battered to death, and Downing Street was strewn with the gruesome remains.

The mob fell silent, their blood lust purged, it seemed, by the horror of what they had done. Yet once again the passion seized them. Two lamp-posts were passed over hundreds of shoulders to those in front. In a few moments the doors of Number 10 and 11 were battered down, and the mob flooded in, screaming for revenge. But to their anger and frustration, both buildings were empty, evacuated the previous night. In a frenzy of rage and hatred they began to demolish the two icons of government, using anything that came to hand, iron bars wrenched from the gates, paving stones, wheel jacks, and, when nothing else was available, their bare hands. In the orgy of destruction no one heard the approaching helicopter. Suddenly it was overhead. A voice boomed:

'Leave Downing Street, or we open fire! Leave the area at once! You have ten seconds. I repeat, if you do not leave the area immediately, we shall open fire.' As the countdown began over the loudhailer, the mob in Downing Street joined in, and the chant was taken up by the huge crowds in Whitehall. A hundred thousand voices echoed derisively: 'Ten! Nine! Eight! Seven! Six! Five! Four! Three! Two! One!'

A long pause, and the mob fell silent, waiting for the count of zero. But no zero came, and no sound of gunfire either, only the steady chatter of the helicopter hovering above them. They began to jeer triumphantly, revelling in their small victory.

'*Zero!*' they shouted mockingly, stomping to the rhythm of the chant. '*Oh, Oh, Zero! Oh, Oh, Zero. Oh, Oh, Zero!*'

The two policemen struck down by scaffolding bars had barely had time to cock their guns. As the helicopter's searchlight swept Downing Street illuminating the shadows, there was the glint of an automatic rifle lying on the ground. One of the mob dived for the weapon, raised it, and fired a long burst. The helicopter exploded in a great ball of flame, and the crowd below ran screaming from the rain of burning metal.

In Moscow and Beijing, Berlin and Paris, in Tokyo, Washington and Brussels, police and the army battled the mobs. Fires raged unchecked, and the cities were enveloped in a twilight gloom fed by great columns of dust and smoke rising thousands of feet into the air, obliterating the sun.

In London, the few TV and radio stations still operating broadcast largely inaccurate accounts of the latest events. Facts were hard to come by, reporters unable to move about the streets, and communication with news rooms brief and intermittent. During the last twenty-four hours rumours had begun to circulate about the disappearance of hundreds of prominent people. The Prime Minister himself, it was said, had vanished; so had several senior members of the government. Not only politicians had disappeared, it seemed, but also high-ranking officers in the armed forces, leading scientists and engineers, doctors and surgeons.

It was all very mysterious and disturbing, though it was generally assumed that all these important people had fled London to save their own skins, callously abandoning less fortunate citizens. There was nothing extraordinary in that. It was simply another example of the cowardice and treachery of the privileged classes. What was new? It was the way they had always behaved.

Soon however, an even more disturbing rumour began to circulate. These people had not run away at all. They had been kidnapped by the Angels of Mercy and were being held hostage. The implications were sinister indeed. How so many people could have been spirited away in the midst of such chaos no one could understand. The terrorists were evidently even more efficient and deadly than anyone had imagined. Such rumours and speculation enraged the mobs still more. Kidnapped or not, their leaders were responsible for what had happened.

Fear overcame all rational thought. To many it seemed that the end of the world had come.

From the Oval Office the US President made a late night appearance on TV, one last desperate attempt to calm the American people, more especially those millions still trapped in Washington. He was, he assured them, still at his post in the White House, and would remain there, confident that a solution would be found. Negotiations were at a delicate and crucial stage, and he had every hope would be successful. Similar messages were conveyed by their respective leaders to the citizens of Berlin and Brussels, Paris and Moscow, Tokyo and Beijing. None of these palliative words had the ring of truth; few were deceived.

Meanwhile the terrorists tantalised and tormented their victims, agreeing terms, then, almost immediately, denying that they had agreed anything. As time passed and the deadline approached, the harassed negotiators were reluctantly compelled to conclude that the Angels of Mercy were toying with them. The frightening truth was that they had no intention of doing a deal with anyone. Their aim, it seemed, was to teach the free world a lesson it would never forget, so that next time – and assuredly there would be a next time – their terms would be accepted without discussion.

Amongst those in the know, the only question now was not whether the devices would be detonated, but where, when, and in what order. Which city would be the first to be devastated? This was mental torture of the cruellest kind. Most worrying and most humiliating of all, eight of the most powerful countries on the planet were powerless to defend their citizens against the machinations of a few wicked men.

In the small hours of the final day, Tuesday, the 28th October, fragmented and incoherent stories of strange events in Tehran began to drift into TV news stations. Reporting from a hotel in the city centre, an excited German reporter – unfortunately cut off in mid-sentence – appeared to suggest that Tehran was under some kind of attack. This however was immediately denied by a Russian reporter on the streets.

Moments later the senior political commentator of ABA, the American global news network, reported that the Iranian government had received some kind of ultimatum, one that was apparently related to the terrorist organisation, The Angels of Mercy. Whoever was responsible had supposedly threatened specific consequences at hourly intervals unless certain conditions were met. According to official government spokesmen the ultimatum had been rejected with scorn by the government of Iran, who also strongly denied any links with the terrorists. The commentator reluctantly concluded that the ultimatum was a bluff, a desperate last-minute attempt by the eight countries under threat to resolve the crisis. If so, it had failed. Hopes swiftly raised were as swiftly dashed.

For a time there was no further news. Then came a flurry of wild stories that seemed to indicate that Tehran was indeed under attack. There was talk of lights in the sky, mysterious flying objects and alien landings, culminating in the most absurd rumour of all – the disappearance of two of Iran's largest oil terminals in the Persian Gulf. As if that were not incredible enough, it was reported a few minutes later that several key buildings in the centre of Tehran had also disappeared.

These stories, flashed instantly around the world, although impossible for most people to take seriously, were lent a certain circumstantial credibility by the conviction with which they were reported. Next came a bulletin from a respected Asian journalist from TAT International, broadcasting live to the world from his hotel room on Imam Khomeini Street, as one by one, he watched the Central Bank of Iran, the Ministry of Foreign Affairs, and finally the Iranian Parliament, vanish into thin air. Less than fifteen minutes later the same correspondent reported that the entire Iranian government had resigned. This news flash was immediately confirmed by several news agencies. The assumption was that this startling development was in some way connected to the crisis precipitated by the Angels of Mercy.

Thirty minutes later it was reported that the President of Iran had resigned, and that at ten a.m. Tehran time, six-thirty London time, his successor would make an important announcement on Iranian television.

Across the world billions tuned in their TV monitors to view the new Iranian President. His message was surprisingly gracious. His country, he declared, wanted better relations with its neighbours and with the whole world. Iran was misunderstood. Far from condoning terrorism, it was doing everything in its power to combat this terrible scourge. As immediate proof of this he was happy to report that the terrorists who had planted bombs in various world capitals had been arrested, and had revealed the exact location of the devices, together with instructions for their de-activation. The government of Iran had already instructed its ambassadors to pass this vital information to their counterparts in Moscow, Peking, Tokyo, Berlin, Brussels, Paris and Washington. Regrettably, he added, the terrorist who had planted the devices in London had only given their approximate locations, refusing to reveal the precise co-ordinates. Under interrogation he had swallowed a poison capsule and died.

Soon after two a.m. Washington time, less than two hours before the expiration of the deadline, the hunt for the bombs began in all eight cities. It was a desperate operation, carried out by helicopter-borne bomb disposal experts guarded by elite paratroopers who had to fight their way through angry mobs to reach their objectives. Miraculously, by two-thirty a.m. Washington time, the devices planted in all seven capitals had been located and de-activated.

It was known that three devices had been planted in London, one in St. Paul's Cathedral, one in The Stock Exchange, one in the Houses of Parliament. During the last two hours, teams of bomb disposal experts had been scouring all three buildings. It was eight-thirty in the morning. In thirty minutes the bombs would explode, and so far not a single device had been found.

In Parliament Square in front of the Houses of Parliament, in Old Broad Street, Throgmorton Street and Threadneedle Street around the Stock Exchange, and in the streets by St Paul's, Cheapside, Newgate, Paternoster and Martin's le Grand, the crowds gathered, fearful, but silent and subdued.

In the last few hours the mood of the mobs had changed dramatically. It was as if the people of London were resigned to their fate, having lost all hope. Hunger, thirst and fatigue had drained their bodies, rage and despair their spirits. They were stunned by the anarchy of the last few days, and ashamed at having been a part of it. Hundreds of thousands had already taken refuge in the sewers that lie beneath the streets of London, in ravaged stores and office buildings, in theatres and cinemas, churches and museums, in underpasses and underground car parks, anywhere that offered the slenderest hope of surviving the catastrophe that was now inevitable.

As the final minutes ticked away, millions sat huddled together for comfort on the streets, parents hugging their children, men and women their loved ones, doing what little they could to protect them from the horror to come.

Five minutes to nine. Through the pall of smoke and dust covering the city, the pale ball of the morning sun was dimly visible. For a few seconds a single ray of sunlight pierced a small hole in the clouds, as if to offer hope. But then more clouds moved across, and the gloom descended once more. In Parliament Square the eyes of a hundred thousand people were focused on Big Ben.

Two minutes to nine. Across London, and throughout the country, millions of men and women who had long since abandoned their faith in God, prayed to Him now. Embracing each other, the crowds in Parliament Square wept and said their last farewells. Lips moved silently, measuring the last precious seconds of their lives.

One minute to nine. The crowd stirred, moved, it seemed, by the same thought. Men, women and children rose to their feet. Everyone was standing now. Heads bowed as the great mass of people began hesitantly to recite the dimly remembered words of the Lord's Prayer.

The minute hand of Big Ben clicked to the vertical. The murmur of voices died. A fearful hush descended. As the massive clock chimed the hour, a hundred thousand souls closed their eyes and waited for death. But the explosions did not come.

Dreading what might happen, people opened their eyes again and raised their heads slowly, inch by inch. Looking about fearfully they stared, first in amazement, and then in disbelief. The Houses of Parliament were no longer there. Nothing was there, nothing but level ground. Across the Thames was an unobstructed view of County Hall, St. Thomas's Hospital and the Albert Embankment. No Big Ben, no House of Commons, no House of Lords. The Palace of Westminster had vanished into thin air.

So had St. Paul's and the London Stock Exchange. It was impossible, it could not be, it had not happened. Across London crowds of people rubbed their eyes and looked away, and then looked back again, not believing what they were seeing, or rather what they were not seeing.

There were no celebrations, only hugs and tears of joy, and heads shaking in bewilderment. No one knew what to say, where to go, what to do. Aimlessly the crowds drifted, some to the smouldering ruins of Buckingham Palace, some to Trafalgar Square, some to Piccadilly Circus, many to the City or Parliament Square, to see for themselves if the incredible rumours were true. When eventually they arrived to swell the already vast crowds, the new arrivals gazed in silent wonder, and looked at each other in amazement, hoping that someone would explain these extraordinary events. But no one did, no one could; for no explanations were possible.

The first bells to ring were those of Westminster Abbey. Then one by one the churches of London responded, until the whole city resonated to the joyful sound of pealing bells. The Deputy Prime Minister appeared briefly on television to urge people to return to their homes so that the streets could be cleared, and public services resumed. He did not mention the disappearance of any buildings, saying only that the danger had passed, and that the government would do all in its power to ensure that life returned to normal as soon as possible.

Television newscasters were naturally less circumspect and so the speculation was endless. Who had made these buildings disappear? And why? Some insisted it must have been the terrorists. Others scorned the idea. What possible motive could they have had? And anyway, weren't they all either dead or in jail? Many were convinced the government was responsible and was concealing the truth. Was that not what governments always did? But then, as others shrewdly pointed out, governments invariably claimed credit for every good thing that happened. In this case they had not, so obviously they were as mystified as everyone else.

One reporter addicted to science fiction suggested that some alien, though presumably friendly entity, had made the buildings disappear in order to locate and de-activate the bombs but since he was unable to explain how such a thing was possible, no one took him seriously.

Still the question remained. Where were the Houses of Parliament? Where was St. Paul's? Where was the London Stock Exchange? Had they really disappeared? How could they? There were no answers, only theories, and of those there were plenty. Perhaps the most popular one was that they had not disappeared at all, and that the whole phenomenon was in reality some kind of mass illusion. Many psychiatrists and medical experts agreed that such an illusion was theoretically possible, and that in the panic and confusion of the moment the crowds could simply have been duped. Those who disagreed pointed out that such phenomena were normally transient; but then, as it turned out, so was this one.

For when the sun rose the next morning, touching with gold the veil of dust and smoke that lay over London, there they were where they had always been – The Houses of Parliament, St Paul's Cathedral and the London Stock Exchange.

At about the same time, the news broke that the three buildings that had allegedly vanished in Tehran had also reappeared, thus seeming to confirm the mass illusion theory.

Those who only twenty-four hours before had seen those vast empty spaces with their own eyes were utterly confused, those who had not were deeply sceptical. But almost everyone now accepted that no buildings had actually disappeared. It was generally agreed by knowledgeable observers that these strange events were the product of mass trauma. Fear, it was said, could paralyse normal rational thought processes, so that people confused fantasy and reality.

It was the sci-fi addict who was the first to ask an interesting question. The devices concealed in London were never found. That they existed was beyond doubt. So what had happened to them?

But even as the TV morning newscasters were attempting to rationalise these extraordinary happenings, stripping them of mystery and magic, and putting everything into sensible and reasonable perspective, something even more extraordinary was taking place in the skies over London. And not only over London. For as the dust cleared, and the sun burned away the mist, a light blazed, a light as powerful as a hundred lightning flashes. Across the world billions witnessed the same phenomenon that day.

In the sky hung a great sword, its blade glowing so brightly that no one dared look at it for more than a second or two, fearing permanent blindness. As the sun rose higher in the heavens, the sword shone brighter and brighter. In the afternoon its light began to dim. At the day's end, when the sun sank below the horizon, the sword glowed blood red, fading from view with the dying light.

There were a few, a very few, who recognised that sword and understood its meaning, proclaiming as it did that the ancient prophecy had been fulfilled, and that Arthur had come again to save the world.

The End of the Beginning